ISBN 978-0-243-93631-1
PIBN 10805596

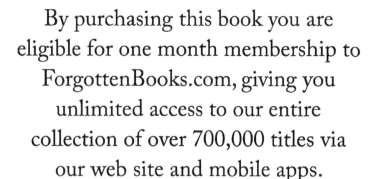

FRANK WARRINGTON

BY

MIRIAM COLES HARRIS

AUTHOR OF "RUTLEDGE"

BOSTON AND NEW YORK
HOUGHTON, MIFFLIN AND COMPANY
The Riverside Press, Cambridge

CONTENTS.

FRANK WARRINGTON.

CHAPTER I.

NEWS.

"This is no world,
To play with mammets, and to tilt with lips.
We must have bloody noses and crack'd crowns,
And pass them current too."—HENRY IV., Act II.

"ENLISTED!" repeated the schoolmistress, not raising her eyes, but not succeeding in keeping down the color in her cheeks.

An ill-favored boy, with big feet and tawny hair, standing at her desk, had been telling her some news, while she ran her eye over the sum on his battered and unpleasant slate, and though the sum was in simple subtraction, she bit her lip, and ran her eye over it twenty times before she knew at all whether it were right or wrong.

The clumsy fellow went on with additional particu lars, and the statement of his authorities, till, with a gesture of impatience, she dismissed him to his seat. A tall, pert girl, in a pink frock, just old enough to be entirely abomin̶̶̶̶̶̶̶̶̶̶̶̶̶̶̶̶̶̶̶̶beyond the limits of human patience, kept her prying eyes on the teacher's face, and whispered something to her neighbor that made her look too and nod. This tall girl in the pink frock was the scourge of the school, and the young schoolmistress' worst trial, gossiping, underhand, meddlesome and precociously acute. She turned around sharply when she heard the whisper and felt the eyes, and said :

"You two girls stay in half an hour after school is dismissed this afternoon, for whispering. Remember."

She of the pink frock sniggered and put down her head, while her comrade pouted and looked scowling at her book. It was a warm, sunny September afternoon ; the little schoolhouse had not much to boast of in the matter of shade, being adjoined solely by one large hickory, whose shadow was only available before twelve o'clock, after which hour it lay tantalizingly along the road and across on the neighboring field. But standing just at the foot of the mountain, and where three ways met, the schoolhouse had always the benefit of the cool, strong wind that swept through the wide valley beneath, and no doubt the sunshine did the children good. It made the schoolmistress' head ache that afternoon though, and she beat her foot impatiently upon the floor, and wondered if the hands of the little clock ever meant to get around to four. There was a vague amalgamated smell of dust, sponge, blackboard and dinner-kettle, brought out in perfection by the hot afternoon sun ; and a dull, monotonous buzz of voices, and shuffle of feet on the gritty floor, to which "the bluefly i' the pane," a dozen wasps on the ceiling, and some bees out side, drowsily kept time. The children had never before been so stupid, so unbearably slow in singing their lessons through their noses; their noses seemed about two yards long, the sounds took such a time in getting out; the younger boys floundered and blundered through their spelling with an exasperating slow ness, the older ones went totally to wreck upon their tables: it was half-past four before the school could be dismissed, and then, retributive justice held the tall girl in the pink frock and her whispering colleague in abeyance till the clock struck five.

It is a question which suffered most under the punishment, the punished or the punisher; at five o'clock they took leave of each other with mutual satisfaction, the younger ones to snatch their satchels, bang their desks, and flounce off impudently; the teacher to close the windows, shut the door, and turn toward home with an involuntary "Thank Heaven!" on her lips.

Not that she usually found her duties so *ennuyante;* she had taught in school ever since she had left off being taught in it herself, and she had never dreamed of thinking it hard work, being of a bright, elastic temper, and being too young as yet to know much about weariness in anything. The news that the boy with the bony feet and tawny hair had given her was in reality the cause of her unwonted impatience to be by herself, with liberty to think. News, indeed, that Louis Soutter was going to the wars; but why need she care, since he had not taken any pains to tell her of it. He had not lived in Titherly for three years past, but it was his home, and he might at least have come back for a night or two, to have said good-bye before he went away.

It seemed, indeed, a hard case for old Humphrey, the uncle who had brought him up and educated him, and who counted so much upon having him come back, and keep up the farm for him in his old age. But Louis had been a restless spirit from his youth; had kept the school in a turmoil during his boyhood, and the whole neighborhood in a state of amazement and doubtful admiration through his early youth ; had run away and gone to sea twice, come back half-penitent, but still untamed, worked a year on the farm, and then, less impatiently, but more resolutely, had again burst the chains of his narrow life, and started off to seek his fortune in the city.

One or two visits he had made home since then, much sobered and far gentler, but with the steady manliness and unconquered daring of early days, apparent still under the better grace and easier manners that his mingling with the world had given him. Reports had come back that he was doing well, getting on in business, and working hard. Nobody in Titherly doubted that he could work hard if he chose : their recollections of him went to show he had been always worth two ordinary men about the farm, when he took a fancy to apply himself, and that whatever he set himself at in earnest, he did better than anybody else. The trouble was, he had not formerly set himself in earnest at anything but mischief, and that the good people thought was not a very paying crop. But almost everybody wished him well, for he was a generous-hearted

fellow, making friends every step he took, and endear-
ing himself to men and women both, by a thousand
acts of good-humoured kindness. Children clung about
him with intuitive affection, and his thoughtful limner
would have painted him with his hand on a dog's head
or in a horse's mane.

Naturally he was quite the hero of his native place,
little as he had given it of his presence latterly, and
from the moment that the war broke out, every one
was certain he was just the fellow to enlist.

The idea, indeed, of his being "the mark of smoky
muskets," had given the young schoolmistress something of a pang at first, but the summer had passed,
and no news of him had reached them. The war-fever
had not raged in that mountain neighborhood—the
excitement had time to cool before it got to them; large
villages sometimes take fire, but scattering settlements
of farm-land seldom; and the township of Titherly,
spread over twenty miles of mountain bottom, had not
a hamlet in its whole extent large enough to produce a
conflagration.

But when old Humphrey, fumbling for his spectacles,
opened Louis' letter, dated the last of August, and read
it to the half-dozen men loafing around the stage house
on the turnpike, there was a little stir and murmur of
applause. Indeed, it was a letter straightforward and
manly as Louis was himself, and deserved a murmur
of applause.

"MY DEAR UNCLE," it read, "you have had a great
deal of trouble with me ever since I came into your

care, and I wish, with all my heart, I had been more
of a comfort to you than I have ever been. It is only
fair to myself to tell you, though, that I have meant to
be. For these three years past, I have been working
day and night to get a little money of my own to lay
out in such improvements as I think would make the
old farm worth working, and I had hoped next year to
come back and settle down on it, and take the trouble
off your hands.

"But I've got to tell you something that you will not
like to hear any more than I like to tell you, and I have
put off telling you as long as it was honest. The fact
is, Uncle Humphrey, I am going into the army. I
can't stand it any longer. I stood by in the Spring and
saw all the men going off, and I said to myself, 'there
are plenty without me, and there is plenty for me to do
at home.' It was harder to stay than to go then, for
people did not know what they were about after that
news from Sumter, and were only wild to get at the
Southerners' throats that instant; they did not know
how many miles, and how many months lay between
them and what they wanted to get at then, but they
know now. And I know; and I am going now because
I know, and because I am sure I am not going for the
hurrah and glory of the thing; and the more yearning
I have for home and the old life and the old place, the
more I mean to go, and the surer I am, I am doing
right to go. And I know you are not the one to put a
straw before me if I see it so; and if you were a young
man, Uncle Humphrey, you would see it so too. You
would feel, it was like standing by and seeing your

mother struck, or worse than that, like looking on with
out a word, when ruffians had their hands upon your
sister. In fine, it has come to that, that I could not
respect myself if I held back, and that I could not feel
I had a claim to the respect of the men and women
whose respect I care to have, if I did not give up my
pleasure and my prospects in the world, and my life, if
there is need of it, to my country in such a time as this.
I should never expect a blessing on anything I did, if I
worked for myself and looked after my own interests,
while the country that I have held by all my life, while
holding by it cost me nothing, was going to pieces in my
very sight. It has been my boast and pride everywhere
I've been, the best country that a man ever claimed,
and the cleanest flag that ever floated; and you would
not think me half a man, if I should just find out I
did not owe her anything.

"Who, all, from Titherly, have enlisted? Tell those
that have not gone already, they had better join my
company: a dozen or so of Titherly men together would
make us feel as if the old place were doing something
for the Union. But we'll talk that all over when I
come up next week to say good-bye. I wish you had
some sons of your own, Uncle Humphrey, and then
you would not mind my going. But you see, if we all
go at it with a will, we shall make short work of it, and
I shall be back the sooner with a clear conscience; and
we shall have something to yarn about over the fire
when the nights are long and cold.

"Your affectionate nephew,
"Louis Soutter."

Louis' large faith in the patriotism of the men of Titherly rather pricked their consciences, but it needed Louis' actual presence to move things that had grown as fast in the soil as they had; their own oaks and ma ples had not struck deeper root. The rural population is generally to be divided into two classes: the slow, easy, good-natured little minds, and the vicious, stubborn, cross-grained little minds. The minds that are not little, like Louis Soutter's, do not long form a portion of the rural population.

Louis loved the old place with a tenderness that had often drawn him back to it from distant lands, but he never found it satisfied him; its narrowness and slowness chafed and discontented him; it cramped him; it was not the life for him, he could not fold his wings so close. And so he was off again, and then tired, again would return to the old nest, till the same longing and weariness drove him out into the world once more. But now it seemed he had grown really satiated with the liberty he had once so pined for; he had taken his resolve, and was working to fit the nest more to his taste, since he could not fit his taste to the nest, and wandering and purposeless as he had hitherto appeared, his resolutions bore the stamp of reality. He had never promised anything before; old Humphrey knew it was not a mere passing whim; and he groaned as he thought what the war had cost him, a faithful son and constant comforter in his childless, desolate old age. How often he had fancied, as he sat at night by his solitary hearth, what it would be to see Louis' children romping round the room and to feel Louis' cheerful sustaining presence always near him. His loneliness was ten times drearier now, when he knew how near he had been to the fulfillment of his hopes, and to what a distance their accomplishment had been thrown.

The schoolmistress seemed in no hurry to reach home that afternoon; there was not a daisy in her path she did not stoop to pick and pull to pieces, and at every rock or fence or other obstacle, she stopped and gazed dreamily over the wide landscape spread before her, or back on the mountains rising near and dark behind her. Her usual path home, shorter by half a mile than the highway, lay down the steep side of a hill, passing through a long stretch of woodland and emerging again into the road, just where the noisy brook, tumbling down from the mountain was spanned by a little bridge, and beside which stood the low white house she had called home from babyhood.

This young girl was an orphan, and lived, together with another orphan, a cousin, under the protection and persecution of an old aunt, a harsh voiced, exacting woman, who had evidently brought up these two girls for the purpose of pitting them against each other and making capital out of the envy she incited in them. They were the children of her two sisters, who had died early and left them to the care of husbands who had either married again, died, gone to California, or practiced some other arts known to youngish widowers in that walk of life, and the little girls devolved naturally on their aunt, unfortunately an old termigant, commonly considered a rich woman in those parts, and very commonly detested. She wreaked upon them the spleen engendered at a very remote period by the better matrimonial luck of her two prettier, softer sisters, and seemed to think she did her duty by them best when she held up to them most strongly the errors and misfortunes of their parents, dead, married again or missing. She had brought them up, however, thriftily and sensibly in many matters, and was in her heart extremely proud of their great good looks, and the uncommon aptitude of the one for learning, and of the other for keeping house.

They had both been named for her, by their weak-minded young mothers, simply because they wanted to propitiate her in some inexpensive manner, and as her name was Frances, and no one had ever dreamed of giving her a nickname, they had followed the bent of their fancies and the suggestions of the children's dispositions in avoiding the strict letter of the law, and calling them respectively Frank and Fanny. Frank, the older by six months, was a pretty brunette, with deep dark eyes and a fine lithe figure, clever and high-spirited, honest as daylight, strong in her loves and hates, and with just enough of the doublet and hose in her disposition to have made it a perfectly unnatural and impossible thing to have called her Fanny. The other, on the contrary, soft, feminine, blonde to the last degree of blondness, coquette to the very heart's core, but demure and tender as a purring kitten, would never have answered to the sobriquet of Frank, but seemed born to go through life as Fanny.

The two, it appeared, were destined to interfere with each other in every imaginable manner: natural enemies, it did not need Aunt Frances' spiteful goads to

drive them as far asunder as the poles. Frank could
bear anything but slyness and insincerity, and Fanny
could submit to any trial save that of being outshone
and dictated to; one was proud and self-willed, the
other was vain and deceitful, and though they slept in
the same white bed, in the same white-curtained room,
and braided their hair before the same greenish per-
verted mirror, they were less sympathetic even, than a
pair of rival generals on the eve of an engagement. Indeed Frank and Fanny seemed always, so to speak, on
the eve of an engagement, and nothing but the whole
some restraint of Aunt Frances' authority preserved a
decent show of amity between them. Their tastes
clashed, their beauty was of violently opposed orders,
their pursuits were in a high degree inharmonious.
Fanny always fell in love with Frank's admirers, and
endeavored to supplant her; Frank always despised
Fanny's friends and avoided them unreservedly. Fanny
grudged Frank her dark eyes, her talents, and her pretty
figure, and Frank was secretly consumed with envy
when she looked at Fanny's white throat, soft eyes, and
baby smile. Fanny undermined Frank's friendships
and made all manner of trouble between her and the
few for whom she cared, and Frank was too proud to
look into the cause, or to do anything but throw
them off and feel bitter and indignant at the fate that
brought her vexation and disappointment from every
source. And so she withdrew more and more within
herself, and learned to cherish most that inner life of
half-shaped dreams and fancies, with which her rival
could not meddle.

gether, and listening attentively. Frank had not a
tinge of color in her cheeks; but a flame went to her
eyes, and they were beautiful. Her voice was low; it
came near not being at all, there was such a strong pain
grasping at her throat, and such a tightening round her
heart.

" How late you are, Frank," Louis said by and by,
uncomfortably. "I thought you let the youngsters out
at four."

" Yes, generally I do, but they have been very troublesome to-day."

" I'll bet they're often that," Louis returned. "Are
you tired of school keeping yet, I wonder?"

" Tired of it? O no."

" It would not be like you to acknowledge you were
ever tired of anything, if I remember right," he said,
glancing down at her.

She did not make him any answer, and there was
a very blank period of silence. Louis broke it at last
by saying desperately, looking at the bunch of daisies
in Frank's unmoved hands,

" I never see a daisy without thinking of the old red
school-house. Do you remember how you used to tell
my fortune for me every day with one when we went
to school together?"

Frank signified that she did remember, by a very
unemphasised " Yes," and Louis went on, stooping
down and picking a bunch that grew by the bridge.

" Do you believe in them any more? For I've a
fancy they're somewhat given to exaggeration."

" No," said Frank, "I do not believe in them at all."

not to look, and thought in her secret soul he was better than all Titherly put together. She gave a little shriek when the pistol went off, and hid her eyes again, only recovering after another period of expostulation on Louis' part, and at last consenting to approach the mark, to see how near he had come to it. She crept towards the old tree on which the paper was fixed, very much as if it were a battery which might open fire on her at any moment, and Louis watched her, and laughed, and admired. When, however, she reached the target she fell into the most artless ecstacies over the skill that had put the bullet directly through its heart, not a hair's breadth to be desired on this side or on that. It is delightful to a man to have a sweet, fair-haired girl in artless ecstacies about him, and Louis was quite human enough to enjoy the homage, whether he believed in it or not. Indeed there was a careless ease in his manner and a laugh in his eye that indicated he was amusing himself with it more than being ensnared by it. He was waiting for Frank and making love to Fanny, *pour passer le temps.*

But how could Frank know this? There was "a knot in his throat" as he started forward to meet her on the bridge, dropping Fanny and the pistol unceremoniously, all the laugh going out of his eye, and all the ease out of his manner as he caught sight of her. He was stiff and constrained for the five minutes that Frank leaned against the birch tree by the bridge and talked to him. Fanny, meanwhile, *piquée* to the last degree, darted revengeful looks at both out of her soft blue eyes, and stood silent, braiding two branches of golden rod to-

and too thoroughly a woman not to feel it. But he did care, and so he was blind and weak as any other man, and his strength of will and steadfastness of purpose promised to be of small advantage to him.

"Do not keep me in suspense any longer, pray," he cried at last, as Frank dropped the last leaf into the stream. "Does she love me, quick ?"

"No,' said Frank, raising her eyes slowly and looking at him for a moment steadily.

"No?" cried Louis with a thrill of something indescribable in his voice, returning her gaze intently. " No ? I don't believe it—I'll stake my life she does !"

A quick flush came over Frank's face as she turned away. "You ought to know," she said with a slight shrug. "I hope you're not mistaken."

" Now !" cried Fanny, in her light girlish voice, such a contrast at the moment to the smothered feeling that the other two betrayed. " Now, Frank, you ought to be ashamed. I counted every leaf you pulled, and on my honor it did not come out no ! Louis, let me tell your fortune for you !"

" Yes, Fanny, that is right," said Louis in a different voice. "You'll take my part: Frank hasn't forgotten how to be perverse, I see. We'll tell her fortune for her, you and I, and convince her she's mistaken if she counts upon the fidelity of any man alive !"

" Oh, I don't count upon any one's fidelity—not even on my own," Frank said with an insincere laugh as she moved away, and Louis turned quickly towards Fanny, who met him with a balmy flood of smiles, and invited him silently to soothe his ruffled temper in her happier mood. He was only too glad to be soothed on any terms, and in the confident assurance that Frank must see them somewhere from the silent house into which she had withdrawn, he lingered on the bridge with Fanny for a full half hour, indulging her generously in her fancy for flirtation, and throwing all the devotion into his manner that he would have shown if Frank had been really in sight.

It was not until Aunt Frances' sharp voice summoned her in to tea, that he started up from his lounging attitude at Fanny's side, and with many low words and laughing adieux, took the path up the hill towards Humphrey's farm. Fanny came in, pouting and slow, to tea; received the old termagant's tirade in silence, and ate her meal in an abstracted manner. Aunt Frances, who was secretly pleased with Louis' attentions to her, scolded all the more, and brought the subject of her loitering up incessantly.

Frank's eyes and cheeks burned so she longed to get away from sight, but that was not to be allowed her. Aunt Frances ordered Fanny sharply to put away the tea-things, while Frank picked up the stitches she had dropped. Thereby Frank's hands were full, and she was kept under the sharp old eyes, whose scrutiny she hated so, while Fanny moved languidly about the room, flouncing and pouting whenever she was spoken to bout her delinquencies of the afternoon, and putting the china down with a thump at every word. Frank would have thrown the knitting work in her aunt's face and darted from the room, but for the pride that kept her still before her rival. Fanny should never see she cared a straw; but Fanny would have been blind indeed if she had failed to interpret the lurid eyes and flushed cheeks of her cousin.

"Ah," she thought with a thrill of triumph, "now I have her; now we'll see which will have most to say about Louis Soutter's fortune!"

CHAPTER II.

HIGH NOON.

"The sunniest things throw sternest shade,
And there is even a happiness
That makes the heart afraid !"—HOOD.

A BEAUTIFUL, clear autumn morning succeeded, and
Frank, in its brightness, and in her honest, earnest work
tried to forget the unhappy phantoms of pain and jealousy that had filled the previous night. During her
quick walk to school, while the cool air was blowing in
her face and the young blood was stirring in her veins,
she almost fancied she had conquered; but when that
passed, and the common worky-day pressure came upon
her, she began to see what a weariness it all was, and
what a strength of hope had gone from her since she
laid it down yesterday.

The children were unusually quiet and docile, the
school-room wore its pleasantest expression, for on a
cool, sunny morning it was capable of a pleasant expression, being very swept and trim in its aspect always
at the beginning of the day, and having the shade of
the great hickory between it and the eastern sun. The
children generally behaved themselves decently during
the first half of their day's incarceration, and did not
begin to be vicious and unbearable till they were hot
and tired and miserable. Frank knew she would have

children write, I beg to know?" he added, tumbling
over the pile of copy-books.

Frank thanked him as she gave them to him, without
looking at him, then told the boys to bring her their
slates. The boys were apt to be extremely trying in
the matter of arithmetic, and she would have given a
good deal to have got rid of them just then; but there
was an indomitable pride about her that made her deny
even to herself that she was unequal to the task. She
tried not to think Louis was listening when he was
silent, and she tried not to hear his low voice when he
spoke to those beside him. She tried faithfully, but the
result was not favorable to the children or herself.
This time, however, they did not suffer very much, for
bending herself to the task, she helped them liberally,
and fulfilled her resolution of getting through it at all
hazards.

"Is arithmetic considered the strong point of the
school, Frank?" Louis said, with a quiet laugh in his
eye, as he handed her back the copy-books; then, without waiting for an answer, half impatiently,

"Isn't it almost time for recess? Do let the young
ones go and play."

"They had their recess five minutes before you came,"
she answered, taking up the books.

"Bother! And they don't go out again till noon?"

"No, not again till noon."

"Well, then, I'll have to write one more copy and go
out myself, for Uncle Humphrey takes his dinner on the
noon mark, as it were, and I must not keep him waiting
this last day."

"You go to-morrow, then?" asked Frank, relenting.

"Yes, to-morrow, 'by the dawn's early light.' Heigho, Frank, I hope you're going to give me a thought now and then?"

"That's the least your friends can do," Frank said, turning over the pile of copy-books.

"Well, I don't ask it of many friends."

"I am sure you might safely; nobody could refuse to remember a soldier kindly now-a-days."

"You haven't sent so many from here that you have to be very economic of your kind thoughts, have you?" Louis said with a little irritation.

"No, I am sorry to say, you have a right to them all, as far as that is concerned."

"Well, see that you are honest in giving them to me, then," and tearing a leaf from a copy-book before him, he began to write silently while she went on with her duties. She soon wondered whether he had forgotten all about her, he seemed so absorbed and absent, but at length he arose, and pushing aside his chair, came to the desk where she was sitting, again in difficulties with the spelling class, but keeping up a brave behaviour.

He took up his cap from the floor where it had fallen, brushed it off, and leaning down a moment to pull the hair of the cherub nearest to Frank's knee, he tossed a folded scrap of paper into her lap, saying, *sotto voce,*

"Read that, Frank, if you can spare the time to-day, and let me find an answer in your desk to-morrow morning. I'll stop and look for it when I pass by here early on my way to meet the stage. Good bye."

He did not look at her nor offer to shake hands, but

turned quickly about, and with a careless parting caress
to the little ones who were in his way, and a nod to the
other children, he strode across the room and disappeared from their admiring eyes.   It was all like a dream
to her; she did not touch the note, but went on with
the lesson without moving her attitude at all; feeling as
if her fate lay in it, but knowing she could not read it
till the children were whooping and shouting at their
play a half hour hence.

At the first stroke of twelve, they started crazily for
the door, pushing, rushing, shrieking.   Save only two
boys whom she had condemned to confinement for some
paltry error early in the day, and the tall girl in the
pink frock, who professed a headache and an intention
of eating her dinner in the schoolroom.   The schoolmistress sat silent, looking over exercises, writing copies,
putting down the morning's marks, with but one thought
in her mind, that of getting rid of the tall girl in the
pink frock and the stupid boys, and being left to herself
for one brief moment.   But that was not to be.   The
hour passed on, other children straggled in to keep that
abominable child company, to ransack their desks, overlook their workboxes; and one o'clock struck, and
Frank's hour of grace was over.

Ah, the length of that afternoon!   But it passed, and
the children once more shouting, rushing, pushing, burst
into liberty, and left their mistress sitting silently at her
desk.   She of the pink calico indeed showed an inclination to linger, but finally all excuses were exhausted,
and she took up her march for home.   Frank gave a sigh
of relief, and sitting down by the open window leaned

her cheek against the frame and looked out. Five minutes more, and she should know what the note contained, whether it were a mere good-bye, more or less
tender, some trifling explanation or apology or—she
feared her fate too much. It was many minutes before
she drew the letter from her pocket and essayed to read
what follows quietly :

"It is not my fault, I am sure you will see, that I have
to write to you to-day instead of speaking to you. However, I suppose I need not regret it very much, for if
you do not know what I am going to say, it is very little
matter how I say it and if you do, and have the right
sort of an answer to give me, it is equally little matter.
And maybe it will be easier to bear my fate, if it's a
hard one, by myself, than if you were looking on and
dealing it to me with your own lips.

"For I take it, a man's pride is not very different from
a woman's, though you all make small allowance for it ;
and while a man has not any right to weigh it a moment in the scale against his love, it may sometimes
hold him back till he sees whether or no he is rushing
into certain disappointment. But now I find I have not
time for that, and I find too, when it comes to parting, I
cannot go away without my answer, whatever it may be

"I am sure you have guessed what I came to Titherly
for ; I believe I have always loved you, Frank, and I
believe too, you have always known it, though of late
we have seemed so far apart, and so like strangers when
we have met, I have sometimes doubted whether you
remembered   I have not at this moment one single clue

2*

to your feelings towards me.   I do not know that I have any reason to believe that you will listen to me; but since you are the only woman I have ever loved or ever shall love, I suppose you have a right to know it, whatever pain it may give me to tell it to you.

"Frank, other men love you; I do not doubt they are in earnest, but their earnest is not equal to mine, though very likely I cannot make you understand it.   It has been the thought of you, growing stronger and warmer ever since I came to be a man, that has kept me from being the worthless wandering fellow every one predicted I should be.   Heaven knows I am far enough from being worthy of you now, but I am not so far as I should have been without the hope of you. Still, if you do not understand me, and cannot return my love, you need not fear for me, and you need not think about the pain you give me.   There is enough to be done in the world to keep a man from ruin, even if all pleasure and hope are left out.   I think now I should stand a firmer soldier and a better man if I had the right to think you loved me; that may be a fancy, and perhaps I shall be worth more to my country if she is my only mistress, and if I like life less than death.   So you need not be afraid to tell me the truth, whatever it is—and I almost know what it is—but you'll give me a kind thought now and then as you have promised, and re-member always what good friends we were when we went to school together.   God bless you."

She sat still, with the letter in her lap, and her eyes fixed on the floor.   It was almost worse than pain for the instant, this sudden, strong rush of joy, for which she was not ready—the crowning of her life at this strange era, the sudden glory of light at this dark hour. Everything was changed; there was nothing left to fear; all hope had for the moment found its consummation, and there was nothing left to hope: a strange moment, the perfection of human happiness, with the vague, unsatisfied yearning of the immortal underlying it.

CHAPTER III.

MIDNIGHT.

"As I have seen a boat go down
In quiet waters suddenly;
When not a wave was on the sea,
Nor in the sky a frown."

LATE in the afternoon Frank shut down her desk upon the folded slip of paper that contained her answer, thinking with a strange rush of emotion of the hand that would next raise the lid and touch the paper she had just laid in it. In the grey dawn of to-morrow morning the departing soldier would be coming there to know his fate—a fate that would give strength and courage to him, and make all the journey light.

It was all misty and unreal to her—the walk home, the meeting with her cousin, the slow passing of the evening. She knew there was no hope of seeing him before he went; his resolution and her infatuation had made that impossible; he was five long miles away that night, the great man of a war meeting that had been threatening to convene for weeks, but which needed the enthusiasm that his presence had supplied. No, she could not see him, before daylight he would be gone; that miserable little letter was all the clue he could have to what was throbbing in her heart. So much for his pride and her temper. But he loved her, and that was happiness enough.

She wondered as she went up to her room, earlier than usual, hoping to be alone, if Fanny saw what she would fain have concealed from all eyes that did not love her. Yes, Fanny had seen, little doubt of that, and Fanny was already in their room, already at the glass, pulling down her long, light hair, and showering it about her shoulders. An indiscriminate litter of col lars, sleeves, ribbons, and nets lay on the table below the glass; Frank took her own off absently, and threw them in a drawer. Aunt Frances' scanty hair would have stood on end if she could have seen the careless ways her two pretty nieces were getting into; all her rigorous teaching seemed to avail them little when they came to have anything pleasanter or more momentous on their minds. Frank was a long while in undressing herself, and when at length she approached the glass, Fanny was before it still, listlessly braiding her hair.

"You need not move," she said in a softer voice than usual; "I only want my Bible." And she put out her hand to reach it from under the heap of muslins on the table.

"Stop," cried Fanny; "it isn't there."

Before the words were out of her mouth Frank had withdrawn her hand, but her quick movement had scattered on the floor the *débris* of her cousin's toilet. Fanny stooped hastily to pick them up, but not before Frank's eye had caught the gleam of a golden chain with a trinket attached, that Fanny flung hastily about her neck and buried in her bosom. The action gave her a vague feeling of suspicion, but took no certain shape, till bending down, that Fanny had overlooked in her hurried search upon the floor. Her eye fell on it as she took it up; the envelope had been torn off; she only caught a few words, but they seemed for the moment, to take her breath away. A few words, and a signature in a familiar hand. With a half-bewildered manner, she held it out to Fanny, who seized it with a guilty flush thrust it in a drawer, and turned the key.

"There is your Bible," Fanny volunteered, pointing to a little volume by the window. She took it and sat down by the light, opening it at the accustomed place. But her face had a vacant look, and Fanny felt certain, as she lay covertly watching her with half-closed eyes, that she did not know a word she read; and when she closed the book mechanically and knelt down, Fanny knew also that she did not say her prayers.

After a few moments Fanny saw her face again, as she arose and went across the room softly, as if she were afraid of herself, and laid down her Bible, picked up a leaf that had fallen out, replaced it absently, and then put out the light, and creeping to bed, lay down quietly.

Fanny would not close her eyes lest she should fall asleep; she hardly breathed, listening for her cousin's movements; but beyond a low, short, uneven breathing, she heard nothing that repaid her vigilance. Her companion did not stir a limb, or turn a hair's breadth from the attitude in which she had first lain down. But she was not asleep; no sleeper ever breathed that suppressed, choked breath, and lay so marble still, and kept such unrelaxed control of breath and muscle. For hours they lay so, within touch of each other, not ten inches space between them, nothing but the darkness hiding their restless eyes, and strange eagerness of look.

But a little after midnight, weariness began to glaze Fanny's cat-like eye; she roused herself and tried to shake off the coming drowsiness, and believed she was quite awake, and then in a few moments she gave a little toss, and a little sigh, and nestled her cheek down on her arm and was fast asleep.

Her companion drew a longer, freer breath, and raised herself softly on her arm, and bent her head down to listen. Yes, that was true sleep, though it was a long time before she could bring herself to trust it. At last she ventured to rise up, and with a cautious hand reach out and strike a light.

Half sitting on the side of the bed, with one foot touching the floor, she shaded the light from the sleeper's eyes with her hand, and bent over her. The sleep of innocence and simplicity it seemed; the soft braids of her hair lay loosely about her neck; the low breath came and went evenly between her pretty lips; one white hand was under her smooth cheek, the other lay exposed and baby-like upon her breast. A gleam of the chain about her neck directed Frank's creeping fingers to the locket hidden in her bosom, and with parted lips and suspended breath, she drew it softly forth. The candle-light shining up from the hand that shaded it, showed a very different face from the sleeper's, as she bent down and gazed upon the picture.

A long deep gaze, and

within the white folds of the dress from whence she had taken it, and raising herself, put down the candle on the floor, and standing up, tried to move softly from the bed. But from some cause, perhaps her painful and long constraint, she staggered and could scarcely stand. She put her hand to her head for a moment, and sat down upon the edge of the bed to recover herself. She soon conquered the dizziness, and rising, went softly to where her clothes lay and began to put them on. A most hurried toilet, over which she threw a grey cloak that hung upon the door, and drew the hood up over her head. Then glancing again at the sleeping face upon the pillow, she satisfied herself she had not been incautious, and blowing out the candle, crept stealthily over to the door.

The passage way was literal night, and the staircase was a narrow, crazy, winding one, that was treacherous at noonday even, but she had climbed it much too often to be betrayed by it. Her aunt's door stood distrustfully ajar, characteristic of the woman within, who grudged the hours of sleep that necessitated a brief respite from picket. But *bon gré mal gré*, the old woman slept like lead, and her niece stole past unchallenged, undid cautiously the fastenings of the door that led into the porch, and was presently out into the night alone.

Without, it was dark and heavy and still : the weather had changed since sundown, and a wild autumn storm had begun to accumulate its forces round the mountain. Its bursting might be two days off as yet; but the intervening time would be more gloomy and oppressive than the crisis. She felt her way down the path and out the gate; it was blindingly black, for she had not yet got the glare of the candle out of her eyes. Once into the road, however, and beyond the shadow of the tree and house, the darkness began to lift a little, and she could discern dimly the bridge and the bars beyond. Hurrying over the fence, she struck into the path which led across the field, keeping it however with great difficulty, for it was too dark to see anything upon the ground; the great black mountain rising before her and sometimes a near tree or projecting rock, were all she could discriminate, even after her eyes were habituated to the gloom. The grass was long and wet, and her feet struggled harassingly through it when she lost the path, but at last she gained the entrance to the wood, and pushed her way into it.

A narrow and sufficiently tortuous path at noonday, it was terrible at night, and its steepness and uncertainty made it entirely unfrequented after sundown, but she had not stopped to think of that. Groping along with outstretched arms to guide herself between the thickly standing trees, stumbling over the logs and rocks that lay plentifully along the uneven ground, there was not much time for thought or fear; it was a hand to hand fight with darkness and solitude and the waking forest. She heard more than once, as for a moment she paused to breathe, the soft step of some prowling beast; once, when she lost the path, her foot sank deep in the loose earth, and she heard the low brood of snakes below, but she was not answered to the name of fear;

and would pay for it long after, but now it was lost in the presence of something stronger.

At last she reached the limits of the forest, and sank down for a moment on the stile where she rested every day on her way to school, where, that very afternoon, she had lingered long and dreamily as she came home. Something that looked to her like a streak of dawn in the distant east made her start up and hurry on. A half mile still lay between her and the school-house, a half mile of clear, open hard road, and in ten minutes her hand was on the latch of the unlocked door.

What a solitude, what a listening silence reigned in this daily tumultuous room, where she had hardly ever been silent and alone in all her experience of it, and which she never before had entered but in daylight, and for the actual realities of working and carrying out the daily business of her life. There were loud echoes and reverberations as she went across the room, and opened and let fall accidentally the cover of a desk. It was worse by far than the solitude and darkness of the wood. She trembled from head to foot as she laid her hand upon the cover of her own desk and lifted it, pausing, listening and looking round. The darkness did not impede her much; her hand touched instantly the object of her search; crushing it between her fingers, she dropped the desk cover, sprang down and hurried to the door, only stopping to close it as she had found it, then flying along the road like one pursued, starting and trembling at every sound, terrified and panting.

When she reached the bars below the bridge, day had begun faintly and distantly to dawn, and she crept into the house, glad to forget in its continued darkness, that light was about to rise anew upon a world grown so blank and bitter to her.

All was still and at rest, as when she went away She climbed, with limbs that almost failed her, up the narrow twisted stairs; listened for a moment, as she entered the dark room, for Fanny's even breath, threw off her clothes, and with the hand that held the note hidden in her bosom, crept shivering into bed, and lay her burning head upon the pillow from which she was not again to lift it, till many suns had risen and set, and many changes had passed over her, and the peril of death had been very near her.

CHAPTER IV.

THE CHILL OF DAWN.

" Fleet-footed is the approach of woe,
But with a lingering step and slow
Its form departs."

THE dangerous illness that succeeded that night was passed, and Frank had come out of it, to the surprise of those who had watched her, unimpaired in mind and with a wonderful remnant of bodily strength. She had left behind, it seemed, beauty and youth and interest in life, and shorn of these, was to begin the world and make her way through it with what courage she could command. Life in any event would have been earnest work to her ; now it had a promise of something more than earnestness.

When consciousness first returned to her, and opening her eyes, she looked around upon the familiar, silent room, her glance went intuitively to the chair beside the door, with a wonder that her grey cloak was not lying on it, and then she felt in her bosom for the note. It was not there, and the empty hand she looked at was thin and white, and she was alone upon the bed, and the room was scrupulously in order, and her aunt sat opposite to her bolt upright, with arms folded, looking at her rigorously. Then it all came to her, and her mind cleared suddenly and with a painful distinctness.

That night, which she had been living over in such multiplied and varied phases of distress, was separated from her by weeks, not hours. She had been at the threshold of escape, but had been cruelly turned back.

The old woman saw the gleam of intelligence that had lighted her face when she roused, and, coming to the bed, said,

"How are you, Frances? You have been very sick, you know—"

"Yes, I know," she said, shutting her eyes and turning her face away, and there the colloquy ended. For hours she lay with closed eyes and averted face, and for hours her nurse sat doggedly and watched her. Once she saw her face work painfully, and her fingers twist themselves with vehemence together, but that passed instantly, and she lay as if asleep.

The first moment that day that she was left alone, she started from the bed and staggered across the room. Supporting herself by a chair, she pulled open a drawer, and lying on the top of it, smoothed out and folded, she saw her own note. She did not touch it, but shut the drawer, and attempted to regain the bed, on the side of which the returning attendant found her, insensible and ghastly pale.

From the moment that she saw the note, her resolution was taken. Since Fanny knew it, all the world, her world, knew it. She wanted to live now, to get away from it. She hated every stone, every tree she looked out at from her window. She loathed every article of furniture in the room she h . . . . . . from a baby. She turned sick at the famil . . . . . daily chit chat that she heard. She shrank from the sight of every one except her aunt, and she only submitted to her presence as a necessity. She looked at her future with a stolid, defiant courage. The momentary softness that had made her yearn for death was gone. She was so changed, even the dulled perceptions of her aunt recognized the alteration. The impatience and wilful ness of other times had gone; but instead had come a resolute, unimpassioned self-reliance, harder much to overbear and thwart.

Early in her convalescence, she had missed, throughout the day, Fanny's voice and step about the house, and one morning, turning to her aunt, had asked the reason.

"Fanny had taken the school," had been the answer, with a doubtful look, to see how the interrogator would receive the intelligence she was supplanted.

An expression of relief passed over Frank's face; that the school was cared for, removed another obstacle from her path. The most serious remained. She desired to go without acting in disobedience to her aunt. To go, she was determined of course; but if possible, she desired to go pacifically and lawfully.

How it was accomplished she hardly knew herself; but one morning, a month after her decided convalescence, she awoke with the thought, almost a happiness, that that day she might begin her preparations. Perhaps Aunt Frances knew she had better yield her consent than have her authority openly set at naught; perhaps she felt that the girl had outgrown her, and could no longer be coerced. At all events, she yielded at last, an ungracious consent that Frank should try her fortune at school-teaching in the city.

The preliminaries were soon arranged. Frank's father had a sister living there, a widow, of middle age, who had often supplicated in vain a sight of her only brother's only child since she had grown to woman hood. To her she was to be consigned, and the world lay before her.

Whether Fanny were pleased, chagrined, or puzzled by her cousin's resolution, it was difficult to guess. They saw little of each other now. Fanny's duties at the school kept her away from home till a late hour of the afternoon. Since Frank's illness they no longer shared the same room, and their mutual avoidance was too earnest to be ineffectual. Frank's recovery had been very rapid; her illness had begun early in September, and by the middle of October even Aunt Frances admitted, grumblingly, there was no reason why she should not go, if she were ready.

It spoke rather ill for her sensibility, the kind-hearted neighbors thought, that she should be going from their midst without a single token of regret; that the girl who had been so much their pride and favorite, should be turning her back upon them without a pretence that she felt sorry she was doing so. If they had known the morbid eagerness with which she counted the days till she should be away, the aversion with which she turned from everything that reminded her of her past life among them, they would have been more outraged even than they were.

CHAPTER V.

TWILIGHT.

"All bright hopes and hues of day
Have faded into twilight gray."

It was the dull twilight of a rainy day; Frank had just arrived in the great city she had decided should be her home; the carriage rolled carelessly and heavily on, in the lolling, heedless manner that hacks assume when they are conscious of an undistinguished traveller within. The mud splashed up sometimes upon the carriage windows, and sometimes the wheels grazed the wheels of a cart or the shins of an omnibus horse, making always a little delay and eliciting a broadside of curses from the drivers of the vehicles. For the first time, her heart began to sink a very, very little. The lamps blinked drearily through the dismal fog; the men and women whom she looked out at were wet and cold and miserable—the children's faces sent a shiver through her. Their route lay through a low and obscure portion of the city; the driver swung heedlessly round abrupt corners, and drove with equal indifference and inattention through choked side streets and crowded crossings. Frank had been very brave in dealing with ideas, it remained to be seen of what sex her courage was when it came to the treatment of material terrors.

The driver rather abruptly drew up before a corner

store, the traffic of which was proclaimed by the low inside shutters, banging baize door, and enticing show of kegs upon the pavement. Throwing the reins upon the horses' backs, he got down, muttering as he passed the window something about asking the way inside, and went into the shop. She started forward and called to him, but it was too late, the baize door closed upon him, and there was nothing for her to do but wait for him. The neighborhood was anything but pleasant, the people who passed were anything but reassuring. Two or three rough looking men went up to the shop, and disappeared behind the baize door; several women, with dirty dresses drabbling on the pavement, and coarse, hard faces illumined by the light from over the entrance, passed under it, but went plodding on, as if even the sorry solace that it offered were denied to them; the very children were haggard and repulsive.

Frank had disabused her mind of any fears that the horses might start, by one glance out at them. With heads hanging down, and the most weary expression in their angular outlines, they stood in a cloud of steam, on three legs each, ambitious of nothing so much as of being let alone, occupants of that one spot till the crack of doom, their only condition, permission to change a leg every century or so, and to lie down, at the final dissolution of mundane things.

After a lapse of five minutes, the driver emerged from behind the green baize, accompanied by a red faced man, who mounted with him on the box, and the horses patiently gathered up their legs and put themselves in motion, their dream of the millennium cruelly

3

been at a dead lock for some seconds, when a new actor appeared on the stage in the person of a half-grown grocer's boy, with a basket on his arm and a cigar stump between his teeth.

"What's to pay?" said this *débutant,* pausing and looking intelligently around. He seemed to command respect in the areas, for the nearest maid, drawing her apron over her head, explained the case at large to him.

"A lot o' doughheads," he said, when she had ended. "Why couldn't you ha' sent to the corner for me, and not kep the lady waitin' here all night?"

For Frank looked like a lady, notwithstanding her surroundings, and the young rascal comprehended it.

"Then you know where I can find her?" she said, moving towards him.

"Think it likely I do," he returned, taking the cigar from his mouth. "Aint apt to forget a customer. Served her, man and boy, these three years."

Frank repressed her curiosity to know what period of his term of service was embraced in the expression "man," and begged to know how long she had been gone from here.

"Better'n a year," he said. "Had to give up her house along o' losin' money i' some o' your rascally banks and things. I took quite a interest in the old lady tho'; she was a clever old party. Some folks might think a little too strong on the preach, but I didn't mind. I've got loads o' tracks she giv' me—me, ye know," he reiterated, with a leer at the maids, who titteied, showing they did. "An' a Prayer-book, with my name writ in it."

They tittered again.

"Six pictur' reward cards, and the Youthful David!"

They laughed aloud, at which he regained his gravity and turned to Frank, with a good deal of manner, and explained:

"She didn't know, ye see, like them young women does, as I wasn't likely to be took with tracks, not bein' one of the early pious myself. But that didn't hinder me from bein' obliged to her all the same, and it'll be a pleasure to me, miss" (with a scrape) "to serve ye any way on her account—bein' her daughter, maybe?"

"No," said Frank. "But I shall be very much obliged to you if you can direct me to her."

"Nothin' easier, miss. Leastways if she haven't moved of late. Ye see, when people get a goin' down hill along o' banks and things, they have to keep a movin', they can't stan' still. 'Taint nothin' 'gainst 'em that they can't, Heaving knows. So ef your aunt aint been a movin'—I think you said she was your aunt, mum?"

"I did not say," returned the young lady, and the boy's eyes twinkled.

"Oh, so you didn't. Strange I should ha' been so mistook. Well, this ere lady then—your cousing, maybe?—ef she haven't moved since May "——

Here the coachman broke in with a great growl, and told him he'd take his horsewhip to him if he didn't hurry up and tell 'em what he knew about the lady, and the females in the area conjured him to be done with his "nawsense," and not keep the young lady on the pavement any longer.

Thereupon the youth's soul rushed to his face, and after being very severe to his late supporters in the area, he concentrated himself upon a reply to the coach- man, and some very strong English being given and received, invited him to decide the matter by single combat, setting down his basket, and pushing up the sleeves of his huge coat, with a view to striking awe into the beholders, and showing the enemy his entire good faith.

Frank made a sign to the coachman to get upon the box, and moved away, saying as she did so, he was an ungrateful boy, and she should never ask another favor of him. This had precisely the desired effect, and gave the crafty youth a sufficient excuse for backing down and abandoning his belligerent attitude. No lady should ever have to say that of him, he said, as the coachman, restraining his desire to swing him over into the middle of the next block, mutteringly mounted to the box; no lady should ever have to say that of him; he'd give up the pleasure of thrashing that rascally coward there rather than she should.

The coachman stooped forward and took up his whip, with a menacing look, at which the boy winced a lit- tle involuntarily, stepped back out of range, and con- tinued the delivery of his proclamation. The proclama- tion was rather labored, as such efforts are apt to be, and wandered a good way from the mark, which was the intention of the orator; but he finally consented to smooth his ruffled plumage (a figure of speech which meant nothing of more outward significance than turn- ing down his sleeves and setting his cap straight on his head), and to tell the lady how to find the plaçe she wanted. The lady had now got into the carriage, and the little sinner saw there was no more glory and very little further entertainment to be gained by prolonging the interview; so after another preamble and resolutions, he told her the street and number to which the old lady's goods had gone from 98; and amid renewed Billingsgate addressed to the driver, and some doubtfu. compliments flung after her, they drove away.

The house to which he had directed them was not very distant, though in a much lower and humbler quarter of the town; down hill indeed—Frank felt sure the boy had not been mistaken as to that. The letter she had written two weeks before, addressed to 98, of course had never reached her aunt; the welcome she had hoped to find prepared for her she could hope for now no longer; but shelter, protection, no matter how humble—ah, that she might find them. Her aunt might be dead, might have left the city; these were pleasant alternatives to face. She knew no other soul in it, she had never thought of the possibility of her present difficulties. But it was time enough to give up to these anticipations when she found herself houseless and friendless, as the next hour would decide.

At their next pause, she said she would ring the bell herself, as she did not care to let the coachman see too much of her perplexity; so, after another battle with the adhesive door, she extricated herself from the carriage and went up the steps.

It was a boarding-house of rather meager dimensions sufficiently grimy and unpleasant, with a deep-seated smell of beef-steak, fried fish and bad coffee, and with a slatternly girl in attendance. The slatternly girl knew nothing of any such lodger, but had only been in the place herself a month; maybe the landlady might know. So while she went to call the landlady at the top of the basement stairs, Frank waited by the door, holding her dress off the dirty oilcloth, and longing to get out of the place, if only into the dreary street again. It was evidently the hour of the evening repast below; there were sounds of voices in the basement, and jingling of cups and saucers, while a pile of shabby hats and caps upon the hall table, showed the social rank of Mrs. Murdoch's boarders. After a long period of suspense, during which the slatternly girl hung over the balusters and called out at intervals to Mrs. Murdoch to come up, Mrs. Murdoch came up, wiping her mouth on the back of her hand, and her hand on the back of her apron, and bringing with her a renewed reminiscence of beefsteak, fried fish, and bad coffee, and looking a good deal out of temper at being brought away from the enjoyment of them.

She was a stout, untidy woman, with a very loud voice and a very sharp eye, and she treated Frank to a good deal of incivility on account of her bootless journey up the basement stairs. Why didn't she send down word what she wanted? She could have told her as well down there as up here that she didn't know anything about the old lady. She had been gone from there these three months; she didn't keep track of all her boarders; she would have her hands full if she did.

"But wasn't there anybody in the house who knew,

wasn't there *any* way of getting a clue to where she was?"

The landlady eyed her sharply, and seeing how g od-looking she was, felt more antagonistic than be)»re "No," she said, turning towards the basement stairs again, "she didn't know any way at all."

"But wait one moment," murmured Frank, appalled at the sudden cutting off of this last thread of hope, "I must find her. Pray try to think—I don't know what I shall do."

"Well, I'm sure I don't," said the woman, indifferently, stooping to deal a cuff to the nearest of a troop of yellow-headed, frowsy children, who were now swarming around the basement stairs. At this moment the man outside shook the handle of the door, and called out,

"Look here, mistress; I can't be keepin' my horses standin' here all night; I've got somethin' else to do."

"One moment," said Frank, in a faint voice, and looked imploringly towards the woman. "You don't know where her things were sent—you don't remember—"

The woman turned her head over her shoulder and gave her a look that was worse than any words, and she put her hand out hurriedly to open the door, but at that moment,

"Stop!" cried a small voice from among the troop upon the stairs. "I don't know where's she's gone, but I know the man as took her things—the Dutch cobbler round here in the alley."

"O," cried Frank, with such a sudden relief in her

voice it sounded almost like a sob. " Show me the way
to him. I will give you some money if you will. Won't
you let him ?"

The landlady muttered it was no concern of hers; the
boy might go if he "was a mind" to lose his supper;
and then she floundered down the stairs again and left
them.

The slatternly maid bustled about, touched with a
little womanly pity for the stranger's plight, and made
the boy presentable as quickly as she could. "O, no
matter for that," pled Frank, as the girl shook him out,
pulling his trowsers up and his jacket down, plastering
his hair smooth, in a manner known to nursery-maids
of that social grade, and scouring off with the corner of
her apron the most conspicuous of the blemishes apparent on his face. "No matter for that; nobody will
see him ; he looks well enough."·

" There, then," said the girl, with a final dab across
his features which made the poor child stagger. "There,
now you'll do."   And catching up a cap at hazard
from the pile upon the table, she crammed it down upon
his head, and thrusting his hand into the lady's, pushed
them towards the door, and followed them out into the
street, watching their career with gaping interest.

" You will stay here," said Frank to the driver, " till
I come back. I shall not be gone many minutes. I
will pay you for the time you lose."

The man growled, but she did not stop to listen;
grasping her little cicerone's hand, she half dragged,
half followed him along, coaxing and hurrying in the
same breath. He was a stout urchin, not used to rapid

locomotion, and he puffed and blew a good deal before they got around the corner.

"I'm sorry to make you hurry so, dear," she said, slackening a little. "But that man is so cross, you see. Is it much further?"

"No-o, round—next block," gasped the child—"second alley-way."

Frank proposed to carry him, but he declined, being turned of eight years, and having a good deal of manly pride inside his greasy jacket. It was raining a little, and the pavement was rather slippery, and the boy's shoes being down at the heel, they made but slow advance.

While she was struggling on thus through a maze of low and dangerous streets, guided only by a helpless child, perfectly houseless, homeless, perhaps penniless, amid perils of which she hardly knew the name, not a soul in the vast city who knew of her existence, or cared whether she failed or prospered, there came the thought of home, its peacefulness, safety, steady protection—and the first doubt, had she done well to leave it? Had she had any right to come away from it? Was she not following the dictates of self-will and pride? Had she not turned her back upon her duty? Has a woman, and particularly a woman of her age, a right ever to take the reins so arbitrarily in her own hands, and plan a life out for herself so widely different from the one in which she has been placed?

"Right or wrong," she muttered, putting down her head to meet a gust of wind and rain that swept around the corner as they turned it. "right or wrong, I have done it, and I will abide by it. I would rather lie down and die here in this spot; I would rather fight out this dreadful battle through a life-time than go back. I will take my chance, it's not much either way."

"Here," said the boy, stopping and pointing with a fat forefinger. "Here's the alley."

She gave a little shudder and drew back. "We have not to go in *here!*"

It was worse than her worst imagination. She could barely stand upright under the low arch through which her guide proceeded; the slimy stones were dripping with moisture above her head, while her feet went ankle deep into the filthy mud below. The dim gaslight from the street did not penetrate beyond the entrance; it was to be hoped the child knew where he was going; she could not see an inch before her; she could feel the stone wall on either side when she put out her hand, and the arch above pressed close against her head; grasping the child's arm tightly, and guiding herself by the wall, she trod cautiously to keep from slipping, till they emerged from the alley into the inner court. The boy plodded on through the ash-barrels and lumber-piles that obstructed their way, till he reached the extremity of the court, where he paused at the foot of a crazy staircase that led up on the outside of a hovel, to what was probably called by courtesy the second story.

"Up there," he said, and Frank saw a shoemaker's sign hanging from the window. At this moment, a villainous little cur, roused from banqueting upon a heap of potato parings and well-polished bones below stairs, bounced out upon them savagely. Frank's guide

and protector set up such a howl on this alarm, that she
was obliged to lift him up and set him on the stairs out
of reach of danger, while the racket brought to the door
a woman with a shrill voice, having a baby tucked
under one arm, and holding a ladle in the other hand.
Seeing the girl and the little boy, she subsided some
what, turning her anger principally in the direction of
the dog, whom she kicked down the stairs and threatened fiercely with the ladle; while the little boy, getting
within the door, yielded to the swelling of his manly
pride, and shook himself clear of Frank's protecting
grasp.

The room into which they were invited was the
lowest, the narrowest, the thickest settled, and the
dirtiest into which the young woman's fate had ever led
her. It was almost filled up by a bed, a stove, a work-
bench, and a table, but on and beside these were piled
all imaginable articles of household and personal neces-
sities, all in the last degree untidy and deranged, and
all indicating a combination of poverty and uncleanness
most revolting. The woman was bitterly plain, red, and
Dutch in appearance, and seemed to be very tyrannical
in her family relations, for the little girl stowed away in
a corner, tied up in a chair, ceased her whimpering at a
glance from her mother, and the baby tucked under her
arm seemed not to call his soul his own, but submitted
like a little saint to the peculiar attitude to which h
was condemned, and only grew red in the face and
squirmed a little when his head accidentally got down
where the feet of babies are ordinarily put. The poor
cobbler, also, from a habit of getting out of the way

and taking up as little room as possible, was bent almost
double over his bench, and looked up a little sideways
at the visitors, and then at his wife, and did not say
anything at all.

Beside him on the bench, sat a girl of twelve, inex
pressibly plain, with a marked cast in her eyes, a very
large mouth, with half developed teeth at irregular
intervals, and straight, rough, short hair, but across
whose ugliness there shone occasionally an intelligent
and sunny smile, and her face, at the moment Frank first
looked at it, was all alive with interest and curiosity.

She gave them as quickly as possible the reasons to
which they owed the honor of her visit, and waited
anxiously for the annihilation of her hopes or their
happy reëstablishment. The woman, whose English
was very puzzling, insisted upon being spokesman, and
Frank at last, turned imploringly from her to the girl,
in whose face she instantly read encouragement.

"Oh, yes, they knew the lady," she exclaimed.

"And a kind lady it wash too," murmured the cobbler, with his head down among his knees.

"And you know where she lives?"

"Oh, yes," the girl replied; "I go twice a week to
do up chores for her."

"Then, you can give me all directions about getting
to her!"

Thereupon the woman interrupted and told "Dod-
oty" to "zhut up," she'd tell the lady; and then followed
such a bewildering splutter of be-Dutched English
names, and unintelligible directions, that Frank felt her
hopes obscured afresh. She glanced down at the cob-

bler, who was shaking his head gloomily among the awls and lasts, and exclaimed :

" You know the way ; you have been there ?"

" Yah, yah," he said, looking up intelligently, " often, many, many times."

" Come with me. then, and I will never forget your kindness."

He started up, but looked doubtfully at his wife, who, after a moment of surprise and opposition, concluded he might go. It had, no doubt, occurred to her that the stranger's gratitude might take a metallic form, and she proceeded to effect his toilette with all possible despatch. She sent Dorothy under the bed for his hat, while she herself pulled out his Sunday coat from between the mattress and the sheets, and dusted it with an ashy whisk that had been lying on the dresser, with the griddle-cakes and cabbage for company. Then, peeling off his jacket, she went on to invest him with it, jerking it up by the collar behind, and ramming his arms down in it while he stood meek and unresisting. After she had hitched it up by the collar and yanked it down by the tails, and buttoned it across the breast, she made a dash at a tin basin on the hearth, half full of slate-colored water, containing a soaked rag in common use among the family, and began applying it to his face with as little regard to his personal feelings in the business as if he had been a saucepan or a baby.

" Dere, dere; ishn't dat enough," he murmured feebly. " De young lady's in a hurry ; dere, dere, now."

She concluded, without reference however, to his

expostulations, and taking the hat from Dorothy, whc had just emerged with it from underneath the bed, she passed her sleeve around it thoughtfully several times, and then placed it on his head, jamming it down to his eyelids and tipping it a little back, which gave him a very funny, helpless look, and conveyed the idea that he had not dressed himself, as few men who dress themselves are in the habit of pulling their hats down to their eyebrows and then tipping them a little back.

"Dere, now you'd petter go," she said, stepping back and looking at him, while she picked up the baby from the bed and tucked him under her arm. "You'd petter go and not keep de young lady waitin' in de cold no longer."

For Frank had retreated to the fresh air meanwhile, and now led the way with alacrity down the steps, followed to the entrance of the alley by the cobbler and the little boy, the woman and the baby, the black cur and Dorothy, leaving the small girl tied in the chair, howling piteously.

They were soon out into the street, and the cobbler seemed to regain himself at every step. He pushed his hat timidly a little higher up on his head, and after they had turned the corner he set it straight, though not without a cautious look behind him as he did it. Frank half expected to find the carriage gone on her return to the boarding-house, but there it stood, though the man was on the box in a very unpleasant frame of mind, threatening to go off every minute. The slatternly girl was sitting on the steps however, with a shawl over her head, watching him very closely, and three or four adjoining windows had heads protruding from them and several of the lodgers were standing in the door.

One of them, a dark, suspicious looking man, with heavy moustache and beard, better dressed than his companions, came down the steps and looked narrowly at Frank as he opened the carriage door for her to enter.

"Where shall I tell the man to drive?" he said, raising his hat.

She shrank back to the other corner of the seat and said:

"This person who came with me will tell him."

She saw uncomfortably that the stranger listened carefully to the directions of the cobbler, and did not turn away till the latter had come to take his place timidly inside, there being no room for him on the box, owing to the coachman's red-faced comrade. In her vexation and embarrassment at the crowd of men upon the steps, Frank had forgotten to remunerate her little guide, so leaning forward, she hurriedly called him to her, and dropped a piece of money in his hand. He had been on the eve of crying for some minutes, but his round face smoothed itself out instantly, and with a deep blush, and a very conscious look, he put both fat fists into his pockets and hurried to the house.

While Frank, with a sigh of relief, leaned back in the carriage, and felt that her perils were over; whereas they had, in truth, but just begun.

CHAPTER VI.

CITY LIFE.

"Alas! to think how people's creeds
Are contradicted by people's deeds!"

WHEN the carriage stopped for the third, and as Frank devoutly hoped, the last time, the little cobbler threw himself heart and soul into the task of opening the pig-headed door, and struggled with and battered at it till he was quite weak, coachee meanwhile having concluded he had played footman long enough, and not stirring from the box. Seeing no immediate prospect of release at this rate, Frank at last, in an evil moment, said to him,

"Press against it, perhaps it will yield."

"Yah, yah, perhaps it vill," he murmured eagerly, and unadvisedly throwing his whole weight upon it, it did yield, suddenly, treacherously, unequivocally, and the poor little cobbler went sprawling on the pavement.

"Oh my, my," he murmured plaintively, trying to get up, as Frank, springing out, stood offering him her hand. "O my, I didn't means to, no, no, no. You will not tinks I did. You vill not, now?"

"Why no," said Frank. "Of course not! That' the last thing. I'm afraid you've hurt yourself."

"O my, O my," he went on, cowering before her, an

abject apology. "To tink I should have ton it, when 1 vent riding mit a lady too. O my, O my!"

The coachman and his comrade were guffawing audibly on the box, and the little Dutchman, looking up at them with a sidelong plaintive glance said, shaking his head mournfully,

"I am very shorry, shentlemen, I am very shorry."

Frank tried to reëstablish his self-respect by changing the current of his thoughts, so she asked him if he were sure this was the house they wanted.

"O yes, O yes," he answered with alacrity, hurrying up the steps. There was no bell to ring; it was a two story wooden house, painted yellow, very neat and decent in its exterior, but very, very, humble. The door opened in an unreserved way that showed it was tenanted by more than one family, and the passage way and stairs were bare, though clean and well swept.

"Von pair pack, miss," said her cicerone, and he shuffled up the stairs and paused before the door and pointed. Frank nodded and thanked him, and paused too before it, her heart beating somewhat fast. She sent him down to help the driver with the trunk, while she knocked faintly at the door.

A low feeble voice said enter, and she turned the handle of the door and entered very softly, feeling there was sickness and sadness and age within. The room was small, but white-washed and very clean. A well patched square of carpet covered the middle of the floor, a slim long legged bedstead stood in one corner and a high brass-knobbed bureau in another; a small stove, a chair, and a 'ittle table completed the

of the apartment.   In the chair by the stove, with the
little table beside her, sat a pale attenuated elderly
woman, who turned her head feebly to the door as the
new comer opened it.

"Aunt Eleanor," said Frank hesitatingly, making a
step forward, then pausing as the sick woman put her
hand, bewildered, to her head for a moment and said
nothing.

"It is not—my little Frances," she said in an uncertain and hesitating manner.

"Yes, dear Aunt Eleanor," Frank said, hurrying forward and stooping down to kiss her.   "I hope you are
glad to see me!"

Her voice choked as she attempted to welcome her;
she held her in a silent embrace for some moments, then
raising her head she said, "You've come to stay with
me?'

"Yes, dear aunt, to live with you, if you will let me."

"Ah, my child," sighed the poor woman, shaking her
head, "Why did you not come before!   Now—this is
no place for you.   You cannot live in it.   I should not
be right to let you."

"Dear aunt, I am not afraid of poverty.   I am going
to work.   I only want you to let me stay with you.   I
don't ask anything better than you can give me."

She shook her head with a deep sigh, "My child,
you do not know—"

Frank answered her by a kiss, and went to the door
to receive her trunk, pay the driver, and give the little
cobbler her liberal thanks and a douceur that utterly
confounded him with its magnificence.

"How came he with you?" said her aunt amazed "How did you find him, and, above all, how did you find me?"

Frank, thinking to amuse her, told her the story of her adventures since she left the cars at twilight, which frightened the poor old aunt terribly, and confirmed her in the belief that the city was no place for her, and that the sooner she was sent back to Titherly the better. It did not take many hours for the neice to find out, however, that she could stay, if she were bent upon it, so she went to work advisedly; first she made herself indispensable to her aunt, and then she coaxed and finessed a little, and then she told her finally, she would not go back to old Aunt Frances, come what might, and she had only to choose between keeping her with her and turning her adrift upon the world. Then she painted a seducing picture of success in her school-teaching, removal to better quarters, the permanent services of Dorothy, new furniture, and an easy state of the money market. And the poor woman listened and shook her head, and said it was impossible, and yielded, as Frank knew she would. And the next day saw her firmly established in her new home, and her new life begun. But not such a life as she had tried to make her aunt believe in, nor even such a one as she had thought she reasonably might hope for. She soon discovered that absolute penury was staring her poor relation in the face, that her once ample household furniture had gone piece by piece to keep her from starvation, and that of the scanty remnant of it, more must soon go, to keep the wolf away. And it seemed indeed to Frank, as she watched her

narrowly, that her life hung by a thread. Illness,
anxiety, and age together had made sad havoc with a
constitution naturally feeble and a mind naturally timid
and dependant. One by one she had lost or shrunk
away from the few friends she had made since her
removal to the city; relations she had none; and thus
was sinking into the grave, a patient, faithful soul, whom
only God and the good angels watched and pitied.

It nerved Frank with a new energy, and she resolved
it was a work worth her best strength to keep this forgotten sufferer a little longer in the world, and to show
her there was love and comfort in it yet. But how
achieve it, how begin her work? Day after day she
started out with resolution and courage, and night after
night she came back gloomy and disappointed. Slowly
but surely, the slender purse that held their all grew
lighter, steadily and continually the weight upon her
heart grew heavier; she was adding to her poor aunt's
perplexities, not easing them; she was a burden where
she should have been a support. She had need of all
the defiant stubborn courage with which she had set
out; she was learning that it is the march and not the
battle that taxes the soldier's strength. She did not
dream for a moment of giving up, her spirit was as
unbroken as ever, it was even stronger, but it was
not a healthy strength, and added neither to her happiness nor profit. One day's record will show the tenor
of her experiences at this time of her life.

She had fancied that the public schools offered a more
independent sort of life than any others, and she had
pplied in innumerable ways for a situation in one of

them. She had no letters and no influence of any kind, but a very strong faith in her own success if she persevered, and a very strong determination to persevere. But a month of the most uninterrupted rebuffs and discouragements had somewhat allayed her confidence, and it was with a very dull step that, one morning, she started out, with Dorothy as cicerone, to obtain an interview with the principal of one of the largest schools, to whom she had been very discouragingly referred. Dorothy had been on all occasions her companion; this had been a strict proviso of her aunt's, who considered her much too young and pretty, and much too ignorant of the city, to be trusted by herself. So with strong inward rebellion she had submitted to the companionship of this bizarre child on all her expeditions, and indeed they were so much to Dorothy's taste that she hung about the house continually, and never allowed Frank the satisfaction of walking around the block alone. The child did all the errands of the family however, and so saved her from the annoyance of mixing herself at all with the small merchants and hucksters of the neighborhood. But though her goings and comings were so unobtrusive and quiet, there were few of the neighbors who did not speculate upon her, and catechise Dorothy whenever they could obtain that young person's ear, which indeed was not a difficult thing to do, seeing she always had one ear inclined to purposes of gossip, and one eye directed to the interests of her neighbor. Being, however, the best hearted and most absurd child in the world, and devotedly fond of Frank, Frank could not help being somewhat fond of her, though at times extremely bored by her society, and uncomfortably conscious of the odd appearance they made together in the street.

Dorothy's taste in dress was not good : she wore her clothes unnecessarily short for a girl of her age, which made very prominent her grey worsted stockings and immense pegged shoes. A short round cloak of other days, and a Dutch built bonnet of her mother's, together with her surpassing plainness, attracted the notice of those few passers-by who did not turn to look at her pretty companion.

"This hateful, hateful place," thought Frank, pulling her veil closer and pushing Dorothy a step behind her. "Don't walk so close to me, Dorothy, the sidewalk is too narrow."

Dorothy dropped back, but Frank's pace being much faster than her own, and being afraid of losing sight of her in the throng, she presently caught hold of her cloak and hurried panting after her, and the people looked more than ever.

"Come and walk beside me, Dorothy," Frank said at last, stopping and biting her lips. "Don't take hold of my cloak, and rest yourself if you are so extremely tired."

The school, which they presently reached, was an immense brick building, with the number of the ward in gilt letters over the entrance. The ground floor was a sort of court-yard, where the children played, the second, and the third, and the fourth floor had to be passed before the principal's ear could be obtained. All the rooms looked busy and orderly, the passage ways were clean and well aired, and the staircases strong and well built.

"My last chance," Frank thought, with a little sinking of the heart, as she paused before the glass door to which she had been directed, and knocked. A pert, mincing girl, who reminded her a good deal of the pink calico abomination of Titherly, opened the door and left her standing within it, while she went across the room and spoke to the principal. The principal waved his hand towards a seat, after a glance at her, and desired the teacher to go on with the recitation. The teacher was evidently a good deal in awe of him, and went on with assiduity, while Frank's heart sank a little lower at the way in which the scholars rattled through their lessons, flying, tripping, picking themselves up, and scampering on without a look behind She knew she had never thought as fast as that in all her life, and she felt herself very unworthy to teach them, if they understood at all what they were saying; but she soon satisfied herself that they did not, and that thinking was not one of the branches insisted on in Ward School No. —.

At the end of the lesson, the principal came up to her and questioned her rather unceremoniously upon her business with him. He was not a gentleman, and his manner made her very uncomfortable, while all the girls in the vicinity peered pertly at her from over their books, and tittered faintly at the open embarrassed looks of Dorothy. The pri moment, told Frank to follow him to his Dorothy brought up the rear, clutching

pauion's cloak, and looking back continually to see if
they were laughing yet.   Their conductor closed the
door after he had shown them into a small comfortable
apartment on the floor below, settled himself in a study
chair, passed his hand through his hair, and leaning
back looked at Frank, who stood before him, and asked
her her name again.   She felt her cheeks burn as she
answered him; only the thought of her dire necessity
kept her civil.   Then he went on and asked her a good
deal about her education and acquirements, and gave
her several rather perplexing questions in history, which
she surprised him by answering very promptly.   She
was quite sure, from his glibness in putting them, that
they were a series of standards, a sort of abridged classic
library he carried about in his mind for use on such
occasions, and she longed to be at liberty to ask him
perplexing questions.   She had no doubt she could
put him to total rout in fifteen minutes.   Finding
her pretty well educated, and with a clear definite
way of expressing herself that betrayed a clear, definite
way of thinking, he prudently left the ground which
seemed to be more entirely *pays de connaissance* to her
than to him, and proceeded to corner her on mathematics.   In this he succeeded, for she was a little out
of practice, and indeed had never been up to the Ward
School standard.   So he told her she would not do, and
began to look over a file of compositions.

She was desperate enough to ask if there was no
chance for her if she perfected herself in mathematics.
No, the small great man said, there was none; there were
no vacancies, and hosts of applicants all the time, who

would come, of course, before her. So, with the sweet satisfaction of knowing she had been catechised for his entertainment solely, she left the room and hurried down the stairs and out into the street.

Presently Dorothy pulled her cloak and told her she was going in the wrong direction, so she turned and etraced her steps. She found she was being closely eyed by a man who was loitering outside the school-house door, and a glance at him recalled instantly the night she came to the city, and the lodging-house of Mrs. Murdoch. They had to pass directly by him, and he gave Dorothy a smile of recognition, and Dorothy, much delighted at having been remembered, grew very red in the face, and looked up sideways at her companion.

"How came you to know that man, Dorothy?" she asked.

Dorothy explained that she had seen him at her father's; that he had been there lately several times to have his boots mended, and that she thought he was a very pleasant gentleman, and that he had given her a quarter more than once.

Their next errand was to answer an advertisement for governess. Dorothy guided her to the house and waited for her in the hall, while she was taken by the servant up to his mistress' morning room, a charming little apartment on the second floor, where there were flowers, and pictures, and books, and a dainty work-basket lined with cherry, and a half cut review on the table, and a low easy chair drawn up by the blazing soft coal fire, and every token of a lady-like presence recently withdrawn.

"If I were mistress here," she thought, during the

half hour she waited for the lady-like presence to reassert itself, " if I were mistress here, what coquettish morning dresses I would wear, and what pretty little slippers. On a dark day like this, what sweet hours, with my book, before the fire, and that pretty embroidery on my lap. I really think I should feel more at home than in the bare little room in G—— street, and like it even better, though the carpet is well patched, and though the stove does shine supremely. What a happy, easy life! I long to see the woman who has the happiness to lead it."

Her desire was at length gratified; an adjoining door opened, and a tall, well-dressed woman appeared, pausing on the threshold, and, looking over her shoulder, before addressing Frank, to give some curt, business-like directions to some one in the rear, about a man who was to come from the upholsterer's and a woman who was to bring back some work. Then she closed the door upon that branch of industry, and coming forward, recognized Frank in a well-bred manner and sat down. Frank scanned her rapidly and curiously; she evidently took life hard; there was a perpetual plait in her forehead just between her eyes, which were handsome ones, and a hard, cold ring in her voice, though nature had made it a very fine one. She was dressed in admirable taste, and had a thoroughly high-bred air, but her pretty clothes were evidently no pleasure, only an inevitable duty to her, and her good manners were too rigid to be pleasing to anyone, least of all to herself, who had had the trouble of forming them. But to do her justice, she was very innocent of any desire to please anyone, even herself, to whom she was inexorably tart. In the ten minutes' conversation Frank had with her, she became convinced she had never had a trial in her life; she had evidently never known anything but wealth, she was too indifferent to it to be new to it; her children were living and were well. Frank knew from the hard way she spoke of them that she had never lost one. Her husband's kindness and consideration for her came out inadvertently, and her own respect and deference for him were apparent in some trifling arrangement that she mentioned; her parents were still living; her own health was good; what did it all mean, this hard drudgery that marked itself on her face, in her voice and manner?

Simply that she was ungrateful, untender, and dutydoing; that she had rigid notions of what the world, her position and her conscience required of her; that she did not allow herself a grain of gentleness towards others nor of indulgence to herself; that she got no pleasure out of her life, and was making of it, altogether, a huge mistake.

She evidently was pleased with Frank's intelligence and good manners, and would have been very glad to have engaged her, but that her inexorable sense of what she owed her children forbade her giving them a governess whose requirements did not come strictly up to her rules for them. Frank's education had been irregular, her judge soon found; she could not carry out that system in which the children had heretofore been drilled, and she had to tell her with decision that she would not suit.

"I could very soon attain what you require," said Frank, with a look of wistfulness, for she saw the struggle. "I could study and improve myself in those branches in which you think I am deficient. I am very desirous of a situation."

It flashed through the lady's mind for a moment that it was a hard case for refinement, intelligence, and beauty to be turned away from her nursery because they had not been moulded on her model; but she repulsed the thought as unworthy of her, fortified herself against the pity she felt for the girl's position, by the thought of what she owed her own; dissected her reluctance to reject her, decided it was a weakness, and reiterated her well-bred refusal.

Frank said good morning, and passed out of the pleasant room with a heart that ached acutely. While the lady stood three minutes after she heard the hall-door close, beating her foot upon the carpet, and wondering if she had not done an unwise thing. "They shall have judgment without mercy who have shown no mercy;" the lady *had* done an unwise thing.

Frank had three other names upon her list; the rest of the day was spent in pursuing them, in being catechised, scrutinized, and sent away by those who answered to them; it was nearly dark, when, grasping patient little Dorothy's hand, she left the last place and started on her long walk home. Bitter and rebellious feelings filled her heart as she thought of the poor invalid awaiting their return. This was justice, perhaps, but it did not commend itself to her mind as such. Who had sinned, this woman or her parents, that she had been born to drag out such a sad, dull life, and end it in such penury and sorrow? The easy lives of the men and women she had that day been brought in contact with, would suffer bitterly in a comparison with her meek aunt's humble walking in the ways of God. Had He forgotten; had He hidden away His face, and would He never see it? It almost frightened her when she found what thoughts she harbored; thoughts that would have seemed impious two months ago; thoughts that many good people go through life without thinking, but which they had better not be too hard upon, till they have tried experimentally to put them down.

Little Dorothy was quite awe-struck by the rigidity of her companion's face; she would not for the world have spoken to her, and she heaved a little sigh of relief when stopping at the door of a shop, she said, "Wait here, Dorothy, a minute till I come out."

She had been thinking, "My head does not seem to avail me much, I will see what my hands can do. I must, I *will* find some employment."

The lamps were just lighted in the shop, which was brilliant with all sorts of novelties in tapestry: she went up to a woman behind the counter, and asked if she had any work to give out, if, indeed they ever gave out any from the shop.

O yes, the woman said, a good-natured little French-woman, they gave out a good deal, but it was all promised, and more, and there were women waiting for it all the time. She was evidently somewhat more familiar with the sight of refinement and poverty combined than our own happy countrywomen are, and she gave the

young stranger a look of considerable sympathy as she
was turning away, and said, knitting on rapidly as she
spoke, " I wish I knew some way to tell you, miss, but
this is a bad city for such as have to work : it's only
meant for rich people, I begin to think."

" I'm afraid so," said Frank, with a half-bitter smile,
as she turned away and went out into the bustling, giddy
street again.

" Did you get what you wanted?" said Dorothy,
timidly inserting her hand in her companion's.

" No," she returned, taking it without repulsion.
" They did not have what I wanted. Shall we go home
now, my little girl, and get some dinner? For I begin
to remember breakfast occurred some eleven hours ago,
and we didn't have anything for lunch."

Dorothy brightened up and quickened her pace, and
Frank devoutly hoped there would be enough to satisfy
her hunger in the house. For herself it was no matter,
she was not hungry, she hated the name, the thought
of food; but she was so weak from the want of it, she
almost feared to trust herself to walk alone.

This day's disappointments and pains were not new,
and they were repeated, on many succeeding days, in
varied forms. On one, a little crueller and longer than
the others, she came home to find a new and worse trial
waiting for her.

The poor invalid was lying on the bed, and turned
her head slightly towards them as they entered.

" You have had an easy day, dear aunt?" Frank said,
stooping down. But she saw at a first glance that some
thing had gone wrong: her aunt's face was deadly pale,

and the handkerchief she held before her mouth was wet with blood.

"I trust it is not anything, dear child," she murmured faintly. "Do not be frightened; it has happened once before."

Frank assured her she was not frightened; she was chiefly sorry she had left her so long alone. She whispered Dorothy to go and ask the doctor if he could come immediately, while she smoothed her aunt's pillow, adjusted everything about the bed, and then arranged upon the table, supper, dinner, or whatever bread and butter and tea as a second meal is called, quietly reassuring her aunt by the tranquillity of her manner, and persuading her to lie perfectly still in her present attitude, knowing that probably her life depended on it.

But, when the doctor came, he shook his head; there was no hope, he told Frank, who followed him out into the hall; she might linger several days, she might not survive the night; he would come again in the morning, early; in the meantime apply the remedies he had prescribed, keep her entirely quiet, watch the changes that occurred and report all faithfully to him.

But when he came in the morning, he found that all was over; there was a white attenuated figure stretched upon the bed that needed his care no more, a simple-hearted child crying beside it, who could not understand his clumsy pity, and a girl with a pale, stern face moving quietly about the room, who did not apply to him for help, and to whom he did not dare to offer it; and so the common-place doctor went away vaguely uncomfortable, and left Frank alone with her dead.

4*

CHAPTER VII.

THE SETTING OF A GREAT HOPE.

" The life of woman is full of woe!
  Toiling on and on and on,
  With breaking heart and tearful eyes,
  And silent lips, and in the soul
  The secret longings that arise,
  Which this world never satisfies!
  Some more, some less, but of the whole,
  Not one quite happy, no, not one."—GOLDEN LEGEND.

Two days had passed since the funeral, and Frank,
standing silently by the window, was looking vacantly
out at the dreary court-yard and the tall, mean houses in
the rear, when Dorothy put her head in at the door, and
with her cross-eyed, queer smile, asked if there was
anything she could do for her before she went away.

"Yes," she said, putting her hand in her pocket;
"you may get a paper for me if you will."

Dorothy would, with a great deal of pleasure, and
did, with a great deal of expedition. Frank said carelessly, as she took the paper and thanked the child,
"You mailed that letter for me this morning, I suppose."

"O yes, ma'am; or, leastways, that gentleman did. I
couldn't quite reach up to the box, and he took it and
said he'd mail it with his own, down town."

"What gentleman?"

"The one we meet sometimes, Miss Warrington—"

"I know, Dorothy. You have done very wrong."

But she stopped, reflecting it was useless to reprove her for what she had done ignorantly, and what she could not have the chance of doing very soon again. For Dorothy was smiling her cross-eyed smile all the time now, having the happy prospect of going to a "place" the day after to-morrow, the delighted recipient of very light wages and very heavy work. Frank therefore dismissed her without more reproof, charging her to come back at night, however, and wondering silently what she should do when Dorothy could come back at night no more.

The letter had only been one to Titherly, conveying very concisely the intelligence of her aunt's death, purposely omitting her own address, and giving no account of her position or her plans; but it was enough, she knew, to give this man who dogged her steps and haunted the neighborhood continually, the information he lacked regarding her. Dorothy certainly had done her as much harm as it lay in her power to do. She drew the shades before the window, and sat down by the little table, looking around with a shiver upon the cold, bare white-washed walls, and scanty, chilly furniture. The empty chair by the hearth gave such a feeling of vacancy, of loneliness to the room. It was all in scrupulously neat order, there was nothing for her to do from now till night. She must just sit there alone and think. And what was there then for her to look forward to? Dorothy's genial company for an, and then a long, still night of wakefulne

thy slept soundly. And in two days more, even this
slender solace and protection would be withdrawn. She
could not live by herself, she knew, even if she had the
means. She leaned her face down on her arms upon the
table, and tried to think. She could not live upon the
money that remained to her after paying the expenses
consequent upon her aunt's illness and death more than
a week longer; the rent was paid up to that time; beyond it she could see nothing. She had only the ghost
of a hope to cheer her, and that was so vague, so distant, nothing but her desperation made her waste a moment's faith upon it.

Since she had been with her aunt she had heard more
than she had ever heard in her whole life before of her
father. She had always clung, with the ardor of an
affectionate child, to the secret hope of one day being
claimed by him again, and having him return, a grand
gentleman, to take her away from Aunt Frances and
Titherly forever. Very secret, however, the hope had
to be, for as the years passed on, and no intelligence
came from him, and no remittances, Aunt Frances' ran-
cor outgrew the limits of her self-control, and the girl
learned to dread the sound of her father's name, but
cherished all the more tenderly her faith in him and her
affection for him. She had not the least remembrance
of him, father and mother were but names to her; but,
with the strange intuitive faith of childhood, she gave
all the love she had to give to those two memories, and
repaid with absolute aversion, the practical but ungracious bounty to which she owed her daily bread. "Wai'
till my father comes back," had been the bitter but con-

fident thought that had swelled in her heart at every childish grievance, and, modified and tempered, it grew to be the unspoken hope that helped her to sustain the pressure of more real trials.

Since she had heard more of him from her aunt, however, much of the romance had gone, and had given place almost entirely to a sorrowful tenderness. He was the poor lonely sufferer's only brother, and so Frank heard the softened story of his wrong doings, and was made to see the heightened picture of his good qualities and misfortunes.

The plain unvarnished truth was simply that Frank's father was a tolerably worthless fellow. With too much talent to remain contentedly in the station in which he had been born, and too little perseverance to attain permanently any higher, he lost, in the young wife whom he really loved, his only balance and an affection which stood to him in the place of principle. From the moment of her death, his course had been steadily a downward one. Full of talent, extremely handsome, and with a certain degree of generous feeling, he was yet practically selfish and without steady principle, and so equally in danger from himself, his friends, and his enemies, and all the three preyed upon him unreservedly. He led a wandering, dissolute life, at first chequered with terrible bursts of remorse and long fits of melancholy, but gradually sinking down into a dull, reckless succession of sins and the consequences of sins, to which he had grown alike indifferent. When he was not heard from at all, it was the best news; his name grew to be the most unwelcome sound in the

CHAPTER VIII.

A FRIEND.

"Give words to thy grief, so art thou relieved of it,
　　Give words to thy joy, so art thou bereaved of it."

ANYTHING was better than that dim, blank, dead room, even the street, dull, grey and grinding, with its rush of feet, its roar of wheels, its sea of faces, under the leaden, cold November sky. She hurried on, now with, now against the current, as her ear caught the guiding sound of the distant bell; she did not heed the vast human ocean through which she was hurrying, her eager pre-occupied face was lifted above it wistfully, listening for the music it drowned sometimes, sometimes lulled enough to let her hear. She followed the sound through a tangled maze of streets after she left the thoroughfare, till it brought her into a broad and open one, in which it was an unspeakable relief to breathe, and above, against the leaden sky, there sprang a free graceful spire, and above it rose a dark and slender cross. The sound of the bell came from within that belfry, and she pressed on through the gloomy doorway into the church itself, which was darker than the street, but not gloomily, only dreamily obscure. Not twenty people were assembled there: a clergyman in his surplice was standing in the chancel, a book open in his hand. Frank went slowly down the aisle, drawn more parental love she had ever known, the only tangible food her hungry heart had ever yet obtained. But in the first interval of quiet after her aunt's death she had written to him, imploring his return, telling him of her desolate and unprotected state, and promising to follow him anywhere, to do anything to serve him, if he would only come and accept her as his child. It had been an eloquent letter, the only vent her heart had had in that dark hour, and she could only hope with a sigh it had not fallen into the same hands that her letter of yester-, day had. She almost dreaded to question Dorothy about it.

For the present, she had only to look over the advertisements again, and to prepare herself for the weary work of to-morrow. But before she turned to the hateful column she was so familiar with, she glanced through the paper. There was an arrival from California, and she ran with interest over the news it brought, the specie list, the list of passengers, the items of political news, the marriages and deaths. Suddenly her eye caught her own name, as the eye always catches the most familiar one, in no matter how confused a list. A very brief and simple record accompanied the name, but it blazed itself into her mind at the first glance, and she laid the paper down, stunned and silent.

" Drowned, in the Yuba River, Cal., August 28th, John Warrington, a native of New York, aged 42 years."

For ten minutes she sat still, with the paper before her, and the fatal words staring up at her; then she started from her seat and paced up and down the room. Had God forgotten? What had she done?

others to merit this! Would He ever see it; did He concern Himself with the miseries of the children of men? Or was it only the dull monotonous wheel of destiny that she had fallen under, a chance that had befallen her, a thing that others had escaped, but she must bear, and bear patiently, sweetly, kissing the rod.

There had been so much need for action, stirring constant battling with necessity, since she had come away from home, that she had had little time for thought, but now there was ample, ample time, and it came crowding, pressing in upon her. It had seemed, an hour ago, as if her trials were heavier than she could bear; within that hour she had seen set forever the hope she had never been without before, the hope with which she had grown up, which was entwined and woven in with everything which came up in her thoughts, and which it cost her a most bitter pang to detach and to unravel. It had never been anything but a hope: orphaned, in reality she had always been; all her life she had endured the actual penalties of orphanhood, and now she was suffering its first pangs afresh, in her darkest, most unfriended hour.

As she sat with her head bowed upon her arms before her, she heard through the distant hum of the busy city, the faint sound of a church bell. That might be a call to her, that might be a voice for her ear, the only one in the vast city that was speaking to her. Poor friendless child: it brought back to her mind a recollection of the faith and simplicity she had lost, the religion she had believed in, the wide Christianity that sheltered all beneath its wings, "though slow and loath to come," the communion of saints throughout the world of sinners, the tender eye of God upon His people.

"I will follow that sound," she thought, starting up. "Perhaps it will bring me to some quiet place where I can say my prayers again; perhaps it will bring me to some kind soul who will tell me what to do"

"I do not like to think we shall never meet again. Can we not be friends?"

Frank returned the generous look with one of gratitude. "I am afraid we cannot be friends exactly, our paths lie so very far apart."

"They need not," said the stranger, pleadingly, "I have been watching you through the service. I know you are not happy. Let me help you. Tell me what your trouble is. *Let* me help you!"

"Help me!" murmured Frank, turning her face away. "I do not know where you would begin."

"I would begin by loving you," said the girl, taking her hand in hers; "I would begin by suffering with you. Give words to thy grief so art thou relieved of it. Tell me what your trouble is."

"It is—my life dead in its beginning," said Frank, raising her head, and speaking with a smothered vehemence. "It is poverty, isolation, desolation, apathy. It is more than comes often in a whole long life come at once into mine. It is youth ended before it had well begun, happiness made a thing impossible, dull indifference the only hope. You do not know what trouble could do all that? Think a moment. Do you believe in any one, man or woman, *believe* as only women can believe? Fancy that belief taken away from you in one moment, and a heavy certainty of treachery and baseness come instead, and see whether you could bear it any better than I have borne it. And then add to that pain every other possible discouragement, distress, and difficulty, and you know what my trouble is. I don't know why I tell you this; I never have told any one before; I never meant to have told any one. If I had died to-day, it would have died along with me, and no one would have known what God had dealt to me. You must forget it."

And the sudden, brief emotion sank down in a moment to the old stern manner.

"I will forget it, except when I say my prayers. Believe in me, tell me of the present, what you are suffering now, and what I can do to help you."

Frank shrank back, chilled again, when it came to talking of the grinding present. She wondered and was frightened at her momentary unreserve. But at last she conquered herself and yielded to her friend's importunity enough to say,

"All that any one could do for me at present would be to help me find a place as governess. I have been unable to get one for myself."

The young lady's face brightened with pleasure. A governess for the children was the thing they needed now at home. They were in town on that very errand. It was so fortunate.

"But," interrupted Frank, with an unconquerable instinct of honesty, "I must tell you I do not know anything about music, and I have not been educated regularly for a teacher. I doubt if I shall suit."

Her companion would hear of no objections. She was certain it was the very thing. As to the music, that was nothing. It was the only thing she knew anything about, and she could teach the children just as well as not herself. She had always known she ought to do something about their education. When should mamma come and see her?

the three younger children of the Thorndyke family, more, it is to be feared, because their mamma was tired of governess hunting, and because their sister had set her silly little heart upon it, than from any conviction of the applicant's peculiar fitness for the undertaking. Her commission was to bear date from that very after noon; it was desirable that she should be ready to accompany them to the country at four o'clock; could she find it possible to do so?

Entirely possible, Frank said, and her new friend's face was radiant.

They should not come in town till after the holidays, Mrs. Thorndyke explained, as the house was to undergo repairs; and as the children had lost much time already since their last governess left, she hoped Miss Warrington could make her arrangements to stay till they moved in, without visiting the city herself.

The daughter blushed and looked pained, thinking this sounded rude and dictatorial, but Frank's unembarrassed assurance that she had nothing to call her to the city, and that she much preferred the country always, served to relieve her mind.

As Frank hurried home, with Dorothy by the hand, and her curious crossed eyes on her face, she revolved a hundred schemes for getting rid of the furniture remaining in her rooms, and disposing of the few things good feeling dictated reserving for the present. She longed to burn the ship behind her, to make away with everything connected with this most painful period of her life; there should be no connection between the old time and the new, no one in that dismal neighborhood should have the least clue to where she meant to go Dorothy, most of all, should be kept in ignorance of her intended residence.

A small shop, with second-hand furniture encumbering the walk in front, suggested a way to get rid of her unwieldy wealth. The man inside the door regarded her proposals favorably; within an hour he was present in proper person in the little back room in G— street, chaffering industriously over the scanty remnants of the poor lady's household goods, and blessing secretly the providence that had thrown in his way such a very acquiescent customer. Of her simplicity he had strong doubt, but of her anxiety to be rid of the furniture and of him, he had none whatever. He humored her in this fancy, and in amazingly short time, the cart was at the door, and the room stripped of its late adorn-ments, while the narrow equivalent for the purchase was thrust eagerly into the young financier's light purse. She packed a trunk and sent it away for safe keeping to the little shoemaker's, and another to go with her, and her arrangements for removal were complete.

She paid and said good-bye to Dorothy, and sent her away in tears, with a slight gratuity and a new frock; then stood alone for one moment to breathe, in the desolate room, with its four blank staring walls and sounding uncarpeted floor. The old life seemed, indeed, to have passed away, like an unhealthy dream; her courage rose again to meet the new; the doubts of the night before were stifled by the busy plans of daylight; no doubt she was doing right, her scruples had been

folly, her wavering absurd; she held her future again in
her own hands, and she must shape it according to her
former plan.

She had ordered the carriage herself, to avoid giving
Dorothy the least clue to her, and when it came to the
door, and the driver carried down her trunk, she followed him out with a strange feeling of emancipation,
a certainty of stepping out of one life into another, and
leaving not a trace behind.   But in this she was destined
to be thwarted: near the door stood the man whose face
was so detestably familiar to her, and which she had
hoped belonged entirely to the old life, and would never
affront the new.   She hurried into the carriage without
glancing at him, but he followed her, and lifting his
hat, closed the door for her and said, with his eyes
steadily on her face,

"Where shall I tell the man to drive?"

Frank's presence of mind forsook her for the moment,
she hurriedly gave the direction, and, turning away her
head, thought with deep vexation, she had herself given
the link between the past and future, that she had done
so much to separate.

CHAPTER IX.

SAINTY.

"Et la grâce plus belle encore que la beauté."—LA FONTAINE.

IT was already twilight when the carriage drove into the gate at Ringmer.

"I am sorry it is dark," said the young lady. "The drive from the gate is very pretty: I know you will like it. Ah, there's the glimpse of the river between the trees, this bend of the road is the prettiest of all. Look forward, I am sure you can see it!"

"My dear," said her mother in a very travel-worn voice, "you can show Miss Warrington the view by daylight. It is hardly worth while to strain your eyes with making it out now."

Cecelia gave a little sigh, and drew back from the window humbly. Her mother was continually repressing her, the little nature doing its best to smother the great one; but its best was ineffectual, except for the moment, and the large, sweet soul expanded and grew even under the cloudy sky, and sprang up bright and elastic, though daily beaten down with misapprehension and indifference.

It is a beautiful thing to see a young woman love her home as Cecilia Thorndyke loved hers; it is an earnest of her future safety, and the worthy turning of her life, "true to the kindred points of heaven and home." From the moment the lights from the house were visible, her eyes had been dancing, her pulses fluttering, and before her foot was on the carriage step, a dog's head was in her lap, a child's arm round her neck an incoherent chorus of welcome echoing all about her

"We thought you never would come back," cried the smallest voice of all upon the steps.

"I've caught a huge moth, Sainty, did you bring the insect pins?"

"Martin's been about the crocusses, such lots and lots of roots!"

"Muff was lost all day yesterday, and only came back at night."

"Four little Maltese kittens, Sainty, at the barn, the littlest you ever saw!"

"A letter's come to you from Cyril, and another for mamma."

"You didn't forget about the paper boxes?"

Cecilia had an answer for every question and a kiss for every mouth, and was laughing and wondering and exclaiming in as sincere earnest as any of them, as they thronged about her on the steps. There were a few dutiful salutations for mamma, whom the maid was assisting to alight, and the boy, the eldest of the party, submitted to remain behind and be loaded up to the eyes with shawls and bundles.

Frank followed silently into the hall, and watched Cecilia with a half envious admiration. She darted first towards a stand of flowers in one of the wide windows, and bent over them as if they were human loves every bud, every newly developed leaf seemed to give her a thrill of purest pleasure: then detaching herself from the children, she ran over to the niche where her bird hung, and cooed and whispered to him lovingly. It all had a very picturesque effect—the children in their white dresses and bright ribbons, the graceful girl bending over her flowers, the wide hall, with its colored pavement, pictured walls and dim niches, with the soft lamps shining down : the young plebeian felt she must have seen it in her dreams before, it was all so familiar and so fit.

The parlor door was open, and Cecilia ran in and kissed, a little timidly, a grey, dried, unprepossessing elderly gentleman, reading his paper by the lamp, who did not seem particularly moved by her coming, and who asked where her mother was, after she had kissed him. Her mother made her appearance at that moment in the door, looking very handsome, *negligée* and discontented, and Mr. Thorndyke, simply glancing up at her from over his paper, said the train was late, and went on reading.

The fact was, Mr. Thorndyke had been very tired of his beautiful wife for twenty-five years or more, ever since he had been married to her, in truth, and wasted as few words upon her as was possible. He was a man of more than ordinary ability, and had originally had a good deal of heart, but the disappointment of finding he had married a silly woman and been desperately in love with her besides, had given his character an unhappy distortion, and he had become a stern, hard man of business, cold and exacting in his family, sneering

and ungenial in the world. He never could believe in
the intelligence and trustworthiness of women after his
great mistake, and he did not suffer himself to regard
his three young daughters with anything but the most
ordinary interest, neglecting no part of his duty towards
them however, but that of loving them, and bringing
them up at arms' length from their babyhood.

He had felt as truly a patriarchal pride in the birth
of his two sons as disappointment in the birth of his
daughters. He found them legitimate objects of interest
and ambition, and built all his hopes upon them. The
elder had grown up a fine, spirited fellow, in whom the
father believed his own incomplete life would be perfected; the younger was a dull, gauche, shy boy, whom
nobody understood and of whom the father even was
unable to be proud. Poor Cuthbert, called familiarly,
and with an irregular kind of nursery justice, Cub, was
remarkably plain in feature, clumsy in frame, and slow
in mind; he was desperately afraid of his father, and
his mother was nervously afraid of him; his teachers
groaned over him, his elder brother laughed at him, his
younger sisters tormented him, his nurses had early
made his life a burden to him. Even Cecilia saw little
in him but matter of commiseration, and with the best
intentions in the world, pitied him out of all self-respect.
She was gentle and patient with him, but he saw she
was only sorry for him, and he groaned and went stumbling on alone.

By contrast with this unprepossessing boy, the heir
the eldest born, the young tyrant of the household,
shone a perfect hero. He inherited his mother's beauty

and enough of his father's mind to be entirely captivat-
ing in society, and entirely idolized at home. His self-
will, however, was a most distinguishing trait, and early
in his career it became apparent that no other will
would have much to do in the direction of his movements. He had entered the army, totally against his
father's wishes, and to the entire heart-breaking of his
sister, and was now on duty near Washington, where,
if not strictly covering himself with glory, he was at
least seeing a good deal of life, and spending his time
very much to his own satisfaction. He was the most
important member of the family, whether absent or
present, and Frank was familiar with his appearance,
prospects and proclivities before she had been a day at
Ringmer.

There had seemed, on the night of her arrival, to be
a perfect bevy of children in the hall, but after a few
hours' residence among them they resolved themselves
into three; the boy Cuthbert, aged fifteen, and two
girls, aged respectively twelve and six. Sylvia, the
youngest, was pretty, and vain, and loveable; Camilla,
the elder, was clever, and self-willed, and unloveable.
All adored Cecilia, who was, however, but a child herself among them, and too young and too humble-minded
to govern them at all, consequently they never were
governed by any one but their father, out of whose way
they kept with great discretion and industry.

Frank looked with good courage upon the materials
before her. She was sure of the Cub and of Sylvie, and
Cammy was of better texture than many she had had to
deal with, and she locked herself into her room that

5*

night with a feeling of satisfaction and security to which she had long been a stranger. What a gulf between last night and to-night!

The room was a simple, square, plainly furnished one on the third floor, opposite the nursery, for which cir cumstances Cecilia had stammered many apologies; but it had always been the governess' room, and mamma thought perhaps it would be more convenient for her to be near the children; there was one opening out of her own room on the floor below she had hoped to have given her, but mamma thought better not—and —that is——

Poor Cecilia got more deeply involved at every step in explaining away her mother's cold-heartedness, and Frank, in pity for her embarrassment and gratitude for her kindness, smothered her excuses with a hasty kiss, and told her this room suited her better than any other in the house. Cecilia clung to her lovingly, expended a thousand cares on her comfort. and left her at last reluctantly. She was so sweet and engaging, Frank almost believed she should learn to love her, and it was something very bewildering to her to find she could care for any one again in that young manner. To have given her the first kiss and received her kindness as she did, seemed almost hypocritical; she must not deceive her by a warmth that meant little coming from such a dull heart.

Indeed it would have been a cruelty in any matter to have deceived Cecilia, and there were few among those with whom she had been thrown, hardened enough to do it. She was so simple, so purely true herself, she startled hypocrisy into honesty, and made the world ashamed to tamper with her innocence. It is impossible to imagine anything more trusting, more earnest, and more unconscious than her manners; educated in a school of life the most hollow, most pompous, and unprofitable, she was unworldly, pure-minded, and *dévote* from her cradle. She was not a beauty for the multitude, but her grace and delicacy of feature would have made her charming in the sphere in which her lot was cast, if she had chosen to charm it; a sphere for which she had been prepared with every care, but from which she turned away with the indifference of a child, bent on some other pleasure than the one that is offered to it. She did not dread the world, as Christians who are learning their religion sometimes do, and Christians who have been involved in it always do; she simply did not like it; she went into it against her heart, made no progress in it, and came back with the thrill and flutter of a happy bird, to her flowers and books, and the children of the household.

Her indifference to society was an abiding trial to her mother; it was the only pursuit that had ever given, or even now gave her pleasure, and she could not be reconciled to Cecilia's entire distaste for it. She had built great hopes upon her eldest daughter's advent in the world; she would live over again in her the triumphs of her youth; she would enjoy again in her the pleasures which time had made it impossible for her to taste herself. An unworthy ambition, a greedy vanity, a narrow worldliness hung over the child's pure cradle, but could not wake it from its dreams of bliss. Sweet, young soul, she made the air around her pure by her own exceeding purity, and grew up defended from the world by her entire unworldliness.

Cyril, partly because he hated the name to which she was condemned, and partly because of the inborn propensity towards self-sacrifice and saintship which she developed even in the nursery, had given her the pretty sobriquet, which was now a household word. Her beautiful talent for music, together with her auburn hair and dreamy face, completed her title to be a St. Cecilia, and for a while, in a very remote period of his boyhood, Cyril had been quite an enthusiast in the matter of the fine arts. Cecilia and he had been very intimate while the fit lasted ; he had painted her again and again, till she had ached from head to foot with sitting in the saintly attitude. Then she had practised five hours a day to please the whim which succeeded his enthusiasm for the canvas, and when that had passed, had sighed humbly and submitted patiently to be thrown aside, while he dashed forward into the pursuits of youth. Everything by fits, and nothing long ; but in everything beautiful and entirely admirable, the meek maiden thought. She had studied to keep up with him, till the doctor had given her father a solemn warning, and the father had smiled incredulously at the presumption of the girl, and had turned her back into feminine pursuits, with a stern charge to keep to them in future. That, she fancied, was the reason Cyril had ceased to care for her, so none of the blame came on him, but all lighted naturally on herself, for being unable to keep up with him, and being so weak and unenduring as to grow pale and ill when she sat up stealthily till midnight over the books he conquered before eight.

This present separation, just when he had begun again to sympathize with her and care for her society, was a very bitter trial; but her patriotism was not of that irrational character that stops just short of prac ice, and demands the sacrifice of every other woman's dearest and best, while holding back selfishly her own. Cyril was her dearest and best, and she sent him away from her with the courage of a heroine and the submission of a saint.

He went, with a rush of pleasure in his pulses, and a sound of glory in his ears; she watched him go, with a deadening chill in every vein, and a fatal terror forever before her eyes; the courage that had the truest ring had not the bravest glitter.

his eyes as he lifted them and asked her if that was true. She felt almost as people feel at the first fluttering sign of life in an inanimate body over which they have been bending doubtfully; she always had a special interest in poor little Cuthbert after that.

The revival was very slow but sure; a few books were retained as outward and visible signs of progress, but Cub learned his real lessons from Frank's lips. She led him on carefully step by step, holding his hand, guiding his feet, till she became far more interested in him than in either of the brighter pupils. They had been educated in a most unimproving manner; constant changes in the governesses had involved constant changes of system—so, between them all, the poor little girls had been sadly bewildered and neglected.

Cammy had strayed off by herself into all manner of frivolities, read novels *sub rosâ*, and filled up the interstices of her school hours with writing spiteful, ill-spelled notes to Cub about the governess. Sylvie, spoiled to the last degree, wavered some days between the nursery cabal, Cammy and Marcelle the bonne, and the school-room authority and attraction. The latter happily prevailed at last, and Frank found herself sustained by the majority.

Out of school hours, the children were not imposed upon her; Marcelle took care of Sylvie, and Cammy took care of herself, while Cub wandered drearily about or came and sat shyly near her, quiet as a shadow and wistfully affectionate.

In a very few days things settled into their places, and Frank fancied she saw her life clearly and definitely his Cæsar a vacation, and making him sit down by her in the pleasantest window, she proposed they should try something new, and leave off the old lessons for awhile, perhaps altogether. He might read some pleasant book of history to her, and then they could talk about it afterwards, and perhaps she should be able to remember some amusing stories to tell him in connection with it. The boy looked dumb and unmoved, put down his books without emotion, and took up the *riant*, little yellow bound volume she assigned him, and began to read in a dull, droning voice. For all the good she expected it to do him it might as well have been " Old Curiosity Shop" or the Leatherstocking Tales—rather better, perhaps; she only wanted to get into his mind . by any means available, and she took the historic lever out of deference to the little girls' prejudices, who would be manifestly disedified by story books in school time.

The book was a very clear and easy narrative, and stopping him at the first striking passage, she commented on it lightly, adding some odd and picturesque fancy, and watching closely to see if it found any lodgment at all in his mind. None, it was evident; the scales of diffidence and dullness had grown too thick for such an arrow, they could only be pierced by a strong, trenchant fact. So she let him read on again, and arrested him the next time upon a point of historical importance, questioning him upon it, and then slowly, clearly, and with emphasis, repeating it to him in easy words of her own. Ah, it had struck a vulnerable point in the tough armor; a slow light came into

Cecilia poured out her heart to Frank, she clung to her, she supplicated silently her love, but she had to accept in return a fitful sympathy, a moody silence, an unsatisfying affection.

And yet, in the household, generally, she was a most satisfactory element; the children showed almost immediately the good effects of her quiet method with them; Cub was waking up, Cammy was softening down, Sylvie was growing less pert and *exigeante*. She was becoming invaluable, too, to Mrs. Thorndyke, for though she could not be blind to that lady's short-comings, not-comings-at-all, as one might say, she could not forget she was Cecilia's mother, and the mistress of the family in which she had experienced unexampled kindness. Conse quently, in a thousand ways, she had slid into an unac-knowledged usefulness, and had assumed many trifling duties for which Cecilia's dreaminess unfitted her, and to the annoyance of which the mother was very much alive. Frank's fine tact enabled her to see just what was burdensome to her benefactress, and just how far she could relieve her, and she jealously desired in some way to return the kindness she felt she had not merited. She very soon, in the matter of minor household arrange-ments, in the superintendence of the children's ward-robes, the ordering and arranging of things outside the province of the housekeeper, the writing of notes on business or of courtesy, became the indolent elegant woman's " bed of down," *un bon lit de repos*, on which she half unconsciously but most luxuriously sank back. Cecilia wondered at her friend's adaptability, and strange aptitude for duties which were most unpalatable to her unpractical taste; she did not comprehend the avidity with which Frank seized on any actual tiresome duty as a relief from the thoughts she was always fighting, and tried to wear herself out upon what her hands and her eyes could combat.

Long dreamy twilights, soft sad poems, pictures of depth and pathos, were the food of the one soul and the keen torture of the other. Indeed, these two young girls were placed at such an incalculable distance apart in their inner lives, that it was wonderful that in their outer lives they assimilated even as well as they seemed to do. No two experiences could have differed more : luxury, refinement, poetry and leisure had made musical and tender the life of one; necessity of living, practical battling with the world, the cruelty of suffering, the dreariness of having suffered, had nerved with power, and yet it seemed forever darkened, that of the other. One, with her dream of bliss yet undreamed, the poem of her life still folded, unread, in her heart ; the other, rudely roused from dreams to suffer, the short tragedy of her life a finished and irrevocable piece of fate ; they were strangely separated, strangely unsympathetic, and yet strangely attractive to each other. Nature even said different things to each ; Cecilia loved the soft, still, sunny October days, the "calm decay" of autumn forests ; Frank was in sympathy with strong rushing November winds, grey, wet flying clouds on a grey, dim firmament beyond. Sunshine mocked her, calm oppressed her, but such a wind gave her strength and courage and defiance.

It was towards the close of a November afternoon.

that the two found themselves miles from home, with
but little daylight left. They had walked on through
the forest with the wind sounding overhead, along the
river, with the waves dashing restlessly below, across
high open fields swept desolate by the gale, Frank eager
to tire out the impatience that possessed her, and Cecilia
nerved for the moment with a spirit as ardent, caught
from such companionship. The walk home was worse
than dull; it was already dark when they reached the
outskirts of the grove beyond the house, and Cecilia
hurried forward a little anxiously to catch a glimpse of
it. The lights were already shining, and they gave her
a premonition of the rebukes that awaited her within
As for Frank, she was *fade* and weary beyond expression, the spirit all effervesced, the defiance worn out,
nothing worth living or dying for, morbidly, exaggerat-
edly exhausted in mind and body.

" How pale you are," began Sainty, opening the hall
door, but her voice was drowned by a rush of children
and a wild hubbub of excitement.

" Oh, Sainty! where have you been ?"

" What made you stay away so long ?"

" What's the matter with Miss Warrington ?"

" Who do you think is coming ?"

" What do you think has come ?"

" Wait till you hear the news !"

" Don't tell her, Cub. Let her guess, Sylvie !"

" Oh, *won't* she be astonished !"

The long walk, the sudden excitement, the unnamed
error that never left her heart, were too much for poor
Sainty. She turned very pale, and, leaning against the

door, tried in vain to induce them to put an end to her suspense. But they danced about her like little fiends, overjoyed to find they had the power to tease her. Cub, indeed, looked relenting, and tried to make her understand by clumsy hints; but Cammy thrust her hand upon his mouth and threatened him if he dared to speak. Sainty at last made an effort to recover herself, and starting to the parlor door, said, agitatedly,

"Mamma, what is it? Is there any news?"

"Yes, there is," said the lady from her sofa, with marked displeasure in her tones. "But let me ask you why you have stayed so late and given me this alarm? I would not have had such an excitement for the world. I am quite unnerved."

"I am very sorry. We went further than we meant to go; we forgot how far it was. But the news, mamma—you have heard from—from Cyril?—"

"Yes, a telegram came an hour ago."

"Yes," cried Cammy, who was performing a war dance between the speakers, "just as we came in from nutting, the man was at the door. I read it first of all."

"Cammy—mamma—you have not told me—has anything gone wrong with Cyril?"

"Gone wrong with him, my dear?" said the mother, with calm irritation. "Camilla, will you be quiet? You are becoming unbearably presuming. Miss Warrington is too lenient with you. Sylvia, stop those antics. You see, Camilla, the effect of your example on your little sister."

Cecilia stood with one hand on the back of a chair,

the other pressed against her heart, her eyes fixed on
the floor. In a moment her mother turned to her, and
said, resuming the tone and subject where she had left
them to repress Cammy,

"Yes, my dear, I have heard from your brother. He
is coming home; he will be here to-night at half-past
nine, with your father."

"He is not ill?" faltered Cecilia.

"Ill? no, certainly not. Who said he was ill?"

"But I thought by his having leave—"

"Only for three days. I do not think you have much
heart, Cecilia. Is it possible it does not give you pleasure to know of your brother's return?"

Cecilia turned her face away, and was going quietly
out of the door, when she paused to listen to a recom-
mendation from her mother to go and dress immediately
for dinner, which had been waiting for her half an hour
already.

Frank gave a weary sigh as she mounted the stairs to
make her own toilet, while Cecilia flew before her,
nerved with a fresh hope. "Why can I not be unselfish? Why can I not be glad for her?" Frank
thought remorsefully. She knew she would be given
up entirely while he stayed, and that a happiness she
could not share—the worst barrier between friends—
had started up between them. But it was not that she
dreaded most. It was the meeting a stranger, a soldier,
a man fresh from the scenes she was always trying to
forget; it was the mixing of a new element in her life,
the breaking of the faint crust of oblivion and stoicism
that had been forming over her heart during this season

of repose. It was the world flaunting itself before her wretchedness again; it was the end of the outward silence that had been flattering her.

She hated herself for her selfishness; but the happy faces at dinner gave her such discontent she longed to get away from the sight of them. The children, extremely troublesome in their happiness, were to sit up to see their brother, and it became Frank's duty to keep them from driving their mother to insanity. Cecilia was in such a flutter of excitement she could scarcely control herself, much less manage the children. She turned from her book to the piano, and from the piano to her embroidery-frame; then she flitted to the glass to alter a rose in her hair, and then she ran across the room to adjust the fall of a curtain.

Frank had given Mrs. Thorndyke's orders for supper, for Sainty never was trusted with anything so practical, and just after nine o'clock, having concluded a weary series of games at cards, she obeyed madam's hint, and went into the dining-room to see that everything was right. A most cosy and tempting table, arranged for five, the candles already lighted, the fire glowing on the hearth. What a warm and beautiful home to be coming back to! what a welcome awaited this spoiled child of destiny! Frank felt she knew his character most thoroughly from the few sketches she had had of it, and she hated to feel she too was helping to smooth and beautify his path. But then, he was Cecilia's brother.

As half-past nine approached, the children became unbearable. Cammy was restless and excited, Sylvia was sleepy and cross, one teased and the other fretted

Cub sat bewildered and silent, oppressed by the shadow already cast upon him by the coming of his clever brother. They heard wheels and they did not hear them; one knew the lodge gate opened five minutes before, and another knew it had not opened at all; they flattened their noses against the panes and peered out into the darkness; they ran to the front door and listened; they disagreed on all points, and bore their continual disappointments without philosophy or religion.

At last Sylvie began to cry, and Frank had to allure her to her lap and coax her into quiet at a great sacrifice of her own personal feelings in the matter, for the capricious little coquette, like all fine ladies, young and old, was quite contemptible when out of humor. The yellow curls subsided on her shoulder, the quarrelling degenerated into whimpering, and the whimpering soon ceased altogether. Then came an interval of quiet, during which Cammy tried her powers on Cub, and Cecilia sat at the piano with her hands clasped above a music-book, listening breathlessly. Mrs. Thorndyke watched the clock, and beat her foot impatiently upon the carpet, as the hour of ten approached. And all for this ungrateful boy, thought Frank, who left them recklessly and rules them ruthlessly!

With all their listening, the carriage had approached within a hundred yards of the house without their hearing it. Coming up the drive rapidly, it was almost at the door before the sound of wheels reached the parlor. Then, presto! how the scene changed. Cecilia, with a low exclamation, darted to the door, her hand tight on her heart. Her mother, rising, followed her quickly, more feeling animating her handsome features than Frank had ever before imagined they could express. Cammy, all alive with eagerness, flashed out into the hall at the first sound; Sylvie, broad awake on the intant, bounded from the governess' lap, her limp, soft limbs nerved with sudden life; Cub, stumbling along in the rear, looked stunned and spellbound. Frank, staying alone in the vacated apartment, bit her lips to keep down the envious sighs that struggled through them. The acclaim, the welcomes, the kisses, the happy voices, the tender words, roused bitterly the feeling of isolation that had recently been slumbering. There was no family circle where she had a right to enter; there was no home where she deserved a welcome; there was no one living whom she could run to greet with welcoming caresses. Alone most bitterly; shut out from all the ties of love, condemned to satisfy her hungry soul with the tasteless husks of kindness and of friendship.

The voices from the hall grew more distinctly audible, as the welcomed and the welcomers approached the door; if she might only escape before they entered! It was too late, they were already in the room, and she should make herself too prominent in attempting to cross before them, so she shrank back into her corner and tried not to feel she was the only one who had no right to be there. But she was quite safe from observation, the family group were all absorbed, and did not heed her presence any more than they would have done her absence. Mr. Thorndyke, indeed, coming in in his

6

usual all-observant, all-indifferent manner, spoke to her very matter-of-factly as he reviewed the furniture, the lamps, the condition of the fire, drawing the paper from his pocket, pulling his arm-chair to the hearth, and settling himself down, as if the enthusiasm of a welcome, the sentiment of a soldier's return, the reunion of a family were weak and pitiable chimeras to which he would not for a moment lend himself. For the time indeed, he seemed almost as much outside the happy circle as the stranger looking on.

Frank raised her eyes, not with curiosity, however, for she felt as if she knew the new brother's face as well as if she had spent her life in the house, seeing that his picture looked down at her from every wall, or smiled up at her from every album, rest, or locket that she stumbled on. But a surprise awaited her; the handsome features, multiplied on canvas, ivory, steel, and paper were handsome and self-satisfied, "and they were nothing more." The face she saw now, looking down into his mother's, was a radiant and an inspiring one, boyish in its *abandon* and beauty, manly in its strength and ardor of expression. She understood in a moment the fascination of the household; she felt as if she never could have resisted him herself, if she had not been dead. She never remembered to have seen anything so handsome as his face. He had Cecilia's auburn hair and eyes, a skin many shades darker, but as clear and finely colored, a profile of the most perfect grace, and a mouth that changed with every thought. He was well, but slightly built, of middle height, graceful, easy, and determined in his bearing. An Adonis—who

could blame him for the vanity that was inevi able?
No one did; his vanity was one of his great ch rms;
for without it, he would have lacked the confide.ice to
conquer. He had not fallen into the usual error of the
nouveau militaire, and did not shine bra' with epau-
lettes and buttons, but the cut of his moustache, the
squareness of his shoulders, the turn of his head, were
soldierly, *sans contredit*.

He had one arm around his mother, and was looking
affectionately down into her face, while Cecilia stood
with her hand clasped in his, and the children were
clinging about his knees. A scene and moment to
make a man's face beautiful if he has a ray of tenderness
or goodness in his soul. He cast an eager, affectionate
look about the room.

"Ah, what a pleasure to be at home again!" he exclaimed with a thrill of enjoyment in his voice. "I
never knew before where my heart really was," he
added, in a lower tone, looking down in Sainty's face.

Poor Sainty, that one sentence, forgotten as soon as
said, repaid her for whole months of hoping, and pray-
ing, and fearing; it was to be her happiest memory for
whole months to come.

"And you!" he cried, lifting Sylvie in his arms.
"Silliest of little sisters yet! Mamma must have your
curls cut. I vow you are too pretty and too vain to
live!"

The silly little sister hid her face on his shoulder and
swept her soft curls across his cheek, while Cammy,
piquée at the compliment to charms of which she could
not boast, endeavored to create a diversion by clamor

ously demanding if he had got her letter and Cub's, and if he did not think Cub was improving in his writing.

"Oh, vastly," laughed the brother, determined not to satisfy her, "vastly; Cub is quite a scribe. Cub, don't relax your efforts, I may need you yet as adjutant."

He glanced over his shoulder at him as he said this with a laugh, and poor Cub looked miserable, and awkward, and red, and as if he wished he could get away from his brother's merry eyes, and the merry, and careless, and pitying eyes of all the world.

"Cuthbert is actually improving, though," said his mother with great dullness, by way of killing him entirely.

"Yes, with Miss Warrington to do his lessons for him," muttered Cammy, maliciously. "I wonder who couldn't get along that way."

"Cammy," said Cecilia, in a tone of reproach; then moving forward a little anxiously, she tried to arrest her brother's attention in order to present him to her friend. But though she was quite within range of his eyes, and much nearer to the group than she desired to be, Sainty could not make him see her; he was so engaged with the many objects of home interest he entirely overlooked her.

" Ah!" he cried, putting down Sylvie on the rug and leaning forward on the mantelpiece, "I see you framed that little assumption—it's an exquisite engraving. Sainty, I've got a lot of camp sketches for you, I know you'll like them; they are really clever. Did I write you? Quite a genius turned up in the regiment the other day, poor as possible, and glad to get work more to his taste than cleaning guns. I'll show them to you to-morrow. Why! is that clock in its right mind! The train was abominably behind to-night. If I were a director on that road "——

"You'd be likely to keep quiet about it, and be thankful that it ran at all," said Mr. Thorndyke, without raising his eyes, and speaking as if he read it from the paper.

Cyril was the only one of his five children who dared to be familiar with him, and he enjoyed secretly the boy's presumption while outwardly meeting it with his accustomed grimness. To-night, the young hero, doubly confident, dashed irreverently forward among his father's time-honored prejudices, laughed at his railway ventures, asked questions about his farming, sneered at the political party to which he was allied, and showed generously his contempt for the social element called old fogy. The father snapped and growled, and set him down repeatedly, but it was evident there was a fascination to him in the young man's impudence, and that he was convinced he saw the making of a man, a man directly modelled from himself, in the self-will and independence that overrode all feelings of reverence and loyalty.

The children always listened to him with awe and admiration, and the mother with a fond and foolish pride, only poor Sainty looked troubled and wistful, and liked her brother less in this than in any other attitude. She longed that evening to get the children all away, for Cammy was drinking in his extravagances with

avidity, and Sylvie, an unconscious mimic, was swelling
with sauciness as she listened.   At last, the mother,
recalled to the lateness of the hour by the announcement of supper, ordered them off peremptorily to bed.
With many remonstrances and much dissatisfaction
they obeyed, and Frank seized the moment of their exit
to effect her own.

But at the door she was met by Thomas, in a condition of agitation; would Miss Warrington step for
one minute into the butler's pantry?   Some mistake
had occurred about the wine, the housekeeper and he
had different views about a certain label which had
slipped from the decanter, and Mr. Cyril never forgave
confusion in the wines.   Would Miss Warrington be so
kind as to decide between them.

Frank followed him into the butler's pantry, where
the housekeeper, red and determined, stood confronting
him with a bottle in each hand.   She began by sub-
mitting the whole question to Frank's arbitration, and
promising to abide by her decision, but took advantage
of her possession of the floor to give a rapid summary
of her estimate of Thomas' acquirements, and the very
slender claims she conceived he had to the position he
presumed to occupy.   A man that hadn't any more
nose than a Newfoundland, that blundered about among
the bottles like an idiot, that hardly knew port from
sherry; a pretty man indeed to serve a gentleman's
table, to tamper with such wines as Mr. Thorndyke's.
She wou'd not for the world have Mr. Cyril know the
confusion things were in; she almost sank with shame
when she remembered how near he had come to know

ing it that very night if she had not interfered. An affront Mr. Cyril never would have overlooked, such a gross blunder as this, and on the occasion of his first return from camp.

Thomas was white with rage, the housekeeper grew redder every minute. " O this precious Cyril," thought Frank, glancing down at the decanters, " he thrills the family even to its extremities." Happily Frank's eye had that evening made acquaintance with the two decanters.

" Where did this smaller one stand this evening, Thomas, when I came out to give you orders for the supper ?"

" Here, miss, just exactly here," cried Thomas, and the housekeeper acknowledged she had seen him take it up from there.

" Very well, I saw the label just beside it on the shelf; you pushed it back a little when you took the decanter up. Here it is." She turned to the light and read it. Thomas was right, the housekeeper was wrong; the former looked radiant, the latter swept away in a dreadfully bad temper.

At this moment the man was called abruptly into the dining room, and leaving the door ajar, Frank, who was fastening the label on another dubious decanter, could not help hearing the voices within.

" Where is Miss Warrington ?" she heard in tones unmistakably the father's. She felt sure he was glancing around in a hard manner as they took their seats at the table, uncomfortable at the sight of the vacant place beside Cecilia.

" I think she went up with the children. It is

scarcely worth while to call her," said the mother
languidly.

"Pray who might 'Miss Warrington' be?" asked
Cyril, carelessly. "Another governess?"

"Yes. O, Cyril you were so perverse," said Sainty's
soft voice. "I tried faithfully to introduce you to her
and you looked every other way."

"I don't wonder," he answered, affecting a slight
shiver. "A happy instinct preserved me from the
shock. I hate the order to that degree, it would have
spoiled the pleasure of coming home entirely."

"Cyril, you are so unreasonable. And she must
think so strangely of the negligence."

"Ah *n'importe*, Sainty," he said. "I'll make up for
it to-morrow. You shall introduce me as often as you
please, and I'll try to see her every time I find myself
breathing the blessed air that's breathed by her."

"Thomas," said Mr. Thorndyke, as if nobody had
been speaking, "send up and let Miss Warrington
know supper is on the table."

"Ah, now let me beg you," cried Cyril with an
impatient gesture. "Spare me my first evening. If
she has the good taste to leave us to ourselves, pray
don't thwart her."

While Thomas paused in uncertainty which orders to
obey, Frank gained her own apartment, and answered
deliberately the knock that in a few moments followed
her retreat. She begged Mrs. Thorndyke would excuse
her, she did not care that evening to come down to supper.

What a fine glow of scorn and anger tingled in the
governess' veins. She had not thought herself capable

of such sharp feeling still. It did her good decidedly it braced her as no softer emotion could have done, Really, the undeceiving this young autocrat gave an interest to her existence which surprised her. It was an object, albeit a very unworthy one, upon which to string some plans and for which to revive some of her former spirit. It broke in, for the moment, upon the blankness of her life, and stirred again the waters that had settled into leaden stillness under the leaden sky.

CHAPTER XL

HOME, SWEET HOME.

"The difference one person more or less
Will make in families, is past all guess."
Legend of Navarre.

MR. CYRIL THORNDYKE did not favor the family with his presence at breakfast the following morning: the fatigue of his journey, the charms of his own room, the luxury of civil hours once more, were "too many" for him, and Gustave sat within hearing of his master's bell hour after hour, ungratified by the suggestion of a tinkle from it.   The children were bitterly disappointed at his non-appearance, and Cammy mounted guard outside his door till school time, applying her ear to the key-hole and then her eye, without any encouraging result.   A soft twilight pervaded the apartment, and a velvet silence: there seemed small prospect of its being violated for the present.

The little girls flounced and pouted when they were recalled to the stern duties of the school-room, and flew down to mamma and importuned her to give them a holiday, and flounced up stairs again and pouted angrily when they found there was no hope.   Miss Warrington's duties, certainly, were not light that morning; Cammy and Sylvie were quite unsettled and ungovernable, and Cub was bewildered and helpless in everything that concerned his lessons.

Even Cecilia, counting every moment of her brother's visit, rather added to the *bouleversement* of the school-room, by passing uneasily in and out of it several times, and trying to occupy herself with things which had not the slightest interest to her. In fact, all that had any interest to her that morning, lay sleeping away the precious hours in that luxurious room, perfectly unconscious of her wistful vigil.

It was a blessing in disguise, therefore, when her mother, about twelve o'clock, summoned her to accompany her in the carriage, to execute some errands in the village.

"But, mamma," remonstrated Sainty, half crying "if Cyril wakes there will be no one to make his breakfast for him."

"There is no chance of his waking for an hour yet. I cannot do without you."

Cecilia bit her lips to keep back the tears, and followed her mother silently.

At one o'clock it was *en régle* for Frank to take the children with her to the dining-room, and see that they ate their lunch without riot or tumult, before they were allowed their liberty. It was rather a difficult thing on this occasion, to conduct them decorously down stairs, as they showed a disposition to spread themselves over the second story, and investigate the chances of Cyril's resurrection, but she was peremptory, and marshalled the unwilling squad direct from the school-room to the dining-room. They were too much excited and too uneasy to be hungry, and she had great difficulty in regulating their repast. Sylvie's diet was a thing of moment, and she invariably wanted to eat just what she could not be allowed to eat, and then cried herself sick when she was refused.   Pie was the rock on which the peace of the party was always stranded, and Frank made Thomas a gesture to take the one on the table away, but not before Sylvie had caught sight of it, and had declared her intention of partaking exclusively of that dish.

"No, Sylvie, not to-day.   You must eat some chicken and a roll."

"No," protested Sylvie, pushing back her plate.   "I won't eat anything if I can't have pie."

"Very well," said Miss Warrington, with unexpected acquiescence, "then you may get down, for you cer-tainly shall not have that."

Sylvie looked stunned for a moment, and then began to cry.

"Do you think that is a pretty noise?" asked Frank with much indifference, as she cut a roll in two for Cammy, who sat upon the other side of her.   "Cub, are you ready for some chicken?"

Cub was ready, and after she had helped them both, she again desired Thomas to take the pie away and bring some fruit back in its stead.   At this, Sylvie re-newed her screams, and told Thomas it should not go, and Cammy began to frown and say she wanted a piece of pie.

It was just at this point, while Thomas was awaiting, pie in hand, the issue of the contest, Sylvie screaming and hiding her face, Cammy pouting and looking like a thunder-cloud, and Frank standing, carving the chicken calmly, that the door opened and Cyril entered, looking nonchalant and slightly *ennuyé*. The dining-room was a handsome apartment, with great windows opening on the piazza, commanding the lawn and the river and the mountains beyond. The group at the table were directly opposite the door, with their backs to the sunshine that broke out that moment from the clouds which had been obscuring the sky since morning. Perhaps it was the sudden light, possibly the sudden sight of the group at that instant in the room he had fancied vacant, that made the young gentleman draw back a little and look amazed. Certainly no apparition could have been more startling to him than that of a pretty, graceful woman in the midst of his turbulent little relatives, instead of the *gauche*, pale-faced, ill-conditioned person, who had previously occupied the position of governess among them.

Frank did not look at him, but she felt instinctively who had entered; there was a sudden hush among the children, and Thomas looked prepared to swoon, that the young master had come down to an unready breakfast. Frank, entirely ignoring any entrance, went on with her directions to him :

"Some figs, Thomas, if there are any, or some apples; and remember never to bring pie up for lunch. It is quite useless, and only creates disturbance. I think I told you so last week."

"Yes, miss," said Thomas, miserably, not understanding a word she said to him, and glancing furtively from his master's face to the blank breakfast table.

"What, children," cried the young gentleman, with

a good humor quite reassuring to poor Thomas, advancing to the table and seating himself *vis-à-vis* to the
group; "what, breakfasting so late? I thought I was
the very last."

"Breakfasting!" cried the juveniles in chorus; "why,
we had our breakfast at least four hours ago. Why,
this is lunch."

"Lunch!" ejaculated the new comer, glancing up at
the clock upon the mantel-piece. "Upon my word, I
believe it must be. Really, I am ashamed of myself.
Cub, you must not think these are regulation hours."

Cub, overcome by being particularly addressed, upset
his plate into his lap, and spilled a glass of water on
Miss Warrington's dress in trying to catch the chicken
bones before they reached the carpet.

"Cub, you awkward fellow!" cried his brother, starting up. "Thomas, bring a napkin. I am afraid,"
coming around the table to her, and moving Sylvie
back with much solicitude, "I am afraid that careless
boy has ruined your dress completely."

"Not at all," she said, taking the napkin from Thomas, and brushing it carelessly off without noticing his
offers of assistance.

"Cammy, you may go on with your lunch. Bring
Master Cuthbert another plate, Thomas."

Cyril sauntered to the window, and looked out several minutes; evidently, he was unused entirely to " this
sort of thing."

At last, with a keen glance at the back of the govern
ess' well-shaped head as she bent again over the chicken,
he left the window and resumed his place. Order was

now restored, and the children became loquacious, the governess remaining quite silent and attending scrupulously to her duties. Thomas, standing obsequiously before his master, ventured at the first pause to ask what his orders were for breakfast.

"Don't let me interfere with the lunch," he said, looking quickly across the table. "I can wait."

There was a pause.

"Or, send Gustave to me, while you attend to the young lady."

"I do not know of anything," the young lady said, quietly glancing around upon the viands, "that is wanted after the fruit is brought. The children, I believe, have everything they need."

Mr. Cyril made a bow, which was a little stiff, but which she did not look up to see, and said he would wait, then, till Thomas found himself at leisure, meanwhile taking up the paper and glancing through it carelessly.

But Cammy was indisposed to let him rest; she talked incessantly, and he did not oppose her desire as sternly as on many occasions which she could recall—indeed, he laid down the paper presently, and played the good brother *à merveille*, when it is considered how new the part was to him. He answered all their questions, and told them several amusing stories, besides asking them a great deal about their lessons and their play, and expressing great interest in all that concerned the school-room.

When Thomas had brought the fruit and placed it anxiously before the governess, she looked up from Syl rie's plate, on which she was engaged, and said, "That will do."

And that was all she said, till rising, five minutes later, she told Cub to see that Sylvie did not hurry through her meal, and ate all the chicken she had cut for her, and charged Cammy not to take another apple, nd not to go out to play till she had called Marcelle down for Sylvie, and then she took up the book she had brought down with her, and quietly left the room.

After that, Cyril found the children's chat annoying, and he requested them to be quiet while he read his paper; and presently Cecilia came in from driving, looking fresh and happy, and he sent them off and accepted her society while he ate his breakfast. She made his coffee, and while he was trying it, he said, nonchalantly, but with a little brusqueness, "What sort of a creature is it, Sainty, that you've got to torture those poor children now?"

"Ah, Cyril, you have not seen her. You will not talk so when you have."

"Oh, but I have seen her. She has been in here half an hour, putting them through their lunch, and if I may be allowed to say so"——

"Don't, please, Cyril," said Sainty, looking pained. "I only ask that, for my sake, you will not say any thing harsh and unkind about her. For my sake, Cyril," with unusual earnestness.

"Ah," he cried with animation, "you consider you are fond of her. I see; you have conceived a friend ship for her *sur le champ*. Well, every one ought to respect a woman's friendship, I am sure; a sertiment so constant, so enduring, founded always on such a sensible foundation! So amenable to reason! so thoroughly under the control of common sense! so justifiable in its course, so profitable in its results!"

Cecilia hung her head, looking flushed and unhappy, but did not answer.

"No matter, Sainty," he cried teasingly, "no matter, I will not interfere. I will promise to be quiet. I give you just two months to be thoroughly weary of your friend. Only you must let me say this, that she is as imperious a young woman as I ever had the happiness to meet, and if you do not take good care, she will ride over all your heads before the two months are ended. Does my mother take to her?"

"I have never seen her so much pleased with any stranger," said Cecilia eagerly, "and really, Cyril, she is doing wonders for the children. Cub is a different boy; she has the greatest influence over him."

"And over Cammy?"

"Cammy is too self-willed to be influenced by any one, but she is better with Miss Warrington than with any governess we have ever had, and Sylvie is wonderfully improved."

"There was room for it, I must admit. But is she thorough? Where did you pick her up?"

"Oh, that is a long story," said Cecilia, evasively. "Wait till we have talked over the thousand things I am longing to hear from you."

But Cyril was not to be put off, when he had set his mind even on such a trifle as this, and poor Sainty had to lay open for his cool criticism, the romantic, unsub stantial foundation on which her friendship had been built. Notwithstanding his promise, he was not sparing of his irony, and did not succeed in his efforts to make up for his teasing as easily as ordinarily.

"Well, well, let it pass," he said. "I will suspend judgment for the present, till I give her a fair chance to earn my good opinion. In the meantime," he added, looking at his watch, "let's go and take a drive. Or, stay: I want to take a look about the stables, we'll put it off till three, and you can ask our lady of the ferrule to go too. Make her understand I desired it, you know. Why don't you look pleased? What's the matter? I thought it would suit you perfectly."

"I hoped you would have ridden with me. Sherry is as fine as silk; Martin has exercised him twice a-day ever since you've been away. No one else has been upon his back, and I wanted you to see how well I've learned to manage Betley."

"My dear! if you had galloped over as many hard roads as I have since last August, you'd be thankful to find yourself sitting in a carriage like a Christian gentleman once more, with no matter what before you in the way of horse flesh. Don't ask me to ride, to-day at least. Now you have an hour at your own disposal, while I am at the stable. Don't forget to apprise the governess, remember. Be ready, 'both of you, at three o'clock, for the days are getting very short, and I'd like to go to Witley and back before dinner."

At three o'clock, Cyril, drawing on his driving gloves, stood waiting for the young ladies on the piazza, and rather impatiently wondering at their tardiness. He longed to hold the reins once more behind his favorite greys, and to be bowling over the fine roads around Ringmer "like a Christian gentleman." The very clink of their clean hoofs upon the ringing ground had an away-with-melancholy inspiring music in his ears. Martin with difficulty kept down their impatient mettle; they were longing, like their master, to be off, in the eye of the keen wind, over the smooth broad roads that had been so often the theatre of their triumphs.

"Why don't they come," he muttered half audibly, with an impatient stride across to the hall door. Cecilia met him at the threshold, hurrying out.

"Have I kept you waiting?" she said, buttoning her gloves as she went towards the steps.

"Not long; it's no matter. But isn't Miss—the governess, you know, almost ready? Why didn't you tell her to be punctual?"

"Oh," said Cecilia, looking uncomfortable, "I forgot to tell you. She isn't going with us."

"Why not?" asked Cyril shortly, stopping on the steps. "Did you tell her I—that is—did you make her understand who the invitation came from?"

"Yes," said Sainty, hesitatingly, "but she said she did not care to drive to-day; I don't know what the reason is."

Poor Sainty had not a very pleasant drive that afternoon. Cyril was quite out of temper, and half frightened her to death with his fast driving and impatience with the horses, who were unable to satisfy him in any of their efforts. Martin got a large share of his dis

pleasure, but as it was tossed back to him across
Cecilia's shoulders, she naturally took the burden of it
doubly, and began to believe that the horses were
ruined, and that everything had been going wrong in
the stables for the past three months. She felt vaguely
relieved when the horses' heads were turned towards
home, and then keenly penitent that she should feel
relieved. She thought with a sigh, perhaps her mother
was right after all, and she really had no feeling. It
was shocking to find herself so far from happy in this
her first drive with Cyril after such an absence. In
fact she hardly had been happy since he came, although
she had had such anticipations, and how she might
reproach herself when it was too late !

Dinner was a little retarded that evening on account
of a change in the train that usually brought the master
of the family to his happy fireside. Cyril came in from
the stable, looked into the parlors and found them
empty, into the library and found it empty, and then
went up to his own room. He heard the voices of the
children on the stairs, and shut his door very sharply
as he heard them coming. When he left his room after
a lapse of ten minutes, he heard them romping in the
hall below; so, with a shrug indicative of disinclination
to their society, he turned away and went up to the
school-room door. The twilight rendered it difficult to
distinguish the figure standing by the western window
as he entered.

" Cecilia," he said, going towards the window, " is
the key of my cabinet of minerals in the door ?"

" Miss Thorndyke is not here," said the governess

starting a little, and then resuming her position by the window. "I think you will find her in the parlor.'

"It is of no consequence. I only wanted to know from her where the key of that old cabinet at the other end of the room has been left. Do you know whether it is in the door?"

"It has been taken out. Mrs. Thorndyke has it, I believe."

"Ah, it is no matter then. I will put off looking in it till to-morrow," walking to the window and addressing her with an air of attention. "I regretted not driving you to Witley this afternoon, Miss Warrington."

"You are very kind," she said with great indifference, turning her eyes to the window. "I believe Miss Thorndyke made my excuses to you."

"My sister told me you had declined. You are not fond of driving, I understood."

"O yes, ordinarily I like it very well, but this afternoon I did not feel in the humor for it."

"I may hope, then, that to-morrow's humor may be more favorable to me? Since women's humors have been known to change in the lapse of four and twenty hours."

"Yes, it is possible I may feel differently to-morrow," responded the young lady, not enough interested, evidently, to trouble herself with repartee.

"Then you promise me, if you do, I shall benefit by it?"

"That I will go to drive with you, you mean?" she asked very matter-of-fact-ly, turning slightly and looking at him.

"Yes, Miss Warrington, that you will go to drive with me," he answered, bending his head a little, and looking curiously and irritatedly into her expressionless eyes.

"I don't care to promise," she said, withdrawing her eyes. "It might be very pleasant if the day were fine, but I think I like walking better, generally, at this season."

"What is your favorite walk at Ringmer, Miss Warrington?" he asked, as he leaned against the opposite casement of the window, and watched the graceful outline of her figure, quite clear still in the fading western light.

"I hardly have any favorite walk, Mr. Thorndyke. I like them all."

"You don't find Ringmer dreary, then, even at this season?"

"Oh no, no more dreary than any country place."

Cyril bit his lip.

"You are more used to the city, I suppose, Miss Warrington."

"I have lived in both city and country," she replied, in a tone that placed, civilly, a bar across the conversation.

For once in his victorious career, Mr. Cyril Thorndyke found himself completely baulked; his curiosity was unsatisfied, his admiration was unnoticed, his importance was overlooked. It was her indifference that provoked him; for there was, after all, nothing really assuming in her manner, only a complete preoccupation and self-possession, in strange combination with her yonth and peculiar beauty. Eyes out of which ought to have flashed coquetry and pleasure, responsive to his admiration, were cold and commonplace and unsympathizing; her voice, that was fine and clear and low, never changed its tone or betrayed a quicker feeling when she talked with him. Indifference in most women, however beautiful, creates nothing but inuifference in their suitors. Men in this age are not given to image worship and idolatry of irresponsive works of art; but there was a suggestion of latent power in this inanimate young woman that was excessively attractive. She could be coquettish and piquant if she could once be roused, her strong feelings were only smothered, her high spirit was only half subdued. Cyril looked with impatience for one kindling glance of her dark shrouded eye. Should he soonest win it by devotion, opposition, or neglect?

It was a dangerous study, but he resolved to apply himself to it, and to ascertain, before the evening ended, in what way to make himself of interest to her. From motives of policy he left the school-room to meet her ten minutes after at the dinner-table.

During dinner she was silent, as a stranger must necessarily be in such a family circle, and Cyril, though showing himself in his gayest and most attractive colors, did not often address her particularly, or call the attention of the table to her. She would have been dull indeed, however, if she had not seen that he was talking for her. She realized her conquest, and was not insensible to the triumph she had promised to herself; but she undervalued it, and regarded with little respect the

preference of one who seemed born to please himself at the expense of the thing that pleased him. It seemed anything but an honor to her that he dared persevere in his attempts to see her, after the coldness with which she had received him. If he had thought her his equal, he would never have presumed; every advance was just so much of disrespect.

After dinner, while Cecilia at the piano soothed her mother into her accustomed doze, and the children, grouped at a table in the corner, played a pacific game of high-low-jack, Frank, with a book in her hand, sat gazing vacantly before her. She was not reading; indeed she rarely read now, filling her time up with studies which fell in with the plan of life she had adopted. She looked with dull apathy upon books which, six months ago, she would have been thirsty to obtain; they were tasteless, wearying, most of them had nothing whatever to do with what she was experiencing in the present; all of them were tame when compared with what she remembered of the past. She had lived far beyond the passion of ordinary books, and those that came nearer to her knowledge only gave her pain. Works of fiction had little interest for her, study had no charm unless it promised to further the only purpose that she had in life—the power to obtain an independence and be mistress of her fate. She felt no healthy interest in the people whom she met; even the little children thrown upon her care seemed just so many curious studies that it behooved her to acquire a knowledge of; just so many parts of a routine that she must be perfected in.

For Cecilia alone she felt affection, and sometimes she doubted even that. When she thought how three months ago she would have loved her, how dear the children would have been to her, how pleasant her light duties would have seemed, she wondered what the end would be of this long death in life. She wondered when she analysed herself, what length of time it would take to cauterize this wound, what state of feeling would succeed this morbid apathy. It could not last forever. How should she come out of it. What would be the new existence to which she should arise, as distinct from this as this was from the one she had lived before.

But such self-contemplation does not enlighten much. When the mind is in its best estate, clear, well-poised, and full of vigor, it risks its balance by turning in upon itself, and contemplating the wonders of its own construction ; but when it is in an amazed and stricken state, when the whole head is sick and the whole heart faint, it is worse than folly to seek within for the cure of the disorder. Only from without, from above, can any light come. The simple act of turning away from the inexplicable problem and acknowledging that, though our sin may have brought it, our strength is insufficient for it, is the first step towards the solution of it. But this simplicity of sorrow, this first lesson in His law, in knowledge of whom standeth our eternal life, she had not yet submitted to receive, though she fancied she had taken her chastisement as it was meant, and that she had long since given up rebellion.

Much before the hour at which Mr. Thorndyke ordi

7

narily released his guests or returned himself from the
dining-room, Cyril came back to the parlor. Frank's
book had fallen from her hand, and her eyes were fixed
on the blazing fire, not dreamily or absently, but steadily, and with a resolute expression ; but when the door
opened, she quickly resumed her book, and fastened her
eyes upon the open page.   The sudden change of attitude did not escape Cyril.   That was a studied indifference and not an impulsive one.   He also took a book
and threw himself down in an easy chair on the other
side of the table.   Cecilia made a movement to leave
the piano and come to the fire, but he begged her
to go back, and made her understand that music was
more acceptable than talking for the present.

For a long space, therefore, there was a dreamy, luxurious quiet in the room, only broken by Cecilia's soft
music, the childrens' low voices, absorbed and earnest
in their game, and the faint crackling of the blazing
lumps of coal within the grate.   Cyril watched Frank
from over his book, and he caught her eye when it had
been absent from the page before her for the space of
twenty minutes.   There was a flash of significance and
merriment in his glance, and a gleam of vexation in
hers as they met.   She held the volume up after this so
as to hide her face entirely, and again outward tranquillity reigned.   At length, however, it was broken by
Sylvie, who had begun to get sleepy and cross, and to
quarrel about her cards, and who, finding she could
spite Cammy by refusing to play, did so, and came over
to Frank and crept up into her lap.   But in doing this,
she managed to knock Frank's book down on the floor

Cyril stooped and picked it up, saying, as he cooly marked the place with a card and laid it down with his own, a little out of her reach, upon the table,

"You should take some relaxation, Miss Warrington. Do you play whist?"

"I don't enjoy whist," Miss Warrington answered, as Sylvie, having arranged herself to her own satisfaction, closed her eyes. and nestled her curls down on her shoulder. She consequently had nothing whatever to do but listen to Mr. Cyril Thorndyke, if he chose to talk to her, being *clouée* to the spot by Sylvie's weight, and deprived of other occupation by that young gentleman's arbitrary policy. So she merely lowered her eyes, keeping one arm around Sylvie, the other in her lap, and said nothing.

"Then I hope you like chess," persisted Cyril.

"No, Mr. Thorndyke, I don't even understand the moves."

"Don't you feel inclined to learn them? It would give me a great deal of pleasure to teach you."

"You are very kind, but I never felt I should be interested in the game at all."

"Let me induce you to try it. I am certain it would amuse you."

"Thank you. I must ask you to excuse me."

"I suppose I shall have to do it, Miss Warrington. Is not Sylvie troubling you very much? Shall I not ring for Marcelle to come for her?"

"Thank you, you may," she said, mo

And Cyril rang the bell, very much own bad play. Of course, as soon as

Sylvie she would make her escape up stairs; so he
called to Cecilia that he had brought down the pictures
of which he had been telling her, and begged she would
come and look at them.   Cecilia came, greatly relieved
at being permitted to join the circle again.   Mrs. Thorndyke woke up and yawned.   The children, hearing
something about pictures, threw down their cards and
hurried over to the table ; and when Marcelle came for
Sylvie, she was wide awake and protesting against
being sent away.   So her good brother begged that she
might stay up a little longer, and the *bonne* was dismissed till called for.   He brought the portfolio to the
table, arranged it before Miss Warrington, while Cecilia
knelt beside her, standing himself behind them and
looking over their heads.   The children, meantime, getting very imperfect and unsatisfactory views from the
extreme corners of the sketches, looking three deep over
each other's shoulders.

The first sketch was of a scene on the upper Potomac,
near their encampment in the summer.   The river made
a bend just at a point where a flat boat, drawn by ropes,
was crossing towards the Virginia side.   A long train
of Government wagons stood waiting to be thus ferried
over one by one, while a knot of soldiers and teamsters
were grouped indolently beside them ; on the opposite
bank, two or three wagons with their white tops, un-
gainly mules and red-shirted riders, were winding up
the steep, while in the distance the woods, the farm
houses and the deep blue mountains, were sleeping quiet-
etly in the lowering sunlight of a summer afternoon.
Then followed the breaking up of an encampment, the

vigor and animation of the scene a striking contrast to the indolent action of the first. Another was a clever caricature, "Released on Parole;" a gaunt, raw-boned, easy-tempered fellow sitting in the door of his tent, with one hand waves away from his untasted dinner a miserable yellow cur, and with the other holds back a great mastiff who is struggling to be let loose on the marauding traitor. And there was a good deal of pathos in another, a roughly made grave beside a lonely pine, with the words

"Whose business 'tis to die,"

written on the margin; and in its companion piece, an ambulance creeping slowly along an arid road under a scorching sky, with the line beneath

"The paths of glory lead but to the grave."

Cecilia shivered and averted her face, and Cyril laughed lightly and turned several over quickly; "*Voilà quelque chose de plus léger*," he said, taking out one "But why do you start, Miss Warrington?"

"I did not start," said Frank, looking very pale.

"That's a portrait," said Cyril carelessly, "an officer of our mess; a capital likeness, and withal a pretty bit of sentiment, don't you think so?"

"Ah," exclaimed Cecilia, "what a fine manly fellow! I think it is one of the best faces I ever saw; so handsome, so strong and yet so sad. Do tell me all about him, Cyril; is he your friend? Have I ever heard you speak of him? Has he been in the army long?"

"Anything more you would like to ask before I begin
to answer?" said Cyril coolly, waiting for her to finish
her scrutiny of the picture over which she bent, and
upon which she had laid her hand, but which Frank did
not touch, nor lean down to scrutinize, but from which
she could not get her eyes away. It was a night scene
the full moon was shining down upon a lonely road,
beside which paced a sentinel; the picket fire gleamed
faintly through the trees; the soldier, resting for a moment on his gun, gazed dreamily towards the starry sky,
his eyes and heart "very far away," and underneath
was written,

"Ever of thee I'm fondly dreaming,"

and half a dozen bars of that familiar air.

"There's the same face again," said Cyril, turning
over to a group of officers playing cards at night around
a camp chest, with the light gleaming up effectively
upon their animated faces.

"Ah, I should have known it instantly," cried Sainty.
"And that is you, Cyril, at the left. How admirable!
Frank, is it not a perfect likeness?"

"Yes," said Frank mechanically, with her eyes upon
the paper.

"But you haven't told us about him yet," said Sainty.
'I know he has a history."

"Well, he has never given me the benefit of it if he
.. ," re. rned her brother. "I'm rather inclined to the
belief his history, the most stirring part of it at least, is
yet to come. And it will be a history, I think, he'l
have no reason to regret, if he keeps on as he has begun

Don't you think he has a fine face, Miss Warrington! He is such a consistent type of the national character the national character in its best phase, I mean; thoroughly American, self-educated, self-reliant, keen in intellect, undemonstrative in manner, at home in every situation, unabashed by any majesty, unmoved by any honor. He entered the regiment in September, a second lieutenant, and I'm prepared to have him rank us all before the war is over, though he's only got as far as captain yet. How he became so great a favorite, I can't divine, for he never seems to trouble himself about anything but doing his duty in the most matter-of-fact way. He's kind to his men, but he doesn't take half the pains to conciliate them that others do, and yet there isn't an officer in the regiment that's as popular."

"But what's his name, Cyril?"

"Soutter, Louis Soutter. Miss Warrington, let me relieve you of that portfolio. I am afraid you have been uncomfortable. Sylvie you are so restless, I shall have to call Marcelle."

"No, oh, no," cried Sylvie, while Frank pushed away the book and drew back hurriedly from the light.

"Soutter," said Cecilia thoughtfully. "You've never written anything about him. What sort of a person is he; highly educated, you say?"

"Why no; rather well, than highly educated. And yet not even well in our sense, perhaps, though I have never seen him the inferior in any company of men; in fact, in most cases he is better informed and better grounded than most of those one meets. He has been every. where and seen everything, and that for a man with such powers of observation and such an iron memory, is equivalent to having been under pastors and masters for a lifetime.   He gives one the impression of knowing men better than books, and yet as I told you, I have never seen him on any one occasion, betray any unfamiliarity with any topic of any kind that happened to be discussed."

" And what of his family ?   Are they of consequence at all ?

" Only because they are his family," said Cyril, carelessly.   " ' Poor but honest,' I'm afraid describes concisely their social attitude.   Plain, country people, somewhere in the western part of the State, I take it, from what I've heard him say."

" But does he talk about them, or do you only guess at it ?" asked Sainty, with a vague hope that the hero's origin might be shrouded in a mysterious uncertainty susceptible of something like romance.

" He never talks about himself or his own affairs, but he makes no secret of his humble origin either. which is greatly to his credit."

" Of course," said Cecilia, faintly, turning back to the moonlight picket scene.   " But has he the—the manners of a gentleman, you know ?"

" When I tell you he is as popular with the officers as with the men, you may be certain his manners are above reproach, for there is not a regiment in the service officered by more high-bred men.   Fancy McArthur, Granger, Arbuthnot, hand-in-glove with anything provincial and uncouth.   But there was a little demur about receiving him, I'm sorry to remember.   Though

It was but natural, for it is asking a good deal of gentle men to overlook all social considerations they've been accustomed to respect, and to admit on terms of intimacy a man coming from the class their fathers' farmers occupy. However, it wasn't long before all that was sunk entirely, and the new lieutenant was acknowledged to be one of us. Not without some rubs and uncom-fortable things happening at first, which I thought then he didn't notice, he seemed so perfectly indifferent and easy, but since I've known him better, I've begun to think he saw through the whole thing, and has a dis tincter recollection of it than the rest of us have now. Not that he bears malice, or anything of that sort, but that he's formed on that his judgment of us, and will not be likely to be shaken from it. If there's any reserve now, it's on his part, for there isn't a man more liked."

"How I wish I could see him!" ejaculated Sainty, with her eyes still on the picture.

"You might be disappointed," said her brother, care-.essly; "his manners may not be as easy with ladies as in the society of men. I've never seen him out of camp you know; but I'll try to get him off for a few days with me sometime, and bring him home. I'd like to have you all see him, if only for the curiosity of the thing; my mother particularly."

"Who is that you want me to see?" said the mother, looking over toward them with slowly awakened in terest.

"My best friend, mother," cried the best I ever had, in fact. A farmer's boy

7*

mountains; capital fellow. You mightn't like his man
ners, but he's all gold."

Mrs. Thorndyke exhibited the resentment that Cyril
desired to produce in her, and said impressively that
she hoped he never would forget himself so far, as to
impose upon his family the acquaintance of any of his
low favorites. One might have fancied they heard the
Queen Dowager remonstrating with Prince Hal upon
his unworthy associates of East Cheap Inn.

"But, mother," cried Cyril, with irreverent enjoy·
ment, "you've no idea what a good fellow he is; some
thing of a rough diamond you might think, but then,
indubitably a diamond. And after all, what if he was
following the plough, when I was following the dancing·
master? We're both following glory now, and that
puts us on a level, you'll confess. And with our Republican equality "——

"Our Republican equality," said the lady, with a
manner almost regal; "our Republican equality does
not extend beyond the ballot-box; no one ought to
know better than you do that the lines of social dis
tinction are as strong and well-defined in this country
as in any other."

Cyril shrugged his shoulders; this had been the text
for so many tedious dissertations he rather wished he
had not brought the subject up. At the same time it
began to dawn on Sainty that they had been pursuing
a theme that must have been somewhat unpleasing to
the governess. She blushed as she recalled what had
been said, and glanced towards her to see if there were
any expression of pain or displeasure on her face. But

there was nothing but entire rigidity and silence in her face and attitude. She might be hearing nothing, or she might be listening intently. Sainty could have cried to think how inconsiderate she had been. She hurried to change the subject by asking if Sylvie should not be sent to bed, and if Cub and Cammy had not something to study for to-morrow.

" Bother!" muttered Cammy with a jet black look, " why need you always be poking up mamma about . us ?"

" Yes, certainly ;" said her mother, who always felt she had done a good thing when she had sent the children to bed. "Yes, certainly ; it is time for them to go. Cammy, ring the bell, my dear."

" And, Cuthbert," said Miss Warrington, rising too, "if you will come up I will get that map out for you now."

" Ah, Frank, not yet," cried Sainty, starting up and passing her arm around her. "Don't go yet."

" It is very early, Miss Warrington," added Cyril in rather a low tone, glancing at his watch.

" Thank you; but I promised Cuthbert, and I have a little headache too."

And Cyril was left *désolé*, with the evening just begun, and no one to help him through it but his mother and his sister.

CHAPTER XII.

DELINQUENT.

"The dinner waits and we are tired."
Said Gilpin—"So am I!"

AT breakfast Miss Warrington looked so pale and ill as even to attract the attention of the lady of the house, who asked with unusual consideration if she had not slept well. "Not very," she had replied, and Cecilia had asked if her headache was no better, and had received for answer that it was not much better, and then the subject had been dropped.

Cyril had taken the seat beside her vacant place when he had surprised the family by coming in, and was consequently too near a neighbor to be in every way ignored. He did not ask her anything about her headache, but he said presently,

"Children, in consideration of my approaching departure, and of your recent good behavior, I am going to ask Miss Warrington for a holiday for you to-day."

Suppressed expressions of delight, and then a period of acute and silent suspense, while Miss Warrington said nothing, and mamma looked disapproving.

"O yes," said Sainty, "do give them a holiday Frank. You are not fit to teach to-day."

"I should not think of it on that account," she returned quickly.

"It was not put at all on that ground, Miss War-rington," said Cyril. "Though, of course, that would be sufficient of itself."

"Of course," said Mrs. Thorndyke. "Of course, if Miss Warrington is not well enough to go through with their recitations, she must not do it on any account But I should be sorry to have them lose a day. They have lost so much time since Miss Dorsey went away—"

"I shall not think of omitting anything," said the governess, very quickly. "I am perfectly able to attend to all their lessons."

"But," reiterated Cyril, firmly. "You must excuse me: I want the children. It is probably the only favor I shall dare to ask either of *Madame ma mère* or Miss Warrington to-day, and I depend upon its being granted. In fact, children," he said, rising, "I think I shall consider that it is granted, so come! Get yourselves ready, and I'll take you out upon the river for a row, if you'll promise to be quiet and not to rock the boat."

There was a thrill of excitement as the children pushed back their chairs and followed their brother to the door, grasping his hand silently and looking back anxiously, lest the edict should be revoked before they got outside. Once in the hall, there was a wild hurrah, and Sainty, very much relieved, followed them, tied on Sylvie's hood and Cammy's scarf, and accompanied them out upon the terrace, and watched them off half enviously. Then she came back to the breakfast room, and meeting the governess just going out from it, she said with a caress,

"Now, let me tell you what you are going to do for

me to-day : you are coming down to lie on the sofa in
my room, and give me a happy morning reading to you
Think how long it is since you have given me a quiet
hour.   Come, *chérie*, I'll cure your headache, nobody
shall come near you, nobody else shall speak to you."

Frank yielded reluctantly : she would far rather have
locked herself into her own room, and have passed one
of those dangerously self-absorbed and self-consuming
days, which were, happily, so seldom within her reach.
She submitted to be led into Sainty's little morning
room, and to be placed upon the sofa, with an afghan
thrown over her and a cushion under her head.   The
light was softened to a pleasant dreaminess, the fire
stirred just enough to show a blaze, the doors closed
and all sounds excluded.   It was pleasant, even Frank
began to feel.   Every room Sainty had any interest in
was pretty ; she hardly could pass through one without
charming it into some unlooked-for refinement, and it
was not wonderful that her own peculiar favorite apartment was as graceful, refined and dainty as she was
herself.   It would be difficult to imagine anything
prettier than the room, anything more harmonious
than its furniture, more charming than its decorations.
Cecilia's chaste and beautiful fancy had worked itself
out in the grouping of the pictures on the walls, in the
classing of the books and bijoux on the étagères ; there
was a sentiment in the droop of every flower, a meaning
in the attitude of every trifle.   In fact, her whole life
had been so unpractical and imaginative, that every
thing about her had naturally and unconsciously become idealized ; and the indulgence of a picturesque and

uxurious fancy seemed in her case entirely lawful and commendable. She would have been perfectly capable of self-denial in the gratification of her taste if it had been required of her, but it never had been required, and it was the pleasure and poetry of her existence. Her innocent and loving days had ever, indeed, been bound together by a natural and most earnest piety, and no one could doubt, knowing the reverence and pureness of her faith, that when the thorns of life came to be exchanged for its roses, that delicacy of sensation which now seemed akin to weakness, would prove itself a silent, steadfast strength.

" Sainty, you are such a wonder to me !" murmured Frank, watching her movements about the pretty room.

" Do you know I like to hear you say so ?" said Sainty, smiling up from a vase of flowers. " I like to hear you say I am anything to you. I sometimes think no one can be anything to you, that all are equally indifferent. But when you look at me 'n that strange, wistful way, and acknowledge I am a wonder to you, I begin to hope I may one day attain to being something more."

Frank closed her eyes and turned her face down upon the cushion.

" Now, my darling," said Sainty, coming towards her with a handful of flowers, " let me put a flower in your dress; you do not know what a pretty picture you are making with the afghan and the cushion. What flowers shall I give you? Let me see. There is a ovely rose, but you are too pale for pink this morning. Ah, here's another, deep, deep red ; you shall wear that

with its glossy leaves," and she knelt down to fasten it
in. "But no," she said after a moment, leaning back
and looking at her. "They are too gay for you to-day,
something tender, something triste and neutral. Ah,
here is the thing I want. This handful of Michaelmas
daisies, the last, the very last ones of the year. Pretty
ittle darlings; see how lovely they are with your lilac
dress."

Frank put up her hand involuntarily to prevent
Cecilia, then, with a half bitter smile, she checked
herself, and submitted to be decorated with the flowers
that she never thought of now without an insufferable
recollection.

"But my 'wee modest' darlings have not leaves
enough," said Sainty, whose artist's eye craved something green. She searched among the loose flowers for
some leaves that would fill the void, and lifting a little
spray said, "'That's rosemary, that's for remembrance;'
it is a lovely green. You don't mind rosemary, Frank?
I like everything that's for remembrance."

"Oh, no, I do not mind," Frank said in a suppressed
voice, leaning her head back on the cushion as the scent
of the herb came to her.

"There, that is exactly right," said Sainty, rising and
looking down at her. "That suits you à merveille.
But you do not like them," she added, looking troubled.
"Let me take them away. Dear Frank, I did not mean
to give you pain."

"You have not," she returned, putting back her
hand. "Nothing gives me pain. Leave the flowers; I
am long past minding any remembrance they can bring."

Cecilia sighed as she rose, and went across the room to find a book; she understood her friend so little, she was in such constant danger of dealing her unintended pain.

"What shall I read?" she said, looking back doubt-fully.

"Anything," Frank said carelessly, the brief emotion passed. "Anything you fancy. I am too languid tc have a choice to-day."

"Then I must choose for you. You do not want an essay, I am sure, nor history either, with a headache: novels always weary you, you say, and I don't know how to please you in poetry. Ah, if you only liked Wordsworth!" she added, taking down a book and turning over its pages affectionately.

"But I don't, my saint."

"Well, then, Shelley?"

"Yes, if you choose. I used to like 'The Skylark' better than any verses ever made. I don't know how they would sound now."

Sainty brought the book with pleasure, and sat down to read; but the exquisite poem hardly was completed, when a short rap sounded on the door, followed by an unceremonious opening of it. Cyril had advanced some steps into the room before he saw, or appeared to see, who was his sister's companion. Miss Warrington pushed the cushion away from her head, and changed her attitude as he paused.

"*Pardon*," he said, "I fancied Sainty was alone. But, Miss Warrington," he added, advancing toward them, "you are not better, I am afraid. You look very pale; Sainty has been tiring you."

His manner was too respectful and solicitous to re
sent; the governess, though, had not the strength or
interest to resent anything. But indeed, since last
night, she had almost forgotten that she had intended
to repel him; that portfolio of sketches had reversed
her plans. She felt as if he were unconsciously nearer
to her now than any other member of the family; as if,
though she prayed he might never know it, as if he
stood as a link between her and what she had found
she could not live without the knowledge of. It frightened her to find the sudden interest with which it
invested a perfect stranger, to know whose comrade and
associate he had been. "He sees him daily, he has
lived months with him; to-morrow he will grasp his
hand, will look into his face." How strong a power in
such thoughts as those! He was indifferent no longer,
but strangely and dangerously of interest to her. She
longed to hear him talk, to study his motives, his character, his power of judging other men. She longed,
yet almost dreaded, to have him speak again of the
man who was his friend, the man whom he believed in
so entirely. The thought of what he had it in his
power to tell her of him gave his presence a perfect
fascination. Every careless word, every trifling reminiscence of his thrilled her, and all the romance and
passion of books, all the incidents and accidents of
life, had failed to do it.

His eyes sought hers as he stood doubtfully behind
Cecilia's chair, and he found no sentence of banishment
in them.

"What are you doing to torment your friend?" he
said, stooping down and looking over the book upon

her lap. "It has the form and style of poetry. Ah, Shelley! Sainty, I am amazed. Who told you you might read Shelley?"

"Only 'The Skylark,'" said Sainty, humbly. "But, Cyril, read aloud to us a little while; it will be so delightful! Not this, I don't mean; something we used to read. I never look at my old 'Andromaque' now without a sigh. You used to read with me every morning that year you left college; do you recollect? I have never heard any one read as well. I had rather listen to you than to any one."

"Well, Sainty, I wish you controlled the sentiments of the world! I should be judged more leniently than I am now, I am disposed to think."

"Ah," whispered Sainty, drawing his arm around her neck, "you know they praise you; who can help it? But they haven't loved you as long as I have."

"Sainty," he said lightly, with a little caress, "is all that flattery a deep-laid plan to coax me into reading to you? You shall not succeed, *je vous le jure.* Have you forgotten Miss Warrington has a headache?"

"You would not mind, Frank, would you?" she said, suddenly remembering. "He reads so well; it could not disturb you."

"Oh, pray don't make any difference on my account; it would give me pleasure," said the governess, with sudden and inexplicable embarrassment.

Cecilia was soon happy, seated by Cyril and looking over the dear old copy of Racine with him, trying to believe he was not changed since those pleasant college days of which she had reminded him, and forgetting

quite that her new friend was looking on and listening
"A rich and mellow voice he had;" Cecilia had said
rightly, it was better than almost any music to hear
him read a poem that he felt the beauty of. The mor-
ceaux that he read from 'Andromaque' had the charm
too of having been early favorites, in a time when there
had been a glory in all things seen and felt, and he read
them with a tenderness and feeling that no new poem
could have inspired. For an hour, perhaps, he read on,
turning from one familiar page to another, unurged and
abstractedly, then suddenly flinging the book aside at
Hermione's passionate ejaculation:

"Je t'aimais inconstant, qu'aurais-je fais fidèle !"

he exclaimed: "Go and play for me, Cecilia. I have
earned two hours of music."

There was a piano at the other side of the room, and
Cecilia went obediently and opened it, and fulfilled the
programme her brother carelessly indicated as she sat
down, "Those airs from 'Martha' that you played last
night, and 'Trovatore,' *ad infinitum*."

"Miss Warrington, may I read you this?" he said
presently, bending a little towards her as he assumed
Sainty's vacated chair beside the sofa.

It was another hour, a generous one, before the cessa-
tion of Cecilia's delicious music broke the spell, and her
brother said, discontentedly, as she rose:

"Pray, Sainty, don't be quite so selfish about your
music. One would think it might please you to give
others pleasure."

"Why, Cyril," she said, sitting down again, "do you know what time it is?"

"No," he said shortly, turning back to his book; but Miss Warrington glanced towards the little clock upon the mantel-piece and rose.

"I had no idea it was so late," she said. "I must go down to the children's lunch."

"You shall not," cried Sainty, starting up. "I shall go myself, and send some up to you. Cyril, will you come down or will you have yours here?"

"Send some up to me," he said, as without waiting for an answer, Sainty ran out and closed the door. The governess looked irresolute, while Cyril, as if divining her reluctance to a tête-à-tête, reassured her by going to the piano and running his fingers lightly over the keys as he sat down.

"Let me give you some of our 'most admired,' Miss Warrington. If you ever happened at Camp —— I assure you you would hear nothing but this all day long."

Frank sat still and listened to the rollicking, devil-me-care, good-fellowish song, and wondered, with a tightening round the throat, whether that air echoed the sentiments in every man's heart who sung it.

"You are a careless merry set at Camp —— I fancy both officers and men," she said with a slight unconscious coldness in her tone as he paused.

"No," he answered with a momentary seriousness, "no, I think you would hardly call us careless, though we are as well disposed to make the best of things as other men. I think jollity is quite as much our duty as our disposition, and music is our grand promoter of

stances never accomplishing their meal in any shorter
time than that, looked dismayed and perplexed at Cyril,
who knowing the same thing looked *nonchalant*, amused
and careless. She was very much obliged to him for
not saying Cecilia was doing duty for her in the dining-
room, but she could not see the necessity for telling such
a very gratuitous falsehood, and keeping his mother
waiting so impatiently.

"Upon my word it's odd Cecilia stays so long," he
said in a few moments, and calling Marcelle from the
adjoining room, he sent her down to ask her to come up.
Mrs. Thorndyke was very easily befogged, and Cyril, by
a multiplicity of little attentions completely confused her
memory about the events of the morning, and made her
forget her surprise at seeing Miss Warrington taking
lunch in Sainty's room, and at finding him in the house
instead of out upon the river, and her vague sense of
impropriety in connection with the tête-à-tête and the
amiability reigning in the apartment as she entered it.
Cecilia came up hurriedly.

"Where have you been so long, my dear?" said her
mother dissatisfiedly. "I wanted to tell you you must
go and pay two or three visits with me immediately
after lunch, and Cyril, dear, you will have to go too,
for the Cuylers and Rosenbaums never will forgive you
if you go away without seeing them."

"I don't know how it would feel to be subject to the
eternal malevolence and enmity of the Rosenbaums and
Cuylers, but I propose to make the trial. I haven't the
distantest intention, my dear mother, of spending this
last and only day at home in making formal visits, and

I beg you will make your arrangements quite irrespect-
ive of my attendance."

"Formal visits!" echoed Sainty. "Dear Cyril, how
absurd. I don't know what Emily Rosenbaum would
say if she knew you talked of going to see them as
making a formal visit. And I must confess, I think
they would have good cause for being hurt, if you did
not go there."

"I have never imagined their feelings of that delicate
order, my dear sister."

"But consider your intimacy in the family, my dear
son."

"I have considered it, my dear mother."

"And your—your—why—Emily, you know."

"Well?"

"O, nothing, but I really think it will seem extraordinary if you do not go."

"The extraordinary is necessary to chequer agreeably
the ordinary, of which there is generally too much in
life. I shall do the Rosenbaums a favor in that way,
you must see."

"But, Cyril"——

"But, Sainty"——

"You really are serious that you will not go?"

"Most serious."

"Then, mamma, need I?"

"Of course, my dear. I have ordered the carriage
and made all my arrangements. I want to bring Emily
back to dinner with us, and ask the Cuylers to come
too."

Cyril drew his brows together, and, turning on his

heel, walked over to the window and looked out silently
Poor Sainty looked as if she wanted to cry, but said
nothing. Mrs. Thorndyke made a final appeal to her
son, as she turned to leave the room.

"Well, Cyril, you will not think better of it?"

"No, madam, I have thought my best of it."

Sainty obediently followed her mother towards the
door, accompanied by Frank, and Cyril followed at a
little distance. At the door of Sainty's sleeping-room,
which adjoined the one they had just left, Frank kissed
her and wished her a pleasant drive, which good
wish Sainty received without an attempt even at a
smile.

Half way up the stairs Frank heard a quick step behind her, and as she reached the school-room, Cyril's
voice said, "Miss Warrington."

She turned, with her hand upon the knob, and looked
back.

"You are not going to shut yourself up for the rest
of the day?" he said. "May I not drive you at three
o'clock? The afternoon promises to be beautiful."

She could not help coloring and looking uncomfortable.

"No, it will be impossible," she said, rather more
quickly than was altogether civil.

"But you half promised me yesterday."

"I don't remember it."

"Ah, that's hard. But, take my word for it, you did,
nd that I remember it very well. You will keep your
promise?"

"No, Mr. Thorndyke, I can't go, really."

She turned hurriedly and went into the school-room, but he followed her, and said, stopping at the table where she laid down her books,

"Is it because Cecilia is not going you refuse? Cammy and Sylvie can go in her place, and you would be making them most happy."

"Why, no; it is you who can make them happy, Mr. Thorndyke."

"But I shall not if you do not go. I shall not drive at all."

"I am sorry," she returned, distantly, going towards the door. But, in leaving the table, her dress caught in a pile of books upon it, and her quick movement sent them flying across the floor, accompanied in their descent by a work-box of Cammy's, the lid of which fell off, and scattered the contents lavishly about. Everything seemed to conspire against Miss Warrington's dignity that morning, for, stooping hurriedly to repair her error, the bunch of daisies fell from her dress, and Cyril deliberately picked it up and put it in his buttonhole before he attempted to assist replace the books.

"Stay, Miss Warrington," he said, hastily tumbling the things into Cammy's box. "You will retract your refusal to drive. It will be such a pleasure to—to the children. I have no right, of course, to ask it on my own account; but this will be the last day of liberty I shall have in a long, long while. You will not spoil it for me?"

"I don't flatter myself I have it in my power," she said, quickly, not raising her eyes as she went out of the room.

Her own looked dreary and uninviting after Sainty s. The fire had gone out, and the furniture, though scrupu lously in order, looked bare and comfortless. There was nothing on the table but an inkstand and some school books. She had never since she had been in it altered the position of an article of furniture, or arranged any thing about it to satisfy her taste, or make it more hab- itable and homelike. It was more the housemaid's room than hers, as regarded any character apparent in its ar rangement, for Betty adjusted it to suit her taste, with out much reference to the occupant's.

"I use it," she thought, glancing around it, struck forcibly by its contrast to Cecilia's, "I use it just as I use the world; it is utterly indifferent to me, perfectly blank and dull. I don't attach myself to it, or feel a throe of pleasure or interest in anything about it; it is just a place to live in, nothing more."

She had stood for half an hour, perhaps, gazing out of the window, with a discontented air, and watching the carriage, with Mrs. Thorndyke and Cecilia, drive away, when a sudden rush of steps outside her door, and a hasty knock made her turn. Cammy and Sylvie and Cub surrounded her instantly, with acclamations.

"O, Miss Warrington, you'll go to drive! O say you will !"

"Cyril says he'll take us if you'll go !"

"Cyril's promised to go to B—— if you only will !"

"He's waiting just for you to say we may !"

"And it's such a splendid afternoon !"

"And he's going away to-morrow !"

"And we'll never get another chance !"

"The greys go like the wind!"

"And he never lets anybody drive 'em when he isn't here!"

"O, Miss Warrington, just this once!"

"But what will your mother say when she comes back?"

"O, mamma never minds; she always lets us go with Cyril."

Cammy's ludicrous earnestness of manner, little Sylvie's dancing eyes, Cub's pleading looks, the sunshine without, the dreariness within, and, above all, a sudden recklessness of consequences, overwhelmed her resolution, and she hastily exclaimed, after a moment of hesitation, during which the tears came in Sylvie's eyes, and Cammy grew pale with apprehension,

"Well—yes—I'll go. You may tell Marcelle to dress you."

There was a shout of exultation, and the children tore down stairs like mad to apprise their brother of the news. A moment after they were gone, came Frank's repentance, but it came too late. There was nothing to do now but make the best of her foolish acquiescence, and hope as little trouble would come out of it as was possible.

The children, gazing eagerly out of the nursery window, were gratified at last by the approach of the greys, 'ed by Martin, coming to the door. They rushed madly down the stairs, and in a moment the servant came to announce that the carriage was waiting for Miss Warrington.

"I hope you have plenty of shawls," said Cyril, who

met her in the hall. "It may be chilly before we get back."

Frank felt perfectly contemptible when she thought of Sainty. She found the children were already safely disposed of, thanks to the forethought of their good brother. All three comfortably bestowed on the back seat, while the place beside Cyril was left vacant.

"Cub, see that neither of the children are spilled out," he said, glancing back at them, after he had arranged carefully the fur robe across Frank's lap. "Sylvie, you must sit as still as if you were in church, for I've often dropped two or three people out without knowing a single word about it, and the greys never stop for anything, you know."

The children were deeply impressed with the danger of stirring hand or foot, or breathing with any degree of freedom, and Cyril taking the reins from Martin, gave the restless horses the liberty they longed for, and in a minute and a half they were outside the gate and bowling gaily along the road to B——.

It was a superb afternoon, one of those rare and mellow days that come sometimes in late November, before the dead leaves are all fallen, or the certain taint of frost has penetrated into earth and air. The roads were in excellent condition, and the air just bracing and cool enough to make it an exhilarating thing to go through it at such a rapid rate. The horses seemed to feel a resentment at their long inaction, and to realize that this was the unique occasion offered them of vindicating their honor and giving to their master and the world assurance of a speed and bottom quite unparalleled in story.

The fine air, the rapid motion, the gay spirits of her companion, were just the combination of stimulants that Frank needed to create a strong reaction from the languor of the morning. She hardly knew herself, she was so different from anything she had been for months.

The drive to B—— was quite a long one, and when there, the good brother thought it necessary to stop at the village inn a little while, to let the children stretch their cramped limbs, and to rest the horses before their return. The inn was prettily situated on the bank of the river; the parlor windows opened upon a little balcony which ran across three sides of the building. Frank had gone out there to look at the sunset on the river, while the children entertained themselves with yawning, warming their feet at the stove, inspecting the plaster images on the mantel-piece, the colored prints on the wall, and the big Bible on the table; when Cyril, coming in from his supervision of the horses, opened the window and went out on the balcony to join her. The scene was lovely, and Cyril seemed in no hurry to leave it, finding 't unwelcome news when Frank complained that it was chilly, and following her back reluctantly to the parlor. Just as he was holding the window open for her and she was stepping into the room, he saw her start and look disconcerted. His eye followed the direction hers had taken, and fell upon a man, well dressed, but indefinably underbred, who stood on the front balcony, leaning upon one of the windows which was open, and which commanded a full view of the room and of the river balcony from which they had just come in. He was talking with Cammy who had on her pertest and most assuming air, but whc was evidently much pleased at being the object of attention even of such a dubious gentleman.

"What is Cammy about?" muttered Cyril, looking quickly at Frank as he spoke.

"She is very forward," said Frank, trying to speak indifferently, "call her away."

"Cammy," said her brother sharply, going forward "come and put your shawl on; we are ready to start."

"My shawl is on," returned the little girl, not moving; "that's Sylvie's shawl on the table."

"Very well, come and put Syvie's shawl on for her then," Cyril answered, with a look that Cammy didn't dare to disobey. She came reluctantly over to the table, while the stranger moved slowly away from the window and sauntered up and down the balcony, keeping a sharp eye upon the party within. Cyril gave Cammy a pretty severe rebuke, which she received in pouting silence, twitching little Sylvie's shawl about her, however, with an eloquent impatience which made the younger whine and fret exasperatingly.

"I will go and order the horses up," said Cyril, giving the naughty children a dark look as he went out.

"Don't stay long," Frank had it on her lips to say, but she turned away without speaking, and walked impatiently up and down the room. "This way, Cammy," she said, significantly, pointing to a chair beside her, as Cammy sauntered towards the door. Cammy gave her a malicious look as she obeyed, and threw herself angrily into the seat, while Frank continued her walk with most uncomfortable reflections.

What a spite fate must have against her, to throw this man in her way again. Here was the old life dragged forth at last. What had he been telling Cammy? Some pleasing recollections, no doubt, of the little house in G—— street; some anecdote derived from Dorothy; some story of that starvation period. What would her dainty friend Cecilia think of her after that; how would her new admirer take it? She had been trying so long to forget that dreary time she had almost succeeded; and she felt that till she did forget it and conceal it even from herself, she could have no honest basis for her self-respect, no reasonable excuse for the pride she cherished.

Presently she began to hope she had been mistaken, she had magnified some trifling resemblance, and this man was not the man she dreaded to encounter; but again the slow sauntering step crossed the balcony, and glancing out, she saw she had not been mistaken. As he came back again past the window he looked in, paused before the door, and after a glance around, entered. Miss Warrington turned her back and stooped over a book upon the table; Cammy welcomed him with a smile, of course. As he began speaking, the governess heard the welcome sound of wheels, and catching Sylvie's hand, said hastily to Cammy without lifting up her eyes,

"Come to the door, the carriage is here."

As she turned, the man made a pretence of surprise and recognition, and coming forward said in a low tone:

"It is some time since we have met; but I flatter myself you will remember"——

8*

"You have made some mistake," she said, turning abruptly away, and pushing Cammy before her through the door, reaching the steps exactly at the moment the carriage drew up before them. There was a little delay while the children were being settled in their places, during which she had to stand upon the steps before the door, not three feet from the stranger, who did not speak again, but whose black eyes she felt upon her face with most impudent intentness. Cyril did not appear to notice this, but just after he had put Frank in her place and had taken his own beside her, the stranger stepped forward, and raising his hat, said:

"Excuse me, but the lady dropped this, I think," at the same time handing him a letter.

"No," she said, "I did not drop anything."

"But it has your name upon it," said Cyril, looking at the letter and then at her.

"Has it?" she said bewildered, feeling in her pocket. Cyril gave it to her with a doubtful look, and then darted a suspicious one upon the stranger, who, bowing, had turned away indifferently. The envelope was torn, and it had certainly the appearance of being an opened and read letter, but she knew very well it had never been in her pocket or in her possession. She had to accept it, though, or acknowledge the man knew her name, and she thrust it as carelessly as she could into the pocket of her dress, while Cyril raised the whip, and the horses started forward.

"Does that man belong here? His face is wonderfully familiar to me," she said with an affectation of unconcern

"No," said Cyril. "I asked the landlord and he says he is a stranger, that he has been here for the past week; for what object has not yet appeared. You say his face is familiar to you?"

There was an indefinable alteration in Cyril's voice and manner, and it alarmed Frank enough to call up all the actress in her.

"Very," she said thoughtfully, "very familiar. And the more I think of it, the more certain I am I have seen it before."

"Cammy," said her brother, abruptly, "what did he have to say to you? Pray how long had you been talking?"

Cammy tossed her head and seemed to decline to answer, but the good brother gave her a look which brought out slowly and unsatisfactorily that he'd asked her what her name was, how old she was, how far she lived from B——, and whether she liked the country.

"Well," said Cyril, "didn't he ask you anything else? Didn't he ask you about any of the rest of us?"

Now, the fact was, he had asked her a great deal about the young lady on the balcony, the length of time she had been with them, whether that gentleman was her brother, where he lived, whether he often took the young lady driving, how soon they were going to the city for the winter, and a good deal more to the same effect. But she had two reasons for suppressing both questions and answers: the first was, that she did not want Miss Warrington to know he had asked so much about her, and the second was, that she felt afraid to confess how many things she had divulged

So she looked indifferently about her and answered, she
did not remember anything else that he had said
Cammy was not very particular about her facts ordinarily, her moral sense having become a little blunted
by contact with the Marcelles of the nursery and the
mesdemoiselles of the school-room, who had been principally intrusted with her training.   She had, moreover,
a natural talent for intrigue, and would have flirted
and plotted if she had been brought up in a convent.
Frank did not put the smallest confidence in her asser-
tion, but she breathed much freer after it was made.

The drive home was a thought less pleasant than the
drive out, to all the party; but Cyril felt the change
less than any one after he had recovered from the suspicions the stranger's manner had at first excited.   He
presently dismissed the subject as one not worth
remembering, and Miss Warrington assisted him to the
best of her ability.

Just as they came through the lodge gate, he looked
at his watch; it was long past six.   "May the dinner
not be waiting!" he ejaculated.

As they drew up before the door, Frank glanced towards the parlor windows; Mrs. Thorndyke stood in
one, Cecilia and some strangers in the other.   Cyril bit
his lip as he tossed the reins to Martin and sprang out,
but assumed a very *insouciant* manner as he took his
hat off gaily to them.

"We must be prepared for some black looks, Miss
Warrington," he said, *sotto voce*, as he helped her to get
out.   "But do not mind them; I assure you they are
as harmless as they will be brief."

Miss Warrington restrained the haughty answer that started to her lips at the suggestion that any one had the right to question the propriety of her going and coming when and how she chose, and gave him instead a careless and laughing answer as she went up the steps, quite aware that she was being looked at critically and not kindly by the spectators in the window. She did not show the least consciousness of them, however, as she crossed the piazza and entered the hall door; but the ease and indifference of her manner ended when she had locked herself into her own room.

She threw off her shawl and bonnet, and pulling the letter from her pocket, leaned down to look at it by the fire light. The address was written hurriedly, in rather a free, man's hand. She did not hesitate a moment whether to look in it or not, but with a gesture of extreme disgust, tore it in several pieces and threw it into the newly kindled fire, and watched it shrivel into ashes with an expression of relief. At this moment, the bell rang for dinner, with a sort of irritation in its shrill tones, as if the cook were out of temper, and Thomas as "mad" as might be; so she bent her whole mind to getting dressed as soon as possible. Remembering Miss Rosenbaum and the Cuylers, she made the best toilet she was able, and went down stairs, trying in vain to take the tingle out of her pulses and the flutter out of her nerves.

In the lower hall she paused and walked two or three times up and down it to recover herself, for between her hurry in dressing, the unusual excitements of the day, her unstrung state of nerves, and the novelty of meeting stylish people, she was not by any means as regal as she desired to be. The hall was very dimly lighted, and with courage nearly ready for the critical *pas*, she had approached the dining-room door, when she heard, with a start, steps upon the stairs, and, turning saw Cyril already on the landing. She had fancied him, of course, at the table; this was disastrous, anything but making her *entrée* with him. She made a desperate retreat towards the parlor, but he saw her, and came up to her immediately.

"You have dressed quickly," he said, running his eye rapidly and with unconscious admiration over her toilette. "I fancied I should be down first, and would have made my peace with Miss Emily before you came. You must not blame me if I deviate a little from that strict veracity which we all admire."

"I shall not blame you for anything," she said, wretchedly, turning away, "if you only will go in."

"And you?"

"I will come presently—I am not ready—I—that is—" Cyril saw the truth, and, laughing, was whispering some reassurance as he left her, when Thomas suddenly threw the dining-room door wide open, and the two delinquents stood petrified, in a full blaze of light, before the eyes of the whole table full.

"There's no help for us," said Cyril *à demi-voix.* "Courage, Miss Warrington. Trust me to make it right."

CHAPTER XIII.

THE OLD LOVE AND THE NEW.

"It's good to be merry and wise,
It's good to be honest and true,
It's good to be off wi' the old love
Before you be on wi' the new."

THE sudden stream of light and the bodily presence
of the objects of her dread, acted most happily upon
Miss Warrington; she entered the room looking neither
to the right hand nor the left, as a governess should, and
took her place silently between Cammy and Cecilia.
Cyril, meantime, was seating himself beside Miss Rosenbaum, who received his eager expressions of pleasure
at meeting rather coldly, and who was eyeing the governess more than listening to him, while he made his
excuses to Miss Cuyler, who sat on his other hand.
Miss Cuyler, not being an aggrieved party, took them
very amiably, and told him he was perfectly excusable.
Mr. Cuyler, opposite, joked him on his fast driving, and
told him he had caught a glimpse of him only two
hours ago on the road to B——.

"Yes, we started rather late," said Cyril, not quite
comfortably. "I trust," he continued, leaning forward
and looking down the table at his mother, "that you
were not uneasy about the children. I had no idea of
taking them, but they clamored and pled so hard, I

finally gave in to their petition for one last drive before
I went away."

The good brother! Miss Rosenbaum was melting
visibly.

"I certainly have been uneasy, extremely uneasy
about the children. It is of the last importance to keep
Sylvie from the evening air; I would not have had her
out to-night for anything."

"I only started out to give them a little turn," said
Cyril, "but for an unfortunate detention we should
have been home long ago."

Cammy opened her eyes; like another member of the
party present, she could not remember any detention
that had not been entirely voluntary.

"I beg you'll take care that no more such detentions
occur," said Mr. Thorndyke, with a disagreeable decision
of expression. "Dinner waits for no member of the
family in future."

"I have very small interest in the dinner hour after
to-day," said Cyril, carelessly.

This apparently random shot brought down, as was
intended, Cecilia and Miss Rosenbaum, and was not
without some effect upon the father. Cyril knew the
only way of mollifying his mother was to make a show
of devotion to Miss Rosenbaum, and so he set himself
at work to mollify her.

But, in fact, his position was rather a delicate one
with her: Emily Rosenbaum had been his very earliest
flame, and he had gone with her just as far as he possibly could go without engaging himself to her. He still
liked her very much, his old fancy was revived when

ever he saw her, and he had a remote intention of marrying her one of these days, and being very fond of her after he had exhausted all the other pleasures that lay within his reach. It was a very favorite plan of Mrs. Thorndyke's to marry Cyril to Emily, and as she always treated her plans as facts, she contributed largely towards keeping up the hopes in the young lady's heart, which would probably have been starved out in time, if Cyril's slender and spasmodic devotion had been their only food. She always acted as if the ultimate connection of the families was an understood thing ; she talked to Emily of Cyril as if she had a right to be informed of all his movements, she sent her his letters to read when he was absent, and brought her to Ringmer when he was expected home.

Emily was a girl of a good deal of spirit, but not of extreme sensibility, and this was a course which naturally bewildered her. She had been very much in love with Cyril ever since her school-days, and being an only child, an heiress, and very much petted both at home and in society, she was naturally incredulous of any lack of sincerity on his part. So many people wanted her, it was absurd to suppose the man she wanted was indifferent to her. She was exasperated and angry at his tardiness in claiming her, but with all her faults and follies, she loved him very sincerely, and refused suitor after suitor without a moment's hesitation, considering herself pledged actually to him. Her father was dead, and her mother lived only to fulfil her wishes and to obey the will which it was her place to have subdued. She was rather pretty, extremely stylish, and her manners had quite a charm from their animation and assurance, but for the rest, though sufficiently good-hearted, as the term goes, she was willful, selfish and no¹ very scrupulous.

Cecilia tried to love her, and be happy in the prospect of having her for a sister, but she was afraid to acknowledge, even to herself, how uncompanionable she found her, and how few points of sympathy they had in common. Of course, with characteristic humbleness, she laid all the blame upon herself, and lamented her want of interest in the ordinary affairs of life, which had such engrossing weight with her companion.

Frank, of course, had known a good deal of this before, but she was not prepared to find Miss Rosenbaum quite so much at home as she seemed to be, and she would not have been mortal if she had not felt extremely *piquée* at the devotion which her recent admirer lavished upon his neighbor. It was, indeed, somewhat humiliating; she, the governess, was to be admired *sub rosâ*, Miss Rosenbaum, the heiress, was to be the object of his attention when the world was by. She knew she had deserved it richly, but it was not any pleasanter for that.

Cyril, before the dinner was over, was really in an uncomfortable position : the object of his new passion accorded him neither look nor word; to the object of his old, he had grown perfectly indifferent. It was very perverse in the governess not to understand, he thought; she ought to have known he was acting a part to get her out of a scrape, and that upon the keeping up of the fiction of his preference for Miss Rosenbaum, depended the possibility of continuing his real devotion to her. He knew, and fancied she must know too, that f his mother caught a suspicion of the feelings with which she had inspired him, she would lose no time in getting rid of her, and so it was obvious he could do nothing but be civil to Emily and be cold to her.

As the ladies left the dinner table, Miss Warrington· walked directly towards the stairs, but Cecilia caught her hand and whispered, "I shall never forgive you if you do not stay: I do not know how to entertain these Cuylers; I have been depending upon you."

Frank shook her head and looked resolved, and Cecilia added earnestly, "I do not ask many things of you, Frank; this is not much. And mamma said, too, this morning, she knew you would help me, that you would accompany me if I had to sing."

"Very well," she said, changing her mind suddenly. "I will stay."

They went into the parlor, where Miss Rosenbaum was playing the very lovely to Mrs. Thorndyke, and Miss Cuyler was looking a little bored, but very polite. Cecilia, certainly, did not seem to know what to do with her; people generally did not. Miss Cuyler was very young, very insipid, and very complacent. She seemed to feel no responsibility whatever about bearing her part in society, never talked, and yet seemed to take it as a matter of course that she should be talked to; always waiting blandly to be entertained, and never stirring hand or foot to contribute to other people's pleasure Cecilia went dutifully up to her, and tried sweetly to engage her in conversation, but that was a thing that had never been done yet by anybody, so of course she failed. Then she proposed showing her some pictures and they engaged her hands and eyes for ten minutes, but not her mind, for she had not a word to say about any of them, and relapsed into vacancy as soon as the book was closed.

There were several Miss Cuylers, all very unexciting, but this was the most tiresome of the series ; they were all blondes, all short, and all wore their hair *crêpé*, so that it was extremely difficult to distinguish a young Miss Cuyler from an old Miss Cuyler, for they ranged along at easy intervals from eighteen to thirty-four, and as they were not troubled with much activity of mind or body, the old ones were remarkably well preserved, and the young ones never had the air of being young. The Cuyler name was a tower of strength, however, and the Cuyler property proved walls and bulwarks ; no family in the country held a better place, and no stupidity commanded more respect than theirs. They gave stiff dinner and dreary evening parties, to which everybody went who could get an invitation. The father held a high place in the church, the mother was the head of several charitable associations, the daughters were always well attended to in society, the son was quite made a lion of, all upon the strength of a good family name, and a good fortune with which to keep it up.

Frank looked upon them naturally with contempt, because she was of inferior origin herself, and had grown up with an undue reverence, perhaps, for intellect, and an undue contempt for mediocrity of mind. She admitted the claims of the Thorndykes, because the father, she knew, held a high position among men of intelligence, which his good birth alone never would have gained him; she even respected the cultivation and art that had made so much of the mother's shallow brain and narrow heart; Cecilia was to her the picture of a high-bred, gentle-hearted lady, Cyril was a fine type of the young aristocrat; the children all more or less showed traits of good birth and good breeding, and Ringmer was, in her eyes, a beautiful and refined home, where wealth had resulted not only in luxury and elegance, but in an elevated standard of taste and feeling. But these dull Cuylers, with their great overloaded house, their clumsy equipage, their unornamented lives, filled her with contempt. On the one or two occasions when they had met before, she had had a good deal of time to study them, for they had not taken any notice of her. The young gentleman of the family, who was in this respect worse than his sisters, that he was silly as well as stupid, had not indeed ever seemed to realize her presence, and had passed her several times, at church and in walking, without any token of recognition. She bore him no malice for this, but it made her civility to his sister that evening after dinner quite a difficult exertion.

The relief she knew she was affording Sainty, however, encouraged her to keep it up, and when the gentlemen came in after their cigars, they found the ladies in two groups, quite distinct, as such after-dinner groups are apt to be; Cecilia, Mrs. Thorndyke, and Emily together, while Miss Cuyler and Miss Warrington were on the sofa, with Cammy an attentive listener. Mr. Cuyler, having discovered probably that the gove

was pretty enough to attract Mr. Cyril Thorndyke, had
concluded to be attracted by her himself, and accord-
ingly, upon entering the room, sauntered confidently
over to the sofa, and took a seat beside her.

Cyril followed him with his eyes, a little dissatisfiedly,
but yielded to the dictates of prudence, and went
towards the other group of ladies. Emily received him
with a smile that in old times would have melted, but
now only irritated him.

"There, Cyril can tell you about it himself," said
Mrs. Thorndyke, moving away.

"What can I tell Miss Emily?" asked Cyril, sitting
down.

"About that dreadful march last summer, when you
forded the river at midnight," said Emily, with flattering interest.

"Cecilia, my dear," said her mother, crossing the
room to join Miss Cuyler, "go to the piano, and let
Miss Cuyler hear that charming little morceau of Schu-
bert's. I really think she will enjoy it."

Cecelia obeyed, while Mrs. Thorndyke, having executed her masterly move, sat down to talk about music-
masters and piano-tuners to Miss Cuyler for half an hour,
while the insipid brother was left to the mercy of the
governess. He differed from his sisters in this respect,
that he had some small talk at his command, but it was
infinitessimal talk indeed, and Frank was almost tired
beyond civility. As she had no greater fancy than
other young women of her age for being left alone,
however, she endured it, and in the course of the even-
.ng became more patient under it.

Mrs. Thorndyke, as long as she could keep Cecilia a

the piano, held the key of the position, and it is difficult to say when the unwilling *tête-à-têtes* on the opposite sides of the room would have been terminated if Miss Cuyler had not unexpectedly had an idea, and announced that she wanted to hear Cecilia sing.

Cecilia had never practiced the accompaniment of the song required, which Miss Warrington always played for her, so Mrs. Thorndyke felt very much vexed while she assented cordially, and asked the governess to go to the piano. This single movement produced an entire disorganization of the party. Frank went over to the piano, followed by Mr. Cuyler, who helped Cecilia to move it more to suit her, and by Cyril, who started forward to help Frank find the sheet of music on the stand, which was heaped with unbound music, and which would probably be very hard to find.

"Miss Warrington," he said, as he bent over it, turning over one after another, heedlessly, "doesn't that stupid fellow drive you mad?"

"No," she said, quite unmoved. "Excuse me; but I think that is the piece you have in your hand."

"Ah! so it is. But I assure you he will drive me mad if he doesn't you. At least, do not look so interested when he talks to you."

Miss Warrington did not say a word to this, but dropped her eyes, and stood quietly waiting till Mr. Cuyler had ended his officious adjustment of piano and music and stool, and given her an opportunity to sit down.

"I hope you understand," said Cyril, in a very low voice, putting the music-book upon the stand, "I hope you understand my efforts to restore my mother to good temper. I will explain my reasons to you, if you will give me an opportunity, by and by."

Miss Warrington opened her eyes with the most entire and blank simplicity. "Reasons for what?" she asked, in a tone to match.

Cyril bit his lip, and gave her a look which promised something histrionic too; but, thinking better of it, he bent his head a little lower, and said, in a tone and manner quite sincere and simple, "My reasons for letting such a man as this enjoy a monopoly of your attention all the evening."

She displayed undiminished blankness of expression, as she took her seat and thanked Mr. Cuyler for his good offices. The music was not difficult, or it would have been beyond her reach, her musical talent being moderate, and her advantages having been extremely limited. She was improving herself with assiduity, however, and never shrank from anything that she fancied would give her confidence and practice. The idea of playing even a simple accompaniment before all those people, more cultivated in music than in anything else, made her quite weak and wretched, but she betrayed so little of her nervousness that Cyril, watching her narrowly from Miss Rosenbaum's side, resolved, before he left Ringmer, to know in what school she had learned such inimitable composure and command, and in what society her life had hitherto been spent.

This curiosity about her, and study of her, became a somewhat dangerous employment, and interfered considerably with his diplomatic plans. He grew very absent-minded when the music was ended, and Mr. Cuyler located himself permanently beside the piano stool, which Frank did not vacate, but merely pushed back against the wall. Emily was not slow to catch the inattentive wandering of his eyes across the room, and the unsympathetic tones that crept into his voice. She, too. .ooked across the room, and began to feel for the dark-eyed girl at the piano that bitter and consuming hatred which only one woman can feel for another. That her rival was attractive, she could not deny, looking carefully to find a flaw in her. Pretty even to a superficial observer, interesting and perplexing to those who looked further, and, upon looking further, it was evident Cyril was intent. There was a sort of deliberation and self-possession of manner about her that exasperated Emily, while it fascinated Emily's ancient lover. It was a manner very far removed from self-confidence, perfectly unassuming, but perfectly impregnable, and which in any one but a governess, would have been called extremely elegant, being a manner generally recognized as the result of high breeding and contact with good society, but which, in fact, is inborn and instinctive, and is no more produced by good society and good breeding than good complexions are produced by washes and cosmetics. How many ladies does one see every day who have never ceased to be gauche and brusque and maladroit, though they have been before the world for years, who know what's right, but only so, and never practice what they know, lacking tact, self-possession, and a well poised mind, gifts which not unfrequently are found in the possession of those in the commoner walks of life, making good women, wherever they may be, invaluable teachers, nurses, housewives, people whose very presence is an assurance of good order and serenity. Now, Miss Rosenbaum was not at all a lady, except in dress, education, and position; neither was Miss Cuyler, except in repose of manner and appearance of refinement. Neither of them had half the talent for fine-ladyism that the young governess possessed, and they felt it, one of them acutely and one of them unconsciously, and both disliked her in proportion as they appreciated her. Emily was not self-possessed, anything else; she was possessed of confidence, determination, willfulness to the verge of bad temper; but she was not possessed of the command of herself.

"Sainty, dear," she said, audibly, as she went over to the piano, to look at some new music Cecilia was showing to Miss Cuyler, "don't be so lazy about your accompaniments; take the time to learn them yourself. You do not do yourself justice."

"Why," said Cecilia, with perfect naïveté, "that is just why I ask Miss Warrington to play them for me. She is so accurate and accompanies me so well, I feel twice the confidence and sing twice as well."

Emily shrugged her shoulders, and said, turning to another pile of music *"Je vois cela d'un autre jour."*

Cecilia colored and glanced involuntarily. towards Frank, who was, however, at the moment taking a cup of tea from Mr. Cuyler, with such an indifferent smile, that she felt assured she had not heard it.

The arrival of the tea had been a boon to Cyril; it had relieved him from Emily, and given him an excuse to hover round the piano for a while, but not, unhappily, to gain a word with Frank. That young person, now, had no consciousness of his presence when he approached her; no one could say she was coquetting with Mr. Cuyler, for she was as quiet and self-contained as ever, but he only could succeed in getting her eye and ear, and to him alone she vouchsafed a moderate and uncompromising share of her attention. It began to shine in upon Mr. Cyril Thorndyke's mind that the governess's favor was not to be attained by surreptitious compliments. "Confound her pride," he muttered, while he admired it more than anything about her. "But then, why can't she see the fix I'm in!"

But she could not see it, *ou mieux*, would not, and so the evening passed away uncomfortably. Cyril was not the actor he had thought himself, for he only deceived his mother, and that was not very much to do. Sainty was unsuspecting, and did not think anything of the matter after she saw Emily and he had not quarrelled; but Emily knew he was fascinated with the governess. Mr. Cuyler knew it too, and Miss Cuyler thought both the young gentlemen ought to be ashamed of themselves for taking so much notice of her. As for the governess, she knew it as well as young women always know their power.

When Cyril heard carriage wheels outside, he experienced unmixed pleasure. "Not yet!" he exclaimed low to Emily, with a pleading look as she arose.

Poor Emily! Could that be insincere? She caught at it eagerly, and determined to believe in it. This was the last time she should see him, perhaps forever: war is a black gulf to lose one's lover in. He could not have meant what she had fancied she had seen to-night. perhaps he had been piqued, perhaps she had not shown feeling enough when she had met him. She loved him so, she knew she was unreasonable; it did not do for a woman to be too exacting. She was certain after all she had deceived herself.

Moments were precious now. She was impatient of the time required to put her cloak on in Sainty's room, and Miss Cuyler, whose carriage had simultaneously driven to the door, never would be ready it appeared. Sainty was unusually affectionate, perhaps feeling that she had some omissions of her brother's to make up for, and it seemed extremely natural that the three young ladies should linger together by the fire upstairs, while the two young men were lighting their cigars and lingering together by the fire in the library below. But Emily could not wait; she beat her foot impatiently a few moments on the rug, then said she must not keep the horses any longer in the cold, and kissing her companions, she twisted her nubie round her head, and hurried to the stairs.

"Why, I am all ready too," said Miss Cuyler, following with Sainty.

At the head of the staircase, Emily paused and gave a little start, for at the bottom of it stood the governess, with one foot on the lowest step, and one hand on the heavy oaken baluster, with her head slightly turned and her eyes cast down, listening silently to the low and hurried speech of Cyril, who stood behind her. What a pretty picture they made under the soft hall lamp, if Emily had only had an artist's eye. But she had not an artist's eye just then, only a very jealous one, though she watched them, bending forward, breathlessly, as if she took great pleasure in the sight. Cyril glanced up and saw her and drew back slightly; then she pulled her cloak about her, and came down the stairs. The staircase was very wide, but she filled it with her flounces so completely that Frank had to draw back too. She really looked very handsome as she came down, her beautiful dress sweeping after her, and her small heeled boots making a coquettish clatter on the stairs. Her eyes were flashing, and her cheeks were burning with a crimson spot.

"Oh, Mr. Thorndyke," she said pleasantly "won't you see if the carriage is at the door, while I speak a moment to Mrs. Thorndyke. I had quite forgotten a message from mamma."

Mrs. Thorndyke at that moment came out from the parlor, and putting her arms round Emily, kissed her affectionately. Sainty and Miss Cuyler coming down the stairs, and Mr. Cuyler emerging from the library, cigar in hand, effectually blocked Frank's way, and she stood quietly at one side, waiting till she could pass up the stairs.

"Dear Sainty," cried Emily, "won't you come over and stay a few days with me? We shall have ever so many people up from town next week. I know you will be lonely after your brother goes away. His visit must have been such a pleasure to you; no doubt you were together every minute of the time, and you will miss him so!"

Cyril bit his lip: "that girl's the very devil when she gets a jealous fit," he thought.

"Mrs. Thorndyke, won't you make Sainty come! You do not know how much I want to have her. And there's my cousin Julian is expected back next week You know what they say of him, dear Mrs. Thorndyke! The best match in America; I'll be generous and give Sainty at least an equal chance, if she'll consent to come. I know what she will say—she is giving the children music lessons, and she cannot leave them; but I hope you will persuade her that it isn't right to tie herself down that way. Do you think it's right, Mr. Cyril?" she added, turning to him. "Three hours of confinement every day with those children; I never heard of such a thing."

"Really," said Cyril, "I haven't heard of it before, but I have no doubt it is all wrong. It would not be Sainty, if she were not over head and ears in some unnecessary duty."

"Cecilia seems to desire it," began the mother— "or"——

"It is my own choice," interrupted Cecilia. "It is no burden, and it is not unnecessary, either, Cyril."

"But it ought to be unnecessary," said Emily, with a significant look. "*Chère petite, tu es trop aimable;* but promise me you will take a holiday, and leave the care of the children for a few days at least to the governess, and come over to Wheatley. Now promise. Let me come for you on Wednesday."

"I cannot promise," Sainty said, uncomfortably. "I will think of it."

Emily shrugged her shoulders. Miss Cuyler made a movement to depart; and after another moment of

adieux and promises, the guests left the hall accompanied by Cyril.

The Cuyler carriage came first and drove off first,
giving Cyril two minutes in the moonlight to make his
peace with Emily.

They were so well improved that the carriage door
closed as she released her hand from his—his words of
affection ringing in her ears; and the horses started forward, while she threw herself back upon the cushions
and burst into a passion of tears, more than doubtful of
his faith, but more than ever loving, reckless and
unwise.

And Cyril, turning back to the house, felt for a
moment that he was a wretch, and wondered that the
earth did not open and engulf him where he stood.

CHAPTER XIV.

OFF TO THE WARS AGAIN.

"I'm quite convinced the field of Mars
Is not a field of clover!"—WATERLOO BALLAD.

REMORSE seldom troubled Cyril Thorndyke long; it was sharp when it first came, but he did not entertain it patiently, and rather made a virtue of turning it out of his mind before it disturbed the settled order of things there, materially.

So he took a turn or two on the terrace before he went in, and succeeded in convincing himself that he hadn't done anything but what any man under the same circumstances would have done, and that if he were in a false position he owed it to his family and not to himself; and that somehow, things would come out right some time, and there wasn't any use in making himself unhappy about what he could not help.

With which conclusion he went into the house in an easy state of mind, destined, however, to be more seriously disturbed by finding that the governess had disappeared, and that his last chance of seeing her before he went was lost.

"Confound her shyness," he thought, glancing eagerly through the parlors and the library. "She will not be up in the morning, and I cannot go without seeing her, and making her understand."

But it began to appear that he must do exactly that: there was not the smallest chance of seeing her; the more he thought of it the more certain it became. He professed himself extremely tired, kissed his mother and sister good-night very unlovingly, gave some orders for the morning, and went to his own room.

What should he do about it? He paced the floor for an hour, lit one cigar from another, knit his brow angrily, and once and again "confounded" his position with his new love and his entanglements with his old. What could he resort to? A note, a skillful explanation, an implied apology? Worse than useless; she would not allow him personally the right to apologize, much less he knew, would she permit him to do so by letter. An open declaration, then? An unconditional surrender of himself, an offer of marriage in good faith?

Though he was rash and desperately in love, he was not rash and desperate enough for that. Then he thought of some blind message through Cecilia, some little souvenir to which no one could attach importance; or else, from town, some anonymous and costly present; anything to soothe the vexation of going away under a cloud; anything in fact, to keep up a kinder recollection of him in her mind, and to do away the unfortunate impressions of the evening.

But that, common sense told him, he could not do in any of these ways; he would stand fairer with her if he went away without a word, without an indication of his feelings, and he would have a better chance of finding her at Ringmer when he next came back, if he held his

tongue entirely now, both to her and to his sister. Certainly he was very much in love, far deeper than he had
ever been before, and it was distracting to have to go
away. He was in the habit of having precisely what he
wanted from men and women both, and the vexation of
being thwarted, the novelty of being baulked in what
was everything to him for the moment, worked him up
quite beyond his own control.

At one moment he was resolved to throw away his
standing in his regiment and outstay his leave; the
next, he blushed for himself and resolved he would not,
if he could, remain another day near a woman for
whom he could forget his honor.

He tried to persuade himself that it was a whim, a
fancy that would soon pass on to die among its fellows,
and be as much forgotten; but in some way there was a
difference between this and them. He could not quite
persuade himself that he was not in earnest. But the
folly—the folly! A penniless governess coming from
none knew where, belonging to none knew whom; it
was worse than folly to suppose himself in earnest with
her.

"But if I want her," he muttered with a sudden
reaction, "if I want her, what do all these things
amount to? If I want her these things shall not stop
me from marrying her; no family considerations ever
have interfered with me or ever shall. But then—I
don't want her you see, and what's the use of bothering
about it! Confound the girl; she's bewitched me, to
make me even dream of such a thing. I'll take good
care no one finds out how near a fool I've been. It's

.ucky I've got to go to-morrow; she might make me
do anything, I swear. Those eyes of hers are *magni-
fique*, and she takes the wind all out of Emily's sails for
style. Emily's a *grisette* beside her. Who says she
cannot be as fine a lady if I choose to make her Mrs.
Thorndyke?

"*Mrs. Thorndyke!* That's a joke. After I'm ten
miles away from Ringmer, I shall forget I ever saw
her."

A very tempestuous night it proved, in Mr. Cyril
Thorndyke's mind, and if he had carried out half the
schemes that he resolved upon, he certainly would have
been a ruined and unhappy man; but the result of the
struggle was more sensible than could have been reasonably hoped for, and he drove away, in the early grey
of the next morning, having kissed the sleepy, uncurled
children who stood waiting for him at the nursery door,
rushed into his mother's room and received her adieux
from within the bed-curtains, taken his hurried breakfast which Sainty, choked and wretched, made for him
in the dim dining-room, held her affectionately in his
arms at the hall door, and sprung into the carriage and
was whirled away, without having committed himself
in any manner, or said or done an unwise thing in the
matter of the governess.

He went, however, cheered by an intention so fixed
that it was first-cousin to a fact; and that was, to
return at or before the holidays on another leave, or
to throw up his commission. He had not entered the
service of his country with any idea of allowing it to
interfere with the service that he considered that he

owed himself, and he found a great many good reasons for the course he proposed to pursue in the event of a refusal to his very justifiable request. However, things would not probably be pushed to that extremity; if any man in the army had influence at the Department, he certainly had, and he could undoubtedly get a dozen leaves if he happened to desire them.

A week ago, he desired nothing less than leave to absent himself from the scenes of possible adventure and positive good-fellowship for which he had had such a relish, but now things seemed to have taken an entirely different turn, and home was the centre of his pleasures, "a private life was all his joy," and military ardor was flickering low in its socket, ready to go out at the first adverse puff of air.

CHAPTER XV.

AN ENCOUNTER.

Supporter peu, pour emporter tout.

AN extremely dull party met at the breakfast table that morning: Sainty's eyes were red with crying, and the children felt the effects of their unseasonable réveille plainly, being out of sorts, pettish, and indifferent to the charms of omelet. Mrs. Thorndyke showed her regrets for her son by an exaggeration of all her ordinary points of weakness, and Mr. Thorndyke was profoundly grim. As for Frank, she felt as if she had been living upon stimulants for the past three days, and was faint from inanition, now they were withdrawn. She was less patient with Sylvie in the school-room, snubbed Cammy with more emphasis, and almost forgot to be kind to Cub.

It was altogether a dull, blue, cross-grained day at Ringmer, and the succeeding week was not much better.

On the Wednesday appointed, Miss Rosenbaum came for Sainty, looking rather heavy-eyed and ill, but very grandly dressed, and very gay and dashing in her manners. Frank was walking up and down upon the errace with the children, when the carriage drove to the door. Cecilia having just gone into the house, the young lady, as she got out, gave a look around before she approached the children, kissing them affectionately, taking Sylvie's face between her prettily gloved hands with an affected and amusing gesture, and asking Cammy where Sister was, in a very gracious manner.

After which she saw the governess, and nodded to her carelessly, as she would have nodded to the nursery maid. "Well," thought Frank, as she continued her walk, with Cub beside her, while the two little girls conducted the visitor into the house, "well, I do not know whether there is any propriety in my hating that young woman, but I believe I do, and in process of time I am afraid I shall make her feel it, if she does not mend her ways considerably."

The morning had been a rainy one, and the sun having come out too late to dry the walks, Frank continued walking on the flags with Cub till the expiration of the hour she had appointed to herself for exercise. It was not quite ended when Thomas appeared and summoned Miss Rosenbaum's carriage, and presently one of the maids came out, bringing Cecilia's box. Frank had felt certain that Sainty would be over-persuaded, and go to Wheatley, though she knew she hated the very thought of it, and she felt impatient and angry at what seemed such weakness.

She came out from the house with her bonnet and cloak on, preceded by Miss Rosenbaum and the little girls, and followed to the door by Mrs. Thorndyke, who had just bidden them good-bye. Miss Rosenbaum swept down the steps to the carriage door, looking back and saying, with a little laugh, to Mrs. Thorndyke, that she need not hope for Sainty under a fortnight, while

Sainty herself, looking very meek and unhappy, went to kiss Frank good-bye.

"You are a coward," said Frank, *sotto voce.* "Why did you not have the courage to say no?"

"I could not," Cecilia answered unhappily. "Mamma desired it, and Emily would have been so disappointed; it wouldn't have been right."

"Right has a good many sides to it," said Frank, with impatience. "Why will you let people impose upon you so! At any rate, be firm and come back before they wear you out: I shall lose all respect for you, if you stay over Saturday."

"You are very hard, Frank," said Sainty with a sigh, as she turned away.

Miss Rosenbaum leaned out of the carriage to tell Cammy to be a good girl, and practise just as much as if sister Cecilia were at home, and then, with another radiant good-bye from her, and a wistful one from Sainty, the carriage drove away. Frank watched it out of sight with a jealous feeling of regret; Sainty was the only friend she had in the world, and Emily the bitterest enemy; it was more probable that the pitch would blacken the snow, than that the snow would whiten the pitch. Sainty would come back less purely her friend than she went away, and what would Ringmer be to her without Sainty's tender and constantly demonstrated affection. Her life would be grinding and hard, indeed, without that one softening influence, and her face grew so dark, that Cub, watching it wistfully, slipped his hand into hers, and tried to ask her what it was that troubled her.

"Troubles me?" she repeated, with a smile that poor Cub did not like or understand any better than the frown. "Nothing troubles me now, my Cub; nothing possibly can. You know you could not see the eclipse last week, because the night was so frightfully black and close."

"Well?" said Cub, bewilderedly.

"O nothing, Cub; you cannot understand how the blackness becomes almost a blessing after all, it hides so many things. But remember, Cub, you need not mind it when you see me look more unhappy at one time than another, for it is all one, and nothing troubles me at all."

When Marcelle came to the door to call Sylvie in, Frank sent the others with her, and, looking at her watch, resolved to walk to the gate and back before she dressed for dinner. The sun was near its setting, the air chilly and damp, and the road hardly dry as yet, but, lifting her dress, she drew her cloak around her, and hurried down the steps. The distance to the gate was little less than a mile, and she had not half an hour.

The road took several turns, winding just a quarter of a mile from the entrance, through a thick standing grove of evergreens, which extended nearly to the gate, and which Mr. Thorndyke plotted night and day to keep dense and sepulchral looking. Nothing could have been finer, if Ringmer had been a cemetery, instead of a country seat, and nothing could have been better planned, if the design had been to frighten people away, instead of inviting their admiration. But Mr Thorndyke, desiring, above most other things, that his place should be admired, had made a very marked mistake in rendering the approach to it gloomy to the last degree, and in building a lodge without any perceptible feature but roof, and a gate without any tangible result but heaviness

Frank felt the chill and dampness of the air perceptibly increased after she came under the shade of the trees; the rain drops were still falling from the branches, and the water stood in many places in the road. About midway in the wood, she was startled by the sound of an approaching step, and, looking up suddenly, she saw a man within half a dozen yards of her. He lifted his hat as he approached her; it was the man who had accosted her at the inn with Cyril. He began to speak, and she stopped and listened to him. When he had ended his common-place and rather unintelligible expression of satisfaction at meeting her, she lifted her eyes and said,

"You have spoken to me more than once before this without authority. I now forbid you ever addressing me again wherever you may meet me," and she moved on.

"Ha!" he said, turning and walking at her side, the slight shade of hesitation gone entirely from his manner. "I'm not a man much bound by what they call authority, but if I wanted it, to speak to you, I have it. You read my letter?"

After waiting due time for a reply, he went on, with a little sneer, still keeping beside her, "I know you did, though you do not mean to say you did. Well, well, young women will put on airs, whether they're governesses or grand ladies; one has to let them have their swing. But, taking it for granted you did read it, as I know you did, you'll find it difficult to prove that I have'nt the very best authority for speaking to you and for telling you some pretty unpleasant truths, what's more. Young women don't do well to hold themselves so high to those who know just who they are and where they come from. It may do very well to put on airs with young blades from the army, who wouldn't take the trouble to inquire into what's gone before, as long as they had liberty to amuse themselves; but to a man that has known all from the first, it's a mistaken policy to say the least, and a policy you'll be apt to see the folly of before you've gone much further.

"You don't say anything. You don't mean to speak, I see. You're walking very fast, Well, you're not convinced I have you in my power? You're not convinced I know your father was a worthless vagabond, who left you when you were a baby, to be brought up on the charity of his wife's relations; that you're now hiding, as it were, from those who brought you up, and who have a right to know what you're about and to have a share of what you earn? You're not convinced I could in a minute bring a word from your low friends *there* to your grand friends *here*, that would open the eyes of both a little?

"Well, well, don't speak; don't notice this man, who has no authority to address you; he's a low fellow, it's best to turn him off; but harkee! There was one once, wasn't there? not much higher, not such a grand gentleman as Mr. Cyril here, who wouldn't have been turned off if he had only spoken, who could have had anything he asked for in those old times, notwithstanding he was nothing better than a farmer's boy, a farmer's boy brought up on the charity of his relations too.

"Aha! I've touched the right chord, have I? Don't turn away your face. I know it's white; but I shan't tell."

They were now almost in sight of the house, and Frank turning to him said, simply, "Will you leave me?"

"Yes, after I have said one word. Remember what has passed between us to-day, remember what I told you in my letter, and promise to recognize me from this time, whenever we may meet, as an acquaintance. You do not consent? Then you know the consequences. Listen. I am an honest man; I have as good a right to you as anybody has; I've as good a right to admire you as Cyril Thorndyke here, has; and what's more, I've a mind to marry you, which I know he hasn't. You've been as insulting to me as you knew how to be since the first time you saw me; but I'll let that pass, considering that most women think themselves entitled to insult the men that want to marry them. I'm as good as you are, in station and in blood, and I'm a good deal better in what makes gentlefolks, and that is money. You may look higher, but you'll never reach higher. I can offer you all you've got a right to ask for and more, and I'll make a lady of you if it's your ambition to be made a lady of, and I'll give you money and a good home, and all that women want to make them happy. You've pos- sessed me somehow, with your black eyes and your grand ways, hateful as they are, and I'll overcome a good deal

to have you; I've always meant to have you since the
first time I saw you, and I'm apt to have what I set myself to get. I'll give you time to think it over, remem
bering and weighing all I've said, and I wont ask you
for your answer till I see you again; it may be some
time hence or it may be in a week or two. In the
meanwhile, don't forget that if you don't have me, I'll
make it hard for you to have anybody else."

And turning on his heel, the man disappeared into
the woods and left her.

She only reached her room in time to smooth her hair
and brush the mud off her dress, when the bell for dinner rang. She was, as usual, very silent at the table,
and afterwards, when the children hung around her,
with their caressing and questioning and teasing, she
was so absent and dull and disappointing, that they gradually fell off from her, fretted and dissatisfied that she
was so unlike herself.

Nor did they find that she recovered the likeness to
herself the next day, nor the next; she seldom left the
house, and never walked off the terrace, and only then
for a few moments at a time, and with Cub invariably
beside her. She looked so pale, indeed, after a few
days, that even Mrs. Thorndyke noticed it, and invited
her to drive with her in Cecilia's place, which drive became a daily thing during the daughter's absence.

Cecilia did not come back on the Saturday appointed
nor even on the next, but she sent for some more clothes,
and she wrote to her mamma several affectionate little
notes that did not sound particularly homesick. Indeed
they indicated pretty plainly that she was enjoying her

self very much, and that Wheatley was the scene of
very continual merry-making, into which she had entered
with zest enough to forget her longings for home and
her habitual distaste for gay society. Frank felt doubly
lonely after hearing of each of these notes, and the constrained little message to herself at the end, made her
more than ever sure that something very engrossing had
come between her and her only friend, something, that
in conjunction with Emily's suggestions, would keep
them very far asunder in the future.

Those last days of November and the early ones of
December were, indeed, longer and drearier for her than
any that had gone before; her duties were growing
heavier as the stimulus of novelty wore off, and though
her determination had not expended itself, her energy
and interest had. She went on through the dull routine
with a stolid and inflexible resolution, feeling herself a
mere machine, and wondering where the immortal part
of her was; a sensation that did not alter for weeks together; hard and dull and dry, no heart, no tears, no
warmth or depth, as if she were not herself but was
some one whom she had in charge, and in whom she
took no interest further than to direct and impel to necessary action. Since the day she met Cecilia at the
church, and since that blessed rush of tears, too soon
checked and governed, she had said her prayers, she
had read the Bible, had gone to church, to the Holy
Communion even, had done religiously the duties that
she supposed were intended for her to do, and had felt
each day further from the God whom she desired to
serve.

"Children, won't you hush a minute? Mamma, please ask Cammy to be quiet. Let me read you this."

But the children could not be quiet, and it only came through gusts of hushes and tempests of hurrahs that Cyril had obtained leave of absence for himself and two of his brother officers for a fortnight at the holidays, and that he gave his mother and sister leave to do their worst in the matter of amusement for that time.

"I won't quarrel with you if you fill the house on this occasion, and you may put just as many suppers, dinners, drives and parties on the programme as can possibly be crammed into the space of fourteen days. The Cuylers don't go to town till January, I believe, and Emily, I know, will stay up till after that, if you persuade her mother. I have promised Bell and Soutter plenty of amusement, and I depend on you and on Miss Warrington to devise some schemes for entertaining them. I pledge myself to be delighted with whatever you propose, and to assist your plans in every way imaginable. I count the days till I am with you."

Sainty's whole face was radiant with pleasure, as, yielding up the letter into Cammy's hands, she turned to Frank and began to say, "What shall we do for them?" But Frank looked so pale, the words died on her lips. "You do not feel well?" she said, rising hurriedly. "Has anything happened?"

"No, nothing," she answered, recovering her ordinary manner, and turning away a little distantly.

"I forgot," said Sainty meekly; "here is a let.er for you that came with the others."

Frank put out her hand for it and went up to the light. It was directed in Fanny's hand-writing, and was post-marked Titherly, and she thrust it in her pocket, for the bell was ringing as she took it. All through dinner, while the family, from the mother down, were talking eagerly over the projected pleasures of the holidays, the governess was revolving all manner of schemes for getting away from the participation of them. The very thought of staying terrified her; but where could she go? It had been understood when she came to Ringmer that she was not to leave it till the family did, and that there was to be no regular vacation at the holidays, but that some lessons were to be kept up through the entire week, and that the children were not to count on complete exemption from school routine, save on Christmas Day and the first of January. Therefore, she could not go away unless she went never to come back to Ringmer as a home. That was open to her; but where should she go? Which way turn her steps, so mercifully directed here? Back to Titherly? Never, never! She dreaded to break the seal of Fanny's letter from a vague fear it might contain some news to disturb her conscience. There was but one way for Fanny to have discovered her address; she had been feeling as if the silence of that terrible man was ominous, and now it appeared he had not been idle. She kept her hand tight over the letter in her pocket, but she had not courage to open it till the evening was ended and she had locked herself into her own apartment.

Fanny's part of the letter was not so disturbing as she
had supposed it would be—only hateful and spiteful in
a purring, innocent, ultra-simple manner, which she
knew of old; but there was a postscript in Aunt Frances' cramped and crooked characters which roused her
into a flame of anger.

. Aunt Frances had heard news of her that did not
please her, news that showed her silence had not been
accidental, and she told her to come home before she
grew ashamed of home, or gave it cause to be ashamed
of her. She said she did not yet believe any ill of her,
but neither did she want the world to believe any, and
the sooner she came back to the protection of her family
the better. It was no proper life for her, the one she
had chosen, even if she carried herself in it in a proper
manner, which she had good reason for knowing she
did not do, and there was nothing for her but to come
home at once and assist Fanny in the school, or apply
for a situation where she could be under her aunt's eye,
and among people nearer her own rank in life.

Frank's eyes glowed as she tore the letter in bits and
showered it over the fire; then she sat down to write an
answer to it.

The answer was resolute, sensible and concise, not at
all as if she were as angry as it was possible for her to
be. She told her aunt she received a good salary, was
in a good home, was kindly treated, and very well contented. She could not, she said, consent to leave it till
something more advantageous were offered to her; ex-
changing a certainty for an uncertainty was what she
felt sure her aunt could not expect her to do, since she
had undertaken to make her own living. The little

school at Titherly could not give employment for two; she had always found it easy work for one, and she knew Fanny would not be satisfied to leave what she had so recently begun. She begged her aunt to be quite easy about her prospects, she hoped never again to be a burden to her; and she assured her that she would take care to conduct herself in a manner becoming her position, and to bring no disgrace whatever upon those connected with her; and she was as ever,

Very dutifully her niece,

FRANCES WARRINGTON.

CHAPTER XVII.

CHRISTMAS EVE.

"Whatever passes as a cloud between
The eye of faith, and things unseen,
Causing that brightest world to disappear,
Or seem less lovely or its hopes less dear;
This is our world, our idol, though it wear
Affection's impress, or devotion's air."

"Now, children," said Sainty in an imploring tone, putting her hand up to her head involuntarily, "*won't* you go away and leave me for a little while? See, it is nearly five o'clock."

The little girls were in Sainty's dressing-room, leaning over her toilet-table, mauling everything within their reach, fingering the trinkets she was going to wear, peering into boxes and drawers, and making themselves unlovely after the manner of all younger sisters.

It was Christmas Eve, and as Sainty had just said, nearly five o'clock. The carriage from the train came in at six, the Rosenbaums were expected to drive up at any moment, and Sainty had but just begun to dress. The little girls had been made beautiful at an early hour, and could not be satisfied with ordinary occupation since they had had their high holiday attire put on.

"Well, what shall we do, then?" fretted Sylvie

'Miss Warrington's dressing and won't let us in, and the fire's gone out in the school-room, and we can't play down stairs, and there's nothing to do in the nursery."

"Go down and sit in the library with Cub, and look at some of your new books."

"We've looked at 'em all," said Cammy, "every one."

Sainty sighed. "I should think you might amuse yourselves with the game that came up in the box last night."

"It's stupid," said Cammy; "and it takes four to play it."

"I think you might tell us a story," suggested Sylvie. "It's Christmas Eve, and you always used to tell us stories Christmas Eve."

"Well, wait till I get my dress on," said the sister, remembering with some remorse how little the children had heard of Christmas this year, save in its present-giving, plum-pudding, festival phase. Her dress lay on the bed, a pretty, light blue silk, and she threw it over her head with a little feeling of shame at having wondered whether she would look well in it. She hardly glanced in the mirror as she fastened her collar on, and taking Sylvia's hand said,

"Come, sit down by me in the window and I will tell you both a story."

But as she passed the long glass in the wardrobe, she caught involuntarily a glimpse of herself, and as involuntarily came a sensation of pleasure at the sight. The shade of blue was perfect, the color of her cheeks was deeper than ordinary, and the pearl pin and the lace around her throat made her fairness almost waxen.

The outline of her figure and the contour of her head were purely graceful, she saw for the first time. First came a thrill of pleasure, and then a throb of shame, and starting forward, she extinguished both the candles and sank down in the window seat.

Sylvie climbed up into her lap, and she leaned her forehead down for a few moments on the child's shoulder. What thoughts, what pleasures for this night, this night when the hosts of Heaven first missed their King, when the angels sang their last hymn over His birth-place and paid Him their last service till the long years of His humiliation were drawing to their close. Was it this flesh, the flesh of which He bore the burden and felt the anguish from Bethlehem to Calvary, of which she should be vain-glorious and fond? Was the night on which He laid down His robes of glory, the night on which, without offending Him, she could innocently find pleasure in the vanity of earthly trappings?

"Where Thou dwellest, Lord,
No other thought should be.
Once duly welcomed and adored,
How should I part with Thee!"

"You have forgotten your bracelets," said the worldly-minded Cammy, groping for them on the table, and bringing them to her sister in the window. She cared very little for the story, for she had a presentiment it was to be one of the kind Cub liked, about angels, and martyrs, and immortal roses, and she would have liked much better to have watched Sainty dress herself, and to have tried on her jewelry, and imagined the enchanting future, when she should be a young lady, and have fine clothes herself.

"I do not want them," said Sainty quickly, putting back her hand. "Come and hear the story."

"There's Cub on the stairs, shall I call him?" asked Cammy.

She called Cub, and he stumbled across the room and sat down by Sainty in the window seat, his wistful eyes upon her face, while Sylvie, regardless of the beautiful new silk, sat curled up on her lap, and Cammy on a low ottoman at her feet, clasped and unclasped the bracelets, and wondered if Sainty would notice if she wore them down stairs herself.

The twilight was gradually deepening, though the whiteness of the snow that lay thick upon the ground, still made it look light without, and the illuminating rays from the windows below were stretching across the lawn. The evergreens looked black and sombre, but upon the naked branches of the summer trees the snow still lay light and undisturbed, fresh and pure, and fit for Christmas Eve, and the faint stars were just coming through the dark blue of the sky.

"What shall my story be about?" said Sainty, leaning forward and gazing out.

"About the snow—Christmas snow," said Cub, following her eyes.

"No, no! Let it be about the fairies," said Sylvie.

"Pshaw!" interrupted Cammy. "You know there isn't any sense in hearing about things that never happened. Let Sainty tell us about little Bertha, and the German children at the festival she saw "

10*

Cub was Sainty's most sympathising listener, and she always looked to him for appreciation in the misty, imaginative stories she loved to tell them. They were rather unpractical, but perhaps not unprofitable, and they were Cub's dear delight, and though Sylvia liked fairies rather better than angels, she still was imaginative enough to enjoy them a good deal, while Cammy found them *ennuyant*, but better than no entertainment, or entertainment purchased by her own exertions. The story that she wove that night out of Cub's text, " Christmas snow," was almost a poem ; her soul was wandering far away from earth, in the blue ether where her earnest eyes were fixed, purified from the taint of worldliness that had soiled it for the moment, " pure lilies of eternal peace" filling the air she breathed, holy thoughts and springing hopes bearing her up above temptation. Cub's eyes swam with tears as he listened breathlessly, Sylvie was as still as marble, and even Cammy dropped her baubles and appeared to listen.

If there had been a brightness around her head, Cub would not have wondered ; the room was dim, but there was enough light from without to show the group around the window, and Sainty's fair, raised face and low, sweet voice were almost angelic.

Suddenly through the muffled stillness without, there came a sound of bells across the snow, rapid and merry sleigh-bells, and Cammy started up.

"They're coming," cried Sylvie, springing to the floor.

" Only the Rosenbaums," said Cammy, bending down and looking at her sister's watch by the faint light. " It's too early for the train."

The little girls started for the door, Cub following slowly with a sigh, and Sainty pressed her hand over her heart as she rose.

"But where Thou dwellest, Lord,
No other thought should be,"

she murmured half aloud, as she went across the floor, and stood silently for a few moments below a picture near the door upon which the light from the hall fell.

CHAPTER XVIII.

THE GUESTS ARE MET.

"Pray how comes love?
It comes unsought, unsent.
Pray how goes love?
That was not love that went."

"DOESN'T it all look beautiful?" said Cub, waiting for her on the stairs, and looking down into the hall. There were wreaths of evergreens around all the pictures and over all the doors, and the lamps shone warmly on the glossy laurel leaves, and the plumy branches of fir, while the marble pavement was lit up by the blaze of a wood fire, recently kindled in a large fire-place about midway in the hall. This fire-place was a mere conceit, put there with a view probably of protesting the house was a country house, and made no pretensions to any-thing but comfort. The wood was only lighted for orna-ment, however, for the house was heated by furnace, and made it entirely superfluous for any other purpose, and it was a great nuisance to the maid whose business it was to look after it. She wished her master's ideas of comfort might take any other shape, but he was inex-orable; the hearthstone never was suffered to grow cold from November till the family flitting after Christmas.

A great ornament the blazing fire certainly was to the large hall that Christmas eve, and the party who entered

it from the cold frosty twilight without were penetrated
instantly with its look of warmth and comfort. Cecilia
had just reached the bottom of the stairs as they came
in, and she went forward to meet them with all her own
unconscious grace of manner, heightened by the earnest
rapt look her eyes had not yet lost since she came into
the light. The children followed her, Sylvie clinging
to her skirts and half hiding her curls as usual, though
she was not in the least afraid, and Cammy, attendant
on the other side, the model of an artless and unobtrusive child.

Cecilia kissed Mrs. Rosenbaum, who looked very tired,
and Emily, who looked very happy, and gave her hand
with a faint smile and downcast eyes, to the gentleman
who followed them. He was a distinguished looking
man, about thirty years old, not regularly handsome,
though generally called so, quiet in manner, unaffected
and wellbred in speech. He was a nephew of Mr. Rosenbaum's, and a special favorite at Wheatley, and having been abroad since Emily was a child, was welcomed
back with great ardor by both mother and daughter as
a most valuable cavalier, companion and counsellor.
He found it doubtless very pleasant to step into such
a comfortable home after his long wanderings, and
had spent most of the time since he returned at
Wheatley.

Whether he would have found Emily entirely com-
panionable if he had ever been in the house alone with
her and her *fade* mamma, may be questioned, but during the four weeks that he had been *de retour*, it had
been filled with company, and he had had quite a wide

choice of companionship. The naïve Cecilia had ap
peared to attract him more than any one, and Mrs Rosenbaum had immediately begun to scheme about it.
He was in every way a desirable *parti;* the Thorndykes
looked very high for Cecilia, but where could they find
any one more unexceptionable than Julian? And it
would be so agreeable to have the families doubly connected in this manner. The dear lady meandered away
into the future with vague and harmless pleasure, till
sharply recalled by Emily, who begged her to remember she had not made up her mind ye' whether she
would marry Cyril under any circumstances, or whether
she was willing to let Cecilia have her cousin, even if
she did not want him for herself. So Mrs. Rosenbaum
subsided, and did not dare even to praise Cecilia in Julian's presence, but delighted herself with watching the
interest that he took in hearing casually of her, and the
readiness with which he acceded to the plan of passing
Christmas week at Ringmer.

"Will you come now to the parlor and see mamma,
or shall I take you to your rooms?" asked Sainty of the
ladies.

"Oh, let us go up first," said Emily, who was impatient to be dressed before the train arrived. "We were
smothered in cloaks and furs in the sleigh and we are
not presentable."

So the ladies followed Cecilia, and Mr. Rosenbaum
followed the servant to their rooms; then Cecilia had tc
run down and make welcome another guest, a pretty
young French girl, the daughter of a distant neighbor,
who was pining with *ennui* in her isolated home, and

who had accepted with more than pleasure the invita
tion of Mrs. Thorndyke.

She was young and coquettish and handsome had
never seen society, and was thrilling with delight at the
prospect of meeting strangers more exciting than her
father's discreet and uninteresting partner, whom she
was intended ultimately to marry, and the few neighbors whom she was permitted to visit formally. Her
mother had been long dead, and her father was a selfish
old Frenchman, with a great deal of beard and very
little conscience, who did not think much about his
daughter at any time, except to forbid her everything
she wanted, and who brought her up as if she had vowed
herself to Heaven; whereas she was most enthusiasti-
cally though secretly a devotee of earth, and was ready
at any moment to become as deceitful and untrust-
worthy as circumstances would permit. The reason of
this unusual indulgence could only be accounted for on
the ground that M. Clèrambeau was sensible of the
honor of an invitation from a family of such standing
as the Thorndykes, and was anxious to secure for himself a better social position in the neighborhood than he
at present held. He had startled his daughter very
much by giving her a twenty dollar bill to get herself
something new to wear, and for ten days she had been
flitting about the house in créping pins and peignoir,
conspiring with her old nurse to squeeze a respectable
wardrobe out of twenty dollars and the scoured remains
of the clothes she had worn ever since she could re
member.

The true French talent, inherent in both the old and

leaving Frank, he went down the stairs, and asked Sainty who was in the parlor. Sainty told him, and he apologised to the young men for leaving them, but said he must go in a moment while Gustave showed them to their rooms.

As soon as Cyril had left Frank, she had started back and hurriedly gained the landing-place, looking so pale and agitated that Stephanie, scenting afar an intrigue, could not resist slipping back to her own door and listening behind it for a moment.

The two strange gentlemen were coming up, close upon the governess, so close that her chance of escaping their notice was very slight. She glanced around, looked irresolute for a moment, and then stopped and remained standing in a corner of the broad landing-place, under the shadow of a huge bronze figure, hoping in the dim light to avoid attention from them.

The first gentleman passed her with a slight glance and a sort of bow, the second passed her in the same way, but looked back again and gave a start. She had turned her head away, but it had not sufficed ; he took a step or two towards her, paused, and then came up to her, while his companion and the servant passed on through the upper hall.

"Frank !—that is, Miss Warrington," he said, in some agitation, "I could not believe at first that it was you "——

"I don't wonder you are surprised," she answered, with a strange matter-of-factness in her voice, "I am living here, as governess." Her manner was not without its effect upon him, for the tone in which he spoke again was less agitated, but still showed an effort of self-control.

"You have been here long?"

"Not long; only since November."

"I thought you were at Titherly. You came away from there only a month ago, though?"

"No, some time before."

"They are well there, I hope."

"I believe so; I hear very rarely from them," she said, coldly, looking down the stairs, as if she rather wished to be released.

He looked irresolute, and then said, "I did not mean to detain you; but it seemed so strange to meet you here. I had never supposed it possible."

"I am not surprised that you had not. I was very much astonished to find you were Mr. Thorndyke's friend."

"You knew I was coming, then?"

"Oh yes."

There was a moment's pause, and then she added, forcing herself to turn towards him and speak distinctly. "I have never said anything about it here, however, and perhaps it will not be necessary to mention our former knowledge of each other. I have no doubt you will agree with me, that we had better meet as strangers now we are among strangers."

A dark flush passed over his face, the whole expression of which changed while she spoke, and he answered firmly, and in a voice that she remembered afterwards,

"Yes, as strangers, if you wish it, for the remainder of our lives."

He bowed, and left her standing in the shadow of the statue, while Stephanie drew the first long breath for several minutes, and softly closed her door as he strode past it through the hall.

CHAPTER XIX.

THE FEAST IS SET.

" If arms engage him, he devotes to sport
His date of life, so likely to be short;
A soldier may be anything, if brave."—COWPER.

THERE was a vacant seat at dinner between Mrs. Rosenbaum and Cub, who was growing too tall to be dined in the nursery, and the governess, who had been destined to the honor of the position, had not much to regret in the conviviality of her neighbors. Cyril asked Sainty, in a low tone, where Miss Warrington was, but Sainty did not know, and nobody else seemed to care, and the dinner passed off quite as if she were forgotten.

The ladies found her in the parlor, however, when they went in, and Miss Rosenbaum said, "O, how d'ye do, Miss Warrington," and Mrs. Rosenbaum looked at her through her glass, and did not say anything, and Miss Clèrambeau, in her charming French way, went straight up to her and began to talk to her, which she continued to do till the gentlemen came in.

Then, if she had had any heart to be amused at anything, she would have enjoyed the sight of the little French girl's total change of manner. From the moment that steps were heard across the hall, her eyes began to dance, she grew incoherent in her talk, she grew vivacious, coquettish-looking, whereas before she had seemed simply amiable and chatty; her eyes grew blacker, her cheeks pinker, everything about her suf fered a change, an intensification.

Cecilia's fears for the awkwardness of the first even-ing were not realized. Nothing could be stiff long where there were such free spirits as Stephanie, Cyril, and Emily. Emily's eyes shone " too happy to be wise," Cyril was merry and reckless, only thinking of the pre-sent, and Stephanie was yielding to the first wild thrill of liberty. She was coquetting with every gentleman in the room before two hours were over, and Mrs. Thorn dyke began to wonder whether the child knew how to behave herself well enough to be invited out without a chaperone.

Indeed, a more discerning matron than Mrs. Thorn-dyke might have felt a little uneasiness as to the result to be produced from the elements she had just been pouring into her hospitable crucible. There were some strong natures, and some very incompatible ones in the mélée, and Mrs. Thorndyke would have been puzzled to predict how they would assimilate, and what would be the result of her experiment. It was well she did not look forward with a prophet's eye, for she would proba-bly have packed the little French girl back to her father without the least ado, to pass the holidays on bread and water, in the cheering companionship of the bats and owls that tenanted the story next the roof, and Stepha-nie would have missed the gayest and most mischievous week of her life.

Cyril had instantly recognized her as a kindred spirit.

and they were good friends in ten minutes. Emily was
so much relieved to find that the governess had not
been fatal, that she was hardly jealous of the merry
intimacy that seemed growing up between them. She
looked with great complacency towards the corner where
Miss Warrington sat quietly alone, or with only Cub
beside her, and wondered that she ever could have feared
her. Cyril took hardly any notice of her, and the other
gentlemen had not even been presented to her. She
seemed indeed in, but not of, the company.

"Tell me," said Stephanie, who was dividing her
smiles between Cyril and Mr. Bell, "tell me, please,
who that young person is. I find her handsome."

"She is the children's governess," said Cyril, carelessly, glancing over in the direction the young lady
looked. "A very charming and pleasant person, I
believe."

"I thought perhaps she was a stranger, I have not
seen you speak to her," returned Stephanie, remembering the interview she had witnessed on the stairs.

"No, I had almost forgotten. I am glad you
reminded me of it," Cyril said. "I must go and have a
talk with her. She was not at dinner, was she?"

"I did not see, I did not remark," said Stephanie,
feeling she had a good deal to do to keep up with Mr.
Thorndyke. "But you may not go now; you may stay
and tell me who the tall gentleman is who talks to Mon
sieur *votre père*. He is martial. I find him very grand,
and he looks as if he had a grief."

Cyril laughed, and Mr. Bell did the same.

"Why do you laugh?" said Stephanie. "I tell you

I am right, ne has a grief, I know. Why, young officers do not talk to—to *Messieurs les pères* all the evening, when there are so many young ladies, if they have not a grief. See, how *triste* he looks when he is silent, and at dinner he did not speak a word to anybody but his neighbor, and only then because of his duty."

" I shall tell Soutter," said Cyril, which was just what Stephanie wanted.

" O no, not for anything," she said, " it would offend him so."

" I shall present him to you at the earliest moment, as soon as my father finishes that long harangue. I am sure you will do all in your power to cheer him."

" O, I do not ambition that. I have no experience, I could not succeed. Present him to the governess; she might understand."

" An admirable thought," said Cyril, starting up. " I will act upon it instantly."

He went across the room, and Stephanie watched narrowly the face of the grave young officer as he accosted him. His brow contracted slightly, he made some demur, which was overruled, then rising, followed his host to the corner where the governess sat. She lifted her eyes with the slowness and deliberation peculiar to her, as the young men stood before her, bent her head a little as Cyril named his friend, and waited for him to speak.

Stephanie made some excuse to get nearer to the group, and Mr. Bell, who was very unsuspecting, preceded her and covered her advance. She was within

easy range of them, when she saw, with dissatisfaction,
Cyril seat himself, and his tall companion reluctantly
follow the example. So pausing over a book of photo-
graphs upon an étagère, she contented herself with
listening attentively.

"You absented yourself at dinner, Miss Warrington," began Cyril. "I flattered myself when I saw
you in the hall, that you were looking much better
than when we parted in November, and that those
vexatious headaches had been discontinued. Make
arrangements to omit them through the holidays, I beg."

"Why no, Mr. Thorndyke, I think it is the very time
for the enjoyment of them, when they will not interfere
with any of my duties."

"But with all of my pleasures," he returned in a tone
a little lower than was consistent with good breeding,
as he stooped to pick up a paper knife that had fallen
at her feet upon the floor. She felt the color flash into
her face, and she felt that Soutter's eyes were on her,
though she could not look up to know what they
expressed.

Cyril saw the blush too, and it gave him a thrill of
satisfaction; she was not cold, though she might be coy,
and his tone expressed involuntarily his complacency,
as, looking up, he said carelessly,

"Soutter will testify I understand the science of
headache. I learned it of you, Miss Warrington, I
think. I never experienced the sensation till I returned
to the Potomac, in November."

He caught Soutter's eye a moment as he lifted his
own from Frank's face, and he saw an expression in it

11

that he had never seen before ; a sudden flame of wrath
that leaped out of an eye lowering and steadfast, and
then faded instantly into the darkness as he looked.
He felt a momentary surprise and curiosity, but it was
a thing so unaccountable, so entirely uncalled for by
anything that had occurred, that he ceased to wonder,
almost before he had given it a sober thought.

"You enjoy your present quarters very much, I suppose," said the governess at last. "Washington is
beginning to be very gay, they say."

"They say so ; what I have seen of it has seemed
rather dull so far. Soutter can tell you better ; he is
there much more than I am."

"Mr. Soutter likes city life better than camp life
then," said Frank, addressing him for the first time.

"My duties call me there very frequently, Miss Warrington," he answered. "I do not know whether I
should leave camp often if it were otherwise, but I like
the change, I believe, very well."

"You do, indeed, Soutter, you enjoy it immensely,
I assure you. You look quite bored when you have a
week at camp in prospect."

"Perhaps I do. I am in the habit of hearing I look
bored a great part of the time."

"That's very true, I believe you do. And that
reminds me, I heard a young lady say, not twenty
minutes since, you were very *triste* at dinner and hardly
spoke a word. If you had had the pleasure of Miss
Warrington's acquaintance before that meal, now, I
should have said it was easily accounted for."

There was a moment's pause, while Stephanie's eyes

danced as she lifted them over the top of her photographic album.

"And *apropos* of sentiment, I made a promise to Miss Warrington last month; I promised she should hear you sing the little German song we all affect so much. Come to the piano now: my sister was just asking for some music."

"You must excuse me," Soutter returned, quickly and firmly. "I cannot."

"Miss Warrington, what do you say to such an answer as that?"

"Miss Warrington will be kind enough to excuse me to-night, I am certain," he said, distantly.

"'I cannot sing to-night,'" hummed Cyril to a sentimental air. "Soutter, it must be true that you have a secret grief, and it will be worth a fortune to you. There's nothing brings a man such éclat as a secret grief, every woman that he meets is pining to console him; he has nothing but to go in and win, society accepts him with enthusiasm. Already, Soutter," lowering his voice, "you have made a conquest. The little French girl is perfectly *éprise;* she will be entirely vanquished if you sing that song. That's a good fellow, come and try it. How can you resist the expressed wish of one lady and the silent sympathy of another?"

"Why, Mr. Thorndyke, you are making me out very persistent, when I believe I never asked for the song at all. I remember I told you that I liked it, and thought you sang it well, but I have forgotten it almost, and should not dream of asking Mr. Soutter to repeat it for us if he does not fancy it."

"Ah, there's the tender sympathy of all the sex for you, Soutter. Why cannot I be *triste* as well! But I have no talent for grief. I cannot get over a certain trick of looking happy —— "

"When you are so, Thorndyke. It is a trick common to the human family ——. Is that your little sister? What a pretty child she is."

"Yes. How comes it she is up at such an hour as this? Miss Warrington, she will be desperately cross to-morrow. O, by the way, I was speaking with my mother a few moments ago about school-room affairs, and she has decided it will be best to give the children a total holiday this week—with your permission."

"Mrs. Thorndyke must have made a very sudden change of plan. Only this morning —— "

"O, my mother is subject to very sudden changes of plan, you know. But she is quite firm about this, and you are to be off duty altogether, please remember. Sainty tells me she owes to you the plan of a very clever set of charades. Will you let me come to the school-room to-morrow morning, and overlook it with you? And I want to consult you about some other things."

This was said as he rose reluctantly, having cast an uneasy glance across the room to Emily, *distraite* and silent beside Cecilia and Mr. Rosenbaum. Frank could not well make any objection to this proposal, and bowed assent as he moved away.

A moment after, Stephanie saw Soutter rise, bow stiffly and leave the governess, to resume his conversation with Mr. Thorndyke *père*.

No wonder that it gave Cyril an unhealthy feeling of his own superiority, when he saw how easily he could banish and call back smiles on other people's faces. Once more beside ·Emily, he could watch Frank's changed manner as she sat alone, and Emily's restored vivacity now that he was with her: his mother and sister turned to him for pleasure, his father's eyes followed him about the room with a secret but devouring pride; he was actually the lord and master of the home in which he was nominally but the son, and the real arbiter of many fates within it. No wonder that he lay down to rest that night feeling that the world, or what he wanted of it, lay within his grasp; and that the man whom he had chosen for his friend, thought, while a sharp pang pierced him for the moment, that to him that had, had been given, and from him that had nothing, had been taken all the hope and worth of life.

CHAPTER XX.

THE CODE OF HONOR.

"Let's do it after the high Roman fashion,
And make death proud to take us."

THE next morning, long before the children had grown familiar with their new toys, or the ladies and gentlemen in the dining-room had completed the task of breakfasting, the sound of the church bell reminded them that it was Christmas morning. Mr. Thorndyke looked at his watch and said the sleigh would be at the door in precisely twenty minutes, and then went off with the morning paper very much as if he did not mean to occupy a seat in it himself. Miss Emily yawned slightly and asked if there would be a sermon. Mrs. Rosenbaum shivered and said she never ventured out in such cold weather, while Mrs. Thorndyke was very sorry she must stay at home and write some letters for the next day's English steamer. Miss Stephanie laughed and said it was not her own church or she should go, of course.

So Sainty and Emily went up alone to prepare, and Cyril, happy at finding himself released, hurried to the school-room, which Frank was just leaving with her bonnet on.

"You are going to church?" he said in a disappointed tone. "The sleigh isn't yet at the door."

" But I am going to walk," she answered.

" Well then will you let me walk with you? You cannot refuse, otherwise I shall not go to church at all."

The three young men, Soutter, Rosenbaum and Bell, smoking in the library, gave curious and laughing glances out as they saw Cyril leave the house in company with the governess.

" Cyril Thorndyke going to morning prayers !" cried Barry Bell; "the pious whelp! He hasn't been inside a church or chapel to my certain knowledge half a dozen times since he left college, and now he goes tramping off a mile or so across the snow to hear a country parson drowse over a spun-out string of prayers, and a country choir sing hallelujah through their noses! O, to what base uses may we come !"

" It would appear then that you do not propose to follow his example," said Mr. Rosenbaum.

" I had not proposed it; the Clèrambeau does not affect the pious you may have observed, and so I'm not obliged."

" Ah these inamoratas !" observed Rosenbaum with a gentlemanly smile. " But what of this young governess ? She seems a fine creature."

" Yes, she's good-looking," said Bell, knocking the ashes from his cigar. " And Thorndyke's badly in for it, I'm inclined to think. I couldn't divine what had put him so out of conceit with things generally down there, and made him so savage about coming home, till I watched him awhile last night. It's plain to see, it's nothing but this girl, and what's the worst of it, he's touchy to the last degree about it. I tried to run him

a little last night, but I found it was dangerous business
I don't blame him. It's best to keep such nonsense
quiet, for the girl's sake as well as for his own, for it's
pretty well known he's as good as engaged to some one
else—that is—well, I beg your pardon, Rosenbaum; I
had forgotten you were a cousin of Miss Emily's ——"

"You are perfectly excusable," returned the gentleman with a reassuring smile. "I believe I understand
it all, and see it in the same light that you do, but I do
not meddle in those matters, and never think of offering
Emily my advice."

"You're right," said Bell, recovering from his confusion under Rosenbaum's well-bred treatment. "You're
right. It's folly ever to waste good advice on people
when they're once in love. I never trouble myself, for
somehow things come out right generally after all.
Now I've no doubt Thorndyke'll settle down into a
model country gentleman, after this fancy's blown over,
and make the best husband in the world. He's too
much sense to let it interfere with his prospects, we all
know, and Miss Rosenbaum's too fond of him to bear
malice when he comes back to her and says he's sorry."

"And the—the girl, as you call her," said Soutter,
standing by the mantel-piece with his back to them,
"what's to become of her, following your programme?"

" O," said Bell with a laugh, "she'll get over it after
a while and marry some psalm-singing parson or other,
who'll keep her busy making him comfortable, and won't
give her any time to remember how fond she was of her
old love, and how near she came to being made a lady."

"It seems hard too," said Rosenbaum, thoughtfully.

"And yet that is the natural course of things; one sees it every day. We have to recognize these inequalities of fate, one class advancing to happiness upon the depression of another; we must not be too squeamish as we go along."

"No, I suppose not," said Bell uneasily, for he was not much at home on philosophic questions. "But I never bother myself about these things, we know they can't be helped; a man can't marry all the pretty girls he thinks at one time or another that he'd like to marry; he's got to make some of 'em wretched, and there's no use in being chicken-hearted and fretting himself about 'em when he's broken with 'em. It's the natural course of things as you say, and a fellow has to go through a certain amount of that sort of experience to make a man of him."

There was a moment's pause, and Soutter, who had been walking heavily up and down the room while the two men talked, stopped before them and said with a certain huskiness of voice, as if he hardly dared trust himself to speak:

"I hope you say that thoughtlessly? I'd be ashamed to think a man lived and called himself a gentleman with such a vile creed as that. I'd strike my brother from my friendship if he dared proclaim in the light of day as his belief that impurity and treachery and selfishness were necessary to a man's experience. I should blush to feel I was companion of a man who could call himself a man of honor, and yet hold a woman's honor lighter than his own, and sacrifice her, even in appearance, to his vanity or passion. I look up

11*

feeds his honor and advancement upon the dishonor, dis
appointment and disadvantage of the humblest woman
living, as a traitor and a coward, unworthy the confi
dence of his country, the companionship of gentlemen,
the friendship of honest men!"

"Sir!" exclaimed Bell, starting to a martial attitude.
"How am I to take your words?"

"In any light you please; apply them as you think
fit, and come to me if you desire a further explanation
of their meaning." And he strode out of the room.

There was a moment's silence as the two men at the
window watched him leave the house and walk impatiently and heavily across the snow, and disappear into
the woods.

"Confound the pragmatical dog!" exclaimed Bell,
looking rather pale as he glanced after the broad
shoulders and firm build of his military confrère.
"What's to be done, Rosenbaum? There's but one
way, I suppose? Eh?"

Rosenbaum shrugged his shoulders slightly, and said
it was unlucky.

"Unlucky!" roared Bell, taking a rapid turn across
the room. "I should think it was unlucky. I happen
to have seen some of his pistol-practice, which I suppose you have not. Confound him; a low fellow just
coming into notice, putting on such airs with gentlemen. I could blow his brains out with such a satisfaction!"

And the young captain groaned as he thought how
slim a chance he had of experiencing that great pleasure, and how much stronger the probability was that
he would confer it on his adversary

"A more uncalled-for insult I never remember to have heard," said Rosenbaum, thoughtfully. "If he had not addressed himself to you, I should think I had done fully as much to entitle myself to his animadversions as you had, unless there has been trouble formerly between you."

"No," said Bell, reflecting, "there is nothing; or yes—but I had almost forgotten. There was some feeling when he was first promoted—he was high in favor with the colonel, and there was a good deal of trouble among the officers, but it all blew over, and now he is prime favorite with everybody. I can't think he remembers it, however, for we have been on good terms ever since, and he has done me a number of—of favors, I might say, helped me through some scrapes, and shown himself obliging and well disposed in a number of other ways."

"Still," said Rosenbaum, "I cannot help thinking there is something of the old bitterness coming out in this. You say he is a common fellow, and if so, you must make allowance for a spirit of meanness and retaliation that gentlemen cannot understand."

Bell shook his head slightly, but Rosenbaum went on.

"Of course you know him better than I do; I merely judge from probabilities. There must have been some motive for his vehemence; men do not throw away their lives for an abstract idea now-a-days; there must be something personal in the matter to work a man up to such wrath as I saw in his eye. He is on good terms with Thorndyke, of course?"

"The very best."

lessly about the room. "Though it isn't particularly cheerful to have such a sword as that dangling above your scalp for a whole fortnight."

"A man has to reconcile himself to these chances in going through the world," said Rosenbaum, calmly, turning towards the door.

"When shall you see Soutter?" inquired Bell with a pardonable degree of interest.

"As soon as possible," said the other, looking at his watch. "I shall walk as far as the church to meet the ladies, and if he is there, make an opportunity to speak with him before we return to the house. I wish to prevent an interview with Thorndyke, which would be most unfortunate. You approve?"

"Oh, yes," said Bell, faintly. "Certainly; you are quite right."

He was somewhat awed by Rosenbaum's calm superiority, and somewhat sustained by a dread of disgracing himself if he held back, which sentiments stood to him in the place of real courage, and helped him to behave himself respectably though not with great force, when Mr. Thorndyke senior entered the library as his companion left it, and seating himself, engaged him determinately in conversation, with a view of judging what kind of a companion Cyril had chosen for himself.

CHAPTER XXI.

CHRISTMAS.

'When once thy foot enters the church, be bare;
God is more there than thou; for thou art there
Only by his permission. Then beware,
And make thyself all reverence and fear."—HERBERT.

THE short path that Frank and Cyril had taken across the lawn and through the adjoining wood, brought them to the church gate precisely at the moment that the sleigh, containing the children, Miss Rosenbaum and Sainty, drew up before it.

Cyril had enjoyed his walk very much; the morning was sharp and cold and clear and still; the boughs, loaded heavily with snow last night, were shedding it down gradually upon the snow beneath, and the whole air seemed full of the glittering particles. The usually well-worn path they had found unbroken, the stile at the entrance of the wood had been almost buried, and once or twice their way had been completely blocked up by wreaths and drifts of snow. But Frank had been indifferent to the delay, and brave about the snow, and the difficulties and incidents of the walk had rendered it altogether delightful to Cyril, whatever it may have been to her.

He was looking very handsome as he laid his hand on the church gate to open it for her, quite flushed with the exercise he had taken in breaking the path, and powdered from head to foot with snow, when the sud den apparition of the sleigh and of Emily made him change color and contract his brow impatiently. He finished the sentence he had begun clumsily, as Frank passed through the gate into the churchyard; and turn- ng back with much less ease than usual, he went up to the sleigh and offered his hand to Emily. Too angry to be wise, she rejected it, and sprang out without a look at him. He bit his lip, and helped Sainty and the children out silently, and followed them into the church.

Frank had gone immediately in, and was already on her knees in the long pew at the left of the chancel. when Emily came sweeping down the aisle, carrying the eyes of all the congregation with her. Sainty fol- lowed humbly with her soft eyes on the ground, and the children came last with Cyril, who was the admired of all the rustic beauties and the envied of all the rustic beaux. When Frank rose from her imperfect and dis- turbed prayers, she found Emily in the pew before her, and she felt for a moment it was almost sinful to kneel in sight of one whom she so nearly hated. She had not fancied there was any room left in her soul for such a paltry passion, but she found it there when she stopped on the threshold of a great and solemn mystery, to know if her heart were prepared " according to the prepara tion of the sanctuary." Ah, what sins separated be tween her and Heaven! and yet she could not fee. contrition for them, could not see the cure for them, she only knew they were there, a thick cloud not blotted out, a dull weight clogging hope, a burden from which no prayer she said seemed to win her any ease. She glanced at Cecilia, and thought what would she not give for a moment of such peace as her sweet face expressed. She sat opposite them at the organ, with a group of red-cloaked charity children around her, and the rich, soft sunlight through the colored windows falling on her head: her very soul floating upward on the full, triumphant burst of song with which the service opened.

Cyril, alone with Emily in the long pew, wished himself anywhere else, and felt as if it were a treasonable act for him to be facing the congregation beside her, when he was so much more than indifferent to her; for their engagement was commonly talked of in the country, and most people were persuaded it was an established thing. And Emily herself felt, with sharp self-condemnation, the falseness and humiliation of the position she had accepted. In some inexplicable way, the three felt then, more clearly and more uncomfortably than they had ever done before, how they stood in reality in relation to each other. Perhaps there was something in the solemnity of the sanctuary, the consciousness of a Presence there, in which it was vain to cloak and dissemble sin, unto whom all hearts are open, and from whom no secrets are hid; but for those moments in which they were forced to keep silence before Him, they might have said, they had never known what they were doing, they had never seen into their hearts.

The service was half over when Soutter entered the

church, and Cyril, glad of some diversion from his harassing thoughts, motioned him to come down, and rising, admitted him into the pew.

" What ails the world this morning ?" thought Cyril, glancing at him. " Everybody looks high tragedy."

Soutter looked indeed as if the storm within had spent itself, but as if the heavy waves were heaving yet with a dull, suppressed, involuntary vehemence, even though the tempest had subsided and the clouds had begun to roll away. His face was flushed with the hard exercise with which he had been trying to tame himself, and his steady hand trembled a little as he bent his head down upon it.

" What has come over Soutter, pray ?" asked Cyril of Rosenbaum, whom he found waiting outside, when after the sermon he, with half the congregation, came away, leaving the real service of the day to go on without them. " He came late into church, looking moody and dark enough, and once during the prayers, commandments or something, I saw him give a start that would have done credit to an hysterical school-girl. Now, our major is not given to nerves ; what the deuce does he mean by it ?"

" A little indigestion, possibly," said Rosenbaum in a careless way. " Where is he now ?"

" In the church there with the faithful," returned Cyril, pointing that way. " That's the only fault I have to find with Soutter. As capital a fellow as you ever met, but as stubborn about that sort of thing as any parson. There's one fact in his favor, however," Cyril added apologetically, " he never makes the leas' allusion to the subject, and you'd never guess he was inclined that way if you didn't stumble on him in church or in his tent on Sunday, or something of that kind. He isn't thought a bit less of in the regiment for it, I assure you. I never knew a man less long-faced and tiresome, and yet, I think, as far as I can tell about such matters, he's perfectly up to the mark, and pious as a priest."

"I did not suspect him of any such proclivities," said Rosenbaum. "But, as you say, I am no judge. I rather understood from Bell that he had been used to a somewhat different life from his present, and that, in fact, he had but recently been brought into familiar intercourse with gentlemen. Is it so?"

"Well, yes, I suppose one might say so. But it seems to me, Bell might have better business than posting people on facts that are generally acknowledged to be unwelcome. Soutter is a gentleman now, whatever he was last year; and moreover, he's been a better friend to Bell than Bell has ever been to anybody, for, *entre nous*, Bell is a selfish rascal, and not the sort of man to count on in any but good weather."

"You were college friends, I think you told me?"

"Yes, college friends and family friends and regimental friends, and I don't wish you to understand me as depreciating Bell in any way. He is a very good sort of fellow, has the best blood of the country in his veins, conducts himself like a gentleman, and stands well everywhere. Only, when it comes to the interior qualities of gentlemanliness, the high principle and moral fortitude which we look for in our associates, I am heretical enough to think I should find them in as strong development in our low-born friend as in our high-bred one. Still, they have both yet to be proved. I am only speculating, and I certainly should not have done it if I had not been a little vexed at Bell's attempting to prejudice you against Soutter, who, I hold, has a right to start fair in any society, and make himself the best place in it that he can on his own merits. I'm not much of an aristocrat now-a-days, Rosenbaum."

Rosenbaum smiled and said some civil nothing, being convinced that he saw through Cyril so entirely that it was not worth while to be biased by him in the least. Cyril, he was persuaded, was trying to convince himself of the worthlessness of birth and breeding, to make his step down to the governess' level a less jarring one ; he was trying to be democratic in theory to excuse his democratic practice; and remembering his cousin Emily, Mr. Rosenbaum did not feel any too much sympathy with his prejudices. In fact, if it had not been for the restraining thought of Cecilia, it is possible he might have yielded to his inclination and invited Cyril to a reckoning for his most transparent perfidy. As it was, he kept the fine control over himself which a naturally well-balanced mind and a diplomatic education had given him, and did not betray in any manner to his companion that he longed to put a bullet through him, and that he considered him at once a self-deceiver and a traitor. He merely said, looking at his watch as they paced up and down upon the snow before the church:

" How soon may we look for the dispersion of the faithful ?"

"Not in less than half an hour. Let us walk home. It will be tiresome waiting for them till the end of service."

Rosenbaum smiled. " I shall have no credit for my devout intentions if I go back without being seen. You came so early, you can afford to claim an indul 'gence. Do not let me keep you; there are the children waiting for you at the stile. I will stay and put the ladies in the sleigh."

" Well, if you insist. I must confess I am a little exhausted with my unaccustomed piety. You will come home in the sleigh."

Rosenbaum bowed, and Cyril hurried off to lift little Sylvie over the stile and commit her to Cub's care, while he strode on far before them, very glad to be released from Rosenbaum, with whom he felt vaguely uncomfortable, and from another awkward interview with Emily, who was a perfect nightmare to him now. But though he was not insensible that he had done an imprudent thing in walking to church with Frank, he was not prepared to feel penitent for it, or wish it was undone. He found himself more in love with her than ever, and more afraid of losing her by the least inattention, and while he desired to keep his devotion secret, it was more from a fear of immediate consequences than from any intention of returning ultimately to Emily. He was aware that he was playing a dangerous game, a game that might be reckoned up, possibly, with such uncomfortable counters as bullets or short-swords; but he was not a coward, and the danger he ran only gave the play additional delight.

"My pretty Warrington," he thought as he sprang up the steps and hurried to his room, "I'll have you if I want you, 'though father and mither and a' should go mad.'"

And he felt nearly sure he wanted her, already.

CHAPTER XXII.

CECILIA'S LOVER.

"The brow should wear a golden crown
That wears her in its thought."—HOOD.

IN the meantime, Rosenbaum paced steadily up and down before the church, well wrapped in furs, and well warmed with indignant thoughts. This quarrel of Bell's he felt to be rightfully his own, and another quarrel that came in the train of it besides. He had long guessed that Emily was trifled with, and now it was made certain. He had heard it carelessly discussed between two men, almost strangers to her, and he felt it was his part to see they had no cause to talk so in the future. Although he knew Emily to be self-willed and unprincipled, he felt that did not relieve him from his obligation to her, and that whatever she might be, she was his cousin, and bore the name he had a pride in keeping clear before the world.

But what a sacrifice! To give up all hope of winning the sister by making himself the deadly adversary of the brother, to sacrifice his love, all his new hopes of happiness, to a sense of honor, a sentiment of family pride, the worn-out fiction of a reverence for woman. And a woman whom he could not respect, whom he did not love. It was a miserable cause in which to die, or for which to live morose and *mécontent*, separated for-

ever from what was just becoming vitally dear to
him

He had come home, tired of the world, having seen
its worst, and faithless of its charms, having seen its
best, and he had met, in the last place where he had
expected it, what all his life he had been dreaming of,
a woman who at once satisfied his taste, his heart, his
intellect.   Cecilia was a poem, a piece of romance to
him ; he studied her curiously, he watched her critically, and he ended, *blasé* as he was, by loving her
intemperately.   He was a man of fine intellect, of firm
will, almost morbidly refined and delicate in feeling,
with a high standard of moral excellence, and with an
utter disbelief in all that he could not master in nature
and in religion.   Cecilia's simplicity of faith was one of
her chief charms for him ; he loved her for it, as we
.ove children for believing in the Christmas saint, and
would no more have interfered with her faith than we
would interfere with theirs.   It made her beautiful, it
belonged to her character, and he was too keen a lover
of all that was mystic and poetic, to be willing to spoil
the illusion and break in upon the spell that made her
unlike the common-place and clever women of the
world, whom he so thoroughly knew and of whom he
was so weary.

He had no doubt that he could win her : already he
knew he had a power over her that no one else possessed ; she was too artless to conceal anything that she
felt deeply, and he was too worldly wise and discriminating not to discover what he strongly desired to fathom.
From her family he anticipated no hindrances : he

knew himself to be in every point unexceptionable, and was too much accustomed to be courted for his wealth, to doubt of his success in entering any family he might choose to favor with his preference. A fine fortune, an influential and aristocratic family connection, high personal position, unblemished moral character—Mr. Julian Rosenbaum would have been a dull man, indeed, if he had not known that the possession of these combined advantages gave him the key to any society in the land.

But, as he thought bitterly, pacing up and down before the little snow-roofed church, from which the music came out to him at intervals low and sweet, but what did all this advantage him, if with it he could not buy what only now he wanted. For a bare sense of honor he must take up his cousin's cause against the brother of the woman he desired to marry, and place a bar forever between him and her. Verily, it was a hard code under which he served, and he resolved doggedly he would not soon be pushed to that extremity. He would try what diplomacy would do in putting down this low-born fellow, who had obtained such influence with Cyril, and in bringing Cyril to his senses about the governess. He would keep Bell up to the vindication of his honor, or, if he faltered, assume the quarrel himself, and teach Cyril in that way what he must expect.

Meanwhile, the twelve days' armistice might work wonders. He would not despair till he had tried a peaceful solution of the family entanglements, and he turned to receive the ladies as they came out of

12

church with his finest smile and most unembarassed manner.

Cecilia's eyes grew a little troubled when she saw him, though she flushed with involuntary pleasure. He went down to the gate to order the sleigh up, and while they waited a few minutes for it, he said in an under tone to Soutter, who had come out last, " A moment's conversation with you, if you are disengaged."

Soutter bowed, and they sauntered down the path a moment together, Rosenbaum talking very indifferently, Soutter assenting stiffly, and both returning to the ladies as the sleigh appeared.

Emily, who had only stayed in church to avoid coming out when Cyril did, hurried down and sprang in unassisted, with a flush on the cheek and a tiger like gleam of the eye, that did not look well for the peaceful solution planned by her cousin Julian. Mr. Rosenbaum gave the governess a narrow look as he offered her his hand and put her in the sleigh. He did not wonder very much at Cyril's preference, as he contrasted her face with his cousin's, but there was an expression of power about her beautiful mouth that he did not like in any woman, least of all in any woman to whom he was opposed. Her movements denoted self-possession, and the general look of her face was cold and unimpressible, but her eye was warm and flashing, and the color varied in her cheeks with every varying emotion.

" A dangerous rival, my self-willed cousin," he thought as he drew back.

Soutter was arranging the sleigh robes for Cecilia on the forward seat, but Rosenbaum, planting himself very firmly in the snow, said, " Allow me," and showed no disposition to give way, as Cecilia approached. Soutter made no attempt to interfere, but stood quietly beside the sleigh, as Rosenbaum, giving her his hand, assisted her to enter it. But, just as her foot reached the step, the horses gave a sudden start, and threw her violently back into Soutter's arms. He caught her promptly, and extricated her foot from the sleigh, before the horses, with whom the coachman was struggling vehemently, had made any progress.

" You are not hurt, Miss Thorndyke ?" exclaimed Rosenbaum, springing to her side.

" No, oh no," she said, looking rather pale however, for she was a miserable coward about horses. " But I'm afraid I cannot get in."

" Give me your hand, Miss Cecilia, there's not the least danger," he continued ; but, as he spoke, the horses gave another plunge and Cecilia another start.

" Oh, Mr. Soutter ! I'm afraid ! Don't you think I'd better walk ?" she said, turning pleadingly to him, as he stood nearest to her.

" Why no, Miss Thorndyke," he said with a re-assur ing smile, " I think I can lift you in very safely, if vou will permit me."

" Thank you," she said, putting her hand in his, but looking doubtfully at the restive horses. Mr. Rosen baum started forward to assist her, but Soutter said, significantly, maintaining his ground,

" You will do. better service at the horses' heads, perhaps."

. A 'ook passed between them, as Rosenbaum dr

back, which was not lost on Frank. These men did
not love each other; what could have taught them so
soon they were antagonistic?

Cecilia drew a long breath when she found herself
safely in the sleigh; and Soutter, walking past the horses,
said something in an under tone to the coachman, while
Rosenbaum, assuring himself that Cecilia was comfort
able, told the man to make room for him beside him, he
would take the reins himself. Sainty brightened considerably at the prospect, and seemed to think they
were entirely safe.

"You will not ride, Mr. Soutter?" she asked, as Louis,
raising his cap, moved away.

"Thank you, I prefer the walk," he said, and Frank,
as they dashed away, looked back and saw him stride
across the road and throw himself over the fence into
the path that led by the short route home. The carri-
age-road was more than three miles, the foot-path hardly
one, and when Soutter, after his rapid walk, emerged
from the evergreens into the avenue, not a quarter of a
mile from the gate-house, he gave rather an anxious
glance up and down the road. He had not liked the
look of the horses, neither had he put great faith in their
gentleman driver, and had lost as little time as possible
in getting across the woods.

He walked slowly towards the gate-house, looking attentively forward and listening. The gate was open,
and a little red-cheeked girl was leaning on it and looking down the road.

Presently he saw her throw up her arms and run
screaming into the house. Good heavens! how well he

knew what she had seen. Those vicious brutes were fulfilling the promise he had seen in their fiery eyes If he could only reach the gate before they did, shut it, and break their course; the sudden turn into the grounds he knew would dash the sleigh with a fatal crash against the stone pillars of the gate, and the mischief would all be done the instant they were in sight.

He ran forward, shouting to the child to shut the gate, out knowing that he shouted vainly, for a group of children and a tottering old woman were cowering in the door, stupified by the little gatekeeper's incoherent story of alarm.

He hardly dared listen for the sleigh-bells, but they came at last, scarcely audible at the lightning speed at which they were approaching him. He threw himself forward—thirty rods between him and the gate yet—twenty, and the tinkle of the bells growing so much clearer every second. One bound more; his hand grasped the latch of the iron gate and pushed it firmly shut, just as a shrill shriek met his ear, and a pair of lowered, straining horses' heads flashed upon his sight around the angle of the road.

The sight of the barred iron gate checked them in full career; they reared, fell back upon the driver, breaking the pole, crashing down the dashboard, plunging and struggling madly; but what of that; the sleigh itself was safe, not even overturned, plunged sideways in a drift of snow outside the entrance.

Soutter flung himself over the fence, grasped at the horses' heads, and, with the help of a man who came running up, succeeded in subduing them and clearing them from the sleigh. The coachman, almost paralysed with fear, but apparently unhurt, was soon roused to usefulness by Soutter's sternness, and recovered himself enough to take charge of one of the lathered and trembling animals, while the new-comer led off the other; and then Soutter turned to the sleigh. A glance told him those inside were unhurt, but that Rosenbaum lay insensible, half in and half out the sleigh, his head bleeding profusely from some sharp blow. Frank was the only one who had caught sight of it, and was struggling to disengage herself from Emily's convulsive, involuntary grasp, as Louis bent over him.

Cecilia, who was half dead with terror, raised her head at the moment, and catching a full sight of his ghastly face and the reddened snow around, uttered a cry, and fell back fainting. Louis motioned Frank away, and said, "Look after her," while he raised the inanimate man in his arms and carried him into the house. He presently reappeared, having despatched one of the children to the house, another for the doctor, and approached the sleigh. Cecilia was just beginning to recover from her swoon, Emily was in a high state of nervous agitation, the governess seemed quite her ordinary self.

"They will be here presently from the house," he said. "Can you bear the cold waiting here till they come?"

"But Julian!" cried Emily, hardly knowing what she said. "Where have you taken Julian! O, I know he's killed! I know it from your face! Take me to him. I must see him. I will not stay out here another minute!"

At this, a dreadful paleness came over Cecilia's face again, and Soutter, going instantly to her, said, in a re-assuring voice, "Mr. Rosenbaum has only a slight cut on the head; there will not be any trouble from it; but he must be kept very quiet. So, Miss Rosenbaum, if you go into the gate-house, you will not go up to him or speak to him at present."

It was too cold for them to wait outside, evidently, and there were no signs of any assistance coming from the house, so Soutter reluctantly supported Cecilia to the cottage. Emily, who was a good deal afraid of him, made her way into the room, and stood awestruck and silent beside the bed on which her cousin lay. In spite of his efforts to prevent it, Soutter knew in a moment that Cecilia had caught sight of his face as they crossed the threshold, for he saw the shiver that went through her, heard a faint gasp, and felt her sinking helplessly.

"Poor child!" he said, laying her down upon a bench or settle near the door. "Can you take care of her while I go to him?"

Frank silently accepted the charge, putting off her bonnet and keeling down beside her.

A few moments later, Cyril, Bell, and Mr. Thorndyke burst into the room, prepared by the awful story of the messenger and the disastrous condition of things outside, for any imaginable scene of horror. Certainly the one they confronted was not very reassuring, though less desperate than they had perhaps anticipated. Emily was sitting by her cousin, her face buried in her hands. Frank was kneeling by Cecilia. Soutter started forward to meet them. Cyril exclaimed, incoherently,

" Soutter, in heaven's name, what is it ! Are they safe ?"

" Everybody's safe," said Soutter. " Rosenbaum has had a slight gash. I assure you, that is all. The rest of us are only frightened, Mr. Thorndyke."

Mr. Thorndyke had made a rapid review of the room, and was satisfied of Mr. Soutter's accuracy, and gave him his hand, saying, " I hear we are indebted to you that things are not any worse."

But Cyril, in an instant at Frank's side, was searching her face anxiously as he interrogated her.

" You are not hurt ? Solemnly and truly ? Thank heaven ! And my sister ?"

" Has only fainted."

" Poor Sainty ! she had no fall ?" he said, bending over her.

" No, she did not leave the sleigh ; it was only fright at the sight of blood. She is recovering now."

" And you—you are so pale. Oh, that villain of a driver ! You are almost fainting. Come away, and let me attend to Sainty."

He took her hands and led her across the room, where she sank into a chair and hid her face. He bent down and whispered some words which she hardly heard ; she was too overwrought and miserable to know anything but that her safety had seemed of no concern to any one but him.

" Thorndyke—your sister—will you lift her into the sleigh ?" said Soutter, beside him, in a constrained and unnatural voice.

He started, and looking out, saw that a covered sleigh

was before the door—the doctor's—in which it was proposed instantly to take Cecilia home, before the sight of
more blood, or the knowledge of more suffering excited
her nerves afresh.

The doctor, meantime, was examining Mr. Rosenbaum's wound, and was apparently very anxious to get
rid of all the fainting sex before he proceeded to repair
it. Emily, with a face perfectly bloodless and rigid,
stood beside the bed.

"There will be room for two of the ladies in my
sleigh," said the little man, briskly, "if Mr. Cyril will
be kind enough to drive. Miss Rosenbaum, you'll go,
won't you? Your cousin'll be all right in ten minutes,
I assure you. We'll take the best care of him; you
can trust him to us."

"Emily," said Cyril, coming in, "there's room for
you beside Sainty in the sleigh; will you come with
her?"

"No," she said, firmly, "I want to stay with
Julian!"

Cyril could not meet her eye, but he turned uneasily
to the doctor.

"Go now, my dear young lady," said the doctor,
urgently. "Go; Mr. Julian will do better without anybody. We'll bring him down to the house
in an hour or two; depend upon us for taking care
of him."

"Emily, my dear, are you ready?" said Mr. Thorndyke, in his unanswerable voice, coming forward. "The
sleigh is waiting."

She bit her lip till the blood started, but walked

silently out and took her place beside Cecilia, who was lying languidly back upon the cushions.

"I will return for you in ten minutes," Cyril had said to Miss Warrington as he passed her.

CHAPTER XXIII.

COUNSEL.

" Je t'aimais inconstant, qu'aurais-je fait fidèle ?
Et même en ce moment ou ta bouche cruelle
Vient si tranquillement m'annoncer le trépas,
Ingrat, je doute encore si je ne t'aime pas !"—RACINE.

BUT Miss Warrington only waited for the sleigh to leave the door, to tie on her bonnet and go out, unobserved by all but Soutter, who picked up his cap from the floor and followed her.

"I do not think you are fit to walk home," he said. "You had better wait."

She shook her head: "There is nothing the matter with me. I prefer to go."

He did not make any answer, but walked on beside her silently. Neither attempted to speak till they were half way to the house, when they caught sight of Cyril and the doctor's sleigh coming towards them rapidly.

"Tell him not to turn," said Frank in a hurried manner. "I do not want to ride. I mean to walk the rest of the way."

So when Cyril, coming upon them unexpectedly, drew up in surprise and sprang out, Soutter said somewhat stiffly,

"Miss Warrington chooses to walk, Thorndyke; we are so near the house you need not turn back, I think."

" I will, by all means," he exclaimed; "surely, Miss
Warrington you will let me drive you; you are looking very pale. How imprudent for you to think of
walking."

Frank resisted firmly and quickly, and Cyril, looking
angry and disappointed, was obliged to resume his seat in
the sleigh and drive on to the gate-house. A moment's
silence ensued, broken by Soutter, who said somewhat
abruptly, " There is one thing I want to say to you, and
there is no time better than this, I suppose. I do not
know how you will take it from me; but when you remember that I have no personal reason for speaking,
you will perhaps hear me without being angry."

There was a moment's pause, and he went on:

" When you placed me, last night, on the footing of
a stranger, you did not perhaps mean to deny me the
privileges of an ordinary acquaintance. And I think
(and I have tried to be honest with myself), I think I
should say the same to you if you had been personally
a stranger to me till last night, and I had had by some
other means, the knowledge of your character and circumstances. I would have run the risk of displeasing
you in that case, and I shall run it now, I am afraid;
but you must let me tell you this: You are in a dangerous position here, a position which you are too inexperienced to understand."

" A dangerous position ?" she repeated in a question
ing tone, the color rising to her face.

" Yes, a dangerous position," he answered firmly,
" and a humiliating one if you only understood it. I do
not mean humiliating because subordinate, you know we

too well to fancy I mean that, but humiliating because
this man who assumes to be your lover, has put you in
a false position in this house. He has no right to think
of you, he only dares address you secretly, he dreads
the suspicion of his family, and yet he has neither tact
nor self command enough to shield you from the com
ments of his friends. It is understood among them tha.
he has no thought of marrying you, that he means
simply to amuse himself, that he is promised to another
I do not know what truth there is in it, and only know
how it places you among them, and what danger the
very suspicion puts you in. If you were aware of this
before and have allowed his attentions, knowing it, it
can only be that you love him, or are ambitious, and
have a hope of marrying him."

"A hope of marrying him!"

Frank's head swam, and for a moment she felt as if
she were in a frightful trance that must end soon or she
should suffocate.

"Of this I have no right to ask, no right and no desire. I have told you what my duty would not suffer
me to hide. I did it without any selfish motive, and I
trust it will not prejudice you more against me. I had
not much ground to lose with you, I acknowledge, but
believe me, I have not done this without a struggle. I
am afraid I have been harsh in my advice; but I have
been in a hard school lately. I have begun to think I
have not much place in the world except among the
hard and practical. Friendship brought me here, friendship for this man against whom I have been warning
you. Good heavens! I little knew what the folly was

that had possessed him. I believe I have done with
friendship too."

"Why do you not warn him as well as me?" said
Frank in a smothered voice, her eye kindling as she
caught his for an instant. "He is your friend more than
I am; he might listen to you, he might be persuaded to
give up this folly—this strange folly that he has fallen
into—a folly beyond all comprehension! Surely you
might cure him!"

A dark flush mounted to his very forehead as she
spoke. "You are right to remind me," he said with a
shade of bitterness in his tone. "I have meddled with
what I had better have let alone. I am the last one
who should have spoken, but henceforth I hold my peace.
I have multiplied mistakes of late, but Heaven knows I
thought I was doing right this time."

"You have done right," said Frank, stingingly. "I
have reason to thank you; you have enlightened me on
what of all things I most wanted to be certain of; I have
tried to be doubtful sometimes; that's all over now."

"You don't say that honestly," he said. "One word
more before we part. Do not go in yet; stop but a moment," as they reached the piazza. "If I could convince you that I had no motive in warning you but your
own good, I know you would respect my warning more.
Truly, most truly, I do assure you, it was nothing of—
of jealousy, no lingering thought of what has passed
that prompted this. You would have reason to despise
me if it had been; but as a brother who fears for his
sister's happiness, as an honest man who sees a woman
endangered by snares she does not see, I have spoken

to you now. Frank, if you had been the merest stranger to me, I must have spoken, I must have warned you of the precipice you stand upon. I know Cyril Thorndyke; this is not his first folly. I know he cannot make you happy even if he marries you. Give up your fancy for him ! Go back to Titherly : you will see reason to thank me one day if you do. There are honest men, men in your own sphere of life who no doubt will seek you, and who are far more worthy of you than he can ever be, and who will make you incalculably happier. This may be my last chance of speaking with you alone; let that excuse my urgency. Have I convinced you of my honesty of purpose and will you listen to me ?"

"You have convinced me fully that you are disinterested," she said, turning to the door. "I have listened to you, and I promise you to be influenced by what I have learned from you."

"I have humbled myself in vain," he thought bitterly, as the door closed upon her and he paced the piazza alone. "She loves him already, she will never give him up; I have only exasperated her pride, strengthened her resolution, made myself more hateful to her than before. Shall I go, and try to forget the pain that her presence has revived keener than ever ; or stay and guard her if I can, force him to marry her, make the world respectful at least while I am by ?"

"Why !" cried the little French girl, meeting Frank at the door, having watched the interview on the piazza from the window. "You have come back à pied ? I feared you were too ill to walk, M. Cyril made us understand you were. Ah, what danger, Mademoiselle!

I tremble but to fancy it. You are quite, quite well, you are sure? And may I come up to your room with you?"

Miss Warrington gave a very tame assent, and Stephanie accompanied her upstairs.

"And they tell me," she went on vivaciously, "they ell me that *le grand monsieur*, the Major Soutter, has saved all your lives. O, I wish he had saved mine. I should like to be always grateful to an officer so handsome."

Miss Warrington did not look particularly grateful, only very tired, and Stephanie resumed again.

"I am sure you must be grateful to the Major Soutter. I am sure you looked as if you were, when you came up the steps. You talked to him so much, so differently from a stranger. *Mais*, I should have believed you had known him all your life! And yet you never saw him, did you, before yesterday?"

With a pleasant sensation, Frank felt the color rushing to her face, while the little French girl looked naïvely on.

"I hardly know how I talked: under such excitement as this, one says anything, one is not responsible."

"O, without doubt," cried Stephanie. "Only you have not the air of being excited ever. But Monsieur the Major seemed so interested, having so much to say you know, so with the manner of a friend, a kind gentleman who knew all about you and cared a great deal 'or you. But the gentlemen in America have that way, perhaps. These are the first of your countrymen that I have ever known. I hope they are not all so *flatteu·*

as M. Bell; I find him very *ennuyeux*. M. Cyril Thorndyke has the beautiful eyes, and is *spirituel, gentil*, a Frenchman almost; but I like *Monsieur le Major mieux que tous*. Tell me, is he not handsome? Oh, if he would talk to me as he talks to you! So much in his eyes, such an *empressé* manner for stranger! Tell me, do you talk about the war? Or how do you make him so absorbed with you? What do you begin about?"

"I cannot remember," she said, lying down on the sofa and turning away her face, which she could not get out of range of Stephanie's bright eyes. "I believe he began the conversation as we walked from the gate-house. He talked first about some of his army friends, if I remember right."

"Ah!" said Stephanie, with interest. "About any that are here? M. Bell or M. Thorndyke?"

Again Frank felt the blood rushing to her cheeks. What was the girl about. All this could not be accident.

So she tried to look indifferent, and said, "Yes, he talked about one or both of them; he seems to be quite intimate with Mr. Thorndyke, from what he said. They are very much together at camp, I fancy, though they do not seem at all alike."

"Not at all," said Stephanie, with energy and great simplicity of manner. "I am not at all afraid of M. Cyril, he is quite *aimable*, quite easy to know, but this tall gentleman is so grave! He does not see me when I am near him, and he only talks to me when I am his neighbor at the table. But you, mademoiselle, he seeks you out, he talks to you of his own *volonté!*"

"Why no," said Miss Warrington, angrily. "He does nothing of the kind, you know. He walked with me to-day because I was alone, because he had no choice; last evening he only addressed me twice."

"Twice?" said Stephanie, innocently. "In the drawing room?"

"Why do you ask so curiously?" she retorted angrily, conscious of another change of color.

"Oh, *n'importe*," said Stephanie, with an infantile manner. "I—but—*eh bien!* I envy you your con quest, mademoiselle! He is the finest gentleman here, I do admire him so. Ah, but I have made you blush! *Pardon, pardon!* I did not fancy that you cared. I am so overcome of shame. I was so rude."

Fortunately, a servant announced lunch.

"Ah," she cried, "then the gentlemen must have come back."

And the curious Gallic compound of malice, amiability, artfulness, naïveté, frivolity and passion, stooping suddenly and kissing Frank, flashed out of the room to make her toilet perfect, before she met those conquering heroes, of whom her imagination was so full.

CHAPTER XXIV.

STEPHANIE.

"Tout blancheur cède à l'éclat du fard,
Et la nature éblouit moins que l'art."

MR. ROSENBAUM's injury had proved less serious than
the doctor had at first considered it, and the third day
he was able to spend a few hours in the parlor, where
he was overwhelmed with attentions from his aunt and
cousin, his hostess, and the pretty Stephanie, who never
willingly omitted any occasion of making herself charming. Cecilia had not been able to come down to dinner
the day before, nor to breakfast that morning, being
still quite ill from the effects of her alarm, and Mr. Rosenbaum had begun to despair of seeing her, when,
about three o'clock, she came into the parlor, looking
like a lily shaken by rough winds.

"Why, Sainty!" cried Emily, thoughtlessly, going
forward to meet her, "you look as if you had had an
illness. I never saw any one so altered in two days!
Julian, isn't it surprising?"

Julian needed all his principles of statesmanship and
his habits of self-control to conceal the alarm her paleness caused him, and the tenderness and solicitude he
felt. She trembled and looked down when she met his
eye, and tried in vain to answer Emily's brusque questions.

"Pray let her sit down, Emily," said Mrs. Rosenbaum. "Do you not see that she is faint?"

Emily gave her a seat, while Stephanie fluttered about her like a fairy, and her mother looked at her with some interest.

"Cyril was asking half an hour ago," she said, "if you would not be well enough to go down to the river with them all to skate this afternoon, but I see it is out of the question."

"I am afraid so," said Cecilia, with a faint smile.

"Cecilia and Julian will have to entertain each other," Mrs. Rosenbaum said, in a tone of subdued satisfaction, "for you and I, Mrs. Thorndyke, are to drive, I believe, and all the young people go on the river, I suppose."

"It's too bad, Sainty," said Emily; "I would stay with you if I had not promised Mr. Bell. It is such a splendid afternoon! And almost time for us to be putting on our cloaks, Miss Clèrambeau."

"There come the gentlemen from the billiard-room," said Stephanie, dropping the screen she had been holding up for Sainty. "And it is after three."

"My dear," said Mrs. Thorndyke, calling after the two young ladies, as they were hurrying out of the parlor, "won't you stop in the school-room on your way up and tell Miss Warrington I wish she would go along, for Cyril has promised to take the children, and there must be somebody to look after Sylvia and Camilla."

"Certainly, dear Mrs. Thorndyke," said Emily, with an amiable smile, which evaporated almost before she closed the door.

"*Le bon frère!*" murmured Stephanie, with a little malicious laugh, as they went up the stairs together, "I have remarked of M. Cyril that he loves his little sisters *avec délire*, when their governess comes with them."

Emily bit her lip, but said, with a careless laugh,

"How keen you are! I am almost afraid of you."

"Is this the school-room?" asked Stephanie, as Emily paused at the door at the end of the hall. "I thought it was M. Cyril's room, perhaps, I have seen him come from here so often."

Emily pushed the door open impatiently. The governess was there, hearing Cub's Latin, and writing rapidly at a little table in the west end of the long room, away from the desks. She looked up as the young ladies entered, and seemed to wait for them to speak, which Emily did, brusquely, advancing into the room.

"Mrs. Thorndyke wants you to see that the children are ready to go with us to skate," she said. "And she also wants you to go down to the river and look after them."

"Yes," said the governess, without any perceptible change of expression, "I will obey her orders. Was there anything further, Miss Rosenbaum?"

"Nothing else that I think of," she answered, carelessly turning over some books upon the table as she went towards the door.

"O," cried Stephanie, lifting a cigar-case from among the books, with an exclamation of admiration, "How pretty! But, Master Cuthbert, you do not smoke, I hope? You are yet so young!"

Emily looked at it eagerly, but turned her head away

sharply when she saw the familiar C. T. embroidered on the back. How well she knew it!

"No," said Cub, with simplicity, "I never owned a cigar-case in my life. That must be brother Cyril's."

"But how should it be here," murmured Stephanie, still examining it with admiration, "in the school-oom?"

"Cyril sometimes comes in here to smoke," explained the boy.

"Ah! Then you do not mind smoke, mademoiselle? *Pour moi, cela me fait tant de mal!*"

"Mademoiselle is not particular, I fancy," said Emily, with a laugh.

"I enjoy the scent of a cigar very much," the governess said, putting away her writing with extreme *sang froid.*

"But you always go out when brother Cyril comes in," said Cub.

"That is not because I dislike the cigar," she replied, and Stephanie could not repress a little laugh, the governess was so cool and Miss Rosenbaum looked so angry. She swept out of the room, humming an air from Traviata, Stephanie following her, looking back to say, amiably, as she closed the door,

"You'll surely go with us, Miss Warrington?"

"O, of course, I have no choice," she answered, and went up stairs to dress.

It was a fine afternoon, less cold than the day before had been, and perfectly clear. Cyril had had a path shovelled down to the river, a distance of a quarter of a mile, not knowing whether all ladies were as brave as Miss Warrington about unbroken snow, and a fire kindled on the bank, and some of the piazza chairs carried down to it. It was nearly half-past three when the whole party mustered around the wood fire in the hall, examining skate-straps, looping up skirts, muffling in furs, and creating all the "merry din" of country pleasure-seekers.

The children were in high spirits, the young ladies looked extremely well in their skating jackets and gay skirts, and Cyril, always attentive to the effect produced by what he wore, had made himself look like a Polish prince, and handsome as the present occupant of the throne of all the Russias. Soutter and Bell were less strikingly attired, but their fur caps and top boots satisfied the occasion, and did not interfere with the spirit of the scene. The children had early discovered who among the guests they could impose upon, and were incessantly at Soutter's side; and while the others talked and laughed and completed their equipments round the fire, Soutter yielded to Sylvie's arguments, and put her up upon his shoulder, and stalked up and down the hall, which rang with her shrill screams of pleasure, while two great Newfoundland dogs, who rarely gained admittance there, rolled and frolicked clumsily about his feet.

"Soutter grows impatient," cried Cyril, slinging his skates across his shoulder. "Are we not ready? Adieu, Sainty! Rosenbaum, we regret you!"

While Rosenbaum and Sainty, from the parlor window, watched their exit without the least regret.

Soutter, with Sylvie on his shoulder, Cammy and the

dogs beside him, led the way, and Stephanie, whose admiration was entirely genuine, was leading the unconscious Bell on at double quick, to keep in sight of him.
Bell was very soft-hearted about the little coquette, who
had him by this time completely at her mercy.   He was
so abjectly devoted, indeed, that all the party had exchanged laughing comments on the subject, and Stephanie had felt herself quite entitled to put on airs about
it, and treat him with occasional contempt.

She was vexed that Cyril and Rosenbaum were so
beyond her reach, but, to do her justice, she would have
resigned all interest in them both, and thrown Barry
Bell over in a minute for the least chance of making Soutter understand her charms and reciprocate her passion.

She had conceived for him the extravagant admiration
that his manliness, his soldierly looks, his continued reserve, and his imagined tristesse, naturally inspired in
one so southern, so young, and so ill-taught as she unfortunately was.   She had tried a thousand arts to win
him, which none but Frank had noticed, for hers was a
tact so fine, an ingenuity so ready, that she could baffle
all who were not watching with their senses sharpened
and their jealousy awake.   At first he had appeared unconscious of her existence, then he had spoken to her
from duty, when she happened near him; soon he had
learned to turn to her when he wanted to be relieved
from constrained and uncomfortable conversation duty,
and now he was beginning to seek her bright, attentive
eyes for sympathy, for amusement, for relaxation, and
the only real smile Frank had seen on his face, she had
seen there while he talked with Stephanie that day at

breakfast. Stephanie's hopes were high, she felt she had made a marked advance, and she wondered whether the governess did not think so too.

Cyril had started out that afternoon with a well-digested intention of keeping up diplomatic relations with his supposed *fiancée*, and shunning Frank as much as he had courage to. He was, perhaps, a little startled at finding how far he had alienated Emily, and how little progress he had made with Frank, and was resolved to be very cautious and deliberate in all his future moves. He loitered behind the others and fell into place at Emily's side, taking her skates, and showing a dutiful intention of being devoted to her, while his eyes followed Frank, some yards ahead of them, with Cub in close attendance. He quarrelled with his fate, no doubt, for Emily was as cold as steel, and none of his old arts of pleasing seemed to touch her. He began at last, however, to think he was half glad she was so distant, she would save him the trouble of breaking with her. She seemed to have got over all feeling for him, and he need not give himself any remorse upon the subject of his faithlessness. And then, with inconsistency worthy of a woman, he found himself feeling a little *piqué* that she had been so soon cured, and a little perverse at losing what he had been accustomed to consider he had undoubted claim to. Then he began to wonder if really she were indifferent to him, if he could not bring her back, if he had lost all his powers of fascination. For Cyril Thorndyke was the vainest of created men, and had been taught to consider himself conquering hero ever since he had left off wearing frocks.

Arrived at the river bank, they all collected around the bonfire which one of the farmer's boys was feeding, piling it high with dry logs and branches, and keeping it within the circle of stones appropriated to it. The river was a vast expanse of ice before them, and beyond, the lowering sun was shining on the distant mountains with a beautiful effect. The sky was entirely without a cloud, and the only color of the horizon was golden. The breeze was very light, and only stirred the stiff and icy branches of the trees upon the bank occasionally, and Cyril said, lifting his hand, "Listen to the stillness for a moment!"

The whole group paused as he spoke, and listened; that winter silence of a vast landscape is always a grand thing. But, after a moment, the fire began to crackle and blaze up impatiently, and Sylvie fretted to be taken on the ice, and the dogs bounced and growled, and the lull was over.

"Ah, M. Soutter," broke in Stephanie's pleasant voice, "do you remember? You promised me a new strap for my skate. I'm sure you have not brought it!"

"Have I not?" he returned, smiling as he put down Sylvie on the rock, and took it from his pocket. "Now let me put your skates on for you, Miss Clèrambeau."

Stephanie had extremely pretty feet, and Mr. Bell had promised himself the pleasure of fitting the skates to them, which was quite reasonable, as he had carried the skates down from the house himself, and had been begging her to let him teach her how to use them, since the first evening of their acquaintance. Soutter very nonchalantly asked him for them, as he knelt on one

knee at Stephanie's feet, and took them without appear-
ing to notice his lowering looks at all. Stephanie was
in a tremor of delight at his attentions, but she did not
forget prudently to throw Bell a smile, and give him
some trivial occupation to keep him out of anybody
else's service. Cammy had to put her own skates on
which made her rather red in the face and rather out
of temper, while Frank went back with Cub to look.for
Sylvie's scarf, which had dropped off on the way down.

She loitered purposely, and when she came back the
skaters were all upon the ice, and the fire was blazing
for the benefit of nobody but the farmer's boy, who
thought it but inferior fun to be a looker-on. Cub
hurried on his skates, and obeyed Frank's direction to
take Sylvie's scarf out to her on the river; then drawing
her cloak about her, she sat down under the shelter of
a rock not far from the fire, and watched the scene in
silence.

CHAPTER XXV.

SUNSET IN THE COVE.

And still the pines of Ramoth wood
Are moaning like the sea,—
The moaning of the sea of change
Between myself and thee !"—WHITTIER.

HALF an hour had passed, perhaps, when the farmer's boy said awkwardly, coming up behind her,

"Here's an extra pair o' skates, miss: don't ye want to try 'em ? I'll strap them on for ye; ye might show them ladies something about skating if ye tried."

Owen had seen her on the river once, and had greatly admired her action.

"O, I did not come to skate; I came to look after the children," she said, with something between a shiver and a laugh.

"But it's dreadful dull fun, sitting there by yerself," said Owen, unconscious of the irony; "besides, yer gettin' cold, and that there gentleman's seeing to the children. Why don't ye go, now ? Lemme put the skates on fur ye."

"Well, Owen," she said, getting up, "perhaps you're right; I think it is a trifle dull, this looking on, though we of the laboring classes ought not to mind it, I suppose."

Owen did not understand much about social distinc

tions, but he did understand he had permission to strap the young lady's skates on, and he entered with great pleasure into even so remote a participation in the general amusement.

"There!" he said presently with much satisfaction, "I'll bet them won't come off, and I'll bet they'll do considerable more goin' than the other folks' skates has done."

Miss Warrington laughed again shiveringly, and he scrambled down the bank to help her on the ice, and steady her a little as she started. But she felt giddy and irresolute when she first found herself alone upon the treacherous surface, and grasping the boy's sleeve, she said nervously, turning back,

"I've changed my mind, Owen, I cannot skate this afternoon, I'm chilled with being still so long ; take me to the bank, don't let me fall."

Owen stared in amazement, remembering her exploits of last week, and cried, in a disappointed tone,

"Why what's the matter, then? Be'nt the straps right? There, there comes Mr. Cyril and his sweetheart, slippin' round and clutchin' at him every time she takes a step. Thunder what a figger. I thought you would ha' showed 'em all women aint like that!"

Cyril, in truth, was just before them, and Emily, who notwithstanding her pretty costume and her recent course of skating lessons, made anything but a graceful appearance, was clutching his arm and tipping uncomfortably forward,

> " As needs they must
> Who cannot stand upright,"

while Stephanie, supported between Soutter and Bell,
approached from the other side. Stephanie knew no
more about skating than Emily did, but she was too
petite to be as strikingly ungraceful, and too vivacious
and *naïve* to be otherwise than interesting, whatever she
attempted, and the merry laughter of the party had
echoed across the river ever since Frank had been
watching them from beside the fire. Soutter had his
eye upon the children, Cub and Cammy, who were
dragging Sylvie on a sled some rods in the rear, and
occasionally called out some direction to them, or
paused to guide the sled awhile himself, and see that
the child was in no danger from the inexperience of her
companions.

The whole party approached the bank at the same
time, but from opposite directions, Stephanie calling
out to Emily that she had learned to skate *à merveille*,
that Major Soutter said so, and that she thought it was
the most delightful thing in the whole world to do!
While Emily, steadying herself on Cyril's arm, said she
was nearly tired to death, and begged to be taken to
the bank to rest.

Frank, on their approach, gave a sudden push away
from Owen, and then stood still, buttoning the fur collar
round her throat deliberately, and tying the tassel of
her fur cap in a knot behind her hair, to keep it firm.

"O, take care," cried Stephanie, in real alarm.
"You will fall, with nothing to take hold of."

"You are at home on skates, Miss Warrington, I
see," said Cyril, as stamping slightly to test the steadi
ness of each skate, she moved aside to let them pass.

"Sylvie, where's your scarf?" she said, stooping as she approached the sled.

"There! it's gone again!" cried Cammy, and Sylvie beginning to feel cold, and cross and sleepy, fretted and twitched herself about, as the governess, stooping down, tied her handkerchief around her throat, and told Cub to take her to the bank.

"Where can the scarf be?" said Cammy, looking about.

"I see it," said Miss Warrington. "Take her to the fire while I go for it."

A light breeze had caught it, and was carrying it slowly from them towards the middle of the river. Cyril saw it a moment after Frank started, and exclaiming,

"She'll never be able to get it! Excuse me an instant, Emily," struck out in pursuit of it.

Soutter had started forward at the same moment, but as Cyril came up beside him, he turned slowly on his heel and came back towards the bank.

"Admirable!" cried Bell, involuntarily, as they stood all eyes fixed on the skaters. "I never saw a woman skate like that before. She's far ahead of Cyril; look, look! She'll reach it before he does!"

Frank's skating was indeed the very poetry of motion; she glided swiftly but softly forward, till the scarf, reaching the middle of the river, met a stronger current of air, and fluttered faster down the stream. Then, with a sudden motion, she flashed away, pursuing it, gaining on it, then losing a moment while it fluttered uncertainly above her in the air, and fell only to be caught away again before she reached it, and to lead her through another fleet pursuit. Cyril, far behind at starting, seemed not to gain a step upon her as he darted rapidly in chase.

"Bravo! bravo!" cried Cub, as he lifted Sylvie up to see, who echoed shrilly his applause, while Owen clapped his hands and shouted hoarsely that he told 'em so; he'd always said she beat creation on the ice, and off it too. Stephanie was eager in her exclamations of wonder and delight, and Bell cried more than once, she was the most graceful skater he had ever seen; who the deuce could have taught her how to skim the ice like that!

The one who taught her, standing near him, watched her silently and with a rigid face. He was thinking of a little frozen lake among the hills, over which the mountain pines stood guard; where Frank's laugh and his had waked a thousand echoes; where there was a silence worse than death to-day; where their steps and their voices would never echo merrily again. He was thinking of the feel of her warm, girlish hand, which he had held so often; of the touch of her soft lips, which he had kissed so often in their childish winter evening games around the fire. The interval was forgotten; shy boy and willful girl, proud youth and haughty maiden—he was back in childhood's careless paradise once more, hand in hand with his little sweetheart—his pretty, dark-eyed, little sweetheart—and envied of all the rest. Ah, why had they ever left that nook of safety! Why had he not kept her there, taught her to love him, lived to make her happy, satis

fied with him and home, careless, innocent and honest
in that true and simple life. It was too late now to lure
her back to the safe nest from which she had escaped;
she had learned too much of life, she had tasted liberty
and pleasure—she never would return. He must
watch her drawn away further and further from him;
he must see her fluttering in snare and trap, and must
hold his peace and know he could not help her.

No wonder that Stephanie, watching narrowly his
face, suspected that the graceful figure on the river, fast
receding from their sight, had something to do with the
secret grief in which she still believed, and that an
angry jealousy prompted her to say softly and with a
pretty little laugh, as Cyril gained somewhat on the
object of his chase:

" *Le bon frère !* How he is careful of his little sister !
How he would be sorry if she lost her scarf !"

Bell laughed a little, spitefully and sneeringly, but
forebore to say what rose to his lips when he thought
of Soutter's unpleasant sensitiveness about his friend's
affaires du cœur. While Cammy, whose particular
mission in life was to say what nobody wanted to hear,
muttered audibly, twisting around on her skates:

" Oh, he doesn't care much about the scarf ; everybody knows what he does care for, though ! "

" What sharp children !" cried Bell, laughing. " I'm
glad *I* haven't got any little brothers and sisters."

" On account of Miss Stephanie, you mean ?" said
Cammy, looking saucily up at him.

There was a general laugh, while Emily exclaimed :

" Oh, you precocious torment ! If you were *my* sister,

I'd keep you locked in a dark closet; I never have a moment's peace when you are anywhere in hearing!"

"Well, then, I am not sorry that you are not going to be my sister," cried Cammy, pertly. "But it's not fair, Miss Emily, for you to go against me. I never told when Cyril used to flirt with *you!*"

Emily turned scarlet, and there was an awkward silence, broken by Owen's shouting:

"She's got it! No—it's off again! There, it's blowed up into the cove—they're out of sight. Hurrah! she'll have it first, I bet!"

The cove into which the scarf had blown was about a mile below them on the same side of the river, running up into a wooded swamp, surrounded thickly by trees, with but a narrow entrance, which Frank knew well, having been there with Cub on boating expeditions in the autumn. She saw the scarf flutter over into it, and she darted in so suddenly that Cyril missed her, and skated on some minutes, bewildered by her disappearance.

The scarf had lit upon the bough of a tree, deep within the little cove, but only enough above her reach to make her sure of getting it; and, grasping a lower branch, she was in the act of lifting her hand for it, when she heard her name called, and saw Cyril pushing his way though the drooping boughs into the icy inlet. The setting sun was shining through the ice-covered trees and bushes, and making them glitter like a crystal forest; and the apparition of Frank, starting back half defiant and half frightened, her cheeks flushed, her lips parted, her whole face changed from gloom to life, had the effect of making Cyril pause and look at her in silence for a moment before he spoke or offered to approach her. If anything had been wanting to complete her power over him, her beauty at that moment would have done it.

But nothing was wanting; self-willed, self-satisfied and self-indulgent though he was by nature and by education, he was yet capable of many generous and manly sentiments, and his love for Frank once acknowledged to himself, no obstacles were allowed for a moment to prevent the expression of it. He knew he risked his father's displeasure, banishment from home and loss of fortune, as well as the chances of a reckoning with Rosenbaum; but all these considerations were insignificant in comparison with the happiness of winning the only woman whom he had ever loved. There was so much doubt, too, whether the sacrifice of all would win her, whether he could at any cost induce her to listen to him, that he was as ardent, as humble, as passionate a lover as if she had been the high-born lady and he the wandering adventurer.

How could any woman turn coldly from the pleading of such eyes as his, the tenderness of his rich voice, the eloquent passion of his words? Frank was prepared to meet him with a cold repulse, her mind full of Soutter's cruel words; but she was surprised, softened, uncertain of herself when she listened to him. Could Soutter have been deceiving her—a second treachery, as un looked for as the first! What had he done to deserve her confidence? She did not love Cyril, she could not marry him; but she would believe in him if she chose.

And then, when he promised his one wish should be to make her happy, his whole life should be spent in teaching her to love him, the thought flashed through her, what a sweet revenge to take on those who had so humbled her, what a triumph over the world that had seemed in league to keep her down!   The little world at Titherly, who knew of her humiliation and bitter disappointment; the greater world at Ringmer, who accounted her subordinate and insignificant.

She thought of the bitter life that lay before her, struggling with poverty and ill-success alone, encompassed by dangers she had learned to apprehend aright, and for a moment the impulse was strong to throw away all doubts and give herself to the protection and faith of the man she now knew really loved her.

But the hypocrisy, the dishonesty, when she thought of Soutter!

"No, I cannot love you," she exclaimed bitterly, turning from him; "do not ask it.   I have no love to give to any one."

"I do not ask it," he said earnestly.   "I only ask you to accept mine, to give me the right to protect you, to teach you affection by my life's devotion—love, perhaps, by my life's sacrifice.   There is nothing in the world that I would not at this moment eagerly surrender for this one hope of winning you.   What can you lose by granting it to me?   You say you are free, you have a right to dispose of yourself; why will you not be generous and trust yourself to me?   Why will you not believe that I can make you happy, that my love will suffice for both till you have learned to care for me?   !

cannot give you up! I will not be repulsed. Frank! one word—they are coming—I hear voices—there is but a moment. You do not utterly refuse?"

Frank glanced up, and through the icy boughs she saw them coming down the river, the sun just glinting on the foremost figures, Stephanie with her hand in Soutter's.

"I do not know," she murmured, pressing her hands before her face and leaning down upon the branch by which she had been supported. "Oh, why will you tempt me!"

Ah, it was too late; it was the one hope he wanted. In the passion of the moment he extorted from her a fatal word which she never had courage to retract, and the sun set upon a new hypocrisy begun, a new misery inaugurated, upon which he was long afterwards to shine.

"Ah, here they are," cried Cub, brushing aside the branches, while Mr. Bell, guiding a chair containing Emily with Sylvie on her lap, paused before the entrance.

"Tell me," cried Cammy, peering over Cuthbert's shoulder, "tell me who got the scarf. "Didn't you, Miss Warrington?"

For Cyril, as they came, they had found standing near the entrance, tying the scarf around his cap, while Miss Warrington, further toward the swamp, had been resting idly against a low branch of hickory. As Cammy spoke, Cyril waved his cap in the air, exclaiming with a thrill of triumph in his voice not at all assumed:

"Can't you see?   I have conquered!"

"You look very pale, Miss Warrington," said Bell, in a detestably polite manner; "but you must allow me to congratulate you.   I never saw better skating.   You must be used to it?"

"Yes, from a child," said she indifferently, bending down to tighten a strap.

"Oh! Miss Warrington," cried Stephanie, who had approached meantime, "we have watched you with so much admiration, we would give worlds to skate as well.   Who was it taught you?"

"Who taught me?" repeated Frank, looking up and turning crimson as she caught Soutter's eye.   "I have almost forgotten—that is—it is so long ago; I cannot say distinctly—a school companion, I believe."

"We have been wondering," said Emily, with a honied smile, "whether you were not used to tight-rope dancing, or something of that sort; you balance yourself so marvellously, and have such a steady head."

"No," answered the governess, with a simplicity that made Emily fear she had not appreciated her insinuation; "no, I never saw a tight-rope dance.   It's very pretty, isn't it?"

"That's according as people enjoy such exhibitions," said Emily.   "For my part, it always disgusts me to see a woman, on the stage or off of it, endeavoring to excite applause."

"Yes, it seems so unfeminine," the governess replied again engrossed with her skate strap.   "Mr. Thorn dyke, may I trouble you to twist this buckle further round? It hurts me, and I cannot manage it without taking off my glove."

While Cyril was on his knees before her, busy with the buckle, Mr. Bell gave an ejaculation expressive of fatigue.

"Well," he said, "having seen all of the race we can and settled who got in first, suppose we start for home? It's growing monstrous chilly, and the ladies, I know, are tired—Miss Clèrambeau and Miss Rosenbaum, at least."

"Yes, we are only *en spectateur*," said Stephanie, quite willing to get away before any turn in the kaleidoscope separated her from Soutter.

Frank, by a sudden and skillful move, got between Cub and Cammy, both of whom, always eager to skate with one who guided them so well, seized her hands and guarded her effectually. The party would have been silent but for Cyril, whose spirits were too light to be repressed, and who was skating in and out among the group, sometimes guiding Emily's chair, sometimes grasping Cammy's hand or chatting *vis-à-vis* with Stephanie, going backwards gracefully and well, and waking them into a faint, responsive jollity.

He sang, first alone, then Soutter joined him, and before they reached the fire, now blazing like a beacon-light upon the dusky bank, the whole party were singing with a delicious cadence as they moved along; and Owen, waiting for their approach, wondered in his honest heart, what could have made them all so happy.

CHAPTER XXVI.

MANY MEN OF MANY MINDS.

" And now go seek thy peace in war—
Who falls for love of God, shall rise a star."—BEN JONSON.

" Has the dressing bell rung, Sainty ?" asked Cyril.
as they entered the hall.

" No, it will not ring for half an hour or more. We
do not dine till seven to-night, you know."

" O, I remember," said Cyril, hanging up his skates.
" Paterfamilias is in town to-day, and the Cuylers are
coming, too."

" Why, yes," said Cammy, " and the Lothrops and
the Chaunceys from over the river. Don't you know,
it's a real dinner party, and mamma is going to have
her hair dressed with feathers."

" Don't anticipate the rising of the curtain," cried
Emily, going to the hall fire, around which there was a
close circle of the red-cheeked skaters.

" We have almost an hour of liberty," said Cyril,
rolling up a mighty sofa; " let's enjoy the fire: and
Sylvie, run tell Thomas not to light the lamps till he
rings the dressing bell."

The tired party readily flung themselves down into
the seats about the fire, making gradually a wider and
more generous circle, as the heat increased, though
Sylvie and the dogs upon the rug, seemed quite imper-

vious to it. The golden-haired child, with her broad
sash and red Garibaldi shirt, put herself into a thousand
graceful attitudes as she lay, now with her arms around
the dog's rough neck, or knelt down at Soutter's feet,
who, sitting at the left side of the fire-place, burned his
fingers with some apples he was helping her to roast
before the blaze.

Cecilia sat on the other side in one of the high-backed
hall chairs, behind which Mr. Rosenbaum stood, with
his arm in a sling, and the scar on his forehead half
hidden by his hair. A little back from the circle,
Frank had thrown herself down on the second step of
the staircase, and Cyril, half reclining on a mat at her
feet, played with the tassel of the skating cap she had
flung off, and watched with a lover's eye the firelight
effect on her beautiful fresh face and careless hair.

"Soutter," he said suddenly, "what do you and Bell
say to giving up that Potomac infatuation, and spending
the winter where we are! There are plenty of insane
fellows who'd enjoy being killed as much as we, and
who'd be thankful to sport our shoulder-straps! Let's
make 'em over to 'em, and stay here by the fire and be
content. Who cares for glory? I'm inclined to think
it's all a vast delusion."

"I've never been inclined to think it was anything
else," muttered Bell, almost inaudibly. "Half the men
in the army wish themselves well out of it, and
wouldn't stay another day for all the glory
if they could help themselves."

"It's well they cannot, then," said
couldn't conveniently spare half ou   But

what has cured you and Mr. Thorndyke so rapidly of
your military ambition, is it fair to ask?"

"The sight of this cheerful fire, and the enjoyment
of home pleasures was the prescription in my case, Miss
Emily," said Cyril.

"And in yours, M. Bell?" said Stephanie.

A low answer and a very lovesick look, which made
Stephanie laugh coquettishly, and turn away to Soutter,
next whom she was sitting,

" And *Monsieur le Major* alone is not cured of his
ambition. Tell me, monsieur, why is that?"

" Perhaps, Miss Clèrambeau, because I never had
any to be cured of."

An exclamation of dismay.

" No military ambition, no desire for distinction?"

" None, certainly, at the start, and very little now.
Not enough at any time to have kept me a fortnight in
the army."

" Come, come, Soutter," said Cyril, " that's all very
fine, but don't expect us to believe it; don't expect us
to believe all these honors have come thick upon you
without your choice or effort. That isn't human
nature."

" Nor soldier nature, I hope, either," mumbled Bell.

" Well," cried Emily, " I hope Mr. Soutter will
excuse me, but if I were a soldier, I don't think I would
confess I had gone into my country's service without
the least ambition, without a thirst for glory, for making
myself a name."

" I will excuse you, certainly, Miss Rosenbaum," said
Soutter, looking down with a thoughtful smile.

"I don't think you understood Major Soutter exactly, Emily," began Sainty, timidly, and stopped when she found nobody else was talking.

"Emily was rather hasty in her conclusions," said Mr. Rosenbaum in his fine, cool voice. "She has only thought of military life in the particular phase which has come under her observation; she has never had brought before her notice any of by far the larger class in our army (and a very worthy class they are proving themselves too,) who have entered it as an occupation, an honest means of livelihood, in which they are determined to do their duty, as they have done it in their shops and on their farms. Experience has proved they make good soldiers, trusty officers; and though their motives fall somewhat short of the heroic, we have no right to question them, seeing the result."

"But," said Sainty, hesitatingly, "Mr. Soutter did not mean—he—that is—I am sure—"

There was an instant's pause, for Sainty lacked the courage to go on with such an audience listening, after which Soutter raised his head and said, "Thank you, Miss Thorndyke," with a smile that repaid her for all the awkwardness of the previous moment. "The people, Mr. Rosenbaum," he said, deliberately, looking at him as he spoke, "the people have not all gone to earn their bread by risking lives which they value as much, perhaps, as gentlemen value theirs; they have not all left homes and families with the simple object of making a scanty living by the hardest trade devils ever invented, or men ever carried out. Many and mixed motives have inspired al. classes to take up this deadly business, but I believe, could it be ascertained, the working men's would be found as pure as the gentlemen's. I am the only representative of that class among you, I believe, and it belongs to me to defend them from a misconstruction. Mr. Rosenbaum is right in saying ambition did not lead them into the army, neither did the thirst for glory, which Miss Emily apprehends as the heroic impulse, for to plodding, hard-working men such impulses do not often come. Neither did avarice, for their sturdy common sense prevented that delusion, nor love of adventure, for toil had taken off in most instances the edge of their enthusiasm. But the motives that have led them unflinchingly into danger, and uncomplainingly through hardships of the hardest sort, are to my mind not far short of the heroic, and they are, a simple love of country, and a steady resolution to do right. And to do right, not for their own advantage or advancement, not to make themselves splendid names, or secure themselves gratitude from men, but for religion's sake, for the sake of conscience. There is a quaint old poet, whom no doubt you know, who calls this motive

" ' The famous stone
That turneth all to gold.

" ' A servant with this clause
Makes drudgery divine :
Who sweeps a room, as for God's laws,
Makes that and th' action fine.'

They have been misconstrued and undervalued ; the hot blood and fiery zeal of men bred to arms, or to indolence,

or to ambition, have thus far outstripped them; but
they are consolidating, and strengthening, and increasing. Sooner than we had any right to hope for it, our
volunteer army, the bone and sinew of the country, ten
months ago quiet in their workshops or beside their
ploughs, will be turned to iron, and will stand a gigantic
power before the world, a power that avarice and ambition could never have created, that avarice and ambition
never can sustain. The mighty principle that has
moulded that mass to order, that is hardening it into
utility and strength, is that same principle that old
Herbert praises. I do not believe men are machines,
armies huge senseless engines of destruction. I pay
that honor to the immortal part of them, that unless it
is enlisted and righteously engaged, I believe there is
no strength or safety in the man, or in the army of
which he is a part. A man fighting for ambition, for
the hope of a distinguished name, is fighting for himself,
for his own honor, and is a fragment detached and
separated from the mass, puny and isolated; but a man
who is animated by the same unselfish impulse that
influences thousands standing side by side with him,
strikes with a doubled force, marches with twice the
courage and endurance, knows himself part of a great
principle, and feels the honor of his country, while he
forgets his own."

"That's very true, part of it," said Cyril, thoughtfully.
"But I am sorry to say I think you are disposed to give
too much credit to the principle, and too much principle
to the men. Forbid them all chance of promotion, half
of them would go home, cut off their pay, and the other
half would follow."

"Yes," said Bell, "and offer them half as much again, and they'd serve on the other side with just as good a will."

"Well, that being a clear matter of conjecture, I won't try to out-conjecture you, only congratulate myself on believing so much better of my countrymen."

"I acknowledge I think your faith must be pretty strong, Soutter, if it isn't shaken by the experience you had last autumn with those precious reprobates in our division. Who do you think now they were fighting for?"

"The devil, if I am any judge," said Soutter, "and a little more such leaven would have ruined us. As it was, they did an infinite deal of harm among the others, and showed me pretty plainly the impossibility of getting good service out of bad men."

"The history of our modern wars does not tend to illustrate your theory," said Mr. Rosenbaum. "Money and skill fight our battles now, and win our victories; piety and patriotism are choice relics of the middle ages, beautiful ornaments for churches and colleges, but of very questionable utility, I take it, in working guns or manœuvring regiments."

"Rosenbaum! Thunder! Hush!" cried Cyril. "Sainty's ready to faint at the mere hearing of such heresy, and the others look perfectly aghast. Don't you know better than to talk common sense before young ladies? O, if they only had a dear young minister here to put you down! The 'Rev. Mr. Dishwater,' with his pale eyes and 'feeble whiskers'; or if Soutter had taken to preaching now, instead of fighting! What a popularity he might have gained."

" Oh, his shoulders are too broad and he's much too brown to be a saint," said Cammy. "Mr. Rosenbaum's much better: Sainty's made a picture of St. Sebastian that looks just exactly like him."

Sainty was in an agony of confusion, while Emily laughed, and said that was a strange honor for Julian the Apostate. While everybody looked around uncomfortably for something else to talk about

CHAPTER XXVII.

THE PEDLAR.

"There is a Machiavelian plot,
Though every nose olfact it not."—HUDIBRAS.

CYRIL gave them something else.

"Thomas, what is it?" he said, impatiently, for Thomas had been parleying five minutes with some one outside the front hall door, and was in a state of much indecision, now inclining to shut it in the intruder's face, and now disposed to call Mr. Cyril into council. He looked relieved when Cyril spoke, and coming forward, said, in an excited voice,

"There's a man' outside there, sir, as will come in. I never saw his like. He won't take no refusal."

"A man?" said Cyril, starting up. "What's his business?"

"His business? Why, sir, if you can call peddlin' a business, it's that, sir—peddlin', sir."

"Nonsense," said the young master, sinking back. "Tell him to take himself off, or I'll set the dogs upon him."

"I have told him so, sir," said Thomas, with excitement. "I have told him just that thing."

"Well, tell him so again," replied Cyril, adding, in a one of vexation, "I thought they had succeeded in scaring those people off the place."

In a moment Thomas came back, saying, breathlessly, " Master Cyril, he will speak with you, sir, if you please."

Cyril sprang up and went over to the door with an impatient step, going outside of it, and half closing it after him. The dogs, meanwhile, were shaking themselves out of a recumbent attitude, and pricking up their ears, but Soutter, laying a hand on the collar of each, kept them at his feet and ordered them sternly to lie down.

Presently Cyril came back laughing, and saying to the man behind him, " Well, come in if you choose; such perseverance ought to be rewarded."

And, with a shuffling, queer gait, a man followed him into the hall. As he came within the light of the fire he made a low reverence to them, twisted his greasy cap off his head, and tucked it under his arm.

" What strange, sharp eyes!" murmured Stephanie, starting closer to Soutter.

" He is rather a suspicious-looking subject, I confess," said Soutter. " I wonder Thorndyke let him in."

Sylvie, in a tremor of alarm, rushed to him and demanded to be taken up; at which the dogs, feeling themselves released, cleared the circle at a bound, and snuffed eagerly about the new-comer's legs, accompanying their investigations with a low, suspicious growl.

The man seemed terribly alarmed, clasping his hands to his head as if to keep it on, shuffling back, and begging in bad English to have the dogs called off. Cyril sternly ordered them back, and they very reluctantly obeyed, withdrawing a little way from him on each side, and, after a moment's hesitation, lying down, with

14

their noses on their fore paws, and their shining, watch
ful eyes never moving from his face. Their attentions
seemed to embarrass him extremely. He gathered himself up so as to occupy as little ground as possible, and
watched his legs jealously, giving an occasional start
and gasp, as his imagination played him some trick
about their safety.

"Don't be alarmed, my good fellow," said Cyril, with
a serious look. "They won't hurt you as long as I am
by. They have been educated with a sort of prejudice
against pedlars, and are apt to make sad work with
them ordinarily; but I'll see you get off safely. Meanwhile, tell these ladies and gentlemen what you've got
for sale."

Thus recalled to his occupation, the pedlar began to
enumerate his wares in very imperfect English, and to
let his pack down slowly from his back, but the constant
surveillance which he was obliged to maintain over his
legs interfered so much with his narrative, that Cyril,
laughing, had to take it up and go on with it.

"He tells me," said Cyril, "that he has a beautiful
assortment of jewelry, toilet articles, perfumery, and
stationery. You may see it for yourselves, ladies and
gentlemen. You are requested to examine. But, besides all this, he professes fortune-telling, and will guar-
antee you, for the sum of fifty cents, the true and verit-
able history of your future life, the success you will
have in love, and the manner of your decease. These
predictions he will deliver to you, already written out
You must break the seal and read them for yourselves
it is a chance that does not occur every day."

Here the pedlar added his voice eagerly but rather unintelligibly, and ended by fumblingly untying his pack and presenting its contents for the examination of the company. There was a good deal of talking and much merriment about the itinerant Delphos, but it was concluded to try the experiment, and the money being made up and placed in the man's hands, he proceeded, with much solemnity, to distribute certain slips of paper which he held folded in his hat.

He looked sharply at every one in turn to whom he came, and selected the paper for each very rapidly, but with precision. Emily received hers very daintily from his greasy old cap, while Stephanie took hers with a pretty smile, and a sentence or two of the best Italian she could master, at which he looked pleased, and mumbled something which might have been Danish in reply. Between Soutter and Rosenbaum he paused ; he looked a little bit bewildered. He turned away from Soutter.

" Well, aren't you going to give Major Soutter any ?" cried Stephanie.

" Major Soutter, eh ?" repeated the fortune-teller, in a low tone, as, fumbling among the papers, he selected one and gave it to Soutter, with a sharp look, a sharp look which fell instantly, however, as he encountered Soutter's eyes.

Miss Warrington, meanwhile, had kept back out of sight, but she had not escaped the pedlar's notice. He made his way out of the circle up to where she sat, and handed her the slip of paper silently, while Soutter said,

" He must have sharp eyes indeed. I thought he saw nothing but the dogs when he came in."

"Now," cried Emily, impatiently, "we each have our leaf from the book of fate, why don't we begin to read them ?"

"Let me have one seat," said the pedlar, getting on the opposite side of the fire from the dogs. Room was made for him in the circle, and he sat down, with his hands on his knees, and his eyes attentive at once to the movements of the dogs and the faces of the readers and the listeners.

"Begin, Sainty," said Cyril, resuming his place near Frank. "You come first."

Mr. Rosenbaum broke the seal, and handed her the little slip of paper open. It was written in a stiff, upright hand, and Sainty, laughing, leaned down and read it by the firelight. She had, according to the prophet, been disappointed in love and almost broken-hearted, but would soon find a new lover, whom she would like better than the first, who was very rich and very handsome, and had been married twice, but who would marry her before the year was out, and take her to Havana, where they would live in great happiness for the remainder of their lives. There was a great deal of laughing about Sainty's widower, and then Mr. Rosenbaum read his communication from the unknown. It came equally wide of the mark, promising him a lady with black eyes and hair, and a great fortune, success in all his plans, and death at the age of forty-five. Cammy and Cub had all that their hearts could wish in the matter of money and sweethearts, and then it came Cyril's turn. He stooped down to get the full benefit of the blaze, and cried, "Hear this," and read :

" You have sinned while young; you will marry while young, and you will die while young; you have been a deceiver and you will be deceived. The woman you love will play you false, and the woman you leave will be revenged on you. Your course is downward from this day."

" Epigrammatic, upon my word," cried Cyril, with a laugh, which seemed a little forced. " Old fellow, you might have done better by me, I think, considering I introduced you to this company."

The pedlar made some voluble and unintelligible protest, which was cut short by Cyril. " Miss Warrington, let us hear whether you are any greater favorite with the fates. You cannot see; shall I read it for you?"

" O no," she said, coming forward to the middle of the circle, and standing on the rug, bending her head down a little to catch the light, she read the following:

" You are trying to reach something too high for you, and you will get a fall. The man you loved has forgotten you. The man you want to marry is a traitor whose name you will never bear; the way is open that you know will save you; take it without delay; twenty-four hours will decide your fate; have your mind made up against an answer is required of you. If you hesitate, you will know disgrace and trouble."

" Upon my soul," cried Cyril, " that's mystery enough for once."

" Who taught you the black art, old man?" asked Rosenbaum.

· " Sainty, it's worse than your widower," said Frank

in a careless tone, twisting the paper up and tossing it into the fire. " Our matrimonial horizon is dark."

" I begin to grow superstitious," cried Emily. " But listen :

" You are to marry happily, to live long, and to die respected. Your youth has been pious, and your future will be blessed."

" Bah !" exclaimed Emily. " That's extremely tame."

" You don't feel superstitious any longer, do you?" said Cammy.

" Well, Bell," said Cyril, who seemed to have lost some of his enthusiasm in the fortune-telling, " what's to be your fate ?"

Bell was to share the fate heaven sends its favorites— early death ; in fact, so very early, that the present week was to terminate his mortal span.

" Infernal nonsense," he muttered, changing color, while a cold perspiration broke out on his forehead. " I don't know what the deuce makes anybody encourage such scoundrel's trade for."

There was a general laugh.

" Bell, I never guessed you were so much attached to life," said Cyril. " It's all a fleeting show, my friend."

" I am afraid you won't enjoy the week very much, Mr. Bell," said Emily, " when you remember it's your last."

" Bell's a philosopher," said Cyril. " I'll engage it won't affect his spirits in the least; a short life and a merry one is what he's always preached."

" It will only make the present more delightful," said Stephanie. " But hear my fortune."

Stephanie was to have a handsome husband, a great many children, and a great deal of money. And Sylvie, who came next, was to die of a broken heart.

"And now for you, M. Soutter," cried Stephanie, looking animated.

"Ah, it is a long story," said Louis, glancing down the paper. "Old man, do you mean all this for me? Well, listen, friends:

"You are surrounded by enemies; you will do well to leave them. You will never be successful in love, whatever your hopes may be at present. You have been fickle, and you must reap the consequences. You will be fortunate in whatever else you undertake; and as long as you let women alone you will be happy. You will not die in battle, though you will see many fights. You will be a great man if you do not lose your time and let others get ahead of you. Be advised and do not waste another day."

"Thank you kindly," said Louis, folding the paper and returning it to the old man, with a little nod. "But I'm not in any hurry. I think I'll stay and see it out."

The man took refuge behind his bad English, and nah-ed and yah-ed and signored him hopelessly, while the others compared their fortunes, laughed at each other, and made a grand confusion till the dressing-bell rang, which was the signal for a hurried and general dispersion.

"You do not leave me," cried the pedlar, "alone with zese animauls."

Cyril laughed, and called to Thomas to take the dogs

away and chain them, which he did to their manifest
discontent, for they hung back and growled as he dragged them after him through one of the side doors. The
man breathed freer after they were gone, but was evidently anxious not to be detained himself, steering particularly clear of Soutter, who lingered by the fire with
Cyril. Cyril plied him with questions, as he accompanied him to the door, and even quietly made some
attempt to win him to greater freedom of speech by the
offer of money; but all in vain, he was impregnable
behind his crazy English, and Cyril had to let him out,
scraping and bowing and hitching up his pack, without
obtaining the least satisfaction from him.

"That strikes me as a precious old scamp, Thorndyke," said Soutter. "And you'd better see that he
doesn't get admittance here again."

"Yes," said Cyril, uneasily, as he pushed back the
sofa from the fire, "it was rather a silly thing to let him
in; I wish I hadn't done it. Come; we have barely
time to dress for dinner."

CHAPTER XXVIII.

MERRY AND WISE.

" The tiny, trumpeting gnat can break our dream
  When sweetest ; and the vermin voices here
  May buzz so loud—we scorn them, but they sting.''
                                        Idyls of the King.

THE next morning proved unpropitious for out-door entertainment. A heavy snow-storm had set iu during the night, with a fair prospect of continuing itself during the day, and the whole party of ladies were lounging around the library fire, with rather an ennuyé appearance. The young ones were embroidering with very long and lazy needles, the old ones were jogging drowsily through the papers, with the help of their eye-glasses and a strong light from the window, and the children were playing a very unsatisfactory game of " wolf and sheep" upon the floor, and coming to the governess every five minutes for the settlement of claims.

The school-room was being swept, and she had brought them here immediately after breakfast out of a conscientious desire to preserve Sainty, who looked pale and wretched, from being annoyed with them in the parlor Everybody had taken to the library, however, and her presence now seemed to be unnecessary, and she was gathering up her work, when the sound of steps outside

14*

and the opening of the door by the gentlemen, return ing from the billiard-room, prevented her going away at that moment. Stephanie looked bright and interested instantly, and glanced up from her work with a pretty smile to welcome Soutter, who approached her instinct- ively, as he always did now, when he entered the room where she was.

"This looks dark for the Cuyler ball to-night," said Bell, going to the window.

"Rather, dark for us," said Cyril, "for we've no es- cape, my friend, if it were twice as deep a snow. The Cuylers are *exigeants* upon such points; I believe they put the observance of etiquette as the highest injunction of the moral law. I think their catechism must have read like this: 'My duty towards my neighbor is to dine him twice a year, and to go to all his parties, as I would have him come to mine; to bore, stupefy, and entertain all strangers in the neighborhood; to give a ball at Christmas, and to make it as stiff as it is in my power to do; never to give countenance to any one who is not wealthy and well-bred, but to learn and labor truly to keep mine own position in society, and to do my duty towards myself to the best of my ability.'"

"O, M. Cyril, what a hypocrite. So *dévoué* as you were last night at dinner to Miss Cuyler, *la cadette!*"

"*Cela ne fait rien*, Miss Clèrambeau, was she not my neighbor?"

"But, seriously," said Stephanie, "do you go to balls at Ringmer when it storms like this?"

"'We stay not for brake and we stop not for stone,'

Miss Clèrambeau, when the Cuylers are concerned. We dare not risk our standing in the neighborhood by breaking an engagement there."

"Cyril is right," said Mrs. Thorndyke, with a discontented sigh. "They're just the people whom it doesn't do to offend, and they always make it a point to give parties in bad weather."

"Always, and it is a source of satisfaction to them, I know, to feel that people are ruining their carriages and risking their horses and endangering their lives, because they don't dare to be uncivil to them."

"Cyril! Pray don't talk so before the children," said Sainty, in a low tone.

"Why not, Cecilia? Don't you teach them the Cuyler catechism?"

"I know why Cyril's so savage at the Cuylers," said Cammy to Major Soutter, in a stage aside.

"Ah! Why?" whispered Stephanie, with zest.

"Because Mr. Richard Cuyler sat by Miss Warrington all last evening, and made him jealous."

"O, you terrible child! How do you know? You did not stay up after dinner."

"O, I heard Marcelle and Thomas talking about it this morning in the dining-room, when we got our breakfast. You were all so late, you know; there was nobody but us; and there's no law against listening, is there?"

Soutter turned away abruptly; was this talked of in the kitchen even! He put Sylvie down from his lap, and rising, walked over to the book shelves opposite, where he stood reading the titles of the rows above him in an abstracted way, while the others talked.

"By the way," said Cyril, "I've just found out that our friend the fortune-teller shared the hospita.'ities of the servants' hall last night. Instead of going off when I dismissed him, he made his way around to the kitchen, and so worked upon the feelings of the cook that she allowed him to remain to dinner, during which repast he made himself so fascinating that he was encouraged to spend the evening and tell the fortunes of all the party, in which he gave such satisfaction that the coachman invited him to sleep in the loft over his apartment. I don't know that he's gone even yet, but I've sent Thomas out to tell him to be off immediately."

"Marcelle says she's sure he wore a wig," said Cammy, "and his eyebrows were pasted on, for one got loose, and she saw the real black ones underneath."

"The deuce she did!" said Cyril, with a frown. "And what else does she say about him?"

"O, she thinks he's a wonderful man; she says he seemed to know everything, and to be so interested about everybody in the house; he asked her all manner of questions, and he gave her such a pretty ring —— but I wasn't to tell that, I forgot ——"

"No doubt, and you weren't to tell any of the rest, I suppose. I should like to know how people are to be sure they are not entertaining the devil unawares, if they keep such a raft of idle servants in the kitchen, with a French *bonne* at their head. Of course, she has invited him to come again?"

"She didn't say, but I suppose she has. I think she's under the impression that he's an Italian prince, and that he's fallen very much in love with her."

"Well, I'll go and make sure he doesn't have a

chance to accept her invitation," said Cyril, going out of the room abruptly.

When he came back he found Miss Warrington had gone from the room, as well as his mother and the children; Soutter, too, was not there, and as the rest paused suddenly when he came in and began in a forced manner to talk of something else, he very naturally concluded they had been talking about him.

"So!" he thought angrily, as he quitted them in search of Frank, "they begin to make this common talk; even the children and the servants have got hold of it; they shall soon have liberty to make it as common as they choose."

He pushed eagerly open the school-room door, but a glance told him that the room was vacant. He was both angry and disappointed; he had not had one moment alone with Frank since the evening before upon the ice, and he felt as if she were further from him than ever, and as if intangible and ever increasing obstacles were rising up to thwart him, now that he had overcome her coldness, and had extorted that promise from her. He was more irrationally in love with her than ever, and therefore felt with double keenness the perplexity and danger of his position.

Certainly, his fate was drawing to a crisis. He saw by the tiger gleam in Emily's eye, and the clouded coldness of her cousin's, that things could not long continue as they were. The insinuations of the fortune-teller indicated some underhand malice, inspired by whom he could only guess, and in this case his suspicions took a wrong direction. He could not long hope to keep his mother ignorant of what was going on and the information allowed once to go through that channel to his father, all was over with him. He knew the storm that would be raised, and he knew Frank too well to feel sure of her, when she was subjected to inso lence and malice, such as were inevitable. She would never enter his family under such circumstances, he was certain, even if she loved him thoroughly. There was only one course open to him; if he could persuade her to an immediate and secret marriage, all might yet be well. The desire to possess her, to be certain of her, made him persuade himself that he was equal to the complications that such a step would involve him in. He knew his father's vindictive temper, he fancied, perfectly, but he thought him possessed of a certain degree of cold, well-weighing common sense, that would make him accept, after the first outburst, an inevitable and accomplished thing with philosophic fortitude. If he could keep his intentions from his father's knowledge till he could tell him that Frank was his wife, he felt he might brave the storm and come out from it safely.

It would, he was certain, be a desperate offence that would induce his father to forego all the hopes that he had had in him ; poor little Cub never could take his place; a thousand errors would be overlooked before he would deprive himself of an heir and a successor of whom he could be proud. As to his mother, she would soon be reconciled to anything that did not interfere with her present comfort and enjoyment, and as to the world, he did not at that moment, care a rush whether it praised him or condemned him.

But supposing, for the sake of argument, that all went, as he knew it would not go, against him. Supposing his father inexorable, unforgiving, his mother outraged and unreasonable, Frank indignant and unbending, supposing all that, he would be beginning the world under as fair auspices as many a man before him had begun it. He had a good position in the army, and the chance of rising in it; he had influential friends, a good connection, which his father's anger would not deprive him of; he was young, he had ambition, talent, and the double incentive of love for his wife and pique towards his family. Besides which, he had received an inheritance from his grandfather, which, though he had overlooked it in his better prospects, he now reflected, would place them entirely above all chance of want, and make their income, even without his pay, far from contemptible.

But this was all a mere *dernier ressort*, to which he hardly feared he would be driven. The question most pressing now was, how to persuade Frank to consent to such a marriage. She had given him last night a half extorted and faint encouragement, and he was planning to induce her to compromise herself by a private and hasty marriage! It would seem like unblushing effrontery, indeed, but his passion carried him beyond reason, and he trusted to convince her. He would have to sacrifice truth somewhat in his argument, but what of that, if the result were happy. He must make her believe that his entanglement with Emily was the only motive that he had for secrecy, and that that entanglement was entirely a family matter, an arrangement to which he had never given his consent, and into which he had been drawn unwittingly He must persuade her that his father had always held it as a principle that his children should choose for themselves, and that this plan was only one of his mother's making, who, after the first disappointment, could easily be brought into any other scheme they chose to offer to her consideration. Cecilia already loved her as a sister, and would receive her with all the tenderness of one. It was not, surely, asking much of her, he would plead, to put him out of his difficulties by such a simple act as this; to cut the knot that had hampered him so long, by a few words of assent at once, that she had promised him to give by and by. He would use every argument that his ingenuity could devise, every persuasive that his passion could suggest; he must, he would, succeed; disappointment had always been foreign to his experience, and it should be impossible still.

It would seem, indeed, as if he carried some talisman that conquered ill success, for circumstances were at that very moment effecting for him what all his eloquence would have failed to do alone.

CHAPTER XXIX.

HONEST AND TRUE.

" Better thou and I were lying, hidden from the heart's disgrace,
Rolled in one another's arms, and silent in a last embrace."
                                                    Locksley Hall.

FRANK had gone up to her room and bolted the door. There was a smouldering dull fire in the grate; she looked at it, but did not go near it, nor near the windows either, before which was falling a thick, steady veil of snow. It was cold, dreary and comfortless without, drearier and more comfortless within.

She did not pace the floor, nor fling herself down upon the bed, nor vent her misery by any of the outward expressions that most women yield to when they lock themselves alone into their rooms. She sat down in a chair that stood by the head of the bed, and pulling a pillow towards her, put her face down on it, and sat motionless for more than an hour. At the end of that time there came a knock at the door; she smoothed her hair, and opened it.

It was a servant with a note; she locked the door and sat down again to read it, and found, with a feeling of relief, that it was only from Cyril, a hurried, ardent, lover-like entreaty for a moment's interview. She had feared it was something from that hateful man, whose warning of last night she had not been able to forget;

sometime during the twenty-four hours then passing
she would have to hear from him, she knew.   Cunning,
unprincipled and daring, what revenge did he mean to
take upon her, if she refused again to listen to him ?

It was not merely now, that she would have cause to
fear him, though his malice could suggest enough, she
did not doubt, to humble her bitterly among her present associates.   But it was by and by, when she
should be homeless again, that she saw cause to fear
him most.   One breath against her reputation, and her
means of livelihood were gone.   She must marry Cyril,
or must leave his family.   If she left it, her position
was a thousand times worse than it had ever been
before; if she married him, she sinned against all laws
her heart had ever recognised.   There was one thing
open to her, one path of escape not yet closed up : she
could go home to Titherly, acknowledge her defeated
plans, sink down humbly a dependant on her aunt,
accept the daily sight and memory of what she most
desired to obliterate from her recollection.   .

" Never," she said aloud, clenching her fingers on the
note, and lifting her head up from the pillow for an
instant, " never, never !"

And then she put her face down again, while the note
fell from her grasp, and the fire in the grate smouldered
on, and the snow shook its dull veil before the windows
for another silent hour.

Again there came a knock; this time it was Cub
who brought a verbal message from his brother ; he
wanted to see her for a moment in the school-room, if she
were disengaged.   While she was giving her answer to

the boy in a low tone, a servant came up with a note in her hand. She was a new laundry maid, and not well acquainted with the names and ways of the family.

"I guess this note's for you, miss," she said, looking stupidly up and down the hall. "The gentleman said it was the door opposite the school-room, but I don't know rightly which that is."

"That's on the floor below," said Miss Warrington.

"Miss Clèrambeau's room's opposite the school-room," said Cub. "I'm going down there, I'll take it."

"Why no," said the woman uneasily. "I think I'd better take it myself. The gentleman said I must see it in her own hands, and I shouldn't like to disappoint him, you know. These officer gentlemen are so particular."

"I don't know what Major Soutter can be writing to Miss Stephanie about," said Cub, meditatively. "She's been sitting with him in the library till an hour ago. But just as soon as she went away, he began to write a letter, and it must have been to her. Why can't people *say* things, I wonder."

And Cub went down stairs, pondering the matter, to deliver the unwelcome message to his brother, while Frank shut the door again and resumed her former attitude, with a face somewhat paler and with eyes more intense and gloomy in their silence. And so the day wore on, interrupted now and then by the clamor of the children without, and now and then by the kitchen maid or Thomas, on an errand from the house-keeper, but she never left the room, or let any one in it, till about five o'clock, when she heard Cub's voice

Miss Warrington shook her head, and turned away from him.

"It was such a strange letter, though," he went on. "I never thought Major Soutter would write such a sort of a letter, he doesn't seem unhappy, do you think he does? He told her —— "

"Stop, Cub," she said, rising quickly and speaking huskily. "You are telling me what you have no right to tell. You must try and forget all this, and you must never repeat a word of it to any living soul. That is the only reparation you can make. It was not your fault at first, but it will be if you repeat it. Go down and tell your brother I will come to the school-room in a moment; and you wait there till I come."

Cub went out, and Frank, waiting till he had left her, went across the room, and held her hands over the flickering fire. They were icy cold, and she shivered as she bent down and tried to rouse a blaze. It was an unavailing effort; the ashes shook down and covered up the faint and trembling flame, and, turning away, she went mechanically over to the glass. But it was only a black oval, reflecting the dark room, and passing her hand over her hair with an unconscious and habitual movement, she went with a firm step to the door. The hall was dark; half-way down the third story staircase she met Cub coming up, while she caught sight of Soutter in the hall below. Not seeing him, and knowing no reason why he should not speak aloud, the simple minded Cub said quite distinctly,

"Cyril is waiting for you in the school-room, Miss

Warrington. He would not let me stay, though I told him what you said."

"Very well," she said, passing him hastily.

Soutter waited at the landing-place to let her pass. She did not raise her eyes as she went by him, but he made a movement forward and an effort to speak, and then stopped, and with a sigh watched her disappear, and then went slowly up the stairs.

The school-room was dim, only the outline of the large west window was visible, and some one watching beside it started forward as she entered. It was not altogether the chill of the cold room upstairs that made her shiver as she felt her hand clasped by her new lover, and listened to the alternate reproaches, gratitude and passion which he whispered as he drew her to a seat.

It had been a tempestuous day with him; he had been vexed beyond endurance by her refusals, exasperated, disappointed and indignant, but more than ever mastered by his passion for her. His dark and moody looks had made him the subject of rallying and teasing in the circle below, and he had left it in bad temper, and spent most of the day by himself in making and unmaking the futile and short-lived resolves of all angry lovers, and in losing every moment more of self-control and common sense.

There is an unconquerable force in the real passion of a strong-willed man: let a woman once consent to listen to it, and, indifferent or loving, sooner or later, she will yield to its demands. Frank was indifferent, more than indifferent, to the lover, but the love was current too strong for her to launch her reasonings and refusals safely on; it swept them away before her eyes. A moment more favorable to Cyril's suit he could not have asked, if he, instead of fate, had chosen it. With the eager instinct of a lover, he caught at the wavering in her mind, and threw into his pleading such strength of passion, such sincerity of purpose, such subtlety of reasoning, that, with an impulse of desperation, she at last yielded a consent.

Yes. she would marry him—when he pleased—soon —that is, by and by—before he went back to the army, perhaps—she did not know—only let her go now, it was late, some one would come in, she *must* go.

But the bell had begun to ring for dinner, before releasing her hand from his, she hurried through the hall, which was now fully lighted. Stephanie, ravishingly pretty in her dinner toilet, came out of her door at the same moment, and gave her a curious but amiable smile as she passed her, while just as she gained the third floor, she encountered Bell face to face, and knew he was wondering why she was not dressed, and why she did not go down to dinner. Dinner; the very thought of meeting them all gave her a shudder; she felt as if she never could go down again; she thought of Stephanie, bright and piquante, in her now regularly established seat by Soutter's side; Rosenbaum and Bell, curious and half sneering, treating her with a supercilious manner of politeness more insulting than any inattention; Emily, with her hateful, keen and cruel eyes, and Sainty, whom she was deceiving so!

Would to Heaven she could escape them all this very night, this very moment! Cyril more than all, to whom she should be grateful, and of whom she was most afraid.

Ah, was this to be her future, was this her independence, her self-reliant plan of life. She had not succeeded well, she feared, in guiding and directing her own destiny, for she had lost even the fortitude and strength of purpose with which she had set out.

The darkness of the room was suffocating. She walked restlessly once or twice across it, then, taking up the candle, went to the hall to light it, listening a moment at the door to ascertain that there was no one near. She vaguely feared a message every moment—a message, or an encounter with the object of her dread in person. Every step, every ring at the bell, every knock at her door, had given her a sensation of alarm; and she felt only safe within her own room, with the bolt slid fast by her own hand. She glanced around as she came out and approached the hall lamp, and had just raised her hand to light the allumette when she heard a door close and a step come up behind her. She gave an involuntary start, the candle dropped, and she turned round.

It was only Major Soutter, who had just come out from his room, and she grew scarlet as she met his eye. What would he think of her emotion. His face was flushed too, and his hand trembled a little, as, picking up the candle, he took the lighter from her and held it up above the lamp.

She did not raise her eyes again; if she had, the look

15

in his might yet have turned the current of her life,
and saved her from the fate into which she was hurrying so fast. But he gave her the candle silently, and
with only a few inaudible words of commonplace she
turned away.

CHAPTER XXX.

LE PREMIER PAS.

"One touch to her hand, and one word in her ear,
  When they reached the hall door and the charger stcod near."

FRANK was bidden to the Cuyler ball. Mr. Richard Cuyler's admiration had secured that high honor for her; and there had not been wanting urgency on the part of Cecilia, and kind encouragement on that of Mrs. Thorndyke, to induce her to assist at it; but it is not probable that she would have yielded either to them or to Cyril's more ardent wishes, if there had not been a secret and strong reason why that night she should not stay at home. The whole family would be absent, with the exception only of Mr. Rosenbaum, who was since morning confined entirely to his room. Even Cub had been allowed to go as a Christmas treat, and Cammy and Sylvie would be in bed by nine o'clock. Mr. Thorndyke was dining out, and would probably not return before eleven o'clock. The house would be entirely alone, in the hands of the servants, Thomas and Marcelle, and all that crew in whom she had so little confidence; and that, of course, would be just the time the fortune-teller would select to make his second visit. By this time she fancied he knew enough of the ways of the house to be confident she would stay at home, this being the first occasion on which she had ever thought of going out to any entertainment, of which, since she had lived there, there had been many.

It was, however, with a very sinking heart that she began to prepare for this, her first sight of the gay world in its high state of decoration. The ball, no doubt, would be a very tame affair to the other members of the party who were used to city gaiety, but to Frank it would have been a thing to take away the breath if she had been less engrossed with trouble. She had but one evening dress to wear, and it was too simple to require much thought; but it gave her a pang to remember what a different heart she had laced it over when she wore it last. That dress! How she had queened it at the country fêtes last winter in it! How all the homely scenes of merry-making rose up before her as she put it on! She could see Fanny's covert look of envy, and hear the murmurs of admiration that had followed her around. That lilac silk had been a heart-breaking source of discontent to many a less favored girl at Titherly. She smiled bitterly to think how dull and simple it would look among the gay dresses at the ball to-night. Better to be great among the little than little among the great. How thankfully, taking one dark thread from the mixed fabric of the past, she would have returned to those old scenes, not perhaps high-spirited and envied as she had been before, but as an humble and less exacting sharer in their peace, their simplicity, and their safety.

A servant from Mr. Cyril came to her room at nine o'clock to know if she were ready; the ladies were all getting in the sleigh. She threw her grey cloak and hood about her and hurried down into the hall. The ladies, cloaked and hooded too, stood at the door, and Cyril with a slight shade of anxiety on his face, was arranging how they should be placed most comfortably. His eyes brightened a little as he caught sight of Frank on the stairs, but he looked quickly away, and went on speaking as if he had not seen her.

"The covered sleigh, I think, will hold all of you five ladies," he said. "The open sleigh is in dry dock yet, you know, and so we shall have to divide ourselves in the two single ones. Bell and Soutter can drive themselves in one, and Cub and I will follow in the other."

"Very well," said Mrs. Thorndyke, with a little impatience; "it is time we were off. We ought to have started half an hour ago. The Cuylers are always particular to be early at our house; it makes it so extremely awkward in the country."

The ladies followed Cyril out upon the piazza; and he was just assisting Mrs. Rosenbaum, who was an unwieldy mass of wrappers, to her place inside the sleigh, when, glancing back into the hall, Emily caught sight of Frank.

"Why," she said, in an affected whisper, "there's the governess! Where is she going to ride?"

"The governess!" exclaimed Cyril, in a tone of dismay, striking his forehead with an air of great perplexity. "Who the deuce thought of her going! Where on earth shall we put her? Can you make room for her inside?"

"Oh, easily," said Stephanie, with ready malice

"There will be place enough between Miss Rosenbaum and me."

"Indeed, Miss Clèrambeau, I think you are more amiable than I can be," said Emily sharply, not seeing Cyril's ruse. "I will be very glad to give her my place and stay at home, but I don't think I could quite make up my mind to six miles in such crowded company."

"Oh," cried Cyril earnestly, "of course I should not think of it; I spoke hastily. I will make some other arrangement. Cub can drive her, and I will ride one of the greys, or something can be done. Don't give the matter another thought."

"You are so thoughtful in ordinary, M. Cyril," said Stephanie, wickedly demure; "how odd you should have overlooked the governess!"

Emily caught the hint and cried: "Why not let Cub ride, and you drive Miss Warrington in the sleigh yourself; it would be so much safer!"

"Cub, unluckily, isn't much of an equestrian. I don't think he ever succeeded in keeping on a horse's back ten minutes. I should not dare to trust him. But don't give yourself the least uneasiness. I assure you Miss Warrington shall be provided for, if I stay at home myself."

"That shall not be," cried Stephanie. "For you engaged me for the first two redowas, and I will not sit still. Major Soutter!" she exclaimed as he approached, "will you make your friend come? Will you see that he does not disappoint me?"

"I will see," said Soutter, coming to the side of the

sleigh, and Frank, stepping out upon the piazza that moment, saw him leaning down to answer some whispered question, and smiling and raising his cap as, closing the door, he gave the word to the coachman, and watched them drive away.

"I am sorry, Miss Warrington," said Cyril, in the most matter-of-fact, master-of-the-house manner, going towards her, as if he had not another idea in his head than that of being as civil as his position required, and not allowing her to feel hurt, "I am sorry you have to go in this open sleigh, but I trust you are well wrapped up, and there are enough buffalo robes to cover you from head to foot. The snow has almost ceased too. I do not believe you will suffer from the cold."

"Oh, no," she said indifferently, going down the steps. "I shall not mind it."

Soutter meantime, buttoning his coat up to the throat, walked up and down upon the terrace, and did not offer to approach them; while Bell, lighting his cigar, watched them with some interest, and occasionally offered a remark as Cyril, after establishing Frank carefully and protecting her in all ways from the cold, gave the reins to Cub and charged him to be very watchful, and to keep close to the sleigh in front. Just as they started, he leaned down and repeated some directions to Cub in a low tone, adding,

"You remember exactly, do you?"

"Yes, I remember exactly, I believe," said Cub, ng the reins with a vast sense of responsibility, looking steadily, as they started, at the sleigh in f now almost out of sight.

"You're not afraid to let me drive you, Miss War rington, are you?" said he doubtfully.

"Oh, no, Cub," she answered, with a sigh, sinking back into the furs. "I would rather have you than any of the others."

Cub felt himself blushing to his ear-tips, but experienced a sensation of relief when he remembered that it was not light enough for Miss Warrington to know it.

CHAPTER XXXI.

THE MAGISTRATE'S.

" What will they think ?
What pleases them.   That argument's a staff
Which breaks whene'er you lean on't."

Saint's Tragedy.

THE snow had almost entirely ceased to fall; since noon, indeed, the violence of the storm had abated, and though it lay on the ground the depth of two feet, the roads were tolerably broken and the sleighing fine. The cold was not excessive and there was a moon, which though not apparent, still showed a good deal of light through the thin clouds and the faint-falling snow.   Frank lay silently resting her cheek against the furs, feeling half soothed by the monotonous music of the bells, and almost safe with such a kind and earnest little friend beside her, trying not to think, and endeavoring only to rest and pacify the aching in her head and heart.   Cub did not dare to talk to her, and so they went silently, smoothly, pleasantly on mile after mile, one unvarying sheet of white below them, and a faint mist of white around and above them, and the soft music of the bells accompanying them drowsily.

Frank had kept her eyes fixed dreamily on the dark-covered sleigh in front, from which they had kept an

even distance ever since they had come up with it at
first; but a few minutes after having made some sudden turn in the road, she missed it. She roused herself
after finding they did not come in sight of it again
though Cub had whipped up a little, and asked him
where it was.

"We've turned out of the main road," he said.

"Why did you do that?"

"Brother Cyril told me to," he answered. "I don't
know why; but he said I must take the first right hand
road after I passed Norbury, the other side of the saw-
mill, and this is it."

"But does it come out at the Cuylers'?"

"I don't know; I never came this way before."

"Then how are you to know—what's to prevent our
being lost?" she said, rousing quickly.

"Oh, I don't believe we shall get lost. He told me
to go two or three miles on the road and I would come
to a lane."

"Well?"

"Well, I could inquire the way if I saw anybody
about, and if not, I could wait till some of the rest
came up."

Frank felt a sinking of the heart as the obedient and
simple minded boy drove on. What blind trap where
they going into? She looked behind and listened
eagerly; but no one was following them. The road
was very narrow—too narrow to suffer them to turn—
and unfrequented and lonely beyond all hope of succor
if danger threatened them. The snow had not drifted
at all, or the road would have been impassable. One

sleigh had evidently passed over it recently, though the tracks were fast being filled up by the light snow falling. Where could Soutter and Bell be all. this time? What could have detained them so long after them? What could Cyril mean by separating her so from all the party? Six miles from home, and going, she was certain, every moment further out of the way of that and of their destination. A thousand misgivings filled her mind, a thousand vague fears beset her; but to none of them could she give utterance, looking at the unsuspecting and ingenuous face beside her.

"When did your brother tell you to come this way?" she asked.

"When he went down to the stables after dinner and told me I was to drive you."

"Was anybody else with him when he told you so?"

"No, nobody."

"Are you sure you understood him right?"

"Oh, yes; he told me over and over again."

They went on, miles it seemed to Frank in her alarm; there was no change in the road, no sign of any house, no friendly light from any quarter. At last, unable to control herself any longer, she exclaimed:

"Cuthbert, you must turn back; we have come three miles twice over—there is no sense in this."

"We shall soon come to the lane, Miss Warrington; it cannot be much further. Ah, there it must be now, by those big trees. And see! there's somebody waiting by the fence."

Frank's heart stood still; some one was waiting—it was Cyril, holding his horse by the bridle. He gave a

quick look up and down the road, then springing for
ward, said:

"Cub, go lead my horse about in the lane for a few
moments. I want to speak to Miss Warrington."

The young driver obediently quitted his place, and
taking the bridle from his brother's hand, led the horse
away down the lane.

"Frank," he said in a hurried tone, as soon as the
boy was out of hearing, "all this is without excuse, if
you cannot understand my love, my fears, the perplexity
and danger in which we are. I have anticipated your
consent, because it is my only hope of happiness; because I cannot live another day, and see you in the
position you now occupy. Once my wife, I can protect
you from all vexation; now I can only watch you
slighted, insulted, pained, without the right to interfere.
Think how I am placed, Frank! Remember I must
leave you in a week, neglected, unprotected—how can
I endure the thought! Do not hesitate; believe in me,
believe in my affection, which dares all, which is capable of all. At this moment it is in your power to make
me happy and yourself safe. We are within stone's
throw of a magistrate; he is waiting for us now. One
word, and all the doubt is over."

She had sunk back and hidden her face in her hands,
a tumult of emotions excited by his words and by the
strange position in which she found herself. Good
heavens! Four days ago, if any one had told her she
would now be on the eve of such a fatal step as this,
how incredulous she would have been! And yet, how
pledged she seemed to be to it; how far drawn in

already! It was useless to prolong the struggle, she felt within herself she had not the strength to resist this passion, of which she had allowed the declaration; she was reckless, bewildered, unbelieving: was there any right or wrong. Was it not all chance, destiny; she did not care. Yesterday she would have thought this trea son, sin; she would have felt, in all its magnitude, her fatal error. But now she had no faith, no heart to pray, and what availed remorse, anticipating her sin! She must go on and harden herself to meet the future; she must try to remember that the world would think she had triumphed and not fallen; that she would be above the pity and protection of the one who had deceived and disappointed her, that she would take the most complete revenge upon those who had humbled and insulted her; that in all views, save in the light of conscience, this marriage was advisable.

Fallacious reasoning, which only gave the strength of a momentary stimulant, and left the sickening lassi- tude of reaction when it passed away.

Cyril, calling Cuthbert to him hastily, charged him to lead the horse up and down the lane till he came back; then springing into the sleigh, he seized the reins, and turning into the lane, passed him at a rapid gait. At the end of half a mile, a fence terminated the lane, and beyond it a light shone from the windows of a little house almost buried in the woods that rose behind it. A more lonely habitation could not well be fancied; a fit place, indeed, it seemed, in which to bury such a dangerous secret.

But Cyril had no mind to give his companion time

for thought or for repentance; hastily securing the horse, he lifted her from the sleigh and led her to the little gate, whose latch, rusted with damp and covered with snow, resisted for a moment his impatient grasp. A narrow path, bordered on both sides with a high hedge of box-wood, overgrown and untrimmed, led to the porch, through the low window at the left of which, there gleamed an unsteady light. The snow was falling silently, the path was thick with it, the box-wood hedge was covered with it, and brushed its cold plumes in Frank's face and over her grey cloak, as Cyril half led, half drew her to the house.

"O heavens," she murmured, for an instant shrinking back as they reached the threshold, "what am I doing!"

Her companion whispered reassurance as he hurriedly pushed open the door and led her into a room, low and dim, only lighted by a lamp in the hand of a rough, dark looking man, of middle age, who turned half round as they entered, and gave them a grim salutation over his shoulder.

"Don't lose any time, Porter," said Cyril, as the man deliberately set the light down on a table, and looked fumblingly over a bunch of keys, as he went up to a thin-legged, old-fashioned writing desk in a corner. "We are late already."

He gave an anxious look at Frank's ashy face as he spoke, and the man, muttering something in an inaudible tone, pointed to a chair, and proceeded to take down an inkstand, some pens, and a sheet of paper. Frank shook her head, and grasped the mantel-piece for support.

while Cyril, hurrying across the room, poured out a glass of water and brought it to her.

Meantime, the man, pulling a chair up to the table, sat down by the light, put on a pair of spectacles, and looked slowly over the paper he had taken from the writing desk.

"You were to be all ready for us," said Cyril, in a tone of suppressed vexation. "Why do you delay?"

The magistrate deigned no reply beyond a kind of involuntary sniff, as he continued his perusal of the paper, and then stamped heavily upon the floor. This clumsy summons brought to the door a woman, lean, wrinkled, and sour-visaged, to whom he said, "Come in; I want you for a witness."

She was evidently used to being a witness, for she came in, pushed shut the door, and stood sulkily behind her master's chair, with no appearance of surprise or interest.

The magistrate cleared his throat, looked up over his spectacles, and asked, first of Cyril, and then of Frank, the usual legal questions.

"I cannot hear ye," he said, leaning his head forward to listen as Frank's lips moved, but no sound came from them.

Cyril's eyes, with burning anxiety, were on her face. He took her hand in his with mute entreaty. She released herself from him suddenly, took a step back, raised her head, and turning it towards the window listened eagerly.

There was a complete silence for a moment; as complete, alas, without as it was within; her imagination had played her false; with a stony look in her eyes, as she turned them from the window, she pronounced the fatal words of assent deliberately and distinctly, and heard and saw what passed after that as one hears and sees things in a dream.

She knew that Cyril put a pen into her hand, and that she wrote her name; that he gave money to the man, and many charges in a low and anxious voice; that he tossed a piece of gold towards the sour-faced, sulky witness, and that then, buttoning the paper up within his vest, he had led her out and down into the lane. His fond words were utterly unmeaning to her, his embrace gave her no thrill of pleasure or of fear; the lips he kissed were icy cold, the hand he held had no life in its clasp. The beautiful image was his, bound to him by indissoluble bonds; sacred to him and him alone; his, while there was life in it, and while he had life to claim it; man could never sunder them, God alone had power to make him lose his hold upon that for which he had sold his honor, his duty, and his hopes of fortune; but the heart, the soul that it enshrined, was far beyond his reach, never less his than when he called himself its master, never more intangible than when he tried to grasp it.

He held the gilded empty cage, but the bird fluttered against another breast, and pined its life away within another prison. All his love could not win it to him; all his will and strength were as unavailing for its capture.

CHAPTER XXXII.

THE CUYLER BALL.

" It is a bad game where nobody wins."

THE Cuyler ball was in the full blaze of its magnifi
cence when Frank made her way into the brilliant parlors. Mrs. Thorndyke, quite out of patience at her
tardiness, was waiting for her at the door.

"What has detained you so?" she said, in a tone of
irritation, as she led her to the hostess. "I have been
on the watch for you almost an hour. Did anything
happen?"

"We got out of the way—we took the wrong road,"
faltered Frank.

"That was just what might have been expected. I
could have told Cyril, Cuthbert was not to be trusted.
I do not know what Mrs. Cuyler will think of a young
person under my protection arriving at this hour."

Mrs. Cuyler bore it without much appearance of emotion however; only giving the young person an inquiring stare and an inclination of the head, as she was
brought up before her, named, and passed on into the
crowd by her chaperone. Two of the elder Miss Cuy
lers stood near their mamma, and also inclined their
heads as the young person introduced by Mrs. Thorndyke passed before them; and there the hospitable duty

owing to her was considered ended, and she was permitted to mix in the crowd, and take care of herse.f or
be taken care of, as the fortunes of war might be.   Mrs
Thorndyke also seemed to regard her duty ended, and
went off, with a very easy conscience, on the arm of an
old gentleman with a frowsy wig and an eye-glass, who
was telling her he considered her son the most distin
guished-looking person present.

Cyril, by very desperate riding, had reached the
house half an hour before Frank and Cuthbert, and was
now dancing with Stephanie, the gayest of the gay ; and
trying, by all his powers of dissimulation and all his
arts of flattery, to appease her curiosity about his late
appearance, and to atone for his breach of promise in
the matter of the redowas.   Emily was dancing too;
and Frank heard some people near her saying how fine
her dancing was, and how striking and stylish she looked
in full ball dress.

" A handsome pair she and young Thorndyke are,"
·said one.   " The engagement isn't denied any longer, l
believe."

" Why no, not denied exactly," replied some one with
the unmistakable Cuyler drawl, and Frank, half turu-
ing, recognised one of the budding series whom she had
seen at Ringmer.   " But Mrs. Thorndyke told mamma
the other day it would not be announced at present: not
till the war is over, I believe.   Things are so uncertain
in such times as these."

" Yes ; I don't blame Miss Emily for wishing to
defer it."

There was a little movement in the neighborhood;

and Mr. Richard Cuyler at that moment passing and discovering Frank, came up to her in a very gracious way, and, after a few moments' conversation with her, asked her if he should not get a partner for her.

No doubt it would have given Mr. Richard Cuyler very great pleasure to have danced with her himself, for he thought her by a great deal the best looking young woman in the room, but there were distinctions which he dared not overlook—*noblesse oblige*. A prince of the blood does not dance with anything below a duchess. It was all very well to allow himself the amusement of making pretty speeches to her, dining *en petit comité* at Ringmer, but on the occasion of a state ball in his own house, *c'était une autre paire de manches;* and Mr. Cuyler gave himself much credit for his strength of principle. The governess surprised him by declining the honor of a partner. She did not desire to dance that evening.

Mr. Cuyler regretted that, and talked with her a little longer, and then excused himself and went away. She hoped he would stay away. She coveted nothing so much as being forgotten and let alone; and she fell back a little way behind the people who were pressing forward to see the dancing, and leaned against a window that was partly open, and tried to feel that she could breathe, and that she was not suffocating in the warm and perfumed air. She turned away from the dancers, for she saw *her husband* only among all the other figures, and she dared not trust herself to look at him lest her eyes should betray her secret. Her over-wrought nerves and excited brain were fairly insubordi nate now, and she felt as if she were walking about in a dreadful nightmare, doomed to say and do what would be most fatal to her. When any one spoke her name, an almost ungovernable impulse seized her to say, "that is not any longer mine." When anything was said of Cyril, she could hardly keep herself from saying, "do you know I am married to that man?" She felt as if the guilty truth, swift-winged and piercing, sat upon her lips, ready to flutter forth if she but opened them. She wondered if she could be losing her senses, if such a thing were possible when she yet felt strong enough to combat it? She tried to test herself by recalling the most difficult rules in algebra she knew, and by conjugating an obstinate Latin verb; and was not satisfied even after she had accomplished the task, for perhaps she might think she was recalling them correctly, when, in truth, she was not; and judgment might be paralyzed, as it is in sleep; and perhaps there was no safety for her, surrounded by so many witnesses.

Suddenly she found Mr. Cuyler at her side again. He asked permission to present a gentleman who had desired the honor.

"I wish you would excuse me to him," she said, uneasily, drawing back.

Mr. Cuyler, giving her a glance of great amazement, was about to turn away, when the thought suggested itself to him, that probably the young person's ignorance of society and awkwardness among strangers prompted this bizarre behavior, and pausing, he said, he should regret disappointing the gentleman, who was a stranger just arrived in the vicinity, having brought letters to hem—a young officer from the Department of the West. No doubt Miss Warrington would find him entertaining, if she felt no personal objection to receiv-ing him as an acquaintance for the moment.

"Oh, none whatever," she said, recovering herself. "I shall be very glad to know him."

Mr. Cuyler bowed with the air of a man who under-stood the world, and in a few moments returned and presented the stranger.

Frank hardly looked at him. She saw he was middle sized and unremarkable in appearance, and a little stiff and constrained in manner, and felt that what he said was rather common-place and tiresome; but she tried to answer him with a decent regard to common sense, and to pay some sort of attention to his observations. At length, after some twenty minutes of this rather unsatis-factory intercourse, he said somewhat abruptly:

"Do you not find it very warm here? The other rooms are much less crowded."

She felt a sense of relief as she followed him into the hall, and, taking his arm, walked once or twice up and down it. There was a small room opening into the con-servatory that looked quiet and cool, and she assented to his proposal to take possession of it. They were some distance from the music now, and consequently from the crowd, which generally agrees to keep as near to it as possible, and have its senses stunned by the braying, and clashing, and strumming of instruments, originally devised for opera houses and concert halls.

The little room was entirely deserted, Frank found, after she had taken the seat her companion placed for

her, and she looked up a little uneasily to see what man
ner of person it was with whom she was in such familiar
tête-à-tête.   At the same moment he was looking at her
fixedly and with a curious expression.

"You do not remember me?" he said, in a voice
divested of its formality and constraint.

"No," she faltered, looking at him with a nervous
start, and then, fastening her eyes upon the ground;
she did remember him though, most distinctly, as he ·
went on ::

"You have a short memory, Miss Warrington, I am
afraid.   I don't think I'm as much changed as you are
since I had the pleasure of walking with you in the
evergreen avenue at Ringmer."   He paused.   "You
remember me now?"

She inclined her head and said, "Yes."

"You may recollect I said that day I should come
back before very long to get your answer to a question
I put you then.   I have come for it now."

There was a pause of several seconds, during which
she made no attempt to speak, and then he went on:

"I am not fool enough to try to get you by soft
words with such a rival in the field as the one you have
been listening to of late.   I know by the look in your
eyes I can't succeed that way.   But there's more than
one fashion of making love, though maybe you've never
known it, for all you've had so many sweethearts.   I've
come to marry you, and if I fail in it, it'll be the first
thing I ever failed in that I set myself about.   In the
first place, I've got the encouragement and consent of
the only person in the world that has any authority

over you ; but I don't count much on that, knowing you are too high-strung to submit to any law but your own will when you can possibly get round it.

"But, besides her encouragement and consent, I've got her orders, written out in her own hand, to the people that employ you, to send you home directly. For it is reported in Titherly, and currently believed, that you are not doing well, and that your connection with the Thorndyke family is no great credit to you. When I deliver that letter to Mr. Cyril Thorndyke's father, I think there'll be a scene perhaps. Then I've got another letter, one to show to Mr. Cyril privately by himself. It isn't to him, but it is to give him a little light.

"You see, he might not mind having for a sweetheart a girl that six months ago was starving in a city attic, whose drunken father had abandoned her, and whose relations were pretty nearly tired of taking care of her ; it don't make much difference, even to fine gentlemen like him, what sweethearts were once, as long as they're pretty and easy now ; sweethearts and wives are two different parts of speech, you know. But I've kind of an idea that he'll be rather black when he finds out how he has been put upon by this same sweetheart, and how six months ago everybody knew she was in love with some one else. And who ? Why nobody but the low-born friend whom he has taken to patronizing—so monstrous condescending—the self-made man whom he cries up so much, and than whom he feels so much better in his secret heart ! He might forgive him for 'most anything but that—getting the better of him in a love affair—for I take it Mr. Cyril is as vain as any man alive, and it'll be a bitter pill to him to find he's been breaking his neck to get a girl that Soutter jilted months before; and he'll chafe and fume a little when he comes to realize they've both been cheating him into believing they didn't know each other, and have been looking on and laughing at him maybe, while he played the gallant lover.

"I've got a little note here, as I said, that'll make it all clear to him; it's very short, on a crumpled, torn-up bit of paper, but it tells the whole story pretty plain, I think. He couldn't want anything much more directly to the point.

"And then, if all this don't do, you know, there's a few words can be added—a sort of embellishment, to be sure! but what won't a man do when he's desperately in love?—a few words that'll keep you from any decent home as long as I choose to breathe 'em; that'll make it hard for you to marry any other man, as I once promised you. And more than that—that'll make it hard for you to earn your daily bread by any honest means. A woman's reputation's a delicate sort of thing, you see, and it doesn't take many words from a man that's bent upon it to make it pretty black and worthless.

"Now, I say all this to you because I mean you tc know that I've got you in my power, and that I mean to use my power if you compel me to it; but if you don't, I'll be as good a friend to you as any one you've ever had. I won't promise you soft speeches such as Cyril Thorndyke gives you, but I'll be as good and kind a husband to you as you need to want, and I'll give you as I told you, money enough to make you fine, and let you have your own way in everything. Ah, you shiver! Well, I see you don't take kindly to it. Follow your own choice, then; but what I've said, I've said."

Frank sat with her face to the door, her companion with his back to it. Twice while he had been speaking Soutter had come up to it and gone away; just at this moment he repassed it again, drawn back involuntarily by the painful expression that he had caught upon Frank's face. She met his eye as she glanced up, and gave him for an instant such an imploring look that he entered the room and came towards her promptly. The other had not seen the look, having just at that instant, for the first time, taken his piercing eyes off her face and lowered them to the ground. He gave a little start and turned round as Soutter came up.

"Will you go to Mrs. Thorndyke a moment ?" he said, offering her his arm. "She is in the middle parlor."

She faltered an assent, and rising, followed him with an ill-concealed eagerness. Her companion rose also, and saying significantly "I will see you again this evening, Miss Warrington," he bowed and watched them leave the room, taking two or three turns across it, and then following them at a distance.

They walked silently into the hall towards the middle parlor, then back through the hall again. Frank was trembling from head to foot, as her companion had not failed to notice. He did not speak to her for several minutes, till, pausing by a stand of flowers at the entrance of the conservatory, he said abruptly :

"Frank, what can I do for you ? You are in some

16

dreadful trouble; I can't help seeing it. Why won't you let me be your friend?"

She withdrew her hand from his arm, and leaning against the pillar beside the entrance, she turned away her face.

"Yes, I am in a desperate trouble," she said in a smothered voice, "but you cannot do me any good. You could not even understand it."

"It must be something very strange in the way of suffering," he said with a bitter smile, "that I cannot understand. If you refuse to let me know your secret, of course I cannot force your confidence; but I must tell you this. I have determined to disregard your repulses of me, altogether. I will instruct myself about you, I will charge myself with the care of you, as far as it is in my power to do. I will not regard your coldness any longer. If you were happy and prosperous, I would submit without a word, you should never be troubled by the sight or thought of me; I would put distance and absence and silence between us to the end of time; I would satisfy you of my acquiescence. But it is different now. I see you miserable, harassed and threatened. I know you to be tempted and beset with dangers. I know you to be without a friend, not one friend, Frank, in all the people round you; and I will not listen to you when you tell me that you do not need my friendship. You do need it, and you shall have its offices whether you consent to them or not. What do you say? You resent it all? I cannot help it; I know my duty, and my right, to protect you, now and always, when you need my pity and protection ——"

"Your right?" she said, with a sudden flame of pride. "What right?"

"A right," he said, looking deep down into her eyes, "a right you gave me long ago, in the old days at Titherly, when we were little lovers; a right that every man has to serve and to protect any woman who has ever loved him, little or much, faithfully or ficklely."

"What," she said, starting back, "you dare remind me—you dare to boast ——"

"I dare," he answered in a low voice, "I dare anything to-night. I have been silent long enough. I warn you that my rôle is changed. I take upon myself to see that you are safer, if not happier, than you have been of late. You need not make any explanations to me; I shall master the mystery myself."

"Listen," she said, turning towards him with ashy lips and cheeks. "I forbid it. I deny I ever gave you any right to care what might become of me. I protest against your claims upon my friendship, and I absolve forever all ties that have connected us."

"That does not alter my resolve," he said between his teeth, as Cyril, catching sight of them, came up towards them. "You may be certain, from this hour, that I never lose sight of what concerns you, that you cannot dissolve the ties that have connected us, that your trouble is mine, and your error my disgrace."

"Come, Soutter," cried Cyril, joining them, "go to your friend, she is *desolée* because of your neglect; she is absent-minded, and her eyes are on the door continually, though I have worn myself out in flattering her.

I have told her it was nothing but your jealousy of Bell, but I don't think she quite believes it."

"Ah, you're kind to clear the way for my return," said Soutter, with a slight sarcastic coldness in his tone. But he did not move, and Frank, turning to Cyril, said hurriedly,

"I want to go up to the dressing-room, I've left my fan there," took his arm, and, without a look at Soutter, went towards the staircase.

Cyril said a great many things to her as they went up the stairs, but of them all, she only heard the few words that were prompted by a casual glance he gave back at Soutter, standing immovable where they left him.

"I do believe Soutter's fool enough to think that Bell is in his way. What folly, when any one not blind with jealousy can see the girl's in love with him to the last degree. I must set him right; I think they must have had a quarrel recently. I feel to-night," he added low, with a soft glance out of his brilliant eyes, "so generous towards all lovers, I would give them all such happiness as mine."

When they reached the dressing-room door, Frank paused and drew back, for Emily, sweeping out of it, gave her no room to pass, and offered no apology, but brushed by her without a glance, giving Cyril one of double malice though, instead. Cyril's brow contracted into an angry frown.

"I am tired of such scenes as these," he muttered.

"And so am I," said Frank, with a languid movement of her hands. "Go down stairs and pacify her I am going to stay up here awhile and rest."

An exclamation of entreaty burst from Cyril. "Every one can have more time with you than I: no one else is sentenced to such moments."

"But you know the reason; you know every minute you stay here is adding to my trouble. Leave me, and promise not to come near me again to-night."

He began a petulant remonstrance, which, catching sight of his mother coming from below, he cut short abruptly and turned away. Frank retired quickly into the room, quite aware that there was going to be a scene, for she heard Mrs. Thorndyke's voice in a tragedy pitch, summoning Cyril to her, and she caught the words, "this cannot go on any longer," and then Cyril's abrupt and decisive accents, too low to be distinguished, and then a sort of plaintive, querulous murmur, and then a long and earnest altercation, ending in the son's pleasant, careless laugh, and a sort of relieved sigh and ejaculation of satisfaction from the mother.

"Well, Cyril, you promise me," Frank distinguished as they turned to go down the stairs.

"Yes, mother, I promise you," he answered lightly, as they passed out of hearing.

CHAPTER XXXIII.

TWO SUFFERERS.

" Some murmur when their sky is clear,
    And wholly bright to view, .
If one small speck of dark appear
    In their great heaven of blue.
And some with thankful love are filled
    If but one streak of light,
One ray of God's good mercy, gild
    The darkness of their night."—TRENCH.

THERE was an alcove in the dressing-room, separated
from it by heavy crimson curtains, and Frank, weary
of the light and sight of people, retreated to it, dropping
one curtain and throwing herself into an easy chair.
By and by she heard the rustle of a dress, and some one
entered the recess without seeing her, dropped the other
curtain, and sank down into another chair, turned with
its back towards hers..

She listened silently, and heard first a heavy sigh,
and then a restless change of attitude, and then another
sigh. How well she knew that it meant an unappeas-
able pain, a suffering that was growing past control and
silence. Who could it be? She felt reproached when
she remembered she had fancied herself the only sufferer
in the gay crowd that night. Perhaps this unknown
comrade in suffering had been near her, passed her with
a smile in her eyes and with the mask of carelessness

upon her face ; they had not recognised each other then, they were each carrying out the prescribed and inevitable hypocrisy of self respect.

How many more of their fraternity they might find among the people laughing, dancing, talking noisily below. How many who would sigh and toss and moan, as soon as they had dropped the curtain between them and the world !

Half an hour passed, the first of partial distraction from her own troubles that Frank had had for many days. At last there came a lull in the sound of dancing below, a movement in the crowd that indicated supper, and struck with the danger of being missed if she prolonged her absence, Frank started up and drew back the curtain she had dropped ; at the same moment, struck, perhaps, by the same thought, her unknown companion sprang up and pulled back hers. There was an exclamation of astonishment as they stood face to face.

"Sainty !"

"Frank !"

A moment's silence followed, as they dropped the drapery over the recess and went slowly forward into the room, now deserted entirely, even by the maids, who were leaning over the balusters and gazing down upon the people in the hall below.

"Sainty," said Frank, abruptly turning to her, "I'm afraid we have both been so engrossed in ourselves of late that we have forgotten our interest in each other."

There was a moment's silence, and Sainty, self-condemned, gave a little sigh.

"What is it?" said Frank, earnestly looking in her face. "Sainty, what can make *you* unhappy? I never dreamed of your having real trouble! You have not been yourself since Christmas day. Tell me, are you really unhappy?"

A deep tinge of pink spread over her fair forehead, cheeks and throat, and then dying away, left them whiter than before. She was perfectly silent, never raising her eyes or attempting a reply ; an evasion or an effort to avert suspicion from what she had hoped, with woman's instinct, that she had concealed, would have been an impossibility to her Frank sighed, and dropped the hand she had taken.

"I ought not to expect it," she said. "Forgive me for asking you."

"At least," said Sainty, raising her lovely eyes, and putting her hand in Frank's, "at least we can be sorry for each other, for I am afraid we are both suffering very much, whatever may be the cause. I am ashamed of the discontent I have felt at what has come to me, when I know you have been silent so much longer, and borne so much more, no doubt. But I am so weak and childish, and have had so much happiness, you must not despise me. I am so ashamed of my ingratitude, when I *know* it is all right, all sent to help me to perfect myself. O, Frank, is it not strange we can ever doubt God's love! But, perhaps, you never did; you will tremble for me then, I fear, for I have found it in my heart to say my temptation was greater than I could bear, and my Lord was cruel to me! But the wicked thought is gone, thank God; it only stayed a moment, but it was worse than all the pain : all the rest seemed light and easy after it, and I know now I can bear any thing but that—*anything*, as long as God gives me the grace to feel it is His love and not His wrath, His yearning to make me fit for Him, and not His anger that I am unfit. Often since then, I have wondered if there were, indeed, poor souls, who bore that burden that I felt then for a moment, all their lives ; who never found out what God really meant, but were struggling always against His discipline, or bearing it sullenly and without His help. I have prayed for them and pitied them, till I have felt that I am almost happy in comparison."

A low groan escaped Frank, as she turned away. "Pray always for them, Sainty. God ought to hear *you*."

Cecilia looked wistfully and anxiously at her. There was always something she did not understand about her friend ; a depth she had not sounded, a recess into which she dared not look, and the last few weeks had deepened and darkened all. There was a few moments' silence, and then they went down stairs together.

Cyril, with his eyes always on the staircase, was talking to Emily and Stephanie, who were occupying themselves with ices and jellies at one end of the hall. Directly opposite sat Mrs. Thorndyke, engaged in conversation with that young officer from the Department of the West, introduced to the governess earlier in the evening. He also had his eyes on the staircase, but he looked another way when the two young ladies came in sight, and did not appear to notice them as they

16*

approached, but continued to listen with very flattering interest to Mrs. Thorndyke's conversation.

There was no one living who could be so easily worked upon by flattery as Mrs. Thorndyke. She had the craving for it that no lapse of years can extinguish in the heart of an educated beauty. From the stable-boy up, she expected homage and admiration from every member of her family. She was discontented without it, though she received it passively, and without an actual consciousness that it was what she wanted. In society she was almost always satisfied; for she was still so beautiful and imposing in appearance, and so gracious and queenly in manner, that she was admired even by the people who understood her, and never failed to produce a marked impression upon those who saw her for the first time. On that evening, Mr. Cuyler, when he asked permission to present Captain Donelson, had taken pains to add, he should not have thought of doing it if the gentleman had not requested it so earnestly; and then he had enlarged a little upon the gentleman's merits and good standing in the army, the highly favorable letters he had brought them, his recent participation in several brilliant actions, and his claims, in short, to being something of a lion. Mrs. Thorndyke had graciously consented to allow the introduction, and in ten minutes had been so entirely carried away by his adroit pretensions that she wondered in her heart that the world did not ring with the name of Captain Donelson.

So patriotic, so gallant, with such an appreciation of the character and influence of woman, Mrs. Thorndyke felt that she was securing for herself a place in history when she made herself the patroness of this young man. She invited him, *sur-le-champ*, to dine with her next day; and she told him that while he was in the neighborhood he must consider Ringmer open to him as a second home. She had always prided herself upon her power of discriminating character, and upon a large-minded rejection of conventionalities when the occasion required; which was very natural, as those were the two points upon which she was more particularly weak than upon any others.

She introduced Cyril to him, and made him reiterate the dinner invitation; she went in with him to supper; she entertained him graciously with her civilest chit-chat and with her best-bred views of things; and she pronounced him, when she went up to say good-night to Mrs. Cuyler, as a young man of uncommon promise and of wonderful intelligence.

"Cecilia," said Frank, in a low voice, as she put on her cloak, "can you not manage to let me ride back in the sleigh with you? I am afraid to go with Cub, it is so dark, and Cub is so inexperienced. But don't say anything, of course"——

"I understand," returned Cecilia. "I will arrange it for you without making Cub feel badly."

Poor Cub's feelings, however, were not the only ones to suffer in the arrangement. Cyril looked dark and lowering enough, and Emily·and Stephanie were both out of temper at having their flounces crushed. Captain Donelson put Mrs. Thorndyke in the sleigh. She said to him the last thing, "Half-past five to-morrow even

ing, Captain Donelson." And as he closed the door of
the sleigh and bowed to Frank, he said, "Half-past five
to-morrow evening then, Miss Warrington," in a sufficiently unmeaning manner, but with a significance
which she could not but understand.

She would not dare to fail at dinner. She would not
dare to say one word to awaken the suspicions of his hosts
about the character of their guest. She must even be
guarded and civil in her manner to him, or she would
pull the ruin down upon her head outright. Anything
to gain a little time. With dogged and sullen determination she set herself to find some way out of this tangled labyrinth; steadfastly resolved to give no room to
fancy or regret, and to conquer herself while she conquered her adverse fate. Occasionally Cecilia's words
came to her mind, but she put them from her hurriedly.
What had they to do with such a case as hers? What
did Cecilia know of real suffering? She was miserable,
no doubt, about some trifling sin, or harassed about
some paltry point of conscience. She understood no
more what trial and what sin meant than the birds and
the butterflies understand them. It was folly to take
warning or take comfort from such innocence as hers.

CHAPTER XXXIV.

CAPTAIN DONELSON AT RINGMER.

"*Julia.* The strait
I'm fallen into my patience cannot bear !
It frights my reason, warps my sense of virtue !
Religion !—changes me into a thing
I look at with abhorring !"—*The Hunchback.*

THE next day passed on uneventfully. The charades that Frank and Cecilia had arranged were talked over, rehearsed a little, and prepared for putting on the stage the following night. A number of invitations for the occasion had to be written out, which fell to Frank's lot to do, also a good deal of basting, and pasting, and contriving of dresses, which work was shared by Cecilia and Marcelle. In the making of pasteboard crowns, gilt paper knee-buckles, sword-hilts and decorations, there was a good deal of promise, and preparation, and consultation in the library below, between Emily and Stephanie, and the gentlemen ; but most of the work came back unfinished and imperfect, and Frank spent the late hours of the afternoon, while the others all went off to ride, in completing and repairing it.

There were two motives, perhaps, for her untiring application to this duty ; one was an eagerness for any occupation that would keep her from herself, and the other was a sort of self-reproach, that was eased a little

by any exertions in behalf of those whom she was
deceiving, and for whom she was preparing such dis
tress. She saw more clearly every hour what Cyril's
persuasions had blinded her to at first. She doubted no
longer that his marriage would occasion a terrible scene
with his mother, and bitter opposition from his father
that Cecilia would be thunder-struck, stunned, pained
beyond expression by it, and that whatever might have
been their previous feelings towards her, the manner of
her marriage would outrage them all.

Why had she not seen all this before? Why had she
allowed herself to be hurried into what she saw so
clearly now was the worst and wildest thing she could
have done? There was one ameliorating clause, Cyril's
love, which was at least *frappé au bon coin*, and which
promised to bear its mark through every test of opposition; but how long could she count upon it after he
had learned she had deceived him? For deceit it
was, she dared not deny it to herself. She had never
told him that she loved him. She had assured him
over and again that she had no love to give him; but
she had not told him she loved his friend with a strength
of passion that had grown with her daily growth, that
had never fastened, through all her life, on any other
object; that had helped to make her what she was,
self-contained, silent, stronger than other women, and
less dependant on friendship and on sympathy. It
would not be Cyril Thorndyke's vanity alone that would
be hurt. She knew his love went through his whole
nature, and that it was, in its ungoverned way, as strong
and inextinguishable as her own. She foresaw with a

thrill of dread, both for himself and her, the horrors of the moment when he should learn the truth—when he should pass through the same fierce tempest in which her happiness had been wrecked six months before. Ah! she was giving him the same bitter cup to drink that Louis had given her, and that he would in turn pass on to Emily. In his case as in hers, the dreadful awakening had been prefaced by a short mockery of happiness. What would the result be? How would the blow fall on his more ill-governed nature? It was impossible to imagine him forgiving, and, with a large-hearted tenderness, still loving her unselfishly; he was selfish even in his love, he would be selfish even in his despair. No doubt he would cast her off, separate himself from her forever, and hurry into all manner of mad excesses to obliterate the memory of what she had made him suffer. Ah, of how many dire entanglements death might at that moment cut the knot!

Mrs. Thorndyke's embryo hero came to dinner, as did Mr. Richard Cuyler. The hero was rather uneasy and constrained in conversation, and the more dashing young people at the table pronounced him something very *outré*, and Mr. Thorndyke humphed contemptuously when his name was mentioned afterwards; but Mrs. Thorndyke continued to think him a young officer of the highest promise, and to patronize him in a most marked manner.

They played at cards during the evening, and she designated him as her partner, also inviting Major Soutter to the table, while fate completed the quartette by placing Frank there also. The captain certainly played a capital game of whist; the very touch of the cards seemed to inspire him with self-confidence and ease, and Mrs. Thorndyke looked at him with growing admiration. Major Soutter was preoccupied and silent, but Frank saw his eye on his neighbor occasionally with a sharp and curious steadiness, and a gleam of sudden nterest lighted it for an instant, as by some unexpected turn of luck the stranger was betrayed into a slang ejaculation, savoring more of faro than of whist. He caught himself up quickly, and cast a glance around the table to see if it had been noticed; but Major Soutter's eyes were on his cards, and Mrs. Thorndyke seemed perfectly unconscious.

After the game—a most prolonged one—was completed, the captain, intent upon one of another and a less familiar sort, made a thousand uneasy efforts to speak alone with Frank; but in avoiding this, she was aided by the apparent dullness of Major Soutter, who began to talk to her about the probable duration of the war and the probabilities of foreign intervention, as if they were the two matters most interesting to her in the world. In fact, he talked with such emphasis, and engaged her so entirely, that, without great rudeness, she could not have given Captain Donelson the attention he seemed bent upon obtaining.

At length, Mr. Cuyler rose and took his leave, asking the captain if they should not ride on together. The captain had no alternative but to accept his proposition, and also rose, making his adieux with considerably less ease than he had shown in dealing out the cards. Mrs. Thorndyke reminded Mr. Cuyler of his engagement fo'

.the following evening, and told Captain Donelson they should be very happy to see him also. Both gentle-men expressed their acceptance in the most amiable manner, and when the door closed after them, Frank drew a long breath of relief, and Major Soutter stopped talking about the chances of intervention.

When Cyril came back into the room, Soutter asked, " Where's that man staying, and what's his business in the neighborhood ?"

Cyril believed his business was in relation to the establishment of a camp of instruction somewhere in the county, but he was not sure. He was staying at the Bluff House at Taunton, if he remembered right. He had apparently interested himself very little in his mother's protégé, and he turned carelessly from the subject, as if it bored him a good deal to have to think up any facts regarding it.

The next day was pretty much dedicated to the per-fecting of the charades; there was a dress rehearsal in the morning, and the afternoon was occupied in com-pletion of the costumes and the erecting of the stage. Cyril assumed the care of this latter duty himself, allowing nobody but Frank to assist him in the direction of the men, the draping of the curtains, the adjustment of the impromptu scenery, and the arrangement of the footlights. All this seemed very right and proper, as upon Frank had come all the work and direction of the affair; for Cecilia, as Cyril observed, had no head, and the other two young ladies found theirs full of other things. They were delighted to cut paper stars with the assistance of the gentlemen, and tumble over pretty things to suit themselves with ornaments, and practice attitudes before the glass; but that was a very different affair from planning and cutting and contriving up stairs in the nursery, with the assistance of Marcella. Frank had kept herself so busy in that apartment, and had given Cyril so much to do himself down stairs, that things really seemed to be going on very smoothly and commonplacely, and Mr. Rosenbaum was beginning to feel strong hopes that the pacific solution might yet be brought about. He had rather dropped his offensive manner towards Soutter, having got a little the worst of it on one or two occasions; but he continued to speak of him always in a slighting tone, that Cyril no doubt would have resented strongly if he had not been too much preoccupied to give it his attention.

In fact, plotting and counterplotting of the darkest nature might have been going on at Ringmer, and this young lover would not have surmised their existence; a stolen interview once or twice a-day in the school-room, a message delivered at the nursery door, a word passing on the stairs, a cleverly contrived neighborhood at table; these were the subjects of his thoughts and plans, the engrossing interests of his days. No wonder that the plans and interests of his companions were forgotten, and that he was blind to all that was going on around him.

And there was a good deal going on around him— enough to have excited the interest of a more unselfish man. No one could look thoughtfully at Cecilia now and fail to see that some change had come over her innocent and happy life; there was a languor in her step

a look of suffering about her mouth, a startled and ner
vous restlessness of manner, all new and unnatural to
her; she was going through some strong trial, and yet,
surrounded by her family, environed by kindness and
protection, she was all alone; no one saw, pitied or
comprehended; an old tale, and often told; the daughter, the sweet bud of a household, burst into sudden
womanhood, and drooping, "blinded by the shining
eye" of noon, while those who think that they are watching, fancy fondly that the dews of morning are still cool
upon its heart.

Even Stephanie, that short-lived tropic blossom, had
flowered into rapid maturity almost as unheeded. She
had come to Ringmer a foolish, ill-taught, gay, young
girl; she would leave it, when the fortnight of her promised visit was at an end, a woman, with her strongest
passions developed, her worst feelings brought into dangerous play. The change was great in her; the mischievous, elfish spirit that had danced in her eyes when
she first found herself in these strange, new scenes, had
given place to a gleam that was far less innocent though
no less dazzling; the intuitive passion for intrigue had
abandoned its aimless, merry play, and now had an end
and a design. And Emily, a little while ago so ungoverned, so ill-judging, was fast learning from her desperate position, discretion and the finer arts of war. She
was less openly insulting to her rival, she ceased to
oppose and nettle Cyril by her constant appearance of
disdain; but her jealousy and her malice had not gone
to sleep.

Rosenbaum, mistaking this for satisfaction and a

growing confidence in the good faith of Cyril, found himself much easier in mind, and gave himself up to the pursuit of the one engrossing object that had brought him to Ringmer, and that he was resolved he would not leave without achieving. He had not forgotten Bell and his entanglements, but he was quite man of the world enough not to embarrass himself with the trou bles of his neighbors; he was prepared to do his part, when the time came, as second in the affair; and, to do him justice, he would have taken the prospect of bearing the principal rôle with almost as much nonchalance. He was a thoroughly courageous man, cool by nature, steady nerved and self-confident, and a life of travel and adventure had added very much to his philosophy and his easy views of life.

To Bell, on the contrary, brought up in the tramelled routine of a city life, a petted and important member of an exclusive and narrow-minded family circle, the thought of risking himself in such an unequal engagement was fairly distracting and unbearable. He felt as if it were an outrage that he should be compelled to do it; it seemed to him a danger of such vast proportions, involving such a heavy damage to the interests of mankind; he could not understand that it could look less deplorable from any other point of view, and upon merely moral and philosophic grounds, he tried to convince himself that he was justified in attempting to evade it. But, there was the code of honor; how to get over that! He was in a most embarrassing position—in fact, he was quite distracted by his doubts, and he had no one to confide in but Stephanie. He dared not name his misgivings to Rosenbaum, and he had promised not to speak to Cyril; but he obtained a ready listener and a gentle sympathizer in the little French girl, with whom he found himself each day more despe·rately in love.

He was quite well persuaded too that she returned his passion, though she made him furiously jealous upon every possible occasion, and led him altogether a most harassing chase. He even began to argue with himself that he had no right to plunge her into such hopeless grief as his untimely fate would cause her; having gained her heart so inadvertently, could he with any conscience throw himself away and leave her to despair? But, though ungenerous and unmanly, it was sanctioned, alas! by the inexorable code, which all gentlemen must square their conduct by. He began to think honor was a hard master, and society a most ungrateful brute.

her a feeling almost of affection towards him. And when the curtain fell and the sound of loud applause came from the audience, and " again, again," was per-sistently repeated, and all the others prepared them-selves for a repetition, she turned to him and whispered,

" I cannot do it, you must save me. It is more· than I can bear."

Soutter saw her pleading look and the gesture of ten-derness and protection with which Cyril leaned down and whispered his reply. It was a reassurance, for she gave a sigh of relief as he started forward, and throwing off his theatrical look, exclaimed,

" A second time would spoil it ; I vote we decline to gratify them."

" Nonsense," cried Bell, who felt that his appearance had contributed very much to the success of the picture, and who was, moreover, in favor of all acting that did not involve talking. " Nonsense, I say let 'em have it as often as they want it."

" Why yes, Thorndyke, it will ·be hardly civil to say no," said Rosenbaum, adjusting his white wig and straightening his knee buckles.

" But you see," said Cyril, perplexed, as host, how to get out of it, " that moonlight must not be examined ; I'm really afraid we shall ruin all by a second exhi bition."

" It is capital," said Rosenbaum. " It will bear five minutes' scrutiny ; besides, no one looks at the sur-rouudings with Miss Warrington's splendid *pose* in sight."

Miss Warrington, pale and agitated, was feeling cer

tain she was ruined if the controversy went against her.
Cyril looked anxious, and tried in vain to get out of the
embarrassment, without calling attention to her, while
the importunity of the audience increased and the
remonstrances from the actors redoubled.

"I agree with you, Thorndyke," said Soutter, coming
forward and throwing off his military cloak. "It is
better to let well alone; we are out of the spirit of it
now. My arm is stiff with holding out this warrant at
you, and I am certain you have struck your forehead
till it is black and blue. I will make them a speech
to pacify them, while you get things ready for the next
charade."

There was something in Soutter's manner, good-
natured and easy as it always was, that carried with it
an assurance that he knew what he was about, and
meant exactly what he said, and though there was a
murmur of dissatisfaction among the dramatic corps, as
they relinquished their cherished attitudes, no one
thought of offering any further opposition as he stepped
out before the curtain, and making a little bow, and
then a little pause, began with the inevitable "Ladies
and gentlemen."

Frank knew very well it was to spare her he had conquered his repugnance to publicity, and the consciousness of his care for her gave her a quick sense of pleasure, and then a sharp pang of penitence. It had
become, within these two fatal days, a sin for her to
think of him at all, a sin to hope he ever thought of her.
She turned away her head, and tried not to hear what
he was saying to the people in the other room, that

called forth such laughing and applause, but his fine voice was too clear and decided, and her own ear too quick and hungry, for her to miss a syllable.

"Upon my word, Thorndyke," said Mr. Rosenbaum, in a low tone, listening attentively, "the stump seems to be quite your friend's vocation."

"I've always told you," said Cyril, his enthusiasm heightened by a warm sense of gratitude at being helped out of a tight place—"I've always told you he was equal to anything he undertook, and I never saw anything yet he was afraid to undertake. You'll hear of him before the war is over, you may take my word for it."

"I have heard of him," said Rosenbaum, dryly. "In fact I may say I have heard of no one else for the past eight days."

Cyril turned away a little impatiently, and began to give his orders for the clearing of the stage. Soutter's speech lasted, as did the favor of the listeners, till the next charade was ready, and then he made the short and rather stiff little bow which was habitual to him and went back behind the curtain.

The next charade was a very patriotic one, and teemed with stars and stripes, cannon, contrabands, and all the accompaniments of conquest; and after it was over the audience clamored for a speech again, and Soutter again, but with reluctance, went out before the curtain. This time he took the cue from the charade just acted, and trod on the edge of the sensational.

All American audiences, in 1861, whether political or social, were smouldering volcanoes, which needed but a well-directed touch to burst out into flaming patriotism

Soutter spoke always simply, but with a good deal of
strength and vigor. His language was remarkably unornamented, pure and literal almost as a foreigner's, and
was a great contrast to the slangy and extravagant style
of his high-bred contemporaries. His manner was as
unpretending, but his bearing was extremely soldierly,
and there was to-night a smothered enthusiasm in his
eye that belied his cool language and his controlled ges-
tures. His wit was always so good-natured, his ease
was so unassuming, that he was an instant favorite,
without an effort, in whatever society he found himself.
Without wanting in self-respect, he appeared entirely
unconscious of himself; and without lacking respect
for others, he seemed entirely unembarrassed by their
presence. Whatever he had to say he said happily and
easily, and whatever he did he did without effort, and
without looking to the effect.

He spoke now with an earnestness and resolution
that would have surprised him had he stopped to review
his words as he went on. He only remembered he was
speaking to Americans—men and women whose hearts
warmed as his did at sight of the dear old flag, to-night,
indeed, their plaything, but to-morrow, if need be, their
guide to danger and to death. His heart was unselfish
with the love of country, that had been growing stronger
and truer ever since the clouds began to gather over her
happiness and honor. The weary march, the wrangle
of the camp, the distance of the goal, never had dis
heartened or unnerved him. He had counted the cost
before he began the enterprise. Till he was stretched
dead upon her soil he had not paid what he knew was

due to her; and all that came short of that was not
worth the name of sacrifice. He did not need victory
to kindle his love for her, or to sustain his courage in
her service, any more than he would have needed to see
his mistress always crowned with flowers, laughing and
happy, in holiday attire, to keep him true to her. There
was a quick gleam from his eye, and a smothered fer-
vor in his voice, that told his love of country was the
real feeling of his soul, and not a fine sentiment to talk
about. There was a storm of applause when he stopped
abruptly, and, making the stiff little bow, went out of
sight behind the curtain. If there could have been a
recruiting office opened on the spot, it is probable there
would have been several volunteers added to the available force of the United States that night.

The audience were not contented with applauding
once; they called him back again and got another little
bow, and Stephanie threw her bouquet to him, and so did
one or two others. And then they called for Sally, the
barmaid, and would take no refusal. So Soutter went
back behind the scenes, and said, going up to where she
sat, languidly leaning back against a pile of shawls and
screens, "Frank, they want you: you'll have to come
for a minute."

She had not yet taken off her jaunty cap and apron;
but her hair was out of order, and she looked so pale
and haggard, as she rose and followed him in a docile
sort of way, that he said, stopping and looking at her
as they reached the stage:

"Can't you put back your hair? It has fallen from
under your cap. There is no hurry."

She pushed it back and smoothed it mechanically, and said, "will that do?" in a patient, humble tone, that made him turn away his head with a sigh, as he said, "Yes," giving her his hand, and leading her out before the curtain.

There was a great deal of applause, and one or two bouquets. Soutter picked them up and gave them to her as nonchalantly as if he had been used to the foot-lights all his life, and led her off the stage just as pale and unnatural-looking as when he led her on.

"Stop a moment, Frank," he said, as they regained the now deserted stage. "You dropped this note out of one of your bouquets. I saw who threw it; and I suppose you can guess, without opening, who it comes from."

She put out her hand for it, with a distressed, flushed look.

"I want to ask you one thing: do you desire to be rid of this spurious captain, who torments you so? I mean, without doing anything yourself—without provoking him in any way. You have only to say the word, and I can send him out of the country in an hour."

"But he would suspect, he would revenge himself," said Frank, eagerly and anxiously. "He could do all the mischief, too, before he went."

"He will have enough to do to take care of himself if I choose to set the police upon his track," Soutter answered.

"Are you sure? There is enough to make it safe?"

"Perfectly sure. I have ascertained enough to-day to rid society of him for the next ten years at least."

"But would it not involve—could he not—I mean—revenge himself by an—an exposure?"

"You must be the judge of that," said Soutter, with a sad and thoughtful look at her troubled face. "You know best what injury he has it in his power to do you."

Frank uttered a low groan and turned her face away. There was a moment's pause, and then he said:

"This much I can do: I can start measures for his arrest, and then give him warning enough to effect a hurried flight. That will save you for the present. It can be but temporary. You know best if the relief is worth the risk."

"Yes, yes," said Frank, with an eager movement of her hands. "I don't look beyond the present; any thing to gain a little time; anything to rid me of him for a week—a month."

"Very well," he said, laconically. "It shall be done."

She caught sight of his clouded face, the stern contraction of his brow, as he turned away, and she put out her hand involuntarily to call him back.

"You cannot understand," she began; and then she stopped, and hung her head. What could she say to justify herself, what explanation that would do any good! She could not tell him that she had only to dread the man's false statements, for there was bitter truth in what he had to say. She dared not tell him that the worst accusation that he had to bring against her was her love of him; that the thing most dangerous to her in the world was in his possession, and that was the letter she had written to *him* when she believed he was her true and honest lover; she dared not tell him she was married to a man whose jealous fury would respect neither wife nor friend if once the fatal secret reached him; she could not tell him she was miserable but innocent, for she was miserable and sinful to a point she dared not credit in her thoughts.

"No," he said, with a sigh, waiting for her to speak, "I cannot understand, and I do not ask to. Only be sure you understand yourself and have the courage to act as if you had no judge short of Heaven. It is never too late there, whatever it may be below."

"It is too late for me," she said, as she turned away from him. "I am less afraid of my judgment here than there."

CHAPTER XXXVI.

MAJOR SOUTTER SPENDS A DAY IN THE SADDLE.

"La parole est d'argent, le silence est d'or."

MAJOR SOUTTER left the house on horseback soon after breakfast the next morning, and did not return till nearly dinner time. Captain Donelson did not visit Ringmer that evening, nor the next, and on the morning following, Cyril entertained the breakfast table with the subjoined extract from the local newspaper:

"The citizens of —— county have reason to congratulate themselves upon a narrow escape from tremendous imposition. It will hardly be credited by our readers that we have, for more than a month, been harboring in our midst one of the most notorious scoundrels in the land. His object in choosing —— as a retreat can hardly be accounted for, as his operations here have been of a very limited character, compared with the enormous frauds in which he was concerned before his 'ast incarceration in State prison, from which place he escaped about two years ago, and since which time he has eluded the constant vigilance of our indefatigable police. He came into the neighborhood about the middle of November, and, under an assumed name, stayed quietly at the Lion Inn at B——. From thence he disappeared, without exciting any suspicions in the

mind of the very intelligent and obliging landlord of
that tavern, and nothing was known or surmised further
concerning him, till a peculiar train of circumstances
led to his identification with a young officer recently
arrived in the vicinity, and putting up at the Bluff
House, Taunton. His disguise was complete, and no
clue to his *alias* could have been discovered, but for the
persevering efforts of a distinguished military gentleman, whose name we are not at liberty to reveal.
Suffice it to say, that by his exertions the villain was
identified beyond a doubt, that the police were instantly
apprised of his whereabouts, that the news was flying
by telegraph all over the State, when suddenly it was
discovered, that by some underhand agency, he had
been admonished of his danger, and had been assisted
to escape. The greater part of his papers must have
been upon his person, for he never returned to the
hotel, and those discovered in his room throw but little
light upon his recent designs and actions. They are
now, however, in the hands of the authorities, and will,
we have no doubt, lead in a very short time to his
arrest, and to a full revelation of all the imposition
in which he has been engaged. . . . much, we are
liberty to state, was gathered . . . . . of the letter
found in his apartment, for h . . . . some desig
that necessitated an accompl . . . . planned
leave the Bluff House secretly . . . . the 8
of January, that a carriage was . . . . . .
horses were to meet him at diff . . .
road from here to the suburbs of th
sage had been obtai

the steamer sailing for Hamburgh on the following day. The accomplice, it is believed, can easily be identified, and, for the comfort of the timid, it may bo added, there is little doubt of the ultimate detection of the principal offender. The occurrence, in any event, will be long remembered in our neighborhood; the presence of such a daring impostor, and tho circumstances of his detection will invest the Bluff House with a sort of historic interest; and the room will long be pointed out from whence the redoubtable Captain Donelson so mysteriously disappeared."

"Captain Donelson!" exclaimed, faintly, Mrs. Thorndyke.

"Captain Donelson!" echoed Stephanie, Emily, Bell, Rosenbaum, and the children, in various notes of astonishment, incredulity, merriment, and alarm.

"Yes, Captain Donelson," said Cyril, with a laugh, throwing down the paper. "That promising young officer, that illustrious young hero! I feel invested with a sort of historic interest myself; I have shaken hands with him several times, I have taken wine with him, I have carved him a slice of mutton, I have offered him caper sauce, I have, in fact, on various occasions, been excessively polite to him!"

"And oh!" cried Stephanie. "Do you remember! He gave me a rose the other evening. I have it up stairs in water, I shall keep it always!"

"Well, I never heard of anything more extraordinary," exclaimed Bell. "Though I always thought his manners were confoundedly low; still, such letters as he brought; it was amazingly clever of the scamp!"

"What will the Cuylers say!" ejaculated Emily.

"It is all a malicious fabrication. I have not the least faith in it," said Mrs. Thorndyke, slowly and with dignity.

"What will papa say to you, mamma?" said Cammy. "He always snubbed the captain so."

"I do not see any necessity for mentioning it to your father," said Mrs. Thorndyke, uneasily. "He can see it for himself in the paper, if he reads it."

Cammy did not mean it should escape his attention by any chance however, for she only waited till the paper was laid down to catch it up, and slip off quietly to the library with it.

"Well," said Emily, "I congratulate myself upon knowing a gentleman when I see him. I always thought him an ill-bred creature, and I never spoke to him after the day he dined here."

"Well, I did," said Stephanie. "And more than that, I flirted with him a little, I believe. And I promised to sing for him the next time he came. O, I wish he would come again. I so much ambition such a conquest. Don't you think he was handsome, M. Bell?"

Bell scorned to answer, and Mr. Rosenbaum said, in his pleasant, well modulated voice, looking curiously at Frank as he spoke, "I think, Miss Clèrambeau, you are hardly justified in hoping for that conquest. I think Miss Warrington would have something to say about it. I always fancied her the object that particularly attracted him to Ringmer. Is it not so, Miss Warrington?"

Frank rallied suddenly; she had felt a moment before

as if she could not command her voice, if she were obliged to speak, but the taunting look in the questioner's eye showed he had been watching her, and the sense of danger roused her.

"Why, as to that," she said, with a little laugh, "it's not for me to decide, but I'm afraid he was flirtatious if he gave Miss Clèrambeau a rose and paid her compliments, for he certainly said some very amiable things to me at various times, and he threw me a bouquet the night of the charades."

"If I'd suspected that, by thunder," cried Cyril, with a rash and jealous impatience, "I'd have invested myself with a perfect halo of historic interest by turning him out of doors, and horse-whipping him as soundly as he deserved. The scoundrel! Who'd have guessed it! I saw he was an uncouth fellow, but I never dreamed of his daring to play the fascinating in society. Why did you not tell me of it?"

His eye fell on Frank, but he transferred it rapidly to Stephanie.

"I did not tell you, M. Cyril," said Stephanie, with malice, making a courtesy to him as she joined the circle by the fire, "because I did not consider you my special defender. I know not what Miss Warrington's reasons were."

"Miss Warrington, what were your reasons, may I ask?" said Cyril, trying to be off-hand and easy as he addressed her.

"Why," said Frank, with naïveté, "I do not believe I had any. I really never thought of telling any one"

There was a half-hour more of discussion and wonder-ment, during which Frank escaped to her room, feeling almost dizzy with the sudden sense of relief from an impending peril, and yet wondering in her stubborn heart from which side the next danger would arise.

CHAPTER XXXVII.

TWELFTH NIGHT.

"Is there a bitter pang for love removed .
O God ! the dead love doth not cost more tears
. Than the alive—the loving, the beloved—
Not yet, not yet beyond all hopes and fears !
Would I were laid
Under the shade
Of the calm grave, and the long grass of years."

IT was the evening of the sixth of January. The day had been glittering and glorious, a true winter sun and earth, and a rare brisk, bracing air. There had been a six-horse sleigh-ride in the morning, and a luncheon party at a neighbor's about ten miles distant. Every one had gone from Ringmer, down to the children, even Mrs. Rosenbaum, who hated sleigh-riding and was languidly averse to luncheon parties, had been seduced into consenting by the brilliancy of the sunshine and the good spirits of the party; and the day had been hilarious, quite a fitting one to terminate the visit. For on the morrow, the party were to separate and go their several ways, the army men to rejoin their regiment, the Rosenbaums to the city, and Stephanie back to the onely old country home of which she so devoutly loathed the memory.

The original plan had been to wind up the festivities

with a merry Twelfth Night entertainment; old games had been revived, and all the ancient customs of the night were to have been carried out *de rigueur;* but there had been a great deal of languor in the matter on the part of all concerned. Cyril was moody and indifferent, and only took it up from duty; Emily impatiently rejected it; Bell seemed to have no heart for anything but carrying Stephanie's shawl, turning over her music, and picking up her handkerchief; and the rest of the company were equally indifferent; so it was generally agreed that the Twelfth Night party should be given up, and the Twelfth Night consecrated to sentiment and music, *en petit comité.*

The luncheon and the sleigh-ride had worn out all their spirits, and every one dressed for dinner, even the most careless ones, feeling vaguely depressed and weary. Frank had almost as much reason for uneasiness as before, for the next day must force her to a decision of some kind: either she must consent to an avowal, of which she did not feel strength to bear the consequences, or she must submit to the beginning of a life of hypocrisy, from which she turned with loathing. Cyril must go; he had pushed his stay up to the very limits of his leave. She knew he would not consent to never hearing from her, and there would ensue a course of deceit about their letters which seemed perfectly revolting to her. He himself seemed driven to desperation by the perplexities of his position. While, in all the hurried moments they had had together, he had pled and reasoned with her on the advantages of an open and immediate acknowledgment, she had not failed to see, by his very vehemence, that he was trying to convince himself as well as to persuade her. That he dreaded it, now that it was near, more than he had while it was distant, she felt instinctively; he was nervous, impatient, moody, unable to bear the thought of leaving her, and incapable of facing the storm that his announcement would inevitably raise. Her own cool common sense warned her that there was but one safe course, that that was the sharpest and hardest and fullest of immediate pain. Their marriage should be instantly acknowledged, let the consequences be what they might; she should then stand honestly with the world, and would be taking the first step towards an atonement to the family whom she was now deceiving.

But there was in her heart a cruel shrinking from avowing that which she could not feel was irrevocable while it was only a formal legal bond; so many things might free her from the humiliation of obeying it, if a long separation were decided on. If either of them died, it fell to the ground unheeded, a harmless secret, sparing a world of misery to others. If absence tested his love too strongly, and he sought to avoid its fulfillment, she would only too gratefully accept the release, and live out the miserable remnant of her days in obscurity and penitence. There had come the terrible reaction of remorse, and she no longer felt herself strong enough to live calmly in the eyes of the world the wife of a man she could not love and did not honor while her guilty heart refused to forget its early, only passion. She had fancied, while she only distantly reviewed the scheme, that she could conquer her lf

enough to live so, quite dead in feeling and quite
strong in purpose; that the pride of silencing her ene
mies. and the ambition of a higher place than they,
might serve to satisfy her soul and fortify it against
recollection. But she had deceived herself, she had
overrated her strength; she found herself now, on the
threshold of her new life, a miserable, heart-broken
woman, the slave of a love she had thought subdued,
the victim of a passion she could not fight against.
With all her faults, strong in proportion as her character was strong, with the grave error that was turning
her whole life to bitterness, she was honest, true to the
very heart's core, and the net in which she was entan-
gled was all the more maddening to her because she was
so. She could not compromise with nor spare herself;
she was too clear in judgment not to know where she
had sinned, and every deviation from honesty of life and
word was a deliberate known sin into which she forced
herself, and for which she suffered all the sure remorse.

The inevitable results of this inward struggle were
showing themselves upon her face. She looked in the
glass, as she dressed herself that night for dinner, with a
keen alarm lest her excessive pallor and her heavy eyes
should attract attention to her nervousness and depression. "I must carry it on one day more," she
thought, extinguishing the light and turning quickly to
the door. She had promised to meet Cyril in the par
lor half an hour before dinner, to give him her fina.
answer; it was the answer that her heart and not her
judgment dictated, and she felt herself a coward as she
went down into the silent and deserted hall.

"The very last day of this misery," she thought. "To-morrow night Ringmer will be peaceful once again."

And then she felt a sharp stab of remorse as her honest heart told her it would be a blank to her, the only one that had ever given it an interest gone. And for how long must the separation be ? She prayed it might be forever; but it was a prayer her heart refused. She was certain now that he had been truly fond of her once, " when they were little lovers;" she felt that he cared for her now, more perhaps than he knew himself; that he was trying to believe he returned the passion of this other, while he was only unworthily playing upon her feelings and trying to excite his own.

Ah, if they were but children again ! If they could only annihilate this space that divided them so fatally, and live truly and simply for each other, for whom they were only meant !

The parlors, at most other times so gay and noisy, were the stillest and dimmest quarter of the house at twilight, and the lower story, for three-quarters of an hour preceding dinner, might have formed part of a suburban residence in Pompeii for silence. The lamps in the parlor were not lighted and the fire was low, and Frank, as she entered quietly, looked anxiously through the dimness to discover Cyril. He was not there, and while she stood by the fire, wondering that he should have lost a moment of the time that he usually seemed to think so precious, she heard, at the extreme end of the other room, low voices in conversation. Wondering if it could be Cyril, and who he had with him, she listened involuntarily for a moment, and distinguished Stephanie's French accent and eager voice. The only words she understood were,

"I have consented to give up everything; and you, what do you give up? Decide between me and the army; I will not support the idea of a life such as you tell me; you must go back alone. *Que m'importe!* I will go home, I will not trouble you."

This was followed by an eager, low remonstrance, so low that Frank could only guess whose it was, and moving forward quickly, she made some noise to arrest the notice of the speakers before she should hear more. Stephanie caught sight of her and uttered a little scream of consternation, at the same time waving away her companion, who disappeared through the farthest door of the parlor into the hall. At the very same instant, while Stephanie came hurriedly forward towards Frank, the middle door of that room opened, and Cyril entered hastily, and mistaking her, in the twilight, for the one whom he had come to meet, exclaimed, taking eagerly her hand:

"You've been waiting for me."

"*Non, monsieur*," cried Stephanie, starting angrily away and pointing to the room beyond, "but there is one who has!"

This little incident was not calculated to add to the ease and pleasure of those concerned in it when, twenty minutes later, they met around the table. Cyril, till now very little used to controlling himself in any way, found it harder than ever to be gay when he felt gloomy, and civil when he was literally savage. Stephanie, in

from the piano. " Come, Soutter, you take Miss Warrington's place, and help me and Bell to give them a
taste of Camp ——."

Soutter sat down at the piano, and soon launched
them off into a favorite and familiar melody.   All three
men sang well, with beautiful accord, and gradually
waking into the spirit of it, they merged from one into
another of their familiar free songs of the camp, drinking songs, marching tunes, negro melodies, Irish ballads,
glees, catches, of all styles and merits.   Mrs. Thorndyke
and Mrs. Rosenbaum were delighted, and applauded
with great warmth.   Even Mr. Thorndyke came in from
the library and sat down by the fire, to listen to what
took him back to those anti-adamantine days when he
sang college songs with as much zest as any of his companions.   Frank took her embroidery, and sat down by
the light, with her head bent over it, Stephanie leaned
back silently upon the sofa and beat her foot upon the
carpet, and Emily, shading her eyes with her hand, never
looked away from the group at the piano.   The evening
was far advanced before Cyril, moving away, said,

" Bell and I have come to the end of our rope, but
Soutter can go on till to-morrow morning, a new song
every seven minutes.   Give us that serenade, Soutter,
and afterwards the little German song," he added, as he
threw himself into a seat near Frank.   Soutter sang the
serenade, and then one or two airs from the Barber, in
an absent-minded way, as if he were thinking them up
as he went along, but with so much grace and accuracy
that Cecilia exclaimed, quite forgetting her recent misfortunes and her habitual timidity,

" Oh, Mr. Soutter, you have been very selfish, when you could have given us such pleasure every day !"

" I am sure I never guessed it, Miss Thorndyke," he said, rising. " I should have gone to the piano long ago, if I had imagined I could have amused you."

" Don't imagine we are going to let you off," said Cyril.

" That German air of which M. Cyril speaks—we wait for it, monsieur," said Stephanie.

" I'm afraid you will be disappointed, Miss Clèrambeau," he said, with a little contraction of the brow, going back to the piano with evident reluctance. " It is quite a trifle, a mere sketch : I never heard it more than once, and that was years ago."

He sang with an *abandon*, a pathos, a power of expression that carried his listeners with him, and when he ended and rose abruptly, no one could come down to commonplace commendation for some minutes.

" It is late," said Mrs. Rosenbaum, rising.

" Ah, not yet !" cried several voices. But no one said it was the last evening, and when at length they parted, no one said, " Think how far apart we all shall be to-morrow;" each one was trying not to think it, and each read the effort in the faces of the others.

CHAPTER XXXVIII.

THE FINAL ADJUSTMENT.

" Well-done outlives Death."

HALF an hour later, Mr. Rosenbaum, walking into the library, found Major Soutter waiting for him there. They both bowed stiffly, and both approaching the fire, stood silent, each waiting for the other to speak. At last Soutter said, beginning rather abruptly,

" I'm afraid, Mr. Rosenbaum, that our interview must disappoint you. I do not propose fighting your friend, and I have no apology to offer for anything that passed on the morning of the 25th. Except, perhaps, for holding out the hope of meeting him, which hope I then entertained, but have now abandoned."

" May I ask," said Rosenbaum, with the slightest possible distention of his fine nostril, " what has induced you to abandon it at this late hour ?"

" I abandoned it a good while ago," he returned. " Two hours after I formed it. The process of reasoning by which I convinced myself of the propriety of declining to fight will not interest you; facts, I suppose, are what are most needed in such an interview as this. I must decline to meet your friend. And furthermore," he continued, drawing his breath from pretty deep down in his broad chest, as he leaned his head on his hand, his elbow on the mantel-piece, and looked across at his companion; "furthermore, I must deny myself the satisfaction of meeting you."

"A satisfaction," said the other between his teeth, "that in some way I think you will have to take."

"No one, I suppose," said Soutter, going on as if he had not spoken, "will be apt to misinterpret the motives that prompt me to avoid an encounter with Captain Bell. I do not fear any charge of cowardice there; the real self-denial lies in letting go unpunished the insults of a man who is known for a man of courage and of honor."

"Then, sir, as a man of courage and of honor, I hold and shall proclaim you as unworthy the regard of gentlemen, unbound by their rules, unfit for their company. You have refused to vindicate yourself in the only mode known to men of honor, and from this moment you lose your rank among them."

"Your influence is not unlimited, Mr. Rosenbaum, but as far as it goes, you have my full consent to use it. If any humiliation or vexation borne by me can in even the most distant way advance the standard of true honor, and put down this most false test of bravery, I shall be contented with the result of my decision. What it has cost me, sir, you can find by looking in your own heart this moment. I am no saint; my passions are, perhaps, more vindictive than your own, my self-love as strong as other men's, my pride a little stronger. And it has suffered at your hands, sir; I have appreciated your intentions fully, nothing has been lost upon me. If I had considered I had the privilege of

settling the account between us in the usual way, I am
afraid I could not have waited as long as you have, for
the hour of reckoning."

" Your words are very stout, sir," said the other with
a sneer, " considering they are unbacked by deeds."

" You are right," Souter said in a smothered voice,
taking a turn across the room. " Men who do not fight,
have, I suppose, no right to speak, The same principle
that holds them back from shedding blood should keep
them from resenting insult."

" I am to understand then, sir, that your purpose is
unalterable ?"

" Entirely so."

" Then our interview had better terminate. This
matter, of course, is no longer secret."

" No longer ; you are at liberty to speak of it with
what publicity you choose."

" And the answer I am to convey to my friend is
definite ?"

" Completely definite. I decline to meet him, and I
am prepared to take the consequences of my refusal."

" Then, sir, it is best for me to say, in future I shall
not feel called upon to recognise you as an acquaintance."

" I agree to it, sir."

And with a stiff bow, they parted: Soutter to his
own apartments, and Rosenbaum to seek his friend.
As he reached the second floor, however, where his own
room was situated, he paused a moment and consulted
his watch. It was already after twelve, the lights
seemed all extinguished on the floor above, and fearing

to disturb those who slept in the neighborhood by groping about to find Bell's door, he concluded it was as well to wait till morning before giving him Soutter's answer.

Besides, he more than suspected Bell's personal repugnance to duelling, and he felt in no hurry to relieve his mind of the alarm for which he so much despised him. It must be confessed, great as was the contempt he felt at that moment for Soutter, he felt even more for the pitiful braggart who was, he knew, only urged on towards the fatal ground by a dread of disgrace and ridicule.

CHAPTER XXXIX.

A GLEAM FROM A LANTERN.

" God help thee, then !
       I'll see thy face no more,
Like water spilled upon the plain,
Not to be gathered up again.
       Is the old love I bore."

FRANK's first restless sleep that night was broken by
a sudden flash of light outside her window, and then a
sudden darkness. She sprang up, tried to convince
herself that she was dreaming, and groped her way up
to the window. The roof of the balcony below passed
directly under it. She put her face close against the
pane and gazed out. She saw nothing; but she heard,
along the pillar at the end, a sound as of some one
descending cautiously, and then the faintest noise of
steps upon the balcony beneath, and the smothered
opening of a window.

Her heart gave a quick bound, and then stood still.
She knew it all in one rapid thought: the note, the
flight Cub had spoken of, the words she had overheard
at twilight in the parlor, Stephanie's agitated and rest-
ess looks, the gloomy abstraction of Soutter's eye. Ah,
the traitor ! How dared he fly from her whom he only
loved? How dared Stephanie claim him when she
knew the truth so well ?

She sprang to the door with a wild meaning to stop them, to rouse the house; and then, with a strong revulsion of feeling, as she remembered all, she flung herself upon the bed and clasped her hands before her eyes. Who could she accuse of treachery; who was branded so deeply as she was with "the heart's disgrace?" Who would be wronged by this flight? What was the ingratitude, the baseness of this marriage, compared with that of hers?

No; Stephanie had the excuse of ignorance, of an undisguised passion; the alternative of flight or of a hateful home; a forced marriage with a man who was insupportable to her; an eternal separation from the man whom she adored. And Soutter! Was it any wonder he sought to be solaced and soothed by a love of which he could not doubt the genuineness; that, despising her whom in early days he once had loved, he let himself be won upon by the exaggerated passion of one who so loved him? Yes, he had consented to save her from her home, to take her with him rather than leave her to be wretched; he was binding himself forever to her from the generous kindness of his nature, and he would succeed, perhaps, in time, in persuading himself he loved her. He would be contented with her, and be fond of her.

Why should this thought give her pain? She told herself she should be grateful for every step on his part or on hers that sundered them more fully now; that if she were not utterly lost to principle she would be happy in the release that this had given her.

The violence of her emotion passed. She crept back

to the window and watched eagerly for some tokens of the flight she had assumed to be a certainty. There was no moon, and but for the snow upon the ground she never could have distinguished any movements from the height she was; but, thanks to the white mantle lying on the earth, she perceived, dimly to be sure, and far beyond all power of recognition, two figures stealing across the lawn. They halted at a clump of trees. Then came again a flash of the dark lantern, the creaking of a sleigh upon the snow, a long silence, and then a man going cautiously behind the shrubbery back in the direction of the stable.

Two struck musically from all the clocks throughout the house, and silence began again after its unnoticed interruption.

CHAPTER XL

ALL ARE NOT HUNTERS THAT BLOW THE HORN.

· " Said Mr. B., I do agree,
But think of Honor's courts!
If we go off without a shot,
There will be strange reports."—Hood.

FRANK arrived late at the breakfast-room door next
morning—late, that is, in regard to time, not late in
order of arrival. She had trusted to find every one at
table, and the dénouement over; but she found on entering that only the Rosenbaums and Mr. and Mrs. Thorndyke had come down. She took her place hastily, hoping to escape a critical revisal; but Emily, whose notice
of her was always ominous, looked curiously at her, and
said:

" Are you not well, Miss Warrington? You are so
extremely pale."

" I have an excessive headache," said Frank; and
then Mrs. Thorndyke looked at her loftily and said
nothing.

Presently Cecilia came in; and Mr. Thorndyke took
advantage of a pair of shoulders that belonged to him,
over which to lay about him pretty heavily on the matter of late rising.

" And where are the children?" said the mother.

" Marcelle is just dressing them. She overslept, 1

18*

think. She seems a little upset this morning from some cause."

Soon the children came straggling in, and, by and by, Cyril. Mr. Thorndyke looked grimly over the top of his paper at him, but said nothing.

"I am not the last," said that young gentleman, seating himself beside Emily. "My superior officer, I am glad to find, is tardy, too, as well as the illustrious Captain Bell."

"Yes," said Mrs. Thorndyke, "I am afraid if they do not come down soon they will have very little appetite for their early dinner."

"Our train leaves at three, and you propose to dine us at two, I suppose," said Cyril, with a grimace, as he drew the toast towards him. "I do not affect early dinners."

"At half-past one, punctually," said Mrs. Thorndyke.

"Do you go on to Washington to-day?" said Mr. Rosenbaum, stiffly.

"Cela dépend," returned Cyril, as if the discussion of his plans annoyed him. "Soutter, I know, will. I may conclude to spend the night in New York if Bell does. And you, Mrs. Rosenbaum, you drive to Wheatley, I believe, and start for the city in the morning?"

"That is our plan."

"What a scattering of the party!" said Cyril, with a shrug of the shoulders. "Ah, well, we shall all meet here again next Christmas with undecimated ranks What is a year after all?"

Emily shivered involuntarily, and Mrs. Thorndyke said, half petulantly:

'Don't talk about next year. I shall never dare to lo k a day a-head while this horrid war continues."

'Wel., that is the Scriptural way," said Cyril, with an uneasy laugh. "But where is Miss Stephanie? We are always dull without her."

"Camilla," said Mrs. Thorndyke, "run up to Miss Stephanie's room, and ask her if she will not let Marcelle do her packing. Tell her we are all at breakfast."

Frank felt her hand shake as she passed Cyril's cup to him. She almost dropped it as the door that Cammy opened admitted *Major Soutter*.

"Good heavens, Miss Warrington!" said Mrs. Rosenbaum, feebly. "One would think you saw a ghost."

"Well, Soutter," cried Cyril; "you, who are always *matinal*, is this the example that you set your juniors? Under marching orders too. Where's Bell?"

"I have not seen him this morning," returned Soutter, taking his place.

"I beg your pardon for forgetting, sir," said Thomas, the waiter, apologetically, approaching Mr. Rosenbaum's chair, "here's a note Mr. Bell gave me last night, and bade me hand you if you got down to breakfast before he did. It passed my mind completely, sir."

Rosenbaum took the note between his fingers with much indifference of manner, but with some curiosity as to what it might contain.

"Pray read it,' said Cyril. "We're anxious to know when we may reasonably expect him down."

Mr. Rosenbaum broke the seal, ran his eye hurriedly

down the page, bit his lip, knit his brow sternly, and
began silently to peruse it again. During this second
reading, Cammy came in hastily with a very shocked
and alarmed expression, holding a letter in her hand.

"She isn't in her room, mamma. She is—gone away,
I think. This note Marcelle found lying on the dress
ing-table."

Mrs. Thorndyke put out her hand impatiently for it,
looking bewildered and stupid, while Cyril gave a start
and glanced anxiously down towards Rosenbaum
There was a movement of surprise, and a few faint
ejaculations, and then there was a silence of suspense,
while Mrs. Thorndyke, looking every moment more
bewildered and alarmed, went through the letter. Mr.
Thorndyke laid down his paper and his eye-glass, and
sat like a man carved out of granite, with his eyes upon
his wife.

"Good heavens!" she exclaimed, after a few moments, looking up helplessly, "What does it all mean?"

"We are waiting for you to tell us," said her husband,
in a voice that rang like steel.

"What does your letter say, my dear mother? Pray
let us hear," said Cyril, with impatience.

"Well, listen," said Mrs. Thorndyke, reading in an
uncertain and hesitating voice:

"I do not know how to tell you, my kind hostess, of
what I am about to do. I am very unhappy to leave
you in this manner. I know you will be troubled by
it, and will call it ungrateful and unwise. But you do
not know what excuses I have for taking any plan that

saves me from going back to-morrow to my home.
The only happy days I have ever passed, have been in
the house I am now leaving. I ask no pardon of my
father, and send him no excuse. Of you only, who
have been kind to me, do I ask forgiveness, for making
this use of your hospitality.

"I am very unhappy: there are few that care. But
I know you have a kind heart, and will not be ungentle
when you judge me. *Dieu vous garde!*

"STEPHANIE CLÈRAMBEAU."

There was a moment of silence, broken by Mrs. Rosenbaum's querulous exclamation, " What a scandal !
If it had happened in my house I should have gone distracted. My dear friend, what will you do about it !"

What to do about it was the serious question. Mrs.
Thorndyke only shook her head miserably, and looked
down towards her husband.

" Does your letter, Mr. Rosenbaum, throw any light
upon the matter?" said that metallic-toned gentleman
politely to his right-hand neighbor, tapping the table
with his eye-glass.

" Rather too much light, unfortunately," returned
Mr. Rosenbaum, with a smile of contempt, " I will read
it to you if you will allow me."

There was a moment's pause and then he said, " I
must, however, with your permission, preface it with a
few words of explanation."

Every eye at the table was on him, and laying the
hand with the open letter in it on the table, and leaning
forward on the other, he addressed himself to Mr. Thorn

dyke, speaking in his usual cool voice, with an almost
imperceptible tingle of contempt in it:

"The day after our arrival here, sir, a few words
passed between this gentleman," raising the letter, "and
another of your guests, Mr. Soutter, which made it
obligatory on the former to demand satisfaction from
him. I was the bearer of a message to Mr. Soutter,
with whom I agreed, however, to postpone all definite
arrangements till the termination of our residence in
your house. It was understood between Mr. Bell and
myself, and I believe Mr. Soutter, that on the 6th of
January, the subject should be revived, and the preliminaries settled for a meeting as soon after as was
possible. I had an interview with Mr. Soutter last
evening, but, owing to the lateness of the hour was not
able to communicate the result of it to Mr. Bell, intend-
ing to see him at an early hour this morning. Mr.
Soutter's answer, however, and the letter which I have
just received, relieve me from all responsibility in the
matter, as well as from all reserve regarding it."

Mr. Thorndyke inclined his head, and Mr. Rosenbaum, lowering his eyes upon the open sheet, began to
read:

"My dear Sir,—I taxed your friendship rather
heavily in imposing upon you the disagreeable office of
second in my little affair with Major Soutter. I have
no doubt you will be very glad to be released, though
I am sure you will believe me when I say it is with
great regret that I relinquish the fulfillment of my
appointment with him. Fully aware of the delicacy of

my position, I am yet unable to persuade myself that I should be justified in peril.ing my life in such an encounter, and thereby sacrificing the happiness of one who has become dearer to me than my life. When I made the arrangement, it was different. Since then, new ties have bound me, new duties have devolved upon me; the happiness of another is committed to my hands, and I sacrifice my own impulses and the demands of honor, and yield to the claims of affection. I leave it to you to explain this to my adversary, and to convince him of the struggle that it has cost me to relinquish the revenge I had promised to myself. It will not, perhaps, surprise you, that guided by similar motives, I have just despatched my resignation to my commanding officer. I am resolved henceforth to live solely to watch over the happiness of one who has generously given up all for me.

"I sincerely trust that no efforts to interfere with our plans may be made; they will be utterly thrown away, as, before this reaches you, our marriage will be consummated, and we shall be on board a Liverpool packet, sailing at 9 o'clock.

"With sincere thanks to my entertainers, and to you, for your recent services, and many regrets for the manner in which I am compelled to terminate my visit,

"I am obediently yours,

"BARNWELL BELL."

A smothered ejaculation of contempt and anger burst from Cyril, and his father's features expressed a sneer, while Soutter exclaimed in a low tone, "unhappy girl," and pushed back his chair involuntarily from the table.

"I ought to add," said Mr. Rosenbaum with a glassy composure, "that Mr. Soutter's answer would have saved Mr. Bell from the necessity of the hasty step which he has taken, as it was an unconditional refusal to fulfill the engagement upon any terms."

Cyril started involuntarily, and checked himself in an exclamation of chagrin, while the others looked awkwardly astounded.

"But Stephanie! Who would have dreamed it possible!" murmured Cecilia, pale and agitated.

"It is the most astounding thing I ever heard," said Emily, subdued and shocked.

"But how to pacify the old man," muttered Cyril "It's an awkward piece of business."

"It is a disgrace we never shall get over," moaned Mrs. Thorndyke, bitterly aggrieved. "Mr. Bell has not the feelings of a gentleman to outrage our hospitality in this manner. And that bold, deceitful girl! O what trouble she has brought upon us! Why did I ever think of sending for her!"

Mr. Thorndyke broke his wife's lamentations off short by a warning look, and touching the bell beside him sharply, summoned a couple of servants, one of whom he sent with a slip of paper to the telegraph office at ——; the other he despatched instantly to the stable for horses.

"Which of you, gentlemen," he said as he rose, "will accompany me to Mr. Clèrambeau's for the purpose of breaking this unpleasant news to him?"

There was no volunteer for a moment, Cyru and Ro senbaum evidently felt no vocation for the office, and Sontter said at last, rising,

" If I can be of any service to you, sir ——"

" I shall take it as a favor, Major Soutter, if you will go with me," returned Mr. Thorndyke, bowing. " Your part in this matter has done you the highest credit. I shall be glad of your assistance in the emergency of to-day. The horses will be at the door in ten minutes. We shall by fast driving, I trust, reach home in time for dinner. If not, let it be served without regard to our return."

The matter of meals never lost its importance in Mr. Thorndyke's mind. He would have insisted upon the punctual serving of dinner for those he left behind, if he had been about to leave the fleshly tabernacle him- self for ever. It was one of the duties and decencies of life in the performance of which he never allowed him- self the smallest relaxation ; so in the midst of the many hurried preparations that this most unexpected catas- trophe devolved upon him, he did not omit to give his orders for the wine to Thomas, and to send some direc- tions to the housekeeper about the game and soup.

Upon his exit from the dining-room, the buzz of tongues broke forth, and Frank, sick with pity for the misguided girl about whom they were so mercilessly busy, rose and hurried to the door.

Major Soutter followed her closely.

" Will you let me speak with you a moment in the parlor ?" he said, joining her in the hall. " We shall probably return barely in time to reach the train; this will be my only chance."

Frank followed him into the parlor, and closing the
door, he said to her, as leaning against the piano, she
waited silently for him to speak,

"This miserable affair has taught me how little I
know of woman's character. I thought I knew Stephanie Clèrambeau. I did not think she could have done
this thing; I did not think she could have entertained
the thought, much less have carried it out unflinchingly.
And it has given me a misgiving—a fear I hardly
dare to name—about you, who, perhaps, I understand
as little. Frank, forgive me! We may never meet
again. I cannot leave you without one more entreaty,
though you have forbidden me to speak. If I loved
you any less I might be angry at your scorn of me, and
impatient at what seems your weakness. But I love
you too deeply to feel that. I have no hope, and so I
am not selfish. I don't think to save you for myself;
but your happiness is more to me than my own; your
safety, your honor —— "

She put out her hands, with a frightened gesture, and
then turned her face away.

"If you should ever," he went on, in an agitated
voice—" if you should ever be led to take such a step as
this infatuated girl has taken, I should feel I had received
a blow from which I never could recover. If I should
know you to be placed as she is—the wife of a man too
cowardly to face the world before he had secured her,
the mark for the opprobrium of those who form his
family, a tale of scandal for the diversion of society—I
should endure more pain than even the discovery of your
coldness gave me; not because it would place you far

ther from me than you are, but, Frank, because my love
surrounds you always; because, through it I should
receive the blow that would fall upon your happiness,
your self-respect, your peace of life and conscience!
Listen, Frank. If this man's love is indispensable to you,
consent to marry him, if he can marry you honorably
and openly, with due warning to those who may oppose
it; but spurn, as you would an insult, his persuasions
to a secret marriage."

There was a movement without, and a sound of sleigh-
bells at the door, and Mr. Thorndyke's voice called,
" Major Soutter."

" I must go," he said, sadly, turning away, " but remember what I have said. I am older than you are;
I see things clearer, and I am only watching for your
good. Only tell me what you desire to do, what plan
you have at heart, and I will do all in my power to
further it. I will use my influence with Cyril, I will
try to influence his family. I will make any effort, if
you will but tell me what will make you happy."

" Nothing will," she said, in a hollow voice, with her
eyes fastened on the ground.

" I had hoped I need not leave you so," he answered,
turning away, and going out of the room without
another word.

Frank stood listening mechanically as he crossed the
hall. She heard Cyril approach him and say, a little
stiffly,

" I will send Gustave up to pack your valise an
attend to things generally for you. I am sorry to have
you go off on this troublesome business."

It was evident that Cyril felt some awkwardness in meeting Soutter after the great shock he had received from Rosenbaum's narration.   He was half ashamed of himself for being ashamed of his friend; and yet sometimes, when he reviewed the circumstances, he felt as if he ought to be more ashamed of him than he actually was.

Frank waited till she heard their voices out on the piazza, and then she hurried to her room and slid the bolt.   It was a brilliant winter day; the snow was glitteringly bright, and the sunshine came in at every window, and lay in long streams of light along the sombre carpet, and seemed to be staring out of countenance the stiff, unornamented room.

She pulled down the shades and tried to shut it out; and taking up a pile of Cuthbert's exercises, written with a faithful perseverance every day since the holidays began, set herself resolutely to correct them, and prepare for the routine which she must begin again to-morrow.   How many months it seemed since the last time she had corrected poor Cub's theme!

CHAPTER XLI.

SAINT CECILIA.

"Oft in life's stillest shade reclining,
In desolation unrepining,
Meek souls there are, who little dream,
Their daily strife an angel's theme;
Or that the rod they take so calm
Shall prove in heaven a martyr's palm."

Christian Year.

THE long, wretched morning was dragging itself on towards twelve o'clock, when there came a low knock at the door, and Frank, opening it, admitted Sainty.

"Let me stay here a little while," she said, in a tired voice. "There is no other place I can be quiet; for Emily is in my room, and I am afraid I cannot bear it just this moment."

"Cecilia, what is it?" exclaimed Frank, abruptly, taking her hand, and looking intently at her, struck by the pallor of her face, and the inexplicable change that had come upon her even since the morning.

"It is—what do you mean?" she said, faintly, trying to turn away. "I am so tired. Let me sit down."

At this moment there came the tramp of a horse, led upon the pavement below; then a pause, long enough for some one to mount, and then the heavy strike of his hoofs upon the hard avenue, quickening rapidly as he left the house behind. Cecilia uttered a low, smothered in them faded out; and Frank, with a vague fear for some immediate ill consequence from the dreadful ordeal which she had just passed through, forbore to answer her by word or look, or to prolong the burst of feeling that had at once relieved her and exhausted all her powers.

"Lie still awhile, Sainty, where you are; quiet will do you good."

"Yes, that's all I want," she said with a faint smile, closing her eyes.

Frank turned away, unable to watch without emotion the patient misery of her friend. She went noiselessly across the room, darkened the windows afresh, and stood motionless beside the last curtain, with her hand upon it as she dropped it; she could not go back to her work again; this new revelation had taken all her stubborn fortitude away. This strength made perfect in weakness she saw as in strange contrast with her own thwarted resolution and self-reliance. This girl, so young and timid, dependent by nature, undeveloped by education, had just gone through a trial compared with which the terrors of the stake and fagot faded. The records of self-sacrifice could show nothing more entire than this: more than all could not be given up; more than living death could not be suffered. There was the help of no ecstasy, no enthusiasm in her trial; it was a victory, but not a triumph; she was "martyr by the pang but not the palm" as yet. She was contented to do right, she did not look for any crown; in her humility she only asked for help to do the will of God, she only hoped to be kept close to Him. Ah! such a faith as hers all the powers of hell could not overthrow, all the reasoning of man could not invade to injure; it was in Heaven's own keeping. She did not guess how great her conquest was, how pure and shining she had kept her faith; she was too simple and too humble to spoil it by the constant solicitude and supervision with which too many count over jealously and daily their chances of escaping punishment and of obtaining preferment in the eternal kingdom.

Since this trial had commenced, and the poor child had begun to see what was required of her, she had passed through almost every phase of mental conflict, and without, as she had said, one soul to help her by counsel or by pity. She had had all the arguments of an intellectual superior to overcome, all the pleadings of one who loved her ardently to steel herself against. She had to give its proper weight to what she knew would be the wishes of her parents, and to decide between affectionate submission to them and the authority that has said, "He that loveth father and mother more than me is not worthy of me." She had to resist the admiration that her lover's nobleness of nature roused in her, the confidence inspired by it; the hope that it would be accepted in place of that which by nature we cannot have, "the holiness without which no man can see the LORD." And then, hardest of all, she had to discredit the clamoring of her heart of the danger to him of her coldness, the fresh perils to him in the world after such a bitter disappointment; she had no right to sacrifice his happiness, whatever right she might have to destroy her own.

19

But, look well before you enter this unequal yoke, said conscience. Satan sometimes weaves our snares for us out of our truest and most pure affections. Are you sure you have strength to resist the daily influence through all your life of what has already tried your faith ? Can you take ice into your bosom and not be chilled by it ? Consider, that he has resisted, all his life, the pleadings of God's grace ; weigh then the chances of his listening to you. Remember, before you give him the right to guide and govern you, what principles govern him, and who he acknowledges as master. Think well before you enter it, what spirit will reign in the home you share with him ; will religion sanctify it ? will the wisdom of God or man direct it ? And yet again :

Can you be satisfied to share in death, as well as life, the portion of this unbelieving man to whom you give yourself ?

Julian Rosenbaum had not feared ill success ; he had never dreamed till that last interview that she could resist him. He relied so much upon her love for him, upon the womanliness and weakness of her reasoning, that he did not suffer himself at first to doubt that she would yield. It began to dawn upon him though, even before that last struggle, that she had some strength he knew not of ; that she could resist herself as well as him. The conflict was almost killing her, he could see ; she drooped and faded before his eyes. The spirit that sustained her he could not reach ; the strength that kept her up was something that he did not understand, upon which he could make no assault. He had imagined that he knew her many-minded sex as well as man could know it; he had amused himself lightly all his life in playing upon it, in touching the varied notes and listening with the keen ear of a connoisseur for the trembling vibration. But this sweet breath of music that he had now called forth, filled the air around him for a moment, and then floated away from him towards heaven, and all his skill and tenderness could not awake another strain as sweet. Baffled and desperate, in that last interview he had thrown into his pleading an almost overwhelming force of passion and of tenderness; he had reproached, pled, threatened, promised; the same low answer, the same frightened, wretched, but unaltered look about her eyes.

He had appealed to every feeling that he knew was strong in her, her tenderness for her family, their trouble and displeasure at this marring of her future; he had striven to show her the advantages to them of this connection, the position she would occupy as his wife; the fortune placed at her disposal, the good that she might do with it.

And then he had touched upon her affection for her brother, and had hinted darkly of danger and trouble to him, which her consent alone could save him from. This had startled and moved her, but not in the way that he had hoped. What threatened Cyril? Would he not tell her? Had he done wrong? How was he in danger? She would die for him, but— The fair head drooped again; she could not sin for him.

" Sin for him !" exclaimed Rosenbaum passionately. " What creed can make such a marriage as this a sin ?

A marriage of true souls, a marriage that love and honor and authority all sanction? Cecilia, dare you defy them all! Dare you break such bonds as these! Dare you say that from this moment all is ended be tween you and me?"

Half an hour later, Cecilia, sleeping on Frank's bed the sleep of utter exhaustion and oblivion, and Julian, miles away from Ringmer, galloping madly in the eye of the strong, cold wind, showed she had dared to do it. and all was over between him and her.

Frank stood and looked down upon the sleeping girl with reverence, and with most bitter self-reproach. Oh, the gulf between them! What, indeed, had pride profited her! What good had strength, with her vaunting, brought her! Ah, how much better to be lying there, bleeding silently to death with the faithful wound of martyrdom, than living and hiding always in her heart this poisoned, rankling arrow!   .

Cecilia had lain down across the bed, without a pillow, and with her face turned downward, her hands lying unclasped, but near each other, her whole attitude expressing a lassitude and lifelessness that a living figure rarely conveys, even in repose. It suggested, unconsciously, the beautiful marble in her church at Rome, of the sweet St. Cecilia, whose name this one had always playfully been made to bear; true martyr now indeed. true saint, in the eternal record of the Book of Life.

CHAPTER XLII.

QUI PERD, PÉCHE.

" A ship aground is a beacon at sea."

THE dining-room at Ringmer was perhaps the finest apartment in the house. Its walls were lined with costly paintings, and its four great windows opened upon pictures grander still without; the lawn, the river, and the mountains, all frosted with the glittering touch of winter, and with a brilliant sky above. There was no glare, for the shade of the piazza and the heavy curtains softened the sunlight from without, but there was a look of cheerfulness and richness about the room, with its dark furniture, its glittering array of glass and silver, the fine colors of the fruits, the wines, the ornamented viands of the table.

Every place, too, was filled. The three blank spaces left by Bell, and Stephanie, and Rosenbaum, had been bridged over, and Mr. Thorndyke and Major Soutter had returned exactly in time to take their places with the others. Cecilia had come down, looking white and lifeless; and Frank, who was her vis-à-vis, watched her furtively, with a feeling of constant apprehension. There was a good deal of talking, and a pretty steady interchange of question and answer among the different people, but the effort not to let silence get a foothold at the board was too evident to make it very cheerful.

"How odd to be dining by daylight!" said Emily.

"Yes," said Cyril. And then a pause threatened, and he bearded it fiercely, and began to talk about the comparative advantages of late and early dining hours, the hours abroad, army hours, country hours, city hours. When that subject could yield no more, and another blank occurred, somebody hazarded the remark that Cecilia looked pale, which fell dead, as every one, except her father and mother, had begun to suspect what was the cause. Major Soutter turned very quickly, and began to ask his host something about the game before him, and that served for another long parry of the enemy's approach; and then Emily talked of the sleighing, and Mrs. Rosenbaum talked about the jelly, and Mrs. Thorndyke was started on the discipline of children; and so the foe was kept successfully at bay till dessert was brought upon the table; then Mr. Thorndyke, who had been more than usually grim and stony, looked down at his wife, and said:

"Where is Mr. Rosenbaum? I had not noticed he was absent till this moment."

Cyril, who had just before dinner learned the truth, in alarm lest his mother should dilate unnecessarily upon his unexpected departure, and overtax poor Cecilia and bring on a scene, took it upon himself to answer and give the rather indefinite excuse that Rosenbaum had left for him. And then, with haste and imprudence, he asked, anxious only to suppress the dangerous topic:

"What was the result of your interview with old Clèrambeau, sir? I have not had an opportunity of asking you."

Mr. Thorndyke's face grew dark. "About the result that I anticipated," he said, as if the machinery of speech within was made of steel, and the springs had been set in motion by a sharp and angry touch. "He has cast her off completely, and swears he will not only disin-herit her, but will never rest until he has been revenged upon the man who has eloped with her."

"He is an old tyrant," said Cyril, hotly. "He did not deserve any better of his daughter, and I only hope his ill wishes will all come home to roost."

"You speak hastily, sir," said his father, with a scowl-ing look. "He is justified in all but troubling himself to punish her. He should cast her off, and then forget that she had ever had existence."

"What!" cried Cyril; "because she dared to please herself, and marry without asking his consent?"

"Yes; just precisely because she dared do that."

"Then women are in an abject condition indeed. I do not see we need boast of our progress much. I hold she had a right to marry whom she pleased; but I ac-knowledge she did it foolishly and rashly, and I blame Bell for his part in the matter more than I blame her. It was an unfortunate business altogether; but as to its being anything more, I cannot see it in that light. With all his faults, he is affectionate and kind, and he will make her a thousand times better husband than the old Frenchman her father had picked out for her."

"That is nothing to the purpose," returned Mr. Thorn dyke, shortly.

"No, indeed," said Mrs. Thorndyke. "If she were my daughter, she should never enter my house again I never could forgive the want of confidence."

"Remember that, my sisters!" cried Cyril, with an uneasy laugh, to Cammy and Cecilia, who sat below him.

"Well, and why not the brother too?" said Cammy, pertly.

"Son or daughter," said Mr. Thorndyke, sternly. "I make no difference between the duty they owe me, and the authority I hold over them."

"A truly patriarchal system," said Cyril, rashly, with an impatient laugh.

"A system that suits my purposes," returned the father, with a growing irritation in his voice, "and to which I shall adhere."

"It is well that we should understand it," said Cyril, below his breath.

"It is well you should," answered Mr. Thorndyke, catching the words distinctly; "and I repeat"——

"Well, sir," said the younger, doggedly, raising his head, and meeting his father's eye defiantly.

There was a storm brewing. Frank watched its rising, white with terror.

"I repeat, that son or daughter of mine, daring to marry without my consent, shall reap to the full the consequences of the act."

"And those consequences?" interrogated Cyril, in a voice trembling with smothered anger.

"Disinheritance, sir, and as complete a separation from the rights and privileges of my family as if they had never been members of it."

"And this I am to understand is your unalterable resolution?"

"You are to understand so," answered the father,

raising his voice, and speaking in a most vindictive manner. " No son of mine need be in doubt as to the course I shall pursue, if he dares to set himself above my commands, and act in defiance of my authority."

" A son of yours has dared to do it," exclaimed Cyril, in a tone of passion, starting to his feet and pushing back his chair.

There was an instant of utter silence, as Cyril, making a hurried step forward, laid his hand on Frank's shoulder, and, with the other, threw down upon the table a folded paper.

" Your name on that certificate, sir," he said, in a voice haughty and defiant, while it shook with anger, " could add nothing to its weight. The law recognizes it, the world recognizes it, and I demand that you recognize it too !"

Frank could not lift her eyes nor see the faces that surrounded her. She sat, white and giddy, feeling only the hand upon her shoulder, with its strongly-throbbing pulse, and its vehement, unconscious grasp of iron ; and hearing nothing but the menacing and defiant ring of voices, whose words she could not comprehend. Suddenly she felt the grasp relax, as, saying something in a tone of thunder, the father rose and left the room, motioning his son to follow him.

She heard a feeble cry, and knew that Mrs. Thorndyke swooned. There was a stir and movement about her, and, struggling to rise and to escape, she saw Cecilia press her hand upon her heart as she approached her mother; she saw the shocked and frightened group of children; and she saw Emily sitting motionless in her place with blanched and rigid features.

She hurried from the door and gained her own room, hardly knowing what she did.

She was sitting alone, stunned and bewildered, her face buried in her hands, when the door suddenly opened, and Cyril entered.

"There is not a moment to be lost," he said, in an agitated voice, which, despite his self-control, showed the storm he had just been through. "Can you be ready in half an hour? The carriage will be at the door."

"Ah, what have you done?" she murmured, turning away her head.

"Freed myself from tyranny and gained you, my darling," he answered, with an embrace. "I only think of that."

She felt as if she were in a dream, when, half an hour later, a man came up, and, dragging her trunk from the corner, where it had always stood since she came to Ringmer, shouldered it and went down stairs. She tied her bonnet on and followed Cyril out without a look behind. There was no one on the stairs; not a soul in sight as they descended to the hall. Only Cub, as they reached the door, came out timidly from the library, and, with a clumsy motion of affection, put out his hand and said, "Good-bye."

Frank kissed him hurriedly; and Cyril, clasping his hand, said, "God bless you, Cub!" while the tears rushed for a moment to his eyes.

That was all. There was no other word of parting or

benediction spoken as the darling son and brother, iant and impenitent, crossed for the last time the eshold of his home.

CHAPTER XLIII.

THE LONG, LONG WEARY DAY.

"' And lang, lang may the maidens sit,
    Wi' their gowd kaims in their hair,
  A waiting for their ain dear loves—
  For them they'll see na mair !"
                    Sir Patrick Spens.

It was a foggy, dull January morning ; the hands of
the little speechless clock upon the mantel-piece, clasping each other, pointed silently to twelve, and Frank,
sinking back into a soft satin-covered chair, looked up
at it, and wondered why they lingered so long upon
that hour. No clock, since the old days at Titherly,
when she watched the wooden school-room time-piece
impatiently from nine to four, had ever seemed so
dawdling and monotonous.

She had been already that morning two hours alone ;
Cyril had left her after breakfast, to write some letters,
as he said, and at eleven he had left her again, not to
return, perhaps, till dinner. The day presented a dreary
prospect to the young stranger, alone in the great hotel.
There was a pile of new books upon the table, three or
four morning papers, and several periodicals with their
leaves uncut, but though she held one in her hand, her
eye hardly rested on it, wandering from the soft blaze
of the fire in the grate to the grey foggy glimpses of the
street, seen from all the tall, heavily-curtained windows.

The room had the unmistakable look of a hotel, not-withstanding the costliness of the furniture; it was only a place to stay in for convenience, and it had a home-sick, unoccupied, ennuyé expression, that nothing could overcome. There were beautiful flowers upon the piano, and a superb basket of fruit upon the buffet, but the piano was hollow-voiced and out of tune, and the buffet was bare of everything but a plated ice-pitcher and two or three tall glasses. The vases on the mantel-piece were so huge and stiff, they overshadowed every-thing beside them, and the little clock was too cowed to utter an articulate sound. There was a heavy cease-less hum from the street outside, and a droning sort of racket from the more distant busy quarter of the house within; but nothing tangible, nothing definite enough to awaken any interest, nothing that was not wearisome and dull.

It was not yet three days since they came away from Ringmer, and it seemed so long! Three days: what a small part of the twenty, thirty, forty years she might have to live without any stronger interest, without any better food for thought and recollection. She felt the burden of her ingratitude to be so great that she wearied herself in trying to lighten it, and to repay the tender devotion of her husband with the best substitute for affection that she could command. She was thoughtful, watchful, gentle, tried to look happy when he sought to please her, and to divert him when any cloud, passing over his new happiness, reminded him what had been its cost. He had given up everything for her, she could not forget; he had broken the dearest ties, renounced the fairest future; sne had nothing to repay him with but a barren loyalty, a cold sense of duty, that in time would make the duty of a cruel weight. She had nothing else to pay, but he should have that, her life, her whole devotion while she lived; she would serve him faithfully; she would strive to help him to bear the change of fortune, which now he did not realise; she would have borne it all for him. If it had been necessary for her to have worked for him, she would gladly have thrown herself into any toil, no matter how wearying and irksome, but she had not that relief. She had to be his idol, while she knew she had ruined him and been the worst influence of his life. She had to meet him with a pleasant smile, and try to brighten the inhospitable hotel for him, for had she not cut him off from every other home! Lest he should miss the care and tenderness that had encircled all his life, she had to watch him and anticipate his wishes, and she longed to be his servant rather than his mistress. It was torture to be so loved, so honored, and to be living such deceit.

And then, she had a vague fear too, that she had blighted his ambition, had ruined his career, that as he felt now he would never return to his duties in the army. She knew his leave had expired, and she had urged him to tell her why ho loitered in New York. Had he obtained an extension of it, did he mean to risk his standing by outstaying it, what were his plans, when would he return to Washington—were questicns to which she could get no replies more satisfying than caresses and evasions. Why should she want him to decide upon anytLing? Was she not happy? People did not have plans in honeymoons; that was one of the exemptions.

The day, with its long imposition of silence and inac-tion was passing slowly on; three hours yet to dinner, and hardly the chance of a human face till then. Cyril had seemed distressed at leaving her so long alone. He had begged her to drive to the Park, to do some shop-ping, to amuse herself in some way out of the house after he was gone; he should be miserable to think she was sitting there alone till night; and at the last moment he had come back to bring her a new book, though the table was already strewn with them, and to beg her to let him order a carriage for her after lunch. His man-ner at parting was, if possible, tenderer than ever, and he came back a second time to say good-bye and to laugh at his reluctance to be an hour away from her.

Now that it was after four o'clock, Frank began to regret that she had not gone to drive; she was getting so nervous and restless from the long silence and isola-tion, that she would have braved the fog and rain rather than have spent another hour alone, if it had not been so late. She walked up and down the long apart-ment, and tried in vain to tire herself and forget her nervousness, and then she drew a chair into one of the windows, and sat down, resolved to interest herself in what was passing in the street. The room was on the first floor of the hotel, directly above the ground floor entrance, on each side of which were shops, now begin-ning to be lighted, and in and out of which people were hurrying, sometimes with umbrellas and sometimes

without them.   The twilight was premature and the
fog was thick, but the rain had nearly ceased and the
air was unnaturally warm and close.   The up-town
omnibuses were hurrying on, full and inattentive, the
down-town ones were lagging and looking out for passengers.   The cars were racketting along, overflowing
with damp umbrellas and waterproofs; the horses were
steaming, the bells continually tinkling, now to let out
a brisk, high-stepping gentleman, and now to take in a
washerwoman, with her big basket and broken-backed
umbrella.   There were newsboys crying extras along
the pavement, whom nobody attended to, and foot passengers jostling each other without ceremony, and carriages carrying people out to dinner, and express wag-
gons thundering up with luggage.

Frank found it hard to be interested after the first
glance, there was such a monotony in the sights and
sounds; but she dreaded to turn away and withdraw
into the grey room, with its lofty ceiling and empty
look.

Presently a carriage approached, and drew up before
the shop, immediately below the window.   There were
trunks upon the rack.   A gentleman got out and went
into the shop.   There was something inexplicably familiar in his air and figure; if it had not been for the
absence of beard and the greater fairness of his com-
plexion, she should not have had a doubt that the
ci-devant Captain Donelson was again before her.   Her
eye was particularly quick, and her memory unfailing,
and she was able to penetrate a disguise that would
have baffled many clever people.

She leaned forward and watched breathlessly for his re-appearance, almost certain, the more she pondered, that her fears were founded. Several minutes elapsed, and he did not re-appear: she knew he had gone into the shop, but, doubtless, there was an entrance through that into the hotel. No doubt he was even then in the office, and would see their names upon the book.

At that moment, a girl leaned forward from the carriage window and looked out, half anxiously, half curiously. The light from the newly-lit street lamp fell full upon her face. Frank uttered an involuntary cry of consternation as she recognised the pretty girlish features.

It was her cousin Fanny.

She pushed up the window and involuntarily called her name. But the roar of the street drowned the warning, and, without raising her eyes again, the girl sank back into the carriage. Good heavens! what was she made of to watch her cousin unwarned thus led off to ruin : she must save her, she must speak. But—what would be Fanny's safety would be her ruin : she might rescue her cousin, but it would be by the sacrifice of Cyril's happiness, of the little that remained to her of peace. It was too great a cost : she sank down beside the open window, and leaned her face upon the casement. Once more she looked up: the carriage had not moved, the girl in the carriage did not look out again. A moment after her companion emerged from the shop and crossed the pavement.

There was a momentary lull in the noise of the street; Frank leaning forward and listening heard him say to the driver on the box, as he tossed a package into the carriage, and laid his hand upon the door,

"To the pier, foot of —— street."

"Havre packet line?" asked the driver, gathering up the reins.

"Yes," said the other, stepping into the carriage and pulling the door shut after him, which closed with a sharp snap, as he sank back beside his young companion

Frank felt her heart grow cold and sick as she watched with straining eyes the carriage roll away through the dull mist, until it was swallowed up in the noisy, hurrying, heedless tide beyond.

Lost! Lost! Poor Fanny! This was the end of her intriguing, her ambitious dreams; how Frank's heart smote her for the envy and vexation she had once striven to inspire in her! How dead all those paltry feelings were; their childish strifes, their girlish jealousies were bitter recollections now. She had been so unkind, so willful, so overbearing; she had never once tried to influence Fanny rightly, to elevate and improve her; she had only, always, been trying to keep above her, and to defend herself. Her whole life at Titherly came back upon her with a vivid clearness; she felt as if she had this, too, to answer for, and for awhile she was overwhelmed with a strong tide of self-reproach.

She lost sight of herself and her own personal danger till recalled to the present by the thought that her husband might now return at any moment. Rising, she hastily closed the window, ran into the dressing-room to smooth her hair and adjust her dress, and then, with a sudden impulse of alarm, she rang the bell and ordered the servant to go to the office and see if there were any cards or letters in their box.

He returned presently with a letter; the clerk said it had just been left for Mr. Thorndyke by a gentleman. She stooped down and read the direction by the blaze. It was as she imagined, the writing was the same she had had thrust upon her recognition twice before. She put the letter in her pocket and sat down. A servant came to lay the cloth for dinner, and she waited quietly till he had arranged the table and lit the gas, and then sent him away, saying she would ring when she was ready for the meal. The light was so glaring, shining through the figured glass globes, that she turned all the upper burners out, and put a paper shade upon the lower one, stirring up the fire and making it break out into a pleasant blaze, drawing an easy chair beside it, putting a vase of flowers on the table, and trying as faithfully as ever young wife tried, to make a cheery welcome for her returning lord.

And then she sat down silently, with her hand upon the letter in her pocket, and waited for him.

How did she propose to welcome him?

With a flagrant breach of duty, the first step in a course of treachery which must go on indefinitely. If she withheld that letter from him, how could she meet him with a smile, bear unblushingly his fond caresses?

Up to this point, the deceit she had to reproach herself with had been tacit, almost involuntary; she had been hurried into everything she did by his impatience, she was not all to blame. But this—it w too palpable, it had given her a shock from which she could not recover; it showed her to what she must descend if she would keep up with him this false attitude. What! Live forever divorced from self-respect? Always in fear, always the slave of chance? Live too, feeling that she had selfishly saved herself at the expense of her deluded cousin? The ruin forever of Fanny's innocence and honor would lay with her, if she withheld this night the secret of this man's dealings from Cyril; for she could not believe it was too late to save her.

It was a long and dreadful struggle through which she went, as she sat silently with her eyes on the fire, feeling that she held in her hand the release she had so long sighed to hold; she knew but too well what the envelope contained—her own lost letter to Soutter, and the full explanation the revengeful wretch had promised her should come. But she knew it would be the last, he was escaping now to the shelter of a foreign shore, it would be years, perhaps, before he would return, his thirst for revenge might then be slaked. Yes! This was a long reprieve. If she once saw that letter curling in the flames, she might breathe free again.

And truth? and honor? and Fanny?

"No, Cyril shall know all to-night," she murmured. rising hurriedly and walking up and down the room. "If it costs me all that is left to me on earth, I am resolved."

Another hour passed slowly on; the silent clock indicated seven; a vague, uneasy fear possessed her. What could have hindered him so long? She gazed out into the dismal, foggy strect, and back into the lofty, lonely room, and shivered when she found how insupportable it was to be alone, how important to her already Cyril's care and presence had become; and she was, perhaps, about to sacrifice both, that very night, forever.

At that moment, she heard a step approaching down the corridor; her heart gave a sudden throb, and she thrust the letter out of sight. Then, with a strong effort, she controlled herself and exclaimed aloud,

"I swear it—I swear it to myself."

And throwing the letter down upon his plate, turned abruptly towards the door to meet him.

After all, it was not his step; there came a knock—a servant entered with a card. She took it and glanced down at it.

"Mr. Louis Soutter."

"Shall I bring him in, madam?" said the servant.

"Wait a moment," she said confusedly, putting her hand up to her forehead. She had prepared herself for one conflict; behold, another thrust upon her, all unready. She had thought Soutter hundreds of miles away, an impossible temptation for a long while to come; she had even fancied they might never meet again at all. What had brought him on from camp? He had come, no doubt, for Cyril; he had feared for his friend's honor, and hoped to induce him to return to duty before his delinquency was noticed. She must forget everything but that he was her husband's friend, her husband's guest, and must appear to make him welcome.

"He asked for Mr. Thorndyke, I suppose?" she said, trying to collect herself.

"No, madam, for Mrs. Thorndyke," said the negro, bowing.

"It must bo a mistake—but no matter—ask him to come in," she said, and in a moment's time the negro bowed him in and closed the door upon him.

"It is a great surprise," she said, giving him her hand and speaking with self-possession. "I supposed you were in Washington."

"I arrived in town two hours ago," he said, in a voice less calm, as his eye turned quickly and rested for a moment on the waiting table and the cheerful fire.

"You have not seen Cyril, I suppose?" she said. "I do not know what has detained him. Dinner has been waiting an hour for him."

"I did not come expecting to see him," said Soutter, in a tone so serious, Frank gave him an anxious and inquiring look.

"You have heard from him since you have been back in Washington?" she said, with a forced composure.

"Yes; I had a telegram from him last night."

"A telegram! Well?" she questioned in a stifled voice.

"Telling me, if I did not hear from him again to-day, I must come on this evening. But I did not wait; I took the first train, and only reached here at five."

"Why did he want you?" said Frank, almost in a whisper.

"To explain something to you, if it should be neces sary. I hoped it would not be; but"——

There was an instant's pause; she tried to speak, but the words seemed to choke her, and she made him a signal to go on.

"I came too late; I— Can you bear bad news, Frank?" he said, in a voice agitated beyond conceal- ment. "I believe it cannot be softened. Cyril will not come home. He met Rosenbaum at twelve to-day —and fell."

There was a moment's silence; Frank's lips moved, but no sound came from them; a slight shudder crept through her. and she fell senseless at her companion's feet.

CHAPTER XLIV.

A LETTER

" He is a friend, who, treated as a foe,
   Now even more friendly than before doth show
   Who to his brother still remains a shield,
   Although a sword for him his brother wield ;
   Wno of the very stones against him cast,
   Builds Friendship's altar higher and more .ast.''
                                        TRENCH.

"MAJOR SOUTTER bade me give this to you," said
Frank's attendant, handing her a letter. " He went
away this morning before five."

" He has gone ?" she said, starting and turning towards the girl, who reiterated her statement, and
receiving no further orders, left the room.

Frank sank back, bewildered and unnerved. This
was, indeed, to be completely isolated ; there was not a
human being to whom she could turn for counsel or for
comfort.

During these last fearful days, she had not raised her
head from the pillow, had not given the future a single
thought ; she had known only that she was safe, that
the dreadful burden of care, entailed by death and
shame, had come upon one who had borne it generously.
She had not seen him since she heard the fatal tidings
from his mouth, but she had known he was near. tak-

ing all care away from her, protecting her from every pain that he could shield her from, directing and arranging everything to spare her most. She had not troubled herself to think what she should do when he was gone, she had not felt it possible that he could go; he would not leave her till she was strong enough to be alone; and so the tidings that the maid brought to her shocked and bewildered her as much as if she had just found herself in the sad and desolate position into which that week's tragedy had thrown her.

She had not strength to open the letter; she sat dumb and overwhelmed, holding it in her hand and looking vacantly at the familiar writing. Alone! with all the teasing care of arranging the routine of every day, with all the heavy weight of deciding upon her future. It was more than her bewildered brain and shattered nerves could bear; it was cruel to be brought face to face with such a sombre destiny, and to be forced to examine its details while still helpless from the shock of meeting it.

From the letter, when at last she opened it, there fell another, written by a hand now cold and stiff in death; she covered it hastily from her sight; it was too soon to bear that pang.

The letter from Soutter, which a few hours later she found courage to resume, was as follows:

" I find myself recalled to Washington earlier than I anticipated. A forward movement is decided on, and I must join my regiment at once. I have endeavored to arrange everything to spare you anxiety and annoy-

20

ance, but you will understand that no arrangements I have made are binding upon you if they do not meet your wishes, which I have only been able to conjecture. I am very sorry to thrust these considerations upon you now; but it seems inevitable since I have to go.

" I have secured temporarily for you the services of a man of business, in whom I have perfect confidence. In his hands I have placed everything, till you shall be able to decide upon such matters for yourself. Upon him, for the present, you can draw for money as you require it, and from him, as soon as you are strong enough, you can obtain a full explanation of the state of your property, and all particulars regarding your income and investments. I have directed him to wait upon you to-morrow, but if it does not suit you to enter so soon upon the discussion of business matters, you can defer the interview any length of time you please. Everything is safely and advantageously arranged to await your leisure and direction.

" You will be made aware, no doubt, by the inclosed letter, of the general purport of your husband's will. His entire property, which I find considerable, is secured to you, and placed under your own control. There is no reservation or condition of any kind; the will is duly executed and attested, and I anticipate no trouble or opposition from any quarter in regard to it.

" I have feared the noise and publicity of an hotel would be uncomfortable to you in your present weak condition, and I have given Mr. Reading directions to submit to your judgment the propriety of renting, for the present, a small country place, furnished and in order for your reception, about an hour's ride from the city, of which I have secured the refusal for you. I have not been able to guess whether you would desire to remain in this neighborhood, for the present, or to return to Titherly at once, and so have been obliged to content myself with very indefinite arrangements for your comfort; but I believe you may rely implicitly upon the disinterested kindness and good judgment of Mr. Reading, who has promised me to carry out your wishes faithfully in every matter upon which you may consult him.

"There are some other details concerning the events of the past week upon which I need not enter now, but regarding which you can at any time obtain full particulars from Mr. Reading.

"I shall hear of you from time to time through him; and I trust that you will not hesitate to call upon me, if in any emergency you require my services.

"My desire is always to be useful to you.

"I am sincerely your friend,

"Louis Soutter."

CHAPTER XLV

THE MORAL.

"True servant's title he may wear,
He only who has not,
For his Lord's gifts, however rare,
His Lord Himself forgot."—TRENCH.

FRANK saw Mr. Reading the next day, and heard from him, in a general way, what income she had to depend upon; what prospect there was of depreciation in the real estate, and what difficulties in obtaining the revenue from it. She listened with great indifference to all, however, and accepted docilely whatever he advised; heard a few of the particulars regarding the residence Soutter had selected for her; told him she would take it; and closed the interview by begging him to consider that she left everything in his hands, and only desired to be directed by him.

This was all very contrary to what Mr. Reading had been taught by Soutter to expect. He had supposed his client to be a clear-sighted and independent woman, with a well-developed will of her own, and he found her a very docile and indifferent young creature, without the least interest in what concerned her property, and with a most blind reliance upon him in everything.

She removed from the hotel at a very early day, taking with her the maid Soutter had selected for her and a man servant whom he had recommended, going into possession of her new home with the listless composure which had become her habitual manner now.

The country house was a miniature establishment, in perfect order, with an acre or two of lawn and a pretty garden. The parlor was a sunny, pleasant room; and here the young mistress of the house sat, day after day, beside the window, watching the waves of the Sound wash upon the beach below the lawn, and the storms, and sleet, and ice of winter give way to the showers, and gusts, and thaws of early spring.

It was a strange, silent life she led; with no companion, with no relief from the monotony of the slowly-passing days. She had no friends, she found no neighbors, she rarely left the house. Few letters came to her, and she wrote none that were not on business matters. The servants, cosy and chatty in their room below, wondered that she did not die of loneliness, and Mr. Reading remonstrated in vain against a mode of life so trying.

The house had only been taken till the spring, even Frank feeling at the time that then she must go back to Titherly; but a change had come upon her since she had found she had something still to live for—a hope that, realised, would bind her with a new bond to life, and give her, if not a right to happiness, at least a talisman against despair. This silent hope, unknown to all the world, gave her strength again. She was no longer listless. Her dreamy days and wakeful nights were filled with one sweet hope, one steady longing. The old self-reliance returned, the old love of making and working out a plan of life, the old shrinking from submission and dependence. She could not go back to Titherly. It was not her duty now, she reasoned. If she had erred in leaving it willfully, she had amply atoned for it by all that it had brought upon her. If the heavy hand of God upon her could be lightened now, if prayers and promises could buy a reprieve from punishment, she might yet be almost happy. Abased, destroyed as she had been, she yet unconsciously was bargaining with Heaven; her life for the child's life; devotion, sanctity, untold self-sacrifice, if she might be allowed this blessing.

Time went on. The beautiful May days came and melted into June; but the glory of the midsummer was shut out from the dim room where the young mother lay alone, with the waxen form beside her, that was only a dream of beauty, only a lovely mockery of the hope that had been her life for all those weary months. No breath had ever fluttered through the lips she kissed so passionately; no light had ever shone from under the transparent lids her hot tears fell upon; the tiny baby hands were marble; it was all death; it never had been life. She had toiled, prayed, hoped, loved, suffered for a shadow, a dream, a soulless, evanescent, unfixed idol. All the immortal mother's love, welling up within her heart, and only this lovely, lifeless, fading clay to spend it on! Her bosom warmed with a welcome for it, only to be frozen with the indefinable freezing touch of death. Ah! if it could for one moment have nestled against her breast, looked in her face with living eyes, breathed once a human cry, she could have felt she had a child forever—a hope which death could not invade, a memory which would be her sacred pleasure till mem ory itself were lost in bliss.

The unworthy dream was passed. Nothing remained to her of the short episode that had been so strangely compounded of error and misfortune but the "ghosts of blessings gone;" the memories, bitter and unavailing, of her disappointments and her sins. Her life had failed; her strength had proved insufficient even to bear her punishment; her hopes had mocked her; her self-reliance had destroyed her. There remained nothing to her in all the world but God's mercy. Her heart now craved the love she had so long refused to understand. In that darkest moment of her life she saw "what sunshine hours had taught in vain;" what chastening and tenderness had both failed before to teach her, that "the heart that loved us to the death," yearns ever for our love; and that that love, however learned, is "the infinite reward of all faithful souls," the promised haven anticipated here, even in the midst of suffering and sinning.

CHAPTER XLVI.

A PARTING.

> " To me the thought of death is terrible,
>   Having such hold on life.   To thee it is not
>   So much even as the lifting of a latch ;
>   Only a step into the open air
>   Out of a tent already luminous
>   With light that shines through its transparent walls !"
>
> *Golden Legend.*

IT was a still, soft Sunday evening: the city noises were all hushed, the summer sun was lowered to the horizon, the last vibration of the chimes still trembled on the air and Frank, with a strange tumult of emotions, stood waiting for Cecilia just within the church door where she had met her first.

A few lines, hurriedly despatched, had reached her the night before, the first communication of any kind that had passed between them since she came away from Ringmer, begging her to be there at the evening service, and to wait for her if she should be late.

It was to say good-bye, she added ; they were all to sail for Europe the next day, with but a distant prospect of ever coming back to live at home.   Ringmer was sold, the town house rented for a term of years, and all arrangements made for a residence abroad.

"Mamma's health, and mine, too, perhaps," she wrote, "have hurried the plan somewhat, though papa

has for some time been resolved upon it. I felt I could
not go without seeing you once more; do not disappoint
me if it is possible for you to come."

The music slowly fell, the service had begun, the few
worshippers scattered about the dim and quiet church
were on their knees, and Frank, watching anxiously,
caught at last the sound of a carriage rumbling through
the silent street. It paused. Good heaven! could that
be Cecilia?

A lady in deep mourning alighted, and crossed the
pavement with a slow and languid step. Frank
thought, incredulously, for a moment, of the light
tread and happy grace of Cecilia fluttering among the
birds and flowers of Ringmer one short year ago; and
when the drooping figure before her paused and lifted
her heavy veil, it was with a pang she recognised the
sweet features of her friend.

Her bright auburn hair waved with its old luxuri-
ance, her soft brown eyes were deep and tender and
serene, her skin was of a transparent purity, and a
crimson spot burned on each white cheek.

She put out her hands to Frank with a tender and
eager movement; they held each other for a moment in
a close embrace, and then, without a word, entered the
church and went together down the aisle.

CHAPTER XLVII.

RETURN.

"So fall the weary years away:
A child again, my head I lay
Upon the lap of this sweet day."—WHITTIER.

THE wind was soft and low; the afternoon sun was
sending slanting beams across the level orchard, and
the shadow of the hill was creeping fast over the little
cottage at its foot.

Frank stood with her hand upon the latch of the low
gate; how could she lift it and go in to the home she
had so willfully abandoned, how could she claim again
the protection she had so long rejected? The scene, too,
awoke such sad and overpowering thoughts: the un-
weeded and neglected flower-beds that she and Fanny
had planted summer after summer; the old bench
under the locust tree, now almost hidden by the long
rank grass; the closed blinds of the parlor and their
little chamber over it. What grief and penitence every
glance at them aroused! The vines were drooping,
tangled and untended, over the little porch, the door
was open, and in the narrow hall an old garden hat of
hers was hanging, with its ribbons faded, just where
she had left it when she went away, and Fanny's
satchel, still full of books, as the last day she came back

from school, hung under it. There was such a stillness, she could hear nothing, as she listened at the half-open door of the sitting-room, but the loud tick of the old clock and the soft purring of a cat upon the window sill

She pushed the door open, and stood silently with her hand upon the latch, looking in. The room was rigidly well ordered; the painted floor shone where the straggling beams of the setting sun crossed it below the deep and narrow window at the west, the straight-backed wooden chairs stood in stiff rows around the wall, and the brass candlesticks on the high mantel-shelf were well rubbed and glittering. There was wood laid ready to light in the large open fire-place an iron tea-kettle was on the hearth; on the mahogany table, which stood between the windows, with its leaves down and the cloth folded up carefully and laid upon it, was the great old Bible, open at the Gospel of St. John, and a pair of heavy silver-bowed spectacles lying on the wrinkled yellow page.

And in a high-backed chair beside it, with her feet upon a rug, sat the lonely old woman, older by ten years, it seemed to Frank, than when she saw her last, bent and wrinkled and feeble. She rocked herself slowly backward and forward, and beat her fingers feebly upon the arm of the chair. Her ear had lost its keenness and her eye its quickness, for Frank had advanced some steps into the room before she raised her head or seemed to notice her. Then she shaded her eyes with her hand, and appeared to try in vain to recognise her at the distance at which she stood, but as Frank approached nearer to her, she suddenly dropped

her hands upon her lap, and shaking her head mournfully, turned it away, saying with a moan,

"You needn't have come back; I haven't got long to
stay now. I could have stood it to the last as I've stood
it all along."

"Oh, Aunt Frances," said Frank, running to her and
taking her hand as she knelt down beside her, " will
you forgive me all that and take me back again? I
never want to go away from you: I will try my best to
make up for all I've done."

"That won't last long," returned the old woman,
with a groan, turning her head away again. "You
won't be contented here, I know. They tell me you're
rich and among great folks now. Ah me, ah me!
My two girls that I brought up! Much good they did
me when I came to need 'em!"

"Dear aunt," cried Frank, covering her hand with
tears, "I shall never be content anywhere but here.
There's never a day passes that I don't wish I'd never
gone away. It's all been wrong ever since I went,
dear aunt; I've come back a great deal humbler than
I was before. You won't have any trouble with me
now. I only want to make you happy: I have not
anything else left me in the world to do!"

"Then it's trouble's brought you to a better mind,"
returned the other, looking at her half distrustfully.
"Trouble brings us all down; but it only bends
us when we're young. It breaks us when we're old;
ah me!"

And putting her wrinkled, trembling hand before her
eyes, she beat her foot upon the rug and shook her

head. There was a moment of silence, ther. looking up, she said, touching Frank's black dress,

" There's worse trouble than that you can wea mourning for. When I was your age, I thought death was the only thing to be afraid of. I didn't think I'd live to see the day I'd ask it for myself and for her that was my flesh and blood. O my poor girl, O my poor Fanny !"

And the old woman groaned aloud, and rocked herself back and forward in her chair, covering her dry, scorched eyes with her trembling, withered hand again.

Frank could not speak. She was appalled by the burden of grief and shame that this proud, upright, self-willed woman had had to bear so long alone. There had been no neighbor to whom she could bemoan herself, no friend near enough to hear the story. Hers was a grief that could be told to none who were not bound by the same ties of blood that she was to the erring one. Of misfortune we can tell, but not of shame. To Frank, at last, she consented to pour out her long-pent sorrow. They together could mourn for Fanny, and talk of her with tenderness, for they were her only family ties; all the rest who knew her were loud in condemnation, and bitter in contempt since the story of her shame had come to light. The young girls who had been her friends now blushed to hear her name; the families where she had once been welcomed, whispered darkly or scoffed openly, whenever she was mentioned; neighbors, once a little envious, now delighted to pity or condole with the old woman who had held her head so high, and given them all cause, more or less, to smart and feel the sting of her sharp tongue.

All winter and all summer these two young girls had been the favorite scandal of the place. The worst was soon known of Fanny, and of Frank much evil had been surmised, till old Humphrey Soutter set the news afloat of her marriage to his nephew's friend, her early widowhood, and the good position and fortune of the family she had married into. Louis' letter had gone the rounds of Titherly, as he had meant it should, and had prepared for Frank, whenever she should choose to return to it, a reception very different from the one she had anticipated.

"That bad man," said the old woman, the recollections all rushing on her as she talked, "that bad man, who came here only to ferret out what he could about you, never left a stone unturned. At first I gave him credit for an honest man that didn't want to see a girl throw herself away, but soon I began to guess at what he was; but Fanny, she never could be made to see he wasn't what he said. He fired her up about your being so fine, and looking down on folks at Titherly; and the last time he came, all in such a hurry, I never have believed she would have gone with him if he had not told her you were married to a man that was rich and was a gentleman; and from that time I saw it in her eye. I knew she would never rest till she could get away from Titherly and get equal with you."

Frank groaned as she hid her face on the arm of her aunt's chair.

"And she was so cunning, so artful, and I was such a

·ool to be deceived by her! Only that night, when she
went up to bed, I think she was a little softened. I could
not quite make out what made her different from usual.
I thought it was because she had said good-bye to him
that afternoon, and I had my doubts but what she liked
him.—She was softened a little, I was saying, and she
left something in her room for you, that she must have
put up that night. Her letter to me told me I must
give it to you. It was something that had come for
you that she had never given to you; a little package
and a letter. It's there, in that little drawer. Go get
it; here's the key."

Frank opened the drawer and took the package and
the letter out. The letter had been opened, and was
addressed to her in Soutter's writing, and the package
contained the miniature and chain she had seen on
Fanny's neck that night. She sank down on a seat beside the window and read the letter through her blinding
tears:

" DEAR FRANK: When I wrote that letter under your
eyes in the school-room this morning, I thought it was
all that could be said; but I find, when I remember it,
it was not half what I meant to say. It was cold and
proud, and I could not blame you if you never answered
it. Too much depends upon it to trust to it. Frank,
you *must* love me; you do love me! I almost know it.
Forget whatever in it sounded cold. You always make
me proud and angry now-a-days when I am with you,
but when I am out of your sight I am humble enough
I am ready to give up everything just for one word--
just to be with you upon any terms.

"I'm desperate now, because I'm pledged not to see you again before I go. It seems to me I cannot go without one good-bye look. It may be so long too—well, it was my own fault, and I deserve it!

"It seems a long while to wait, till to-morrow morning, for my answer. Let it be a kind one, Frank. Remember how long I have been your lover. Forget all but that. It will almost kill me to know you do not care for me. Try to care for me—promise to love me—don't send me off without any hope! There's nobody else cares for you half as much, nobody whose love means anything compared with mine!

"Keep this picture, Frank, *and send me yours some day.* I do not think there is anything in the world I would not give for it to-night. Shall I ever have a right to it? Heaven knows I'd serve faithfully and long enough to get the right even to your shadow!

"Good-bye. God bless you always! Remember that I love only you—that it lies with you to make me most happy or most miserable.

"Yours, with all the love of all my life,

"LOUIS."

CHAPTER XLVIII.

SUNSET ON THE BRIDGE.

"Oh, playmate in the golden time !
 Our mossy seat is green ;
 Its fringing violets blossom yet,
 The old trees o'er it lean.

"The winds, so sweet with birch and fern,
 A sweeter memory blow ;
 And there, in spring, the veeries sing,
 The song of long ago."—WHITTIER.

An hour later Frank stole out of the little porch and went down the narrow path. The gate stood open as she had left it, and, invited by the familiar babble of the brook, she went on slowly till she reached the bridge. There was a log across it that had often served her for a seat, and at the bank, just peeping over into the water, grew a bunch of daisies. She looked away from them with a heart-sick regret.

What a sweet, soft evening ! The rose-colored clouds were fading to the faintest pink ; the distant mountains wore the deepest violet ; the cool feeling of dew was already in the air, and such a stillness as is dew to the tired brain and thirsty heart. All on which she looked was so unchanged ! The low cottage, with its curl of smoke, nestling under the hill. and shaded by the great

tree in front; the winding road; the cows waiting
beyond the bars; the brook tinkling over its stony bed,
the scent of the buckwheat; the murmur of the sleepy
beehives in the garden; how all brought back the even
ing when she had last seen Louis here!

There is something cruel in the placidity and un-
changeableness of nature. A few months ago she could
hardly have borne these sights and sounds; but now
there was a better spirit teaching her, a better hope
lightening the burden of her self-reproach. The peace
she felt, she had not earned; "it was the gift of God."
What was not His gift who now, in the midst of desolation, had given her the content she had sought in
vain before? She had learned of Him who was meek
and lowly in heart, and she had found rest unto her
soul. The sting was taken from the past. Her sin in
it was forgiven; her misfortunes in it were understood
and pitied. She must ever look back upon it sadly, but
with bitterness no longer.

There were blinding, but not burning tears between
her and the little picture that she held, whenever she
tried to look at it; the brave, manly face, with its happy
smile and laughing, loving eyes, that had never loved
any one but her! that had never been happy but in the
hope of her. Ah! were they looking on the light of
day now, or were they shut down to bear in darkness
the long weight of silent ages till the eternal morning
dawned?

She tried to read again his loving, ardent, hopeful,
almost boyish letter, and then she recalled the last lines
she had had from him, their sober, thoughtful kindness

the absence of everything but manly pity for misfortune, humane consideration for a woman's suffering. She tried to banish the ever recurring conjecture, whether this long silence meant forgetfulness, or a resolution to cure himself of what had hitherto been nothing but a curse to him. Or, whether it meant, that in all these months some danger had overtaken him, some chance had befallen him that had rid him forever of sorrow and disappointment.

"But if he lives, he loves me," murmured the woman's heart within her, jealously. "He cannot cure himself. He will be always mine."

There was a movement on the bridge, a step upon the furthest plank. Frank looked up, thrusting the letter out of sight.

She sprang, gave a cry, then another bewildered look of joy, as she found herself standing with both hands in his, and his own true eyes bent earnestly upon her face.

He breathed hard and quick for a moment before he let go her hand, and sat down beside her on the bridge.

"Well, are you glad to see me, Frank?" he said, trying in vain to speak in his old, easy manner—a manner which no shock of battle or chance of war had ever surprised him out of. "I almost thought you would not know me."

The tears, hardly dry from gazing on the beautiful image of the youth, rushed again to Frank's eyes as she raised them to the changed face of the man. Time, sickness, exposure, all the thousand ills of war, had done their work with him; his hair had threads of grey in it, his forehead was seamed deep with an irradicable scar, his browned cheek was thinned, his mouth had a stern, enduring, patient look; but over all, sometimes there gleamed the winning, cheerful smile of old, like the momentary quiver of sunshine on a dark, storm-beaten battlement.

He checked a rising sigh as he caught sight of his companion's tears.

"Six months in a Richmond prison, I suppose, have not made me any younger. Shall I tell you what the surgeon said who dressed that wound for me on my forehead?"

"What did he say?" repeated Frank mechanically, trying to speak indifferently.

"He said, 'Poor fellow' (for he thought I was unconscious), 'his sweetheart'll never know him!'"

"Well, did she?" said Frank, lifting her head with a faint flash of the old defiant coquetry.

"Yes, Frank, she did; God bless her!" he said, as their eyes met for a moment and then fell, strangely uncertain of each other even yet.

"You have not told me how long you have been home," Frank said at last, listening to the ripple of the brook with a bewildered sense of suspense and happiness.

"Only a fortnight. No one had told you?"

"No; Aunt Frances cannot have heard; she sees so few neighbors now-a-days."

"I have been meaning to go in and see her," he said. ."I have been down as far as the bridge a good many times, but I have never had courage to go in the house. And to-night——Frank, how came you here?"

"How came I here?" she repeated in a low tone. "Why did I ever go away, you mean!"

"Ah," he said with a little sigh, "you have come to see it, then."

"Yes, Louis," she said with an effort, turning to him. "I have come to see it. I have come to understand all. You cannot blame me more than I blame myself; but there is one thing—if I could tell you"——

She faltered and looked down. He was listening so silently; there was such a rush of doubts and misgivings in her mind, she could not speak. What if he were changed—what if he cared no longer to know that she had loved him? All the womanly instinct in her rose to baffle and defeat the honest, honorable impulse that commanded her to tell the truth, whatever it might cost her pride.

There was another moment's struggle, and then she said, in a tone almost inaudible, turning away her head:

"You sent me a picture and a note the night before you went away. They never were given to me—I was deceived, I thought they were for Fanny."

There was an utter silence, only the brook murmured softly on, and the wind whispered low over the sweet, white buckwheat fields.

"It would have been different if you had known the truth, Frank?" he asked in a low, stifled voice, leaning down with his hand on hers and looking in her eyes.

THE NEW YORK PUBLIC LIBRARY
REFERENCE DEPARTMENT

This book is under no circumstances to be taken from the Building

Lightning Source UK Ltd.
Milton Keynes UK
UKHW010146310119
336487UK00010B/599/P